T0089183

TALES OF MANTICA

STEPS TO DELIVERANCE

By

MARK BARBER
from a story by Mark and Leo Barber

**ZMOK
BOOKS**

Cover Art from Mantic Games
Tales of Mantica: Steps to Deliverance
By Mark Barber
This edition published in 2019

Published by Pike & Powder, LLC
Zmok Books
1525 Hulse Road, Unit 1
Point Pleasant, NJ 08742

ISBN 978-1-950423-002
Library of Congress No: 2019940468

Bibliographical References and Index
1. Fantasy. 2. Action. 3. Adventure

Pike & Powder Publishing, LLC 2019 All rights reserved
Copyright by Mantic Games

For more information on Pike & Powder Publishing, LLC, visit us at:
https://www.wingedhussarpublishing.com
Https://www.pikeandpowder.com

Kings of War and Mantica are trademarks of Mantic Games and used under license

This book is sold subject to the condition that it shall not, by way of trade or otherwise, be lent, resold, hired out, or otherwise circulated without the publisher's prior consent in any form of binding or cover other than that in which it is published and without a similar condition, including this condition, being imposed on the subsequent purchaser.

The scanning, uploading, and distribution of this book via the Internet or via any other means without the permission of the publisher is illegal and punishable by law. Please purchase only authorized electronic editions, and do not participate in or encourage electronic piracy of copyrighted materials. Your support of the author's and publisher's rights is appreciated. Karma, its everywhere.

For Leo, thank you so much for helping me imagine and create these characters - I hope you enjoy reading this when you are old enough!

One

As the dry earth gave way beneath his feet and he lurched down toward his death, Orion could not help but wonder at the beauty of the Mountains of Tarkis at sunset. The low, golden sun painted the jagged horizon to the north in shades of orange-gray; the harsh lines of the mountains cascaded down to the foothills to the east overlooking the calm, clear waters of the Low Sea of Suan. The Three Cousins – the islands of Eruks, Kurros, and Ge – sat just offshore, the angular roofs of their little fishing villages just visible even from this distance. The beauty of the surroundings did nothing to calm the sickening fear which shot up through Orion's gut and into his hammering heart as that jagged horizon took on an unnatural aspect while he tumbled over the edge of the treacherous mountain path.

With an audible grunt escaping his lips, he somehow stopped dead in his tracks, dangling over certain death as his thin arms flailed wildly to each side.

"I've got you!" Antoni's reassuring voice called steadily from behind him.

Only now noticing the vice-like grip at the base of his neck, Orion allowed himself to be dragged clear of the edge of the path and flung to the safety of a small plateau to his left. The evening breeze kicked up the pleasant and soothing scent of the lilac, mountainside lavenders as Orion fought to control his breathing. He looked up at Antoni with gratitude.

"Th... th... than..."

"Quite alright," the dashing paladin's lips cracked into a charismatic and contagious smile. "We're here to safeguard each other, after all."

Clad in the distinctive garb of a Basilean paladin, Antoni cut an imposing figure. His highly polished plate armor was lined with a gold trim, while the blue robes of their Order were pinned at his chest by a decorative golden chain. His longsword hung at the hip to one side; to the other was chained his copy of the Eloicon, the sacred text carried by all paladins. Long locks of black hair framed his perfect face; the prerogative of a full paladin in contrast to the obligatory shaven heads of their squires.

"Thank you," Orion finally managed, slowly staggering back to his feet. "That was...well..."

"What happened?" a concerned voice bawled from the path ahead.

Orion turned to see Jahus carefully picking his way through the rocks to make his way back down to them. Jahus' garb was all but identical to Antoni's, but at nearly twice the age, the veteran paladin's paunch had a slightly ruinous effect on the splendor and nobility of the Order's armor.

"Orion stumbled, that is all," Antoni said. "All is well."

"Yes," Orion nodded, "I am fine, uncle."

A relieved smile emerged from either side of Jahus' broad, black mustache as he clamped his armored hands on Orion's upper arms.

"Take care!" he bellowed, his tone sitting in between admonishment and care. "If I do not bring you home alive, your father will kill me!"

"Yes, uncle," Orion felt blood rush to his cheeks as his gaze fell to the ground.

This was the first time he had ever been allowed to accompany the paladins on an actual task. At sixteen years of age, he was already badly behind schedule for completing his training as a squire – assuming he would ever be successful – and he had spent the last week hampering Jahus and Antoni with various acts of clumsiness and ignorance, without being of any help.

"Go on ahead, Antoni," Jahus nodded. "We shall catch up."

Antoni flashed Orion an encouraging smile. In his mid twenties, Antoni was everything Orion wanted to be – charismatic, respected, proven in battle, and possessing a humility and charm which made it impossible to begrudge him his success. Antoni was already rumored to be considered for promotion to Paladin Defender.

"Keep smiling!" the young paladin winked. "Anything you can walk away from is just a story to impress the ladies when you get home!"

"Enough of that!" Jahus warned. "Go on, up ahead."

Orion watched Antoni vault effortlessly through the gaps in the rocky pathway as he forged ahead. Shifting the strap of the heavy shield on his back so that it cut into a different part of his bony shoulder, Orion set off slowly after him. Although only weighed down by a thick, padded cotton jacket and a coat of mail – less than half the weight of a proper paladin's armor – Orion was already feeling the effects of the hike. Awkwardly, he was already a full head taller than both Jahus and Antoni, but with barely a muscle on his body, he often struggled with the physical aspects of squiredom. Which was pretty much every aspect.

"If you must idolize anybody, you could do worse," Jahus remarked as he followed Orion along the path, their long shadows dancing across the sharp rocks that flanked their path in the late evening sun.

"I don't idolize him, uncle," Orion said honestly.

"He did say one thing which was very sensible."

"What's that?"

"To keep smiling," Jahus said softly. "You'll find in life that there are many things beyond our control. Many things. But what we can always control, with a little discipline, is our outlook. How we react to things we can't control. And for a man to keep smiling no matter what the adversity? That is something special. The ability to keep smiling no matter what is truly a gift from above."

Orion opened his mouth to voice his disagreement but thought better of it. The sun was half hidden below the jagged, tooth-like horizon now, its fiery orange fading into soft reds and pinks. The chill evening breeze already seemed a little cooler.

"We should stop for..."

Jahus held a hand up to silence his nephew. On the path up ahead, Antoni was stood still and had a hand on his sword. Orion turned to look at his uncle quizzically. Jahus' eyes suddenly widened and he took a quick step forward. An arrow thudded into the aging paladin, slamming against one of his pauldrons before falling harmlessly to the ground.

"Get back, Orion!" Jahus shouted. "Stay clear!"

Orion's jaw dropped open as three armed men sprang from the shadows up ahead to assault Antoni – the paladin firmly stood his ground, and in one rapid motion he unsheathed his sword and hacked down his first assailant. Jahus was already scrambling up the path toward the melee, unsheathing his own sword and grabbing his kite shield from his back.

Orion froze. He stood rooted to the spot as a second trio of bandits leapt out to attack Jahus; he tried to will his legs into action, to force his hand to drop to the sword by his side, but his body seemingly refused to obey his mind's commands. That was when he saw the third group, another three armed men, scrambling down the rocks to his left toward him. A thousand thoughts danced through his mind as he watched the three men in their battered coats of mail and dented helmets drawing ever closer to him; he wanted to bring his sword up and leap into action, to turn and run for safety, even to shout to his uncle and plead for him to come back and save him. But in that moment, as the three bandits ran roaring toward him, their axes and hammers held high over their heads, the first time Orion had ever faced a real enemy in his life, he remained completely frozen in place. Completely silent. For the second time in only a few minutes, he was sure he was going to die.

A figure from out of nowhere appeared, no more than a flash of blue and white. With the swing of a heavy flail, the first of the bandits flew back in an arc of crimson spray as the spiked metal ball of the weapon connected with his chin and snapped his head back. The remaining two bandits stopped and took a step back, cautiously pacing around the new arrival. The woman – that much was evident in her lithe form – was tall and powerfully built, her limbs covered in white with a blue gown worn over the top, extending up into a blue hood and mask that covered her features. Battered boots of faded brown leather extended above her knees, and a heavy two handed flail swung menacingly in her grasp as she watched the two bandits.

Both men charged at her, the first swinging a warhammer at her head while the second man swiped at her gut with his axe. The tall woman ducked beneath the hammer blow and swung her flail to wrap it around the wrist of her second assailant. She dragged him over to bring a knee crashing up into his rotund abdomen before slamming an elbow into his face with an audible crunching of bones. The first, taller bandit swung his heavy hammer around again, but the slim woman was faster, lashing out with her flail to slam the heavy metal ball into the man's ribcage. He dropped to his knees, clutching at his chest and wheezing.

The second bandit saw the fate of his comrades and turned to run. The woman pulled a knife from her belt, slit the throat of the bandit choking helplessly on his knees, and then threw the same blade after his fleeing comrade. The knife thudded into the man's back – his run slowed to a drunken totter as he weakly reached back to try to grab at the blade embedded between his ribs before he fell face down, crying out for help. The woman dashed over, span her flail around to build up momentum, and then brought it crashing down to cave in the man's skull.

Up on the path ahead, two surviving bandits fled as Jahus and Antoni sheathed their weapons. Orion stared down at the three dead bodies by his feet, feeling bile rising rapidly to his throat. Gasping for breath, his body finally obeyed his commands to move and he turned away, desperate to drag his eyes away from the bloodied and broken corpses ahead of him.

"You, boy!" the woman behind him shouted. "You're armed! You shouldn't need me to save you! What were you thinking? Well, boy, speak!"

Orion turned again. The hooded woman paced over to him, her face hidden but her body language betraying her anger.

"I...I..."

"How old are you?" she demanded, standing in front of him and folding her arms.

"Fif... sixteen," Orion managed.

"Sixteen?" She almost spat the word out. "You should be wearing spurs by now, not groveling around as a squire! When I was your age, I'd already fought a full campaign against the orcs!"

"Orion?" Jahus called as he dashed back over. "Are you hurt?"

"Orion?" the woman laughed. "Your parents named you after the patron of courage and hunting? I hope the irony isn't lost on you."

"And your name?" Antoni demanded as he approached, a liberal amount of blood spattered across his gleaming plate armor.

"My name is unimportant, paladin," the woman said, "I'm a sister, you will refer to me as that."

A sister. Orion had of course met nuns from the Basilean Sisterhood's many convents before, but he had never met a fighting sister. While most nun's duties were of spiritual and medical care, there were a few convents scattered across Basilea whose role was to augment the country's legions of men-at-arms and paladin orders. Tales of their prowess in combat were clearly not exaggerated.

"What brings you up this mountain, Sister?" Antoni asked suspiciously.

"My business is my own," the hooded woman said, pacing back down the narrow path to recover a backpack she must have discarded before the fighting began.

10

She also picked up what looked like a heavy sphere of iron, covered in studs and fitted with a buckled pair of shoulder straps. She slung it over her back, staggering a little under the weight as the metal ball sat painfully across her spine.

"And why are you here?" she demanded as she walked back up the path.

"We are here to serve the Hegemon's authority," Jahus replied coolly. "We are here to bring a criminal in for a hearing."

"Dionne?" the sister exhaled. "So he has finally been declared a criminal? I suppose it was only a matter of time. Don't look so shocked, who else would you possibly be all the way up here to apprehend?"

The hooded woman pushed her way past the three men and carried on up the rapidly darkening mountainside. Antoni shot a quizzical expression at Jahus, the corners of his lips hinting at amusement. Orion saw the butchered bodies by their feet and again felt he would be sick.

"That iron ball she carries," Jahus remarked under his breath, "have either of you ever heard of the Six Steps? The Sisterhood's first three steps are good, positive: the first step is acceptance into a convent, the second is completion of all rights of passage to being confirmed as a full sister, while the third is a little more subjective but is more often than not dying a righteous death."

"And the other steps?" Antoni asked. "Steps four, five and six?"

"Those are a little darker," Jahus said as the three began walking back up the path after the nun. "The fourth step is a formal reprimand, a sign of disgrace for poor performance or violating the Order's rules. The fifth step is a last chance – a penance involving carrying a great weight to a place of spiritual significance. She is carrying out the fifth step."

"And the sixth?" Orion asked.

"Damnation. Expulsion from the Sisterhood."

"Well, well," Antoni nodded, "somebody's been a naughty girl."

"You go on ahead, keep an eye on her," Jahus nodded to Antoni. "We will catch you up soon enough. There is very little light left, and Dionne knows we are here now. This can no longer wait until morning."

Antoni nodded and picked up his pace to close the gap with the woman ahead. Orion let out a sigh and felt his head drop as he realized why Jahus wanted to speak to him alone. He had fallen short of the required standard. Again. He wondered if he would ever become a paladin. Plenty of young men and women failed, so why not he? Perhaps this too was his fifth step.

Jahus placed an arm around Orion's shoulders.

"Don't be so despondent," he said warmly. "You have ended up on a long and difficult road, and there will be plenty more obstacles. Any path without obstacles will never lead anywhere exciting."

"I did nothing!" Orion said shakily, fighting hard to keep back the tears of shame. "I stood and did nothing!"

"You didn't run!" Jahus gave a brief laugh.

"All I've done is get in the way! I've been no help, only a burden! You heard

11

that woman; I should be a paladin by now! Instead, I'm barely halfway through my time as a squire!"

"Pay no heed to her, she's clearly not without fault herself," Jahus grimaced. "And this, all of this, it is what the Shining Ones have chosen for you. There is a plan! Have faith! You are meant to feel this hardship so that one day you can understand how it feels and will be better placed to help others in their time of need."

Jahus stopped and stood in front of Orion, clasping his hands on the taller boy's shoulders.

"Look at me, lad. Your father knew hardship and failure. I've known failure too, many times. I'm forty years old, and I never made it to Lord Paladin! But this was meant to be my lot in life and for that I'm thankful. I think you will be a paladin. I may be wrong, but I have faith in you. But whatever you become, all of this is what is forging you into the man you are meant to be. All of this will give you heart, soul, humility, everything you need to help others. And that's why we are here. To help others."

Orion swallowed and nodded. Jahus smiled broadly.

"Come now, let's catch up with the Antoni. Hopefully we can avoid another altercation, but if we do not, you may yet have your chance to use that sword arm."

*****

A full moon hung high in the clear sky, reflecting the glare of the sun that was now hidden beneath the horizon. It painted the whole sky in shades of dark but vivid orange, giving nearly as much light as that one would see on a bleak, overcast day. It was one of the many things that Dionne loved about Basilea, he reflected as he gazed up at the twinkling starscape above him. It was why Basilea was worth dying for. His eyes drew down to the jagged panorama of mountains that stretched out to the north and the west. The calm seas to the east reminded him of his childhood, his father, and many long days spent battling the elements to bring in a decent catch. His smile faded as he turned to look to the south.

There, the mountains petered out into gentle hills where farmers grew olives, grapes, hops, and myriad other crops that were the lifeblood of the nation. And it was these crops that were the final blow in the ever escalating clash between him and the corrupt bureaucrats which lay further south still, in their extravagant mansions and town houses in the twinkling cities of Basilea's heartland.

"Captain?"

Dionne turned to face the familiar voice addressing him.

Lourne, his most loyal lieutenant who had fought by his side on a dozen campaigns, stood awkwardly on the rocks a few feet below the mountain precipice that Dionne used to view the world around him. Lourne wore the same mail coat and white tabard as the rest of Dionne's men, but as a unit leader, he was allowed some extravagance. He had three blue feathers emerging from the helmet he carried under one arm, rather than the standard single feather. His cool, gray eyes appeared tired but had lost none of the spark that sustained him through ten years of fighting.

"What is it?" Dionne asked.

"Four armed men, approaching from the south."

"Our own deserters?" Dionne stepped down from the rocky precipice. Lourne shook his head.

"Too well equipped, sir. From this distance, they look to be paladins."

Dionne stopped, a burden of responsibility suddenly falling on his shoulders that was so heavy he could physically feel it.

"It was always inevitable," he whispered, mainly to himself, before glancing across at Lourne.

The blond haired soldier fixed him with a defiant glower.

"We all knew the consequences of our action, sir. We stand with you now, as always."

Dionne allowed himself a brief smile as he stepped down from the precipice, patting Lourne on the shoulder as he passed. The two made their way awkwardly through the rocks back to the main encampment on the mountainside below. A ring of wooden stakes, taller than a man, had been driven in between the rocks to form an uneven defensive palisade that acted as the encampment's perimeter. A rickety guard tower stood over the one gateway leading into the camp, where a motley assortment of tents and wooden huts acted as accommodation and storage. Some forty soldiers had chosen to side with Dionne after he had struck out and began to act on his own initiative following a series of disagreements with his seniors in the Basilean Legion; but while many of his men had chosen their loyalty to their senior commanders over their own captain, some locals who had heard of Dionne's exploits and choices had thrown down the tools of their trades to join his cause.

The buzz of conversation immediately died down as Dionne and Lourne approached, replaced by the calm crackle of torch flames and the distant chattering of mountain bats rising from their slumber for the night. Dionne's forty soldiers stood in a loose semi-circle ahead of him, looking at him expectantly. Some stood rigidly to attention, while others pulled on their mail hauberks and strapped their sword belts to their waists.

"You've no doubt already heard that armed men are only moments away," Dionne addressed the soldiers, "only four, but it is the principal which concerns me the most. This is but the beginning."

A mixture of emotions greeted him from the faces of his men – some were visibly scared by the reality of official intervention into their actions; others seemed cool-headed or even proud of the attention.

"The lookouts believe they are paladins," Dionne continued. He held up a hand to still the nervous conversation that was immediately and predictably generated by his last statement.

"We're expected to kill paladins, sir?" an aging swordsman standing in the front row asked incredulously.

"I pray it won't come to it," Dionne replied earnestly. "The paladins fight honorably for what they believe is right. It is the system that is corrupt, not them. I hope they will see reason, but I doubt it. So alas; yes, if necessary. Have your weapons ready. This is our direction now. More men are on the way to join our cause, many more. We are but the vanguard; the foundation of what is right and just. Remember that, if we are forced to draw blood tonight."

The assembled soldiers parted wordlessly to allow Dionne and Lourne through as the two leaders walked to the rickety guard tower by the camp entrance. By the time Dionne had clambered up the crooked ladder to the tower's exposed lookout platform, four silhouettes were already visible on the winding path leading up through the rocks to the encampment entrance. Dionne's heart pounded in his chest, more so than before any battle he had faced for the last decade. This was merely four men; but it was not the physical danger that scared him.

The two lookouts glanced across to their leader for guidance, their crossbows at the ready. Dionne nodded to them but held one hand up. Both men raised their weapons and aimed at the approaching warriors. As they drew closer, the features of their arms and armor drew more visible in the bright twilight. Two of the men were undoubtedly paladins, clad in shining plate armor trimmed with gold and wearing robes of deep blue. A third man, taller and thinner than the others, wore a simple coat of mail and carried two heavy packs on his back. A squire, most likely. The last of the group was a woman, clearly identifiable by her feminine physique, although she too looked tall and powerful. Her white and blue robes and hood marked her out as a fighting nun; very nearly the equal of a paladin in open combat, but perhaps more dangerous in Dionne's opinion due to their fanatical zeal.

"Stop there!" Dionne bellowed out as the four approached the encampment gates.

The group halted by the gates. One of the paladins stepped forward and removed his helmet. A broad, sturdy looking man in his forties, the warrior's face was dominated by a thick, black mustache that hung over his upper lip. Dionne noticed one of the two crossbowmen on the platform next to him was fidgeting uneasily. This was not the time for proceedings to be ruined by an accident.

"Lower your weapons," he mumbled under his breath.

"My name is Brother Jahus, of the Order of the Sacred Ark," the paladin called out. "I'm here to talk to Captain Dionne."

"I'm Captain Dionne. What have you come here for, Brother Paladin?"

"Perhaps you could come down here and talk to me face to face, rather than leaving me at your gates like an enemy?" Jahus called up.

"You come bearing arms," Dionne replied.

"We were attacked," the paladin replied. "Not far from here. Do you have men guarding your perimeter?"

"You were not attacked by my men," Dionne answered, hoping that none of his patrols would be stupid enough to attack paladins.

Jahus looked up at Dionne expectantly. Dionne looked across to Lourne.

The old soldier narrowed his eyes suspiciously.

"Be ready," Dionne warned the two crossbowmen before making his way back down to the ground.

At the foot of the ladder, all of his men waited expectantly by the gates. Dionne gestured to Lourne and picked out six of his best soldiers.

"Come with me. The rest of you, be ready to fight if this negotiation breaks down."

The hastily constructed gates were drawn open to allow Dionne and his seven men through to face the four visiting warriors. Dionne walked boldly forward, making a conscious effort to ensure his gait did not betray his apprehension. He stood in front of his men and cast his eyes across the visitors. Next to Jahus stood the second paladin, his armor resplendent and one hand ready at his sword. Much of his face was visible through the slit at the front of his helmet – a dashing man in his mid twenties whose eyes looked eager, excited, and ready for confrontation. The man worried Dionne more than the older paladin.

To the other side stood the nun, a strange companion for a group of paladins sent to negotiate with a suspected traitor. Under her hood, a mask covered much of her features except for beautiful, crystal blue eyes. Her expression was cold, even callous; utterly dispassionate. Behind her stood the tall, thin squire. He was visibly terrified; his eyes darting from man to man in front of him as his narrow shoulders quivered.

"We've been sent to bring you in, Captain," Jahus said, his tone regretful.

"Under whose authority and what charge?" Dionne demanded.

"The charge is Willful Disobedience of a Lawful Order. It comes from the Duma."

"And what would you have had me do, faced with such orders?" Dionne snarled, his fists clenched in fury at the wording of the accusation. "Let innocent women and children die?"

"They did die, Captain!" the younger paladin retorted. "When enemy forces broke through defenses which were weakened by your orders!"

Dionne opened his mouth to snap back a response, but Jahus stepped forward between the two men.

"Gentlemen, please. We are all just soldiers. I am not here to pass judgment, Captain, merely to carry out my orders. My orders are to bring you in to address the charges which have been brought against you."

Lourne stepped forward to face the younger paladin whose words had angered Dionne.

"The captain isn't going anywhere," he growled. "None of us are. Three warriors and a whelp won't move us."

"That saddens me to hear," Jahus said, "as it forces me to depart and return with many more men. Captain, does this man speak for you? Will you not resolve this peacefully?"

Dionne looked across at Lourne. His lieutenant faced the younger paladin, both men's eyes locked on each other's. A decision was needed. It did not take long to formulate.

"Return with more men, if you must," Dionne replied. "The Duma is well informed. It already knows that hundreds of men are on their way here now to flock to my banner. Allow me to take the fight to the Abyss in my way. If you do not, you are an army who stands in the way of good. And that, Brother Paladin, makes you my enemy's friend."

"There may be a few dozen on their way here, but not hundreds," Jahus began.

His response was cut short when Dionne heard the almost simultaneous ring of two swords being unsheathed. Who drew first, he would never know. Lourne and the younger paladin brought their blades slashing out toward each other with well-drilled expertise.

"Wait! Stop!" Dionne yelled in desperation as he witnessed the violent reaction to a clear misinterpretation by one party.

Lourne, the very best of Dionne's warriors, brought his blade around in a second, faster attack. The young paladin raised his shield to deflect Lourne's vicious attack, and then followed up with two lightning fast strikes of his own. The first severed Lourne's sword arm at the elbow; the second took his head clean off his shoulders.

"You bastard!" Dionne screamed as he watched his friend's headless body crumple down to the ground.

Unsheathing his own blade, he tried to run at the paladin, but a body moved in to intercept him. Jahus stood before him, sword and shield raised for combat. Then his men screamed as one and charged, and all hell broke loose.

*****

Staring in confusion and disbelief at the melee that escalated from nothing, Orion fumbled clumsily for the sword at his side. He watched with pride as Antoni kept three soldiers at bay, skillfully trading sword blows with the trio of warriors as he held his ground. Jahus faced Dionne, the two leaders slowly and methodically circling each other while aiming precise, well measured attacks. The nun had charged forward, forcing two men back toward the gate to block off any reinforcements attempting to provide support from inside the encampment.

That left one soldier. His hands shaking, Orion looked up as a tall, powerfully built spearman advanced confidently toward him, the broad blade of his traditional koliskos spear gleaming in the moonlight. Orion drew his sword. It immediately slipped out of his fingers and clattered down into a narrow crevice in between the rocks at his feet. The spearman laughed and dashed toward him.

"Orion!"

Antoni shouted out the warning, batting aside an attack from one adversary

16

with his shield to create an opening. The paladin stepped across to cut off the advance of the spearman, lashing out with his sword to cut open a great wound across the rebel soldier's torso. Immediately one of the three soldiers behind him took advantage of his opponent turning his back and plunged his own sword through Antoni's ribcage to emerge through his chest. A cry of pain escaping his gritted teeth, Antoni turned in place to hack his killer dead before the remaining two soldiers descended on the mortally wounded paladin to cut him down.

Orion let out a cry of anguish and found himself sprinting toward the two soldiers, flinging his left arm out to smash his shield into the back of the head of one of his adversaries. The short man collapsed forward, allowing Orion to viciously kick at the soldier's ribs until his second opponent lunged forward to attack, forcing him to raise his shield. Still enraged, Orion let out a long cry and charged at the taller rebel soldier, crashing his shield into the man's body, He pushed him back against the wooden palisade and slammed a clenched fist into the man's face again and again.

A powerful grip wrenched Orion off the wounded soldier and he was flung back. He looked around and saw that he was surrounded by ranks of enemy soldiers, perhaps thirty or forty armed men in mail hauberks and white tabards. The nun, bleeding from a wound on her arm, had also been pushed into the center of the circle of rebels. She stood her ground, her back to Orion, her heavy flail raised and at the ready.

"Stop!" a commanding voice boomed out. "Stand fast!"

Orion looked across to where Dionne, the rebel captain, stood by the gateway behind his men. The soldiers parted and Orion saw a crumbled body at Dionne's feet.

"Uncle!"

Orion threw his shield aside and dashed across to crouch down next to Jahus, who lay at Dionne's feet with blood trickling from both sides of his mouth. His eyes, clearly struggling to focus, shifted across to Orion as a shaking hand slowly raised. Orion took the armored hand in his own and looked down in desperation at the bloody wounds which covered Jahus' body. A faint aura of white surrounded his uncle's hand as he pressed it against the vicious wounds across his chest. The flow of blood stopped a little as Jahus used his powers of divinity magic in an attempt to heal himself. But even Orion could see that it was not enough.

"This wasn't supposed to happen!" Dionne snapped, whether it was aimed at Orion, the rebel soldiers, or himself he did not know.

"You'll burn for this!" the nun pointed a finger of accusation at the rebel captain. "You'll burn in the fires of the Abyss for what you've done!"

"Take your uncle and go, boy," Dionne closed his eyes and shook his head. "Just go."

Orion stared wordlessly at the soldiers who surrounded him and his dying uncle. All stared at him, some clearly sympathetic, while others glowered with their weapons ready. Orion looked up at the captain but found no words. He placed his hands under Jahus' arms and dragged his armored bulk away from the encampment, back down the path they had taken together. The nun walked to his side and assisted him, hissing in pain from her own wound. She, too, held a glowing hand to the aging paladin's wounds and used her own mastery of healing magic, but again it was not enough. Orion looked over his shoulder with every few paces. The rebel soldiers watched them in silence until the darkness swallowed them up with their encampment.

It was only minutes until Jahus grasped frantically at Orion's arm. Orion gently laid his uncle down and dropped to one knee next to him.

"I...I..."

"I'm sorry, uncle!" Orion blurted out as tears streamed down his face. "I'm so sorry! This is all my fault! I dropped my sword and Antoni..."

Jahus shook his head, his face twisted in pain.

"No... you must..."

He fell silent as his eyes closed.

"I know, uncle!" Orion urged. "I know what I must do! I'll never let anybody down like this again! I'll never let down my brothers! I'll be a better warrior, a better person! I'll be the best soldier the Order ever saw!"

His uncle again shook his head. He opened his eyes one last time.

"Please... don't forget me."

His eyes shut. Orion held his uncle's hand and stared down in disbelief. He did not know how long passed, whether it was minutes or hours. He was numbly aware of the nun speaking.

"You need to grow up, boy," she said with contempt, "and quickly."

The nun walked away, leaving Orion knelt by his dead uncle.

Two

The midmorning sun blazed unopposed in a cloudless sky, reflecting off the gold trims off the rooftops and sparkling across the surface of the Sea of Eriskos beyond. Some miles away from the hustle and bustle of the Precincts, the Temple Quarter of the City of the Golden Horn lay in relative peace for much of the day. The splendor of the temples was the envy of the known world. Their opulence, even decadence, stood as a proud testimony to Basilea's love and respect for the Shining Ones; the gods of morality and virtue who came to power after the great schism ended the era of the Celestians. Twenty three towering temples of differing designs and aesthetic appeal formed a rectangle which defined the boundaries of the Quarter, each breathtaking structure standing as a tribute to one of the remaining Shining Ones and housing hundreds of clerics, servants, slaves, and guards. Within the boundaries stood countless shrines, chapels, and other places of worship, as well as monasteries, convents, and chapter houses of fighting orders.

On a small balcony of one such chapter house, Tancred looked down the shallow hill of the Temple Quarter and out across the Sea of Eriskos to the south, watching the endless lines of trading ships coming and going from the city's harbor; the hub of the entire world. Weaving lines in between the creaking cogs and caravels were tiny fishing boats, equally as vital in keeping the great city alive. From his vantage point on the balcony, Tancred looked down into the courtyard below where a dozen squires had been assembled in a neat line, ready for instruction at the hands of the Order's paladins. On the far side of the courtyard, a quartermaster bellowed commands to men and a handful of lumbering ogres who unloaded supplies from wagons which had arrived an hour earlier; stable hands tended to the huge warhorses housed in the north of the complex; while an order priest led a small, intimate service in the open air chapel near the chapter house's guardroom. The Order of the Sacred Ark was one of the largest and oldest fighting orders in all of Basilea, being made up of twenty cohorts each consisting of hundreds of paladins, squires, and supporting personnel made up of storemen, cooks, cleaners, clerks, and a dozen other trades. The 15th Cohort currently occupied the Chapter House of the Golden Horn.

Tancred turned from the hum of activity below and caught his reflection in a tall, gold trimmed mirror that stood by the doorway back inside the Chapter House

Command Quarter. Standing a little shorter than average, he still cut an impressive figure in the plate armor of a paladin. The sun shone off the highly polished silver surfaces of the expertly angled metal that covered his body from neck to foot, while shining chains of gold held his blue surcoat in place over his breastplate and secured his copy of the Eloicon to his hip. A heavy sword hung at his left side, its ornate pommel obscured by the grand helmet that he held under one arm. The helmet was new, completely unblemished, specially commissioned to mark the occasion of his recent promotion to Lord Paladin. The helmet protected the entire head and curved around to cover the wearer's cheeks, leaving the face open to allow maximum visibility. Atop the helmet, Tancred had ordered a splendid plume of black and white griffin hair to echo the style of the legion officers of previous ages who had forged Basilea. While his armor was resplendent, Tancred felt his heart grow heavy as his gaze fell upon the reflection of his face; his nose was broken in three places from previous battles while his freckled cheeks were crowned by a mop of red curls. His mother had always doted on him for his fiery golden hair which she said made him look like one of the beautiful, immortal Elohi who dwelled atop Mount Kolosu, while the same hair had caused him to be bullied remorselessly as a child.

If only those bullies could see the armed figure that stood before him in the mirror now. Growing up as the oldest son of a prominent senator of the Duma, Tancred was accustomed to wealth and prestige – even though the other sons of senators who he was educated alongside had as well. However, Tancred was the only boy in his class who was accepted into the illustrious ranks of the paladins, and now stood proud as a Lord Paladin – even if, at the age of twenty five, he considered himself two or three years behind schedule in terms of the advancement path he had chosen for himself.

"Lord Paladin?"

Tancred's attention was taken away from the mirror to a short servant girl, about his age, who stood by the doorway to the balcony. Tancred immediately found himself sucking his gut in, puffing his chest out, and turning away from the mirror.

"Yes?"

"The High Paladin will see you now, my lord."

Tancred followed the servant inside and along a long corridor lined with sculptures, tapestries, and trophies from foreign lands. They arrived at the High Paladin's audience chamber where Tancred was admitted without ceremony. The room was spacious, with a large balcony allowing an abundance of sunlight to augment that which poured in from the dome shaped skylight in the roof. The chamber's furniture was austere enough, but ample grandeur was provided by the ceremonial armor that hung behind the High Paladin's desk and the racks of displayed weapons and shields liberally sprinkled around the room.

High Paladin Augus stood and walked out from behind his desk to greet Tancred. Augus was a tall, lean man in his early forties with cropped silver hair and a thin, hawkish nose. He wore simple leggings and a shirt of blue, matched by a slightly more flamboyant cloak emblazoned with the symbol of the Order – a white phoenix. Tancred stood stiffly to attention and saluted, raising his right hand to shoulder height; the symbolic gesture that showed he carried no weapon. Augus returned the salute.

"Tancred, welcome!" He flashed a warm smile. "And congratulations on your promotion!"

"Thank you, High Paladin," Tancred forced a smile, well aware that as High Paladin and commander of the entire order, it was Augus who would have vetoed his previous recommendations for promotion.

"That's quite a statement," Augus nodded to the helmet Tancred carried under his arm.

"The men need to know where I am on the battlefield, if I am to command, High Paladin," Tancred offered, realizing too late how defensive his tone was.

"The men, and women, will know you well enough; it's your foes who will benefit most from you standing out," Augus warned. "But you must lead in the manner which you deem most suitable. Would you like a drink? Spiced tea, lemon water?"

Tancred shook his head.

"No, thank you, High Paladin."

Augus shrugged and walked back to his desk, pouring a glass of water for himself and adding a slice of lemon before walking out onto the balcony. Tancred followed him.

"I've summoned you here to discuss your first command," the taller paladin said as he looked down at the sprawling city below. The noise levels rose from below as a minor commotion was caused by an argument between a trio of bearded dwarfs and a street vendor selling religious artifacts outside one of the smaller temples. Tancred paid little interest. The High Paladin's words were what captivated him. Perhaps this was the apology he felt he was owed? Overlooked for promotion for several years now, he had been summoned to The City of the Golden Horn itself, to where the 15th Cohort was based in the most prestigious of all the chapter houses. He was to take command of the 15th? Aside from the elite 1st Cohort, there was no greater command for a Lord Paladin.

"Certainly, High Paladin," Tancred replied. "Which cohort am I to command?"

"Oh, I'm not giving you a cohort, not just yet," Augus smiled. "I have a task for you."

Tancred felt his entire body tense, his muscles clenching and twisting in rage. His face felt unbearably hot and his jaw ached.

"I am not to command a cohort?" the statement narrowly escaped through his clenched teeth.

Whether the High Paladin noticed the rage he had caused, Tancred could not ascertain.

"You're young and newly promoted, there's plenty of time for that yet. No, I've got something important I need you to do for me. I need you to command a detachment to carry out a special task. Only a small group of soldiers, but this is important. The tasking has come from the Duma."

Tancred exhaled slowly. He took a moment to compose himself, relatively content that his status was still being taken seriously.

"A special task? What is required?"

"You've heard of Dionne of Anaris, no doubt?" the High Paladin asked as he took a sip from his glass.

"Of course."

Everyone who had ever visited northern Basilea had heard of Dionne. A legion captain who had disobeyed his orders and sent vital supplies back to the local population, he was a folklore hero who had sacrificed himself and his men to stop a famine from tearing through the countryside. However, from a military point of view, it was a disaster, as the subsequent weakening of defenses had allowed an Abyssal force to smash through his area of the defensive line, and many of the now well fed peasant population instead ended up victim to the ravaging invaders.

It was difficult to separate fact from myth with Dionne, but after he disappeared – probably starved to death in the Mountains of Tarkis – he had become a hero of the people, praised every time local bandits were repelled or Abyssal forces to the north were pushed back. It had been eleven years since a small expedition had been sent to bring him before the Duma, resulting in the deaths of two paladins, both from the Order of the Sacred Ark.

"The Duma believes he is alive," Augus said grimly. "I want you to lead our contribution to a force which is assembling to apprehend him and bring him before the Duma."

Tancred's emotional journey plunged from the peak of a wave down into a trough for the second time in nearly as many minutes.

"You want me to go wandering around the Mountains of Tarkis to look for a man who died a decade ago? Is this a joke? Am I being punished?"

The High Paladin's smile faded instantly.

"I think you forget yourself," he said simply.

Tancred stood up straight again, inwardly cursing himself.

"My apologies, High Paladin. Sincerely."

Augus regarded him through narrowed eyes for a few long, uncomfortable moments. Seagulls cawed in the sunlit skies above, the buzz of conversation from the temple merchants continued unabated from below.

"You are to lead the paladins I am sending to this force," Augus continued coolly. "Thirty paladins, with warhorses and logistical support. The entire force will be under the command of Dictator-Prefect Hugh of Athelle. He will be leading some fifty men-at-arms from the 32nd Legion."

"Do we have ranged support?" Tancred asked, hoping his interest in the tactical considerations would detract from his earlier insubordinate outburst.

"The Dictator-Prefect has hired a group of mercenaries, all ex-legion men. You'll meet them on the road north," he paused. "This task is important to the

Duma. You know as well as I do that there are many legends about Dionne, and we know few actual facts. But information that was recently acquired would indicate that he is very much alive and well. Eleven years ago, when he first struck out rogue, it was our very order that dispatched two paladins to bring Dionne before the Duma. He killed both of them. That's why I volunteered to provide assistance to Dictator-Prefect Hugh. This rebel bastard killed two of our brothers. You find him, you bring him to justice in a court of law before those appointed by the grace of the Shining Ones themselves. But if he resists, you take off his head. Clear?"

Tancred felt his anger rising again, but this time in was in support of the High Paladin rather than at him.

"Yes, High Paladin."

"Good. The detachment will be ready to leave tomorrow. One more thing. Your deputy. I want you to take Brother Paladin Orion of Suda with you."

"*Orion?* That animal from the 9th Cohort?"

"Your *Brother Paladin*," Augus snapped in response to Tancred's baleful glare. "And I've moved him from the 9th to the 15th to give him a fresh start. He's a good man, he just needs some guidance. Some responsibility will do him well. That's why I am making him your deputy. Provide guidance. Don't look at me like that, man! What did you expect from your elevation? Did you honestly expect you'd just be given a cohort and a cushy garrison in the sun so you could prance around in your new hat? Promotion comes with responsibility! And sometimes – more often than not, in fact – those responsibilities are things we'd rather not do! Now stop sulking and follow me!"

His teeth grinding, Tancred followed the older paladin out of the chamber and back along the corridor in uncomfortable silence, broken only by the echoes of their feet on the cool, marble floor. Augus led Tancred to the southeast corner of the building and down to the ground floor before emerging onto the training ground he had viewed earlier from the balcony. Wincing in the ferocity of the sunlight, Tancred followed the High Paladin out onto a square of freshly cut grass where a group of five squires surrounded a single man.

"Ah," Augus said, his tone indicating that his temper had settled during the brief walk, "here he is."

The five squires were all in their mid to late teens – young men of fighting age who were undoubtedly at the end of their training and ready to win their spurs as fully fledged paladins. They wore padded armor, off-white in color, and carried wooden poles cut to the same length as the two-handed greatswords carried by paladins on foot. The squires formed a loose circle around one man who, even though he was on one knee, was nearly as tall as some of them. The warrior in the center was a bear of a man, built of solid muscle with broad shoulders and powerful arms. He wore the same padded armor as the squires; like them, his head was also shaven, but his features were largely hidden behind a thick, blond beard. Tancred knew from others that Orion was only two or three years older than him, but the huge paladin could easily pass for a man of forty.

Tancred and Augus watched as Orion looked around at the squires.

"Ready... go."

The five young men charged at the kneeling paladin. Orion surged forward to meet the first two, snatching up a wooden pole that lay in the grass by his feet. He swung the proxy wooden sword up into the belly of the first squire, lifting him off his feet to arc through the air and slam painfully down on his back. With a speed and precision which seemed impossible from a man of that size, Orion stabbed the tip of the wooden pole out to slam into the stomach of the second squire, sending him gasping to his knees and clutching at his chest. In the same motion, he brought the pole across his own back to deflect an attack from one of the squires behind him, and then turning in place to lash out with a back fist, sending a third youth crumpling to the ground with blood gushing from his nose.

The two remaining squires stood their ground, their wooden poles held ready as they regarded the shaven headed brute with terrified eyes. Orion dashed forward and hammered down a reign of attacks into the younger of the two squires, forcing the boy's guard open with brute strength before slamming a foot into his torso and sending him crying to his knees. The final squire dropped his pole and held up his hands.

"I... yield!" he stammered desperately.

"Pick up your damn weapon!" Orion bellowed with a ferocity that turned the heads of all others in the training field.

Augus stepped out into the grass square.

"Hold," he commanded.

The wounded squires staggered to their feet as Orion stood up straight and nodded courteously to the High Paladin.

"Go take a few minutes to compose yourselves," Augus said to the battered squires before turning to the colossal man in their midst. "Orion, come walk with us."

Tancred looked up and met the piercing gaze of the taller paladin as he walked over.

"Orion, this is Lord Paladin Tancred of Effisus," Augus said. "He will be taking charge of our contribution to the expedition I briefed you on yesterday. You will act as his deputy."

Orion looked down at Tancred and nodded.

"Excuse me, High Paladin?" a gruff voice came from behind the assembled group.

Tancred turned and saw one of the quartermasters who had been taking charge of unloading the wagons earlier, a short, balding man dressed in simple robes of brown. Augus looked at him expectantly.

"May I have a moment of your time, High Paladin? It is rather urgent."

Augus looked at the other two paladins.

"Excuse me."

Tancred watched the two walk away before turning to face Orion again.

This could be a problem. From the spectacle he had just witnessed, Orion was clearly a better swordsman than he was, and that was no mean feat. But Tancred had plenty of skills where he excelled. What he needed now was to establish authority from the outset, to ensure that Orion was well aware of who was in command.

"What was the point in...that?" Tancred asked coolly, pointing at the battered squires who had formed a huddle, poorly concealing the fact that two failed to hold back tears.

"What?" Orion exclaimed, his eyes narrowing.

"'What, 'Lord Paladin'," Tancred corrected sternly. "Address me by my rank. Now explain what you accomplished with that barbaric display of bullying five boys. Was it simply to satisfy your own ego?"

"They are not boys, they are men," Orion retorted, "and if you think that I am the biggest and most intimidating thing they shall face on a battlefield, you are sorely mistaken. They are only days away from their final trials, and after that, they will stand in line with our brothers in battle. They are not ready. That is what this is about. Lord Paladin."

Tancred did not miss the contempt with which Orion almost spat out his title. It pained him that Orion was right – five men should be able to take down one, and if they were not ready, they were a hazard to themselves and the men they stood beside. But Tancred was not going to lose any credibility by backing down.

"Go and get your equipment sorted," he ordered. "We leave tomorrow morning."

Orion turned wordlessly and strode off toward the barrack block.

"Problems already?" Augus enquired with a thin smile as he returned to Tancred's side.

"No, no problems, High Paladin," Tancred replied evenly. "He is nothing I cannot handle."

"Good. Let us go and discuss the finer details of your task."

*****

The mid-morning sun reflected off the highly polished armor of the lines of soldiers, stood ready to march out in front of the assembled crowds. Orion allowed himself the smallest of smiles. While the marching out parade was becoming fairly routine now, it was at least something he could mention in his next letter to his mother. His smile grew a little at the thought of her, proudly boring the other ladies of the surrounding households with tales of her youngest son and his heroic escapades across Mantica. At least one member of his family seemed genuinely proud of him.

The men-at-arms had arrived at the barrack courtyard late, and the procession was already nearly an hour behind schedule. Word had only just reached them that Dictator-Prefect Hugh of Athelle would be joining them in a few days, leaving Tancred in sole command until then and adding further delays to the proceedings. Three ranks of men-at-arms stood smartly in line, their white tabards scrubbed to perfection and their mail armor glinting in the midmorning sun. Each soldier wore a helmet adorned with a single blue feather and carried a metal kite shield of blue and white, with an intricate winged design at the top. This design had no practical use but did at least display the unparalleled wealth Basilea possessed, where common foot soldiers could be issued shields that would be the envy of noblemen in other kingdoms.

The clock tower which dominated the center of the barrack building chimed ten times as the men-at-arms' captain, a short, portly man named Georgis, dashed along the lines of his fifty soldiers in what appeared to be something akin to panic.

Lined up behind the men-at-arms were thirty paladins, also in three ranks, waiting atop their armored warhorses. Orion sat in the lead rank, watching the freshly promoted Lord Paladin with interest as the younger knight glared at the legion infantrymen, shaking his head in disapproval every few minutes. Tancred sat atop a magnificent gray warhorse, speckled with white. Orion knew nothing about horses beyond what was necessary to control them in battle, but he could recognize a thoroughbred warhorse worth more than most paladins could afford when he saw one. The paladins wore their full battle armor and rode atop their warhorses, but it was purely for show whist exiting the city. For the long trek north, only minimal armor would be worn while the spare horses would be ridden, leaving the best warhorses fresh and ready for battle.

For those who did not know better, the fighting men and women in blue and white all appeared to be of one force. In actual fact, it was two allied forces under one national banner; the legion took its commands from the democratically elected Duma, while the paladin orders were under the direct control of the Hegemon himself. The paladin orders were often thought of merely as the legion's mounted contingent. Indeed many orders were attached to specific legions for years on end to form an unbreakable bond. Technically, however, the authority that the Dictator-Prefect would exercise over the paladins was a courtesy, and one that Lord Paladin Tancred had the right to revoke if called for.

Behind the eighty fighting men and women were forty mounted squires, some too young to even be considered auxiliary soldiers, and behind them the baggage train made up of a dozen horse drawn carts with food, tents, money, and other vital equipment. Somewhere toward the rear of the procession was Kell, Orion's own squire. He sincerely hoped the boy had properly prepared his equipment for the march, for his own sake. Kell had served Orion for nearly two years now, firmly establishing himself as bumbling if at least relentless in his pursuit of his master's approval.

Finally Orion saw Georgis gesture to the two drummers at the front of the procession. The heavy, familiar boom of the bass drum echoed across the courtyard; three steady beats followed by a silence, then a repeat of the three bangs and a pause. On the next bar, the snare from the second drummer rattled into life at the precise moment that every soldier and warhorse marched forward, left foot first for all the infantrymen. The column of men-at-arms and mounted paladins followed the banging of drums out through the gatehouse and into the streets of the City of the Golden Horn, the crunch of feet and hooves on the cobblestones thudded almost into submission by the drum beats that echoed through the narrow streets and tall buildings.

The pavements to either side of the narrow road were lined with citizens, merchantmen, and other visitors to the sprawling city; a curious concoction of those well used to paying their respects to a military force marching to war and those who watched with gleeful excitement at what was, to them, a complete novelty. The houses to either side of the road were typically angular three story buildings that lined many streets in the city, their wooden walls painted an off white and leaning in to lurch over the road.

Captain Georgis marched smartly out at the front of the parade, his footwork in perfect time with the two drummers behind him. The men-at-arms were an impressive sight, their moves executed with well-drilled precision and their spears held perfectly stationary across their right shoulders.

Dwarfs, elves, ogres, and even salamanders and naiads mixed in with the crowd of humans that flanked both sides of the street, evidence of the impressively cosmopolitan nature of the city, the bastion of justice in the world of Mantica. A few isolated but enthusiastic cheers were issued from the crowds – mainly from children – as the soldiers marched toward the city gates. The youthful exuberance seemed to rally the assembled hundreds, who began a crescendo of cheers and encouraging shouts. The drumbeats echoed and reverberated off the walls of the surrounding buildings, confusing the regular sounds into a wall of noise. Orion saw one of the men-at-arms up ahead – a freshly trained replacement soldier, most likely – lose his timing and frantically stumble and hop in a desperate attempt to realign his limbs to the same timings as the men-at-arms around him. His struggles in turn caused a second soldier to lose his timings and begin the same, almost comedic hop and arm swing. Their failings caused much merriment in the crowds of citizens who guffawed at their misfortune. To Orion, it was an indicator of a deeper problem, a warning of the lack of training and experience accumulated by these men and women.

Orion narrowed his eyes as he detected a commotion up ahead. Two children, a boy and a girl of perhaps five and eight years old respectively, forced their way through the crowd and latched onto one of the men-at-arms, running alongside him and sobbing as they tugged at his arm. A woman in her thirties ran after the children, desperately trying to pry them off the soldier.

"Captain Georgis!" Tancred bellowed above the din of the drums and the crowds. "Take charge of that man!"

Before Georgis could respond, Orion nudged his warhorse into a canter and left his place in the parade, riding up to the children who had pulled the soldier out of his rank. The sobbing children looked up at Orion as he approached, their expressions of sorrow and despair instantly transforming to fear as the bearded, armored rider towered above them and cast them into shadow.

"I'm so sorry, my lord!" the red headed woman sobbed. "Please don't be angry at them! Please!"

"Back in line," Orion nodded to the soldier, a man of perhaps thirty years with a neatly trimmed beard.

Orion leaned over in his saddle and looked down at the terrified children as the soldier hurried back into line.

"Your father will be fine," he forced a slight smile and nodded curtly to the children's mother.

"Thank you, my lord," the pale woman smiled uncomfortably, her words only just audible over the crowd and the drums.

Orion returned to his own place in the line of mounted paladins; he saw Tancred swivel in his saddle and fix him with a disapproving glare. Orion pointedly ignored the glower until the younger paladin turned away. The city gates were visible a few hundred yards ahead, at the foot of a steep hill; and beyond them, the green countryside and the road north to the mountains. Orion let out a long breath. He had grown accustomed, even complacent, to a life on the road and campaigning. But this was different. He had never forgotten his uncle Jahus. And he had no intention of bringing Dionne back alive.

Three

The chirping of birds in the trees by the edge of the shallow pond accompanied the gentle babbling of the trickling waterfall that led from the hills. The flow of water was so gentle that there was not even so much as a ripple by the edge of the pond. The long journey the water took over the rocks of the high ground above did at least mean that it was clean enough to drink by the time it reached the scenic pool, half hidden by the colorful trees which formed a loose ring around it. .

Constance leaned over and held her stitched leather waterskin down to the pond to refill it, catching her reflection on the surface of the pool as she did. She saw mediocrity in so many ways. At twenty-eight years of age, Constance was of average height and build, and was neither beautiful nor ugly. She had been raised in a family of moderate affluence, possessed mediocre intelligence; even her brown hair seemed to sit exactly halfway between blonde and black. There was only one thing she truly excelled at, but that one thing was enough to earn her a living.

She dipped the brown pouch into the cool water, nodding to herself and letting out a breath as the drums she had been expecting to hear all morning finally drifted through the trees from the main trade road to the south. Tying her hair back in a rough ponytail, Constance attached her waterskin to her belt and stood, her mail armor chinking. She heard heavy footsteps pounding from the direction of the farmhouse to the east, so she took a moment to close her eyes and inhale the sweet scents of the yellow flowers which surrounded the pond, taking full advantage of her last few moments of solitude.

Jaque, one of her longest serving and most trusted soldiers, appeared at the start of the little dirt path that meandered through the trees, his lanky frame covered in a jacket of brown, quilted armor.

"Constance!" he called across. "They're here!"

Constance nodded and jogged over to catch up with Jaque. The two walked back toward the farmhouse where the rest of her soldiers waited. Blossoms twirled down from the trees, seeming almost to shine as they drifted down to the lush blanket of green grass below in the pillars of bright sunlight that permeated the leafy canopy above.

"You ever been to the Tarkis mountains before?" Jaque asked as they walked briskly along the path.

"No," Constance admitted, "but it's only the southernmost extent of the ranges, and its summer; so I'm not worried. From what I hear, we might see the odd sprinkling of snow, but nothing too bad. I'd imagine it'll be tough going on the legs, though. Still, the contract is more than worth the tired legs."

"And we're back in Basilea," Jaque flashed a gap-toothed grin, his gray eyes sparkling enthusiastically. "It's good to be home after so long away."

Constance emitted a noise that indicated her contrary opinion. She certainly appreciated the warm weather in Basilea, but while it was the country she was born in and grew up in, her deep resentment at much of the social and political construct left her unable to consider it her 'home'.

The drums from the main road grew louder and more distinct as they two reached the farmhouse. Thirty mercenaries, Constance's entire band, lazed in the morning sun on a patch of flat grass between the farmhouse and the roadway. Some used their packs as pillows, others sat atop them while gambling, but all had their weapons close to hand. Each mercenary carried an arbalest; a heavy crossbow with an even heavier punch, able to propel an iron tipped bolt through the thickest armor. However, the huge force required to draw back the string for each shot necessitated the use of a windlass to wind the weapon, which greatly slowed down a unit's rate of shooting.

Hayden, Constance's musician and the oldest man present, breathlessly joined her as the first ranks of Basilean men-at-arms appeared over the horizon on the road. Hayden was as tall as a bear and with a belly built on decades of ale consumption to match, his few strands of gray hair and his thick iron mustache framed a face made up of an oversized nose, lips, and jawline which gave him a comedic, friendly demeanor.

"Shall I get them up and on the road?" Hayden asked as he approached.

"No," Constance replied, "these men and women aren't in the legion anymore. We don't have anything to prove with pointless displays of pomp and ceremony. Let them relax."

The trio of mercenaries watched the procession of soldiers as it approached. Three ranks of fifty spearmen led the way; behind them was the ever-impressive sight of mounted paladins, their gold and silver armor twinkling in the sunlight. After them rode their squires on the spare warhorses, with the tail end of the force being made up of the supply train of wagons. With a bellowed command, the drums stopped and the small army came to an instant halt on the road by the farm. A portly man in mail armor with a highly polished breastplate and pauldrons, perhaps a few years Constance's junior, with a clean-shaven but sweat soaked face, walked out in front of the ranks of soldiers.

"Detachment! Fall out! Ten minutes, get some water!"

The well-drilled precision of the marching soldiers was instantly replaced with men ambling off in small groups, striking up conversation as they took waterskins from their packs. Their leader walked down from road and, after asking a question to the first mercenary he reached, was directed over to Constance. He paced over and stood formally in front of Hayden.

"I am Captain Georgis of the 32nd Legion," he said crisply. "We are…"

"She's in charge, not me," Hayden nodded at Constance.

"You're in command here?" Georgis asked incredulously after a brief pause.

"Women have been allowed to fight in the Basilean legion for over a decade now, so it shouldn't come as a surprise to you," Constance folded her arms. "So yes, I'm in charge, Georgis."

"One doesn't see many women in the mercenary trade," the captain responded coolly.

"Perhaps it is because so few women leave the legion on account of how well they are treated," Constance countered with a sarcastic smile.

Hayden and Jaque failed to suppress laughs. The legion captain looked around at where Constance's mercenaries lay idly in the farmer's field before flashing an exasperated glare back at her.

"Some semblance of military order would be appreciated here," he snapped, "and I was promised forty men."

"Yet you shall have thirty as that is the size of this unit," Constance planted her fists on her hips. "And if anybody has reason to complain here, it's us, not you. While we arrived at the meeting point on time, you failed to do so. You're late."

"I'd prefer you to refer to me as 'Captain'," Georgis leaned in aggressively, "and while we have been unavoidably detained, the fact of the matter still remains that this is not the unit size we were promised, and therefore your pay will be cut accordingly. In addition, the Dictator-Prefect insists that you wear the white and blue of the Basilean Legion, seeing as you are seconded to it."

"If we are being formal, then you may also refer to me by my rank of Captain, *Captain*," Constance snapped, "but you'll be the only one bothering to do so! My soldiers respect me just as I respect them, so I have no need to hide behind formalized titles. But in your case, I'll make an exception. And as for the blue and white…"

"Dictator-Prefect Hugh insists upon it," Georgis folded his arms.

Constance froze, as if an icy claw had clamped itself around her throat. Her heart pounding in her chest, she let out a labored breath.

"Who is the Dictator-Prefect in command of this task?" Constance managed.

"Dictator-Prefect Hugh of Athelle."

"The deal is off," Constance spat. "Hayden, get the men and women together! We're leaving! Now!"

Constance turned on her heel and took three or four unsteady paces. The world seemed to swim, the sky above and the grass below seemed to close in on her as painful memories forced their way into her mind. A strong hand rested on her shoulder to steady her, but it did little.

"What?" Georgis scoffed. "What difference does that make? You are

31

contracted for a job and you'll damn well carry it out!"

"You heard her," Jaque said, "the deal's off."

Emitting a string of profanities, Georgis turned and stormed back to the road. Hayden walked around to look down at Constance, clamping both hands on her shoulders.

"You alright?" He forced an uneasy smile.

"Yes… yes, I'm good," she managed as her breathing slowly returned to normal.

"I'm with you," Jaque said seriously, "I'm not fighting for that bastard, especially if they're cutting our pay as well."

Constance turned and watched as one of the paladins dismounted from his horse and commenced a heated discussion with Georgis. The legion captain flung his arms to either side in desperation periodically throughout their conversation before finally pointing in Constance's direction and striding off to the other side of the road. The knight – a Lord Paladin judging by his unique attire - sauntered over toward them, his blue cloak fluttering in the light wind.

As he drew nearer, Constance could see he was in his mid-twenties - young for a Lord Paladin - with an unruly mass of red curls falling to either side of an unpleasant face made even worse by a nose that had been broken several times. The paladin was far from the childhood stories of dashing, handsome heroes, as were indeed the vast majority in Constance's experience. The red headed man looked more like a mischievous adolescent who had been packed into his father's armor. He stopped in front of the trio of mercenaries.

"I'm Lord Paladin Tancred of Effisus," the paladin said in a tone that Constance figured the young lord felt commanded respect. "I have heard things have gotten off to a bad start. We really need you with us. Tell me what I can do to make this situation work for you, and I'll do all I can. Please."

Constance looked to either side at her old friends. Dealing with a petulant junior captain of the legion was one thing, but a Lord Paladin was something entirely different.

"My lord," she began with a respectful nod of her head, "I have brought my soldiers here at the agreed time and place. Captain Georgis has informed us that we are to have a significant portion of our pay docked due to an incorrect assumption of our unit size on his part. In addition, he now expects us to wear the colors of the Basilean army, a demand that many of my men and women will be uncomfortable with."

The red headed paladin nodded slowly, keeping his eyes fixed on hers.

"You'll get the pay you were promised, irrespective of the number of soldiers you have with you. I'll personally pay the difference. I believe you were already being paid very well, so given that, you will now receive payment for forty soldiers to be divided among thirty."

Tancred paused, his brow furrowed thoughtfully before he continued.

"I'd never dare of accusing mercenaries of being driven solely by profit,

I'm well aware that there are a great many other factors involved here, but this is a significant wage we are discussing. I hope that does at least demonstrate the value with which you and your company are held."

Constance looked up at Hayden. The big man raised his brows and nodded slowly. She looked across at Jaque but deduced that the wiry mercenary was far more undecided. The money was more than she had ever been paid for a single job, but her principles meant far more to her than the payment.

"Twenty-four of my soldiers are ex-legion," Constance continued, "the rest are former soldiers from their own home nations. However, many of us – myself included – have run afoul of Basilean justice once or twice. We are not on good terms with the Hegemony, and we will not wear its colors."

Tancred raised a fist to his closed mouth and fell silent for a moment.

"I am afraid I cannot resolve that," he finally admitted. "Hugh of Athelle is commanding this detachment and those are his orders. I do not have the authority to rescind them. Basilean blue is also worn by my order – perhaps you could think of yourselves as attached to the Order of the Sacred Ark rather than the legion?"

"With pride, my lord," Jaque spoke up, "but that does not make it any easier to stomach having to wear the white tabard again."

Constance looked across at the paladin with a degree of surprise, realizing her initial impression of the young man was unkind. He did at least appear to be doing all he could to assuage the company's concerns, and she realized that she was in danger of crossing the line from standing up for her principles to being pig-headed and stubborn. The fee was excellent and her soldiers deserved it; she was also keen to move the conversation on before Hugh was brought up again.

"We will honor the contract," she conceded, noting Hayden narrow his eyes as she spoke. "I'll request my soldiers wear your colors, but I won't force any of them, my lord."

"That is all I ask," Tancred replied. "Thank you for talking this through. The next settlement we pass, I will pay for the outfitting myself."

Constance watched the paladin walk back over to his magnificent warhorse and vault back up into the saddle. She turned to face her two comrades, forcing an uneasy smile. Hayden beamed broadly.

"That," he grinned, "is a lot of money! I'll be able to buy my daughter some good land with that!"

"Aye," Jaque nodded bitterly, "and I don't begrudge you that. But I'm not comfortable with this. Not at all. And I won't wear their colors. Not after what they did to us. You should feel the same, Constance."

"I don't need you to tell me how I should feel," Constance replied, politely but firmly. "My chief concern at the moment is making sure that my company is paid well enough; these men and women should not lose out because of my principles. I've made my decision. Hayden, get them up on the road in three ranks."

The tall man turned to bellow a string of orders out to the waiting mercenaries.

*****

His eyes narrowed in concentration, Dionne watched from his secluded vantage point as the mass of orcs navigated their way through the narrow mountain pass below. The late afternoon sun forced a few pillars of light through the thin, broken layer of clouds above that glinted off the battered, dirty armor of the twenty green skinned warriors. While there were as many variations in the heights and builds of the orcs as there were in humans, the general physique of the creatures was constant – hunchbacked, taller and broader than a man, with bald heads, flat snouted noses, and a lower jaw packed with tusk-like, sharp teeth. Dionne smiled grimly as he regarded the huge orc close to the front of the patrol, a gargantuan monster clad in thick plates of armor edged in rust and carrying a vicious, serrated axe with two heads. He was a Krudger; an orc so violent and dangerous that he had managed to fight his way up into their society's – if such a word could be used – ruling class. Dionne wondered for a moment why a Krudger had chosen to lead a mere patrol of twenty orcs. Then he ruefully remembered that he was out on a patrol of his own with just thirty men.

Dionne's men formed a thin line along the rocky ridge above the mountain pass. He had personally selected the choke point three days before and had spent the last two nights waiting for news from his scouts concerning the orcs and their movements. He had expected a far larger party, given the extent of the atrocities committed against the mining villages along the mountainside, but the opportunity to eliminate a Krudger was worth showing his hand and launching his ambush. The narrow pass snaked along the mountainside below them, allowing only two orcs to move from left to right below the human soldiers as they trekked south toward the area's mining villages. Below the path lingered several thin sheets of mist that had clung to the mountainside since dawn.

"Are we taking them?" a hoarse whisper came from next to him.

Dionne glanced across at Teynne, a relative newcomer to his group who had rapidly established himself as invaluable with his seemingly endless range of skills. His long, blond hair framing a thin face with red, perpetually fatigued eyes, Teynne looked at him expectantly. Dionne nodded. He turned to his right and gave another nod to the three soldiers who waited at the end of the line by the rock fall trap they had prepared, their heavy hammers at the ready.

The line of orcs carried on heedless below them, the stench of their sweat drenched clothes combined with their rusted armor and blood smeared weapons drifted up in the easterly wind that issued from the seas to impact against the foot of the mountains and force its way up toward the heavens. Ten of his men slowly and carefully tilted their crossbows down to aim at the silent line of greenskins below. Dionne watched as the trio of orcs at the head of the column edged ever closer to the spot on the path directly below the trap. He had little concern for them – it was the Krudger just behind them that he wanted. He raised one hand above his head and waited patiently until the huge orc was only a few paces from the trap. There – he brought his hand down in a swift, cutting motion.

The three men by the rock fall trap swung their hammers down to knock

34

away its wooden supports, allowing the collection of jagged boulders to tumble forth and drop down over the lip of ground. A guttural shout of alarm was issued by an uncharacteristically observant orc toward the rear of the group, but the reactions were too late. The boulders slammed down to crush the two orcs at the front of the line, their hunched bodies swiftly disappearing beneath the cascade of falling rocks and dense cloud of dust which blossomed up from the unnatural rock fall. Dionne swore – the Krudger appeared unscathed.

Dionne's crossbowmen did not need an order to react now the trap was sprung. A wave of ten crossbow bolts whistled down to cut through the ranks of the orcs, sending a trio of the muscular warriors twirling down over the edge of the narrow path to fall yelping to a violent demise below.

"Get down there!" Dionne yelled as he leapt to his feet, brandishing his sword above his head. "Cut the bastards off!"

A series of gruff commands was bellowed from the Krudger, and the line of orcs turned in place to quickly retreat back along the path to escape the killing ground Dionne had created. His first few men skidded down the steep slope to confront the orcs on the pathway below but were quickly overrun by the lumbering greenskins; three of his men were savagely hacked down while a fourth hapless soldier was lifted above the head of one of the orcs and tossed screaming off the mountain side.

Dionne and Teynne were the next two to arrive to confront the retreating tide of orcs. Dionne brought his sword and shield up to face a pair of the greenskins who seemed intent on charging through him as soon as his feet hit the path below. With a snarl, Dionne ran headlong to meet them. He took a heavy axe blow on to his shield and deflected it to one side to open up the defenses of the first orc, and then swiftly dispatched the creature with a clinical slash across his neck; he then ducked under a hammer blow from the second orc before lunging forward and piercing the greenskin's torso with a well aimed strike to the heart.

Teynne dashed past Dionne, his longsword held aloft. The blond haired man brought his own blade down unnaturally fast, severing the creature's sword arm. The orc staggered back, holding onto his bleeding stump with a look of surprise that provoked a sharp laugh from Teynne. The blond warrior held out a hand, uttered a few words under his breath, and a stream of orange flame issued from his palm to set the wounded orc alight and running blindly in terror as his bass screams rose above the shouts of battle. Dionne watched as the orc tripped and tumbled down the mountainside, the flaming creature bouncing and rolling off the jagged rocks before disappearing into the mist below.

It was then that Dionne saw the orcs had followed his example and had dropped down to take advantage of another pathway below, where they now fled back to the north.

"Follow them!" Dionne yelled to his men as he lowered himself over the edge of the pathway to slip down the mountainside in pursuit. "Don't let them escape!"

Wincing and ignoring the terrified screams of one of his own men who mistimed his descent and plummeted to his death, Dionne led his surviving soldiers down the mountainside and after the remaining orcs. Their retreat was orderly, suspiciously so for a foe Dionne knew was reluctant to retreat or use orderly tactics. He sprinted after the orcs as the lumbering creatures followed the path into a broad opening on a shallow slope before disappearing into a dark, jagged cave mouth in the rocks. Dionne stopped and allowed his men to catch up as the last of the ten orcs disappeared into the cave. He repressed a pang of sorrow as he quickly counted the men as they arrived; he had lost six. Six good men who had trusted him and looked to him for leadership. There would be time to dwell on that later.

Before he could issue his next wave of orders, Dionne watched as thick, wooden barricades were quickly erected across the mouth of the cave ahead.

"They've got defenses prepared?" asked Phellius, a tall, dark haired soldier who had been with Dionne since his days in the legion.

"That's not like these scum," Dionne hissed. "Something's amiss here."

The powerfully built Krudger appeared at the mouth of the cave, giving Dionne a clearer look at the enemy leader. An angular breastplate and pauldrons added to the creature's already imposing frame, while scraps of holed mail added extra protection. A bandolier of severed heads crossed from the orc's shoulder down to his waist, tied to the band by their hair.

"You wanna fight?" the huge orc yelled. "Come in here and fight proper! No more skulking 'round with yer traps!"

Dionne regarded the barricaded cave with seasoned eyes. The orcs had higher ground and an easily defendable position. It was nothing Dionne had not seen countless times before. He turned to issue his orders.

"Crossbowmen, load!" he shouted.

The crossbow armed soldiers rapidly formed up into two ranks and took their pulleys from their belts to ratchet the heavy weapons, ready to shoot again. "Teynne, burn them out!" Dionne commanded.

The blond warrior gave a slight smile and held out both hands, muttering his incantations before twin pillars of fire leapt from his fingertips and enveloped the wooden barricades with an audible whoosh. The dry wood of the defenses ignited immediately, lighting up the mountainside with a column of flames. The heat of the blaze warming his face, Dionne watched as a pair of burning bodies stumbled out of the cave mouth. The guttural screams of agony rose over the roaring of the flames as the tragically familiar smell of burning flesh filled the air.

Howling in despair, the Krudger, who had stood at the cave entrance, turned to watch as his last few orcs died agonizing deaths before his eyes. His own back now ablaze, the flesh of his face blistering in the heat, the Krudger turned again and stomped purposefully down from the cave toward the band of human fighters. He pointed his axe toward Dionne and roared.

"You!" he demanded. "Get out here and fight! Show me what yer made of! Fight me!"

A few of Dionne's men glanced across at him. He was aware of the customs of the orcs, of the need to die a good death and the unadulterated hatred of any enemy who fought using ambushes rather than brute strength. But even though he was confident that he stood a better than even chance against the Krudger, Dionne had nothing to prove. War had nothing to do with honor and certainly was never worth taking unnecessary risks for something as pointless and idiotic as ego. War was only about results. About victory.

"Crossbows, take aim!" Dionne ordered. "Loose!"

Dionne did, however, have to admit that he felt a grudging respect for the Krudger who continued to swear and rant as he staggered toward Dionne, still somehow alive and willing to fight after being punctured by ten crossbow bolts. But injured gravely, the Krudger could do nothing to stop Dionne pacing forward and slicing off his head.

Four

An enthusiastic cheer erupted from the three ranks of legion men-at-arms as the trio of horsemen cantered along to the crossroads from the west. Afternoon was turning to evening on the third full day of marching, but the long, summer days preserved the warmth in the air until well after sunset. The road north was flanked by low foothills and farmland with neat, picturesque olive groves set out in rows that seemed to wish to compete with the soldiers for orderly precision. A few isolated farmhouses and the occasional windmill were the only evidence of habitations; and without a town or village in the area, it would no doubt be another night of sleeping in tents. The relative discomfort did not bother Tancred; it was the wasted time in setting up the encampment only to be packed up again the next morning that irked him.

The three horsemen who approached the detachment were all well dressed, their cloaks, boots, and feathered hats showing that they were men of status. Tancred noticed with interest that their horses were also animals of good quality and breeding, but nothing that matched his own steed. A murmur of conversation rippled through the ranks of mounted paladins as the trio of horsemen approached; not without excitement but certainly not matching the enthusiasm of the legion infantrymen. Tancred glanced across to the crossbowmen; the thirty mercenaries regarded the newcomers in complete silence; sneers, disapproving glances, and folded arms being among the more noticeable signs of animosity.

Tancred spurred Desiree, his warhorse, away from the other paladins to catch up with Captain Georgis as the legion officer walked out to meet the new arrivals.

"Your Grace," Georgis bowed to the closest of the three men as they approached, "thank you for joining us. I am Captain Georgis of the 32nd Legion."

"It is a privilege to serve with your men," replied Dictator-Prefect Hugh of Athelle as he stepped down from his saddle.

The Dictator-Prefect was just a touch above average height, with a thin beard punctuating his dashing features. The flecks of silver in his hair and the first few wrinkles at the corners of his green eyes put him at about forty years of age, but those signs of age made his countenance all the more distinguished. Pulling a thick, leather glove off his right hand, Hugh stepped forward to shake hands warmly with the legion captain.

"Sorry for the delay," he smiled. "I had to tend to a family matter. Captain Georgis, these are my aides, Platus and Trennio."

Tancred looked across at the two aides, both of whom were of a similar age to the Dictator-Prefect and were similarly well armed and armored. Their names seemed familiar; the penny dropped quickly in Tancred's mind, and he remembered that they were both famous names in the dueling and tournament circuits, expert swordsmen and riders. The two men nodded courteously but remained silent. More than a little annoyed that a mere legion captain was taking center stage over him, Tancred lowered himself down from his warhorse and walked over to the gathering. The Dictator-Prefect was a powerful man with great political influence, and given Tancred's ambitions, favor from the nobleman would do him well.

"Your Grace," Tancred bowed, "allow me to present myself. I am Lord Paladin Tancred of Effisus, commander of the knight paladins of the Order of the Sacred Ark that have been placed under your overall command."

The nobleman again flashed his charismatic smile and shook Tancred's hand.

"I'm thoroughly delighted to have elite knights of one of the most prestigious orders in all of Mantica at my side. It is a pleasure to meet you, Tancred. I know your family name, of course."

"Your Grace," Tancred bowed again in acknowledgment.

"Let us not stand on ceremony," Hugh replied, "a simple 'sir' will suffice from here on in. So, onto the task in hand. What are your thoughts?"

"The reports that have filtered back to the Duma place Dionne to the very east of the Mountains of Tarkis, not far from the coast," Captain Georgis began. "We know very little of the size of the force he commands. I'd suggest we make haste to the area and set about patrolling the mountains to locate his base of operations."

"That will take too long," Tancred countered, ignoring the look of irritation his contradiction garnered from Georgis, "and we need to acknowledge that we are not dealing with an overt enemy force. This is more akin to small bands of skirmishers who will harass a conventional military force. This man has made himself something of a legend in the area, a real hero to the people. We would do better by establishing ourselves in the area with a proper show of force, and putting down any insurrections that might stand against the Hegemon's authority."

Hugh nodded slowly.

"I think the paladin is right," he winced. "Given the reputation that the self styled 'Centurion' Dionne has made for himself, we need to be prepared for the fact that we will be facing hundreds of peasants and farmers who will stand against us with every weapon they can muster. These simple folk genuinely believe that Dionne is a hero who stands on our borders, killing orc warbands and hordes of Abyssal demons to protect them where the armies of the Hegemon have failed them. They don't see him for the skulking traitor he really is."

"Our force is small but better trained and equipped than anything we will face," Tancred continued, "but if Dionne gathers enough support in one place, we can still be overwhelmed. Even though these are our own people, I believe we need to make a statement as soon as we are in the area. A very obvious one."

"Agreed," Hugh exhaled, scanning his eyes across the ranks of soldiers on the road behind them. "Where is our war wizard? I assume the Duma would not dream of sending us off on such a task without magic to support our soldiers?"

Tancred exchanged a concerned look with Georgis.

"Sir, a mage was not assigned us," Georgis said quietly. "We were told that none of the Schools of Magic could spare any war wizards beyond those that have already been committed in other tasks and campaigns."

"So what of attacking our enemies at range?" the Dictator-Prefect demanded, more than a hint of annoyance bursting through his otherwise calm and collected demeanor.

"At the back there," Georgis gestured, "behind the paladins' squires. We have a contingent of mercenaries with crossbows. Thirty of them, all experienced."

"Oh, good, good," Hugh's furrowed brow lifted. "With over one hundred soldiers including heavy cavalry and crossbows, I'm confident we can deal with a horde of peasants, even if they are led by a self-proclaimed strategic genius. Still, although the mercenaries are only temporarily attached to Basilea's military might, I'd still welcome their thoughts and input. When we gather on the march, I would have their captain with us."

Tancred again exchanged a look with Georgis, but decided he would speak this time.

"The mercenaries have been very clear about how they see their role in this task, sir," Tancred said carefully. "They are simple men and women with experience, bravery, and skills on the field, but none of them are planners and leaders, by their own admission. They are more than content to leave the planning to us and follow your orders."

Tancred exhaled, relatively happy with his diplomatic twisting of the facts.

"Nonetheless, they bring a different perspective to ours, and outside eyes may well reveal glaring errors in our plans. Ensure a suitable representative from the mercenary contingent is made available for all future discussions. That is all for now. Let us proceed north and take advantage of every minute of sunlight we still have."

Grinding his teeth uneasily, Tancred watched Hugh swing himself back up into his saddle and take his place at the head of the columns with his two aides. As Tancred vaulted back up onto his own horse, the drums struck up again as the soldiers marched north.

*****

Summer in the Mountains of Tarkis was something that Dionne had never grown tired of. Whatever happened in the cosmos above, whatever the Shining

41

Ones had decided to do with the heavens, resulted in the moonlight illuminating the lands in a golden hue for two, sometimes three, hours after sunset and then again in the hour leading up to dawn. He sat alone on a rocky perch at the edge of one of his encampments, looking out to the east across the Low Sea of Suan where the gentle ripples of the waves reflected tiny flecks of orange-white on the midnight blue surface as far as the eye could see. The islands to the southeast, the villages in the foothills to the south, all of them benefited from his protection. He looked up to the northeast where, leagues beyond the horizon but still too close for comfort, lay the enemy of his people. The scar that was wrenched across the earth – both literally and metaphorically – where evil poured forth to sweep down toward the Hegemony and plague all the nation stood for.

Dionne swore and shook his head. The evil threatened all Basilea once stood for. But not anymore. Now, corrupt politicians used the once noble Duma to further their own objectives, line their pockets with gold, and abuse the principles of the system to further their own malevolent and debase families. The Hegemon, that great dictator, sat above it all, hiding behind a web of lies and exploitation of faith. The Hegemon – perversely born into power rather voted by the people – was both emperor and high priest. His will was intractable, beyond contestation by any below him. He lived in the most corpulent luxury in the City of the Golden Horn, the very center of all corruption in the so-called civilized world. Dionne wondered what was the true threat – the Abyss to the north or the Hegemon and his politicians and fanatical followers in the heart of Mantica's most advanced nation. At least the demons of the Abyss were honest in their intentions.

"Centurion?"

Dionne looked over his shoulder to see Phellius stood with two thin young men in the battered garb of simple farmers. Phellius himself wore a coat of mail, battered and overdue for a replacement, over which was an ill-fitting breastplate of basic quality. Like all of the others, he looked thin and tired, but his eyes still held the same spark of determination that was there when Dionne had first met him some thirteen years ago.

Behind them, the subdued twinkling of lights betrayed the carefully controlled campfires of some three-dozen of Dionne's soldiers. How many he actually had altogether, scattered across his numerous encampments and bolt holes hidden away in the mountains, he was not sure.

"Two men from our latest supply visit to Astennes," Phellius ushered the men forward. "They have volunteered to join us."

Dionne regarded the two men with more care and attention. The first was a tall, broad man of thirty years with a thick, black beard and nervous eyes. His coarse hands were clamped in front of him and his eyes shifted from meeting Dionne's appraising stare to looking down at his feet. The second man was in his early twenties, with copper hair and a thin mustache. His stance appeared more confident, almost eager.

"You know who I am?"

42

Both men nodded but remained silent.

"Do either of you have any military experience?" Dionne asked.

"None, sir," the older man said gruffly, "I've worked mines all my life."

"I know how to operate a crossbow," the younger man said, excitement and optimism in his tone, "and I served a month's worth of an apprenticeship with a blacksmith in Tmoskai. I didn't learn much, but I can do basic repairs on armor."

That piqued Dionne's interest, but only momentarily. It did not take long to train a man how to use a crossbow, and he had a good smattering of people who could repair armor.

"Do you have family?" Dionne asked.

"No, sir," the miner said. "I had a wife and a son. They're gone now. Orcs attacked our village."

"I'm married, sir," the young man with the red hair said. "My wife is with child. But she supports me in coming out here. She knows how important it is... what you are doing here."

Dionne heard the creaking from his fists as they clenched, his eyes narrowing as he stared the young man down. He had never married, had never fathered children, but he had spoken to enough fathers and mothers to know the earth shattering importance that parenthood brought with it.

"Go home to your wife, boy," Dionne said with a tired sigh. "Go and see to your family."

"But I..."

"Go and do your damn duty as a father!" Dionne erupted with enough force to make the young man take a step back in alarm. "You've already got a job, so go and do it!"

His face a picture of confusion and bitter disappointment, the young man looked to Phellius for support, but on finding none, turned silently to leave. Dionne watched him go before switching his gaze back to the taller man.

"What's your name?"

"Castus, sir."

"I'm sorry for your loss, Castus. Truly, I am. Do you still hold onto your anger with the orcs for what they took from you?"

Castus held Dionne's stare for a few moments. The nervous glances were replaced with deep sorrow, and then hatred. He nodded.

"Aye."

Dionne held out his arm to offer his hand to the miner.

"You're welcome to join us, friend. I can make a soldier out of you."

Castus shook his hand, his eyes warily flitting between Dionne and Phellius as if he was making a pact with a demon from the Abyss.

"Go get him settled in," Dionne said to Phellius before turning to look down at the sea to the east again.

Phellius walked the new addition to their small army over to another soldier before returning to stand by Dionne again. Phellius said nothing, but the uncomfortable atmosphere was enough to nudge Dionne's mind toward the problem he had come to discuss.

"What is it? Come on, man, you've known me long enough. Spit it out."

"It's Teynne, sir," Phellius said quietly, but with conviction. "The men don't trust him. I don't trust him."

Dionne shook his head and turned to face the younger man. Phellius' eyes betrayed his nerves, but he met Dionne's stare unflinchingly nonetheless.

"We've been here before," Dionne explained, aware that his irritation was creeping through what he had planned to be a patient tone. "He's been with us for over a year. He's proved himself time and time again. What more do you want from the man?"

"He turns up out of nowhere, very conveniently, when we most need soldiers. He knows magic and he knows how to use a sword. Men like that are beyond rare. And he just happens to cross our path when we're surrounded by a horde of undead legionnaires, outnumbered and all but doomed?"

"Fate favored us, it seems," Dionne answered, remembering the incident well, when he had led his men into a complex of caves only to encounter ranks of legion soldiers, dead for centuries, still looking for their lost eagle standard.

"I think a man largely makes his own fate, and Teynne has done just that. Whatever his motivation."

"And what do you think his motivation is?" Dionne snapped. "What has he done that is so sinister to incur the wrath of you and the men?"

"He's spying on us, Dionne!" Phellius exclaimed. "Can't you see? We're rebels! We left the legion, we followed you because we believed in you! We still do! We left everything for you and your cause! A legion captain disobeying orders and taking his men with him? We know that is so incredible that it would have been reported to the Hegemon himself! And here we are, a decade later, still in hiding, still outlaws, and still wanted for trial by the Duma!"

"And still holding back demons, orcs and a thousand evil bastards from pillaging our country and our people, because that same Duma won't send enough men to do the job properly!" Dionne shook his head in frustration. "You can't doubt our cause, surely?"

"Never!" Phellius hissed. "None of us do! But this man who you have accepted and given a position of authority and power, we don't trust him! We won't follow him! He's a spy, sent here from the Duma to report on us! You mark my words, it won't be long until there are legion men scouring these mountains to hunt us down!"

Dionne took a deep breath and nodded. He knew that elements of what his old comrade was saying were undoubtedly true. He had made too much noise, had attacked too many invaders, to remain undetected. The Duma knew he was still out here, and it would not be long before troops were sent to apprehend him. He was surprised that it had taken so long for a reaction from the capital, but it made some sense. After the incident with the unfortunate deaths of the two paladins, he had fled Basilea for the better part of nine years, completely disappearing from the eyes of the Duma.

"I'll keep a closer eye on Teynne," Dionne said softly. "I trust you and I trust the men. I value your instinct and your loyalty. I do not for a second think he is a spy sent here by the Duma, but I will watch him closely."

"Thank you, sir," Phellius replied, "that is all we ask."

*****

Constance attempted to push her way to the front of the small crowd that had gathered in a loose circle at the center of the encampment. The detachment was still three days from the Mountains of Tarkis, but now they were in the northern provinces, and she was still wary as the area had a proud history of rebellion against the rule of the City of the Golden Horn. Half a dozen large camp fires lit up the night, around which were scattered tents of varying sizes, from the cramped shared tents of the paladins' squires to the large tent used by the Dictator-Prefect, no doubt crammed with luxury within.

A handful of Constance's mercenaries had dashed over to see what had prompted twenty of the men-at-arms to form the circle at the far end of camp. She cursed her curiosity as she levered her way in between two of her soldiers – she realized that an element of aloof detachment had its time and place for a leader, but days of marching had left her thoroughly bored despite the good company of the men and women in her band.

"What's going on?" she asked Jaque, raising her voice over the excited buzz of conversation as she nudged in to stand next to him.

"Fight!" The lanky man flashed his gap toothed grin. "One of the legion fellows was shooting his mouth off about how he's unbeatable in a fight, some nonsense about having never taken a hit in five years of fighting. All his boys backed him up; said he is that good."

Constance looked into the center of the circle and saw a tall, powerfully built man in his mid twenties with a strong, chiseled jaw and dark eyes. He wore only blue leggings and leather boots, leaving his torso exposed to show off a muscular physique. Standing opposite him, towering over the legion soldier was a colossal warrior of perhaps forty years of age with a thick, blond beard and a head shaven to the scalp. The huge man watched, unimpressed as the legion warrior showed off his skills as he flourished and twirled a wooden practice sword around his body in a series of impressive displays.

"Who's he?" Constance nodded at the huge, bald man.

"That's the thrilling part!" Jaque's eyes flashed in excitement. "It's one of the paladins! He said he'd fight him!"

"Are paladins allowed to do that?" Constance asked.

"That's the least of his worries!" A legion soldier stood to Constance's left grinned broadly. "Eustace has never lost a fight!"

Constance watched as the legion soldier identified as Eustace by his friend advanced boldly to face the hulking paladin. Eustace span the wooden blade around his body and shouted out a challenge – while the show was ostentatious enough to cause Constance to roll her eyes, she could not help but be impressed with his obvious skill and agility. The legion was famous the world over for its ability to fight and win as a team, in rank and file, but it was a fool who presumed that there were not world class fighters within its ranks.

The warrior leapt forward to attack, stringing together three precise strikes aimed at the paladin's head and torso. The paladin did not step back an inch, but he countered each strike with a solid defense that seemed far too swift and fluid for a man of his size. Undeterred, Eustace brought his wooden blade crashing down at the paladin's head, forcing his guard high before changing the course of his attack to sweep up at the gut. Again the strike clattered off an unmovable defense.

Without pausing for a moment, Eustace again brought his ersatz blade around to strike at the paladin's flank, maintaining momentum and keeping the initiative of attack well and firmly on his side. Constance watched, jaw agape in surprise as the paladin batted the legion soldier's attack to one side and opened up his guard before slamming a fist into his jaw and sending him crumpling to the ground, out cold.

The assembled soldiers fell completely silent as their champion lay senseless in the long grass. The paladin's stern eyes scanned across the circle of soldiers around him before he spoke.

"He's good," he admitted in a gruff voice, "but I've faced far better."

Constance watched as the huge man walked off toward the paladin's tents while two of the legion soldiers set about reviving their unconscious friend. Jaque turned to Constance.

"Well, that wasn't the most satisfying end to the entertainment."

"Come on," Constance shrugged, "see if any of our lot want a story or two around the fire before we call it a night."

Jaque grinned and nodded before dashing off to the south end of the encampment, where the mercenaries had set up their tents. Constance turned her back on the encampment and looked out over the olive fields, still visible in the bright moonlight and the reflected campfires. The land to the north gently undulated up to where the Mountains of Tarkis now dominated the horizon, their saw-toothed profile looking like the lower half of the jaws of some monstrous creature waiting to devour them.

At least it was summer. The Mountains of Tarkis were brutal, utterly lethal in winter, and that served as a major line of defense for the Hegemony against many of the threats that poured out of the Abyssal scar, leagues to the northeast. Many, but not all. Some things that came out of that huge hole in the ground did not feel the cold. Constance suppressed a shiver at the thought, thinking back to the last time she faced Abyssal demons on the field of battle. She turned back and walked over to where her mercenaries had pitched their tents, thinking through a dozen different tales her father had told her when she was growing up. It made her smile to think that her men and women, a motley assortment of tough, scarred warriors from several different kingdoms, still liked to hear her stories around the campfire. But that was culture; that was tradition; without the age old custom of telling the stories, the messages they conveyed might be lost forever, especially given how few of her mercenaries could read and write.

Constance found eleven of her men waiting by one of the fires, all of the usual audience members when it came to storytelling: Hayden, Jaque, Wulf, Mallius. A few newcomers also sat ready for the tale telling. A bottle of wine, the base of its green glass wrapped in a simple lattice of straw, was passed to her as she sat down and crossed her legs.

"As we've got some newcomers to our gathering, I'm going to start with perhaps the most important story of all," Constance began. "We all know it, but it defines the age we live in, and any time spent reciting it is always time spent well."

A few murmurs of approval were exchanged before Constance began.

"The Celestians were eternal, and eternity was the Celestians. The Celestians were omnipotence and ruled over all. Before our own concept of time even came into being, the Celestians created many worlds, and our world of Mantica was the very first, created out of clay and water but infused with the very power of the Star of Heaven itself. Mantica was peopled with three great races – the elves to bring intellect, the dwarves with their industrious nature, and men to bring wisdom and sound judgment overall. Just as Mantica was favored by the Celestians ruling from above, so was the race of Man."

"Unless you hear this story told by elves," Hayden smiled as he lit a long pipe of tobacco, "as funnily enough, their history of events claims the elves were favored…"

"Regardless!" Constance laughed. "Mantica prospered for years, centuries, ages. At the center of the world was the Grand Republic of Primovantor, entrusted with the Tome of Judgment to cast fair and proper verdict over all men. Harrett was Primovantor's greatest king, for it was under Harrett's rule that the people were first given the right to choose their representation, and the foundations of our Duma were established. Harrett had ten sons, and his first and greatest was Okestes. Okestes second son, Marcon, was made the Tribune of Esk, and under his leadership and the paternal love he held over his people, the city of Esk saw its most golden and prosperous years."

"There was the slight matter of his choices during the Great Flood of the West, but let us not besmirch the noble soul's honor," Hayden winked as he puffed a rich, aromatic smoke from his long pipe.

"After many years, Marcon left the care of Esk to his first son, Jarek," Constance ignored Hayden and the smirk of the regulars at his well-practiced interruption to continue, "and left his lands to visit the elven city of Therennia Adar, accompanied by his three daughters. His youngest daughter was Elinathora, famed across all of Primovantor as the most beautiful woman of her age, wise beyond her years, possessing a heart filled with virtue and a mind able to judge the good or evil in a man's soul with but a single glance.

"Elinathora caught the eye of the mighty elven sorcerer Calisor Fenulian, vain and ambitious. Calisor pursued Elinathora, his unwelcome advances firmly but politely rebuked for forty days and forty nights. Unable to accede this rejection, Calisor fled Therennia Adar in a fit of rage."

"Again," Hayden mused, "when I've heard elves tell this story, it does take a slightly different trajectory at this point. Predominantly over the issue of Elinathora's virtue and wisdom."

"Calisor fled to the Groves of Adar!" Constance leaned forward, injecting more of a theatrical tone into her voice in an attempt to override Hayden's latest interjection. "And it was here, under a full moon, that he entering a clearing in the great forest and chanced upon Oskan, the most fickle of all Celestians. Oskan listened to Calisor's story of woe, but whether it was sympathy or a want to meddle that saw the Celestian's interjection into mortal affairs will forever remain unknown. Oskan plotted with Calisor under that full moon in the forest clearing! Together, they hatched a plan to use the full force of Calisor's magic to craft an artifact of great power, a mirror that would show any who gazed into it the future, or at least a possible version of the future. A future that showed Calisor without flaw or vice, so that any who gazed into it would see an ideal, an impossibility, and would love him."

Constance paused, letting the words sink in. Her audience leaned in, hanging on her every word. She saw the same spark in their eyes that she no doubt had when her father told her the tale, even though they knew the story and its ending well – just as she had.

"Calisor Fenulian traveled the length and breadth of the world for a full year to gather the components he needed to craft his mirror. Then, a year to the very night and in the very same forest clearing, Calisor brought the Fenulian Mirror to Oskan. It was under a full moon that Oskan completed the sorcery required for the mirror; the light of the Star of Heaven itself. He left Calisor with one final warning. *'When the golden bird sings, look into the mirror no more.'* Again, for forty days and forty nights Calisor begged to see Elinathora, but on the eve of the Feast of All Souls, her pity won over her wisdom, and she met him in the Gardens of Auroaya. Calisor, driven by obsession, tricked fair Elinathora into looking into the cursed mirror.

"Elinathora saw a world where Calisor was dedicated, virtuous, loyal, and devoted. She saw a world where they fell in love and were married, and where they lived happily and raised many sons and daughters side-by-side, happy and devoted to each other. Her heart thawed as she was deceived by the cruel trick, and she fell in love with the elven mage. Calisor watched in awe and delight as his trick worked and the object of his obsession was bent to his twisted will. He forgot Oskan's words. He did not heed the song of the golden bird. Elinathora's smile slowly faded as the images in the mirror continued, showing her death and Calisor descend into the depths of inconsolable sadness. She saw her son raise an army and go to war against Calisor, and she saw her husband slay their own son before taking his own life when he realized what he had done.

"In a fit of desperation, Elinathora flung the mirror against the wall, crying out in desolation as she tried to blind herself to the images she had seen. But the cursed Fenulian Mirror contained within it the light of the Star of Heaven, and with it, the very power of the Celestians themselves. At that moment, at the very instance the mirror shattered, the heavens and everything below them was changed forever. Many immortal Celestians were slain, consumed by the power that escaped from the accursed artifact as it was destroyed in a great wave of darkness. Those Celestians who remained were torn asunder, ripped in two, and separated into both the purest and the vilest aspects of their very being. In one mortal act, the Shining Ones and Wicked Ones were born, conflicting aspects each born of the same being, who watch us from the very heavens and from the depths of the Abyss to this very day."

*****

The monotonous scraping of metal on metal broke through the crackling of the campfires and the conversations from the groups of soldiers around the camps. The night was mild, even for this time of year, but Orion knew from experience that it would soon change with the onset of the fall and the harsher climates ahead. The metallic scraping continued as Orion's squire carried on in his clumsy attempts to sharpen his swords from where he sat on the other side of the small campfire. Orion truly despaired of Kell. The boy had been a squire for years and still showed no real promise, no advancement, no potential for greater things. There was a very real chance that Orion would have to end Kell's career before it had even truly begun.

"Angle the stone, boy!" Orion bellowed across the orange flames. "How many times have I told you?"

The paladin looked down at the letter in his hands. A courier had caught up with the detachment a few hours previously, and a handful of letters had been distributed among those wealthy enough to possess friends and family who could read and write. His heart thumping in his chest, Orion broke the wax seal of the letter and unrolled the scroll.

"Dear Son…"

Orion skipped ahead to the very end and saw his mother's signature, eliciting mixed feelings. Of course he was always glad to hear from his mother, but with every letter that arrived highlighted the lack of communication from the rest of his family. As the youngest of three sons, he was little in his father's eyes. Leoni was the heir to the family estate, and from what Orion had heard, his oldest brother did a grand job of the day-to-day management. Godfrey had already been given his own chapel in the capital, so his career in the priesthood was assured of success. But Orion, in his father's eyes at least, was not even the spare in case anything befell Leoni. He was the spare to the spare. Perhaps he should consider himself lucky that his father had deemed him worthy of training as a paladin's squire. At least Uncle

Jahus had always shown faith in him.

Orion exhaled and closed his eyes. Uncle Jahus. If only Orion had possessed the strength, skill, and speed back then that he had now. He could have easily bested Dionne's thugs and protected his uncle. Jahus would be alive now. Flashing Kell another admonishing glare for slowing his efforts on sharpening the weapons, Orion returned his attention to the letter from his beloved mother.

"...was only yesterday telling the ladies how proud I am of you... you are always in my thoughts and prayers... must take care and come back home to us safe and well..."

Orion smiled. The letter said both nothing and everything. There was no real news, nothing from back home, but the tone of the letter told Orion all he needed to know. Orion folded the ltter carefully, deciding to save it for when he had more time to truly appreciate the time and effort that had gone into the words. For now, he had his evening prayers, and then a longer night of properly servicing his weapons and armor after the brutal attempts at care exhibited by his hapless squire.

Five

The musty scent of hops drifted across the dusty road as the easterly breeze swept across the fields from the sea. Sunlight poured down, unopposed from a crystal clear sky as the detachment continued north toward the foothills leading up to the mountains, and their destination. The men-at-arms continued to march at the fore in three ranks, Captain Georgis still at the lead but now riding atop a borrowed horse from the paladins, having given up on the long march by foot. His fifty men-at-arms enjoyed no such luxury.

Some halfway along the column, Tancred rode alongside Hugh and his ominously silent aides, occasionally glancing over his shoulder at where his paladins rode smartly behind the legion soldiers. Having spent days on the march in the unforgiving summer heat, the paladins wore their light robes of blue, armored only by their shining breastplates. The rest of their armor was carried in the baggage train, as attack was considered highly unlikely. Tancred had spent the journey alternating between his two other horses, but he now had returned to his primary steed, Desiree. Behind the paladins were the squires, and then the mercenaries. The mercenary crossbowmen ambled along without order or discipline, laughing and joking as they walked.

"Shame we had to resort to them," Hugh remarked, nodding in the direction of Tancred's glance, "but it's understandable."

"The problem with the north," Tancred remarked as he swatted a fly away from his face, "is that the people take too much pride in rebellion based on ignorance. The Hegemon has the overwhelming majority of his armies scattered all across the northern provinces, keeping the forces of the Abyss at bay from not only Basilea, but much of the world. Yet, because these farmers and miners occasionally suffer at the hands of a small orc or Abyssal raid and they do not see a legion man instantly appear to defend them, they jump to the conclusion that the Hegemon does not care."

"These peasants think the Hegemon lives for nobody but himself," Hugh agreed, "and that could not be further from the truth. He is a wise man who does not take his responsibilities lightly, not in the slightest. It takes a great man to head the most powerful nation in the world, and he does it with the right blend of care and force. Our men fight and die to protect Basilea, but these simple country folk

51

don't see great battles on their very doorsteps, so they think the Hegemon and the Duma are idle. They look at those with wealth and power as foppish and lazy. I cannot tell you how much I resent that assumption."

Tancred nodded, agreeing in principle with the nobleman but finding a gnawing of unease within at his choice of words. Still, Tancred's father had spoken highly of Hugh, and the need for Hugh's backing and favor was paramount. Returning to the City of the Golden Horn at the head of a victorious task, with Hugh speaking well of Tancred in the Duma, would no doubt get his advancement back on schedule.

The soldiers rounded the crest of a small hill, and Tancred looked down to see a collection of buildings in the shallow valley below. Situated at a crossroads, the settlement was just about large enough to call itself a town, although the complete absence of any stone buildings marked it out as less than prosperous. A pair of large buildings, possibly an inn and an administrative building, formed the core while the ramshackle, sun bleached houses of farmers expanded out untidily to meet the carefully tended fields in the land around. A gentle and scenic sequence of small waterfalls cascaded down from the hills to the north, terminating in a pool in the center of the town, while a broad, shallow river ran to the east with a long, low wooden bridge spanning it abeam the town's mid point.

"Emalitos," Hugh confirmed as he looked down at his map. "We're still on schedule. I think it would be prudent for the men to wear armor from this point onward."

"Agreed," Tancred said as he looked down at a pair of farmers who leant on their pitchforks and watched the marching soldiers in silence from a crop field to the right of the dusty road.

More farmers moved to the stone walls at the sides of the road as the soldiers advanced to the town, all of them watching with stony faced silence. Their looks made Tancred feel more like he was an invader rather than arriving to apprehend a dangerous lawbreaker. Captain Georgis bellowed a command to halt from the front of the procession before allowing the legion men-at-arms to move off the road and reach for their waterskins.

"Tancred, take a couple of your fellows into the town and find out how much room there is at that inn," Hugh leaned forward in his saddle. "Paladins are more… liked than the legion up here, so the question would be better coming from you."

"Of course," Tancred smiled, happy to be trusted with even a menial task.

He turned in his saddle and picked out two paladins to join him.

"Sister Jeneveve, Brother Orion, with me."

Jeneveve spurred her brown warhorse into a gentle canter to catch up with her commander. With striking, freckled features and long, brown hair, Jeneveve was one of only two sister paladins in Tancred's command. Disciplined, pious, and highly intelligent, she was everything Orion was not. Orion arrived some time afterward, his hulking warhorse seemingly as disinterested in proceedings as his rider.

"This is Emalitos," Tancred said, "we'll stop here for a rest before moving north. Let us go and see what we can find."

"Aye, Lord Paladin," Jeneveve replied.

The three paladins rode past the rickety wooden houses on the outskirts of the town and past the sun kissed waters of the lake near the center. As they rode along the thin road winding through the houses, a small group of children ran out from behind one of the buildings, waving and cheering. Jeneveve stopped her horse and turned to face them, leaning over in her saddle and smiling warmly as they approached. An authoritarian female voice growled a reprimand from the doorway of the building and the children turned silently to file back toward their home, leaving Jeneveve alone for a moment as her smile faded before she rejoined the other two paladins.

The trio of riders arrived in the small town square. Ahead of them, an elderly, robed man walked down from the entrance of the austere town hall, accompanied by two younger figures. Orion brought his warhorse to a halt and stepped down to the ground, his eyes fixed on the figures by the town hall. Jeneveve jumped nimbly to the ground, her features more passive as she turned in a slow circle to look at the town around her. Tancred dismounted his own horse and took the reins to guide the animal to the stable block next to the inn.

A moment later, three men in mail hauberks with swords at their waist walked out of the door before them. The first armed man, a muscular warrior in his mid-thirties with dark, cropped hair, looked up; and his eyes widened in surprise and alarm as soon as he saw the paladins.

"Go!" the dark haired man yelled. "Run!"

All three sprinted for the stable block. Whatever had caused the alarm was a complete mystery to Tancred, but nonetheless he was the first to react, planting a foot into one of his horse's stirrups and hauling himself back up in the saddle.

"Come on!" he urged. "After them!"

The three armed men shot out of the stables on horseback as Tancred was spurring his own animal into a gallop, kicking up a cloud of dust behind him as Jeneveve and Orion were still dragging themselves back into their saddles. Digging his spurs into Desiree's flanks, Tancred shouted an encouraging command to his warhorse as he accelerated after the three men and through the narrow streets of Emalitos. He glanced over his shoulder and saw Jeneveve galloping after him, but she was already too far behind.

The three riders spurred their horses around the corner of a large grain house, scattering a small crowd of locals to each side of the road. Tancred followed on their heels, steadily but slowly closing the gap between them as he coaxed every gasp of energy out of his horse. The riders headed east and down the shallow banks of the river, splashing into the knee deep water and hurtling off to the north with Tancred still not far behind. Children playing at the water's edge cheered and shouted as they passed, the severity of the situation completely lost on them.

The sunlight shone brightly in his eyes as the light rays reflecting off the spray of water left behind the three riders, painting a rainbow of color in the water droplets kicked up by the charging horses. The leading two riders disappeared from view behind a corner of embankment as the river bent sharply to the left. Frantically digging his heels into his horse, the last of the three riders looked over his shoulder with terror as he saw Tancred continue to close, only perhaps three horse lengths behind him now. The rider looked forward again as he rounded the corner, just in time to let out a panicked cry before his head slammed into a low hanging tree branch, snapping his neck and wrenching him from his saddle.

Tancred threw himself into the turn and over to the left side of his horse, dragging the frenzied animal over to one side as he narrowly avoided the same fate. Pulling himself back up into his saddle, he looked back over his shoulder as he overtook the riderless horse; the dismounted rider lay dead in the shallow water behind him. Up ahead, the remaining two riders galloped up and over the embankment to the left of the river to leave the water and disappear into a wooded area to the west. Tancred followed them, kicking at his warhorse again for more speed to make up the ground he had lost in the turn.

Through the wood, he saw the two armored men continue to gallop away, picking their way through the trees and surrounding foliage as the undergrowth grew more dense and treacherous. The shorter of the two men shouted something out to the other rider – the dark haired man who had raised the alarm initially – and then peeled away to drag his horse around to face Tancred. The man drew his sword, fixed his eyes on the approaching paladin, and with a snarl, kicked his horse into a charge.

Tancred almost pitied the man as he drew his own sword from his side – facing a Basilean paladin on horseback in single combat was as good as suicide. Tancred watched the man approach, gauging his attack. As the two closed, he saw the mixture of sadness and desperation on the young man's face as Tancred leaned into the attack and plunged his sword straight through the man's chest, killing him outright and barely slowing down in the process. With one man left to face, Tancred blinked the sweat out of his eyes and continued the chase.

Threading through the trees as blurs of lush green and earthy brown flashed to either side of him. Tancred closed with his quarry again. Pillars of sunlight broke through the canopy of leaves overhead, shining down in columns of misty white. Up ahead, the trees opened out into a small clearing, but at the far end a sheer cliff face of dusty brown rock barred any further progress. The final horseman hauled back on his reins, dragging his steed up onto its hind legs into a frightened halt. He turned to face Tancred as the paladin entered the clearing, slowing his horse but holding his bloodied sword aloft.

"Stop!" the dark haired man shouted, holding his hands to either side in a gesture of surrender. "Enough!"

"Throw your sword down!" Tancred yelled as he closed with the rider. "Do it, now!"

The tall man obeyed, casting his sword aside before slowly climbing down from his saddle. Tancred rode over to him, keeping his own blade held at the ready and looking anxiously around him for other enemies. He heard the drumming of galloping hooves from the woods behind him.

"Who are you?" Tancred demanded as he looked down at the dark haired man. "Why did your man attack me?"

His vanquished opponent offered an insolent smile but remained silent. The rumbling from the woods was replaced with another rider as Jeneveve galloped into view at the far end of the clearing. Orion appeared only moments later, and the two paladins rushed over to Tancred.

"What is going on?" Jeneveve breathed. "And who is this man?"

"That's what we are about to find out," Tancred kept his eyes fixed on the smiling man who stood in the center of the three mounted paladins. "We'll take him back, the others will be wondering where we have disappeared to."

"Not likely, my lord," Jeneveve replied, "the river was clearly visible from the hill to the south of the town, they all would have seen us pursuing these men."

Orion's eyes narrowed pensively before opening wide.

"I should head back to the town," he said suddenly, a note of something akin to panic in his voice, "with your permission of course, Lord Paladin."

Tancred eyed the older paladin suspiciously, feeling his anger rising at the mockery he felt was intended in the use of his title.

"Go," he commanded, "Jeneveve and I are more than capable of bringing this thug back."

Wondering what he was missing, Tancred watched in puzzlement as Orion dragged his horse around and kicked the animal into an urgent gallop back toward the town.

*****

Orion's suspicions were confirmed the moment he arrived back at Emalitos. Six legion men-at-arms were gathered in front of the inn, with a crowd of perhaps fifteen townsfolk in a loose circle around them. Two of the soldiers restrained a fair-haired woman in her thirties, who was screaming and pulling frantically at the men who held her arms, blood dribbling from her mouth and nose. Three of the soldiers were gathered around the crumpled figure of a man of a similar age who lay curled up in a ball in the dust as one of the soldiers kicked him repetitively in the ribs. Orion was enraged but not surprised. He knew of Hugh's reputation. He knew of Hugh's role in putting down the Peasant's Revolt of Karathos three years earlier.

The crowd hurriedly opened up as Orion arrived, galloping his warhorse to the inn before hauling the reins in to bring the animal to an abrupt halt.

"What do you think you are doing?" He yelled as he dismounted, pacing toward the men who were assaulting the injured farmer.

One soldier paid heed to the paladin as he arrived and walked out to confront him. Orion pushed him down into the dirt before arriving at the man-at-

55

arms who was kicking the injured man. He picked the legion soldier up by his throat, dragging the choking man to his feet and staring into his terrified eyes as he closed his hands around the man's neck.

"I asked what is going on here!" Orion bellowed, throwing the soldier down to the ground and turning to face the rest of the soldiers. "You two! Release that woman, *now!*"

"Orders from the Dictator-Prefect!" exclaimed a short soldier, barely out of his teens. "The townspeople have been harboring criminals! We were ordered to get information out of them by any means!"

"Release that woman, boy!" Orion pointed a finger at the young soldier, feeling the rage rise up within him at the injustice that had been allowed to transpire. "I will not tell you again!"

The soldier let go of the woman's arm, but the older legion man next to him stood firm and continued to restrain the panicked woman, even as she smashed her hands ineffectually against his armored sleeve. The other four men-at-arms shuffled around to stand with the first two men, leaving the injured farmer to crawl over to the edge of the growing circle of townsfolk who had gathered to witness the spectacle.

Orion paced toward the soldier who refused to release the woman, his fists clenched. The soldier looked up at him, his resolve finally breaking, and let go of the frightened woman. Orion looked down uselessly at his left hand, wishing not for the first time that he had spent more time studying divinity magic. As it was, he knew only the most simple of spells, whereas many paladins of his experience could easily have utilized their powers to heal the woman's injuries. But Orion had dedicated every spare minute to using the weapons of war. Healing magic had never been his priority. Time studying the arcane was wasted time that could have been spent on swordsmanship. Arcane mastery would not have stopped the sword that killed his Uncle Jahus.

"Go and gather every man-at-arms in this town!" he yelled as he turned his attention back to the legion men. "Tell them that their orders are rescinded! Get them back to that hill to the south of the town. Right now!"

Not waiting to find out whether his commands were to be obeyed, Orion flung two of the soldiers to either side and stomped over to the front of the inn, kicking one of the doors off its hinges and striding inside. The scene that greeted him was not dissimilar to that outside. Hugh and his two aides stood by the inn's bar while ten men-at-arms restrained or beat four bloodied townsmen in a space cleared in the center of the floor. Two serving girls cried in the far corner of the room, cowering at the foot of a staircase leading up to the next floor. Smashed furniture and spilled drinks littered the room.

"Stop!" Orion shouted. "Now!"

The room fell silent. All eyes turned to face him. The Dictator-Prefect's eyes flashed in a rage.

"Just who in blazes do you think you are!" he roared. "I'm in command here, not you!"

Orion turned to two of the soldiers who had been assaulting a gray haired man of fifty until his arrival.

"Put him down, or I will put you down!" Orion pointed a finger at the men-at-arms.

"I give the orders here, not you!" Hugh screamed as he barged his way past one of his men and rushed toward Orion. "And these men are carrying out my orders! These bastards here are providing shelter and food to rebels! Scum who have betrayed the Hegemon and Basilea! You don't have the authority to…"

"You do not have the authority to assault these people! The Hegemon's citizens, who are innocent until proven guilty by a trial conducted by their own magistrate!" Orion snarled.

"I've heard enough!" Hugh spat. "Restrain this man!"

The soldier closest to Orion, a stern looking man in his mid-twenties with cool eyes and a scar across one cheek, reached for his sword. Orion turned to face him and glowered down at him, well aware of his terrifying appearance and how best to use it.

"Son," he growled, "if you go for that weapon, one of two things is happening. Most likely, I shall tear your damn head off with my bare hands. If that does not happen, and by some miracle the Shining Ones favor you in a fight, you will hang for killing a paladin. Do you understand, boy? Either I will rip your head off, or the hangman's noose will! So what will it be?"

The soldier gulped and slowly moved his hand away from his sword. The ringing of metal echoed from the far side of the room as Hugh's two aides drew their own weapons. Galvanized into action by the statement, four of the men-at-arms also drew their own blades. Orion scanned his eyes from man to man, assessing each and every warrior in front of him.

There was not a single man he thought he could not beat, but even in a cramped fighting area with his back to the wall, he faced thirteen armed men alone. Some looked too afraid to enter the confrontation, but even with the odds slightly evened, he knew he could not win. Orion prioritized his targets, picking the easiest kills out of the men who faced him, so as to quickly even the odds further and possibly panic a few of them into running. He still did not favor his chances, but it was the principle of defending the helpless against oppression. It was everything that his Order had drilled into him; everything that Uncle Jahus had taught him was right and true. It was something he was willing to die for.

"You," Orion stared at Hugh as he drew his heavy, two-handed sword from his back, "have exceeded your authority."

The remaining door behind Orion swung on its hinges, causing the paladin to turn in place and raise his sword. Tancred looked up at him, an expression of utter bewilderment plastered across his crooked features. The young paladin stared from man to man, his red hair plastered with sweat against his face.

"By the Ones!" he exclaimed. "What is going on here?"

"Your man has raised a sword against a Dictator-Prefect!" Hugh spat. "And I'm having him restrained for trial!"

"These men have assaulted innocent..."

"Shut up!" Tancred growled forcefully, cutting Orion's retort off. "I've seen what happened outside!"

"Lord Paladin," Hugh seethed through gritted teeth, "restrain your man. Now."

Tancred looked across at Orion. He turned to face Hugh and then looked across the room, his eyes finally coming to rest on the two girls crying in the corner. His eyes screwed up tight and he let out a gasp of frustration before swearing under his breath.

"Dictator-Prefect," Tancred said slowly as he opened his eyes again, "you are carrying out an illegal act. Have your men lower their weapons immediately."

"What?" Hugh roared. "I am a Dictator-Prefect! I'm well aware of the law of the land! I answer only to the Duma! I enact the laws here! I do not answer to you!"

"Oh, you very much do," Tancred took a pace forward, "you forget that my father is one of the most shrewd politicians the Hegemony has ever seen. I, like my father, fight with my words first and my blade second. So let us examine your words in more details. Your legal authority is only in place with the permission of the local magistrate. I am sure you intend to counter that with your right to enact the law in the magistrate's absence, but both you and I know that the law states that every effort must first be made to contact the magistrate, and you have made no effort. Thus, you are carrying out an illegal act."

The Dictator-Prefect's face dropped as Tancred recited the law of the land. Clearly not satisfied, the red headed paladin took another step forward before continuing.

"In addition, the Hegemon himself has empowered every holy order of paladins with enacting his will. Not the will of the Duma that you answer to. The will of the Hegemon himself. So to that end, in matters of the law you do answer to me. You also answer to Brother Paladin Orion. You all do. This is your last chance before I escalate this. Put down your swords."

The seething Dictator-Prefect looked across at his aides and gave a curt nod. The two men sheathed their swords. Without a word, Hugh stormed past the two paladins and out of the inn. His aides followed, both men fixing threatening glares at Orion as they left. The ten soldiers sheepishly followed, leaving the four injured men to limp over to the bar where the two serving girls immediately set about tending to their injuries. Tancred immediately paced over to the injured men and waved a hand of glowing white over the first of them, using his expertise of divinity magic to heal the man's cuts and bruises.

Still surprised at his response, Orion turned to face Tancred.

"Well, that was..."

"Shut up!" Tancred snapped as he spun to face Orion. "You idiot! You bloody fool! Drawing a sword against a Dictator-Prefect! What were you thinking?"

Orion felt his temper flaring again as his shoulders hunched up and his teeth clenched.

"What would you have me do?" he growled. "He ordered our soldiers to attack innocent people!"

Tancred shook his head, one hand dropping to the Eloicon at his hip. Orion heard the younger man mutter a brief prayer quietly as he turned his back. For a moment, he felt some genuine respect for the man who so far had earned nothing but resentment from him. Outside, the unmistakable rumbling of a large group of horses came from the south. Orion moved over to the doorway and breathed a sigh of relief as the thirty paladins of his group rode along the narrow street from the edge of the town, coming to a stop in front of the inn before dismounting and quickly separating into smaller groups to offer assistance to the townsfolk. It was abundantly clear watching them that the assistance was not welcomed.

"Go and help the others," Tancred said quietly. "I need to think."

Orion opened his mouth to speak, but he thought better of it and turned to leave.

*****

A staccato series of thuds sounded as the handful of well-placed bolts from the salvo found their targets. The line of ten crossbowmen peered across the hastily constructed butts, staring at their targets to assess their accuracy. The wind whipped across the exposed mountain plateau, rustling the clumps of long grass that sprouted up between every nook and crevice amidst the jagged rocks. A veteran crossbowman who had been in Dionne's service for nearly a year now paced along behind the shooters with his hands clasped at the small of his back, bellowing advice and reprimands in equal measure. Half an acre down from the crossbow range, another twenty men practiced spear drills as Vassia, another of Dionne's veterans, bellowed out commands, expecting them to react with precision as one unit in unison. He seemed disappointed.

From his vantage point at the edge of the plateau, Dionne watched his latest batch of volunteers respond to their training. He cast his mind back to his own training in the legion at the age of sixteen, remembering the fire and fervor that came with volunteering to travel the world with a professional fighting force, expanding the Hegemon's influence and defeating evil. Dionne allowed himself a sad chuckle at his naivety back then, and then cast his eyes across the motley collection of the middle aged and unfit men who he commanded now. They did not have the gullibility of youth that could be molded into fanaticism, but they did have maturity and, to a man, the insurmountable sense of drive and purpose that only stemmed from true loss. That in itself was enough to give Dionne confidence that they could be trained into effective soldiers. He had spent the last year doing just that, and it worked well.

"Dionne?"

He turned to face his addresser. Teynne stood before him, his red robes flowing in the wind and his perpetually tired, red-rimmed eyes narrowed pensively. Dionne had not had a chance to confront Teynne since Phellius' accusation, and now seemed as good a time as any to have that discussion.

"We need to talk," Teynne said before he could speak.

"Strange, I was about to say the same thing."

Teynne's brow lifted a little.

"Oh?"

"Something Phellius brought to my attention."

Teynne suppressed a smile as if the response was one he was suspecting.

"Perhaps we'd better go somewhere more private," he suggested.

The two men walked in silence away from the plateau, picking their way along the rocks to a small, shallow cave not far from the path leading up to the peak. Despite his trust for the man, Dionne gestured for Teynne to enter the cave first. Again, Teynne suppressed the smallest of smiles at the gesture and entered without a word.

"I'll come straight to the point," Dionne began as he entered the cave, shuddering a little as a small trickle of moisture from the earth above the entrance caught the back of his neck. "The men think you're a spy working for the Duma."

Teynne paused, nodding slowly.

"I can see how it looks that way. But I'm not."

"Not the most compelling defensive argument."

"What do you think?" Teynne enquired calmly.

Dionne fixed his eyes on the blond warrior mage. The younger man looked back without a hint of fear.

"This came from Phellius," Teynne said, "but that is part of what I wish to talk to you about. Phellius is gone. He took some men to Emalitos for supplies, as you ordered. The Duma has sent a force of over one hundred soldiers to apprehend you. They have Phellius in custody. Your other men are dead."

Only a mere moment's shock at the words caused Dionne to pause. Not only was this bound to happen one day, but he had also faced worse a hundred times over. He knew he would have to face the legion at some point and that had always pained him greatly, as he had nothing against the soldiers he once stood alongside and led; it was the leadership he despised.

"When did this happen?" Dionne demanded.

"Less than an hour ago."

"How could you possibly know that?" Dionne said with deliberation. "I know you have arcane powers, but nothing I've seen that indicates to me that you are a great sorcerer who can see all over incredible distances."

The corners of Teynne's pale lips lifted slightly into an uncomfortable smile.

"And so we reach the critical point. The reason why both of us needed to

60

have this conversation. Your men were correct about one thing, Centurion. I haven't been completely honest with you."

Dionne felt his facial muscles twitching in anger. One hand lowered to rest on the pommel of his sword.

"You've kept things from me? Or you have deceived me?"

"I am on your side," Teynne moved his hands out to either side passively, "I am not what you think, but I am not your enemy and I mean you no harm. I want nothing more than for us to continue to work together just as we have been for this past year. With this Basilean force here to take you away, you need me now more than ever."

His eyes narrowing, Dionne stepped forward and looked down at the shorter man.

"Stop mincing your words, man!" he seethed. "Your very life depends upon it! Now tell me, plain and simple, who you are and what you want!"

"Alright," Teynne replied calmly, his tone almost apologetic, "if that's what you want. I need you to stay calm, Dionne. Remember, we are on the same side. We want the same thing."

Dionne watched in horror and amazement as Teynne's body transformed before his very eyes as he spoke, growing taller and more muscular, the skin changing tone and the hands turning to claws. Only the face remained the same.

Six

The creature was taller than Dionne, far taller than any man he had ever faced; large enough for the curved horns that sprouted from its forehead to nearly skim the top of the cave. Its body, red-skinned and broad, was made up of knotted muscles clad in scraps of crude armor of spiked metal. A row of sharp teeth defined a thin-lipped mouth beneath obsidian black, eerily calm eyes. Bat-like wings were folded behind the being's torso. But it was not the metamorphis that was the most unsettling – it was the face of the demon that remained the same.

Dionne needed no more evidence. He had faced Abyssal Champions before. Drawing his sword, he charged forward.

"Dionne, stop!" the demon urged, raising a hand.

Dionne swung his sword up at the monster's head, forcing it to take a step back and draw its own viciously curved blade. Following up with a second strike at the champion's abdomen, a dull clang echoed across the cave as the two heavy blades of the expert warriors impacted. The demon was good, but Dionne fancied that he was better. Undeterred, he linked a series of lightning fast strikes aimed at the creature's head and torso to force it on the defensive before he managed to create an opening. The champion let out a howl of pain as Dionne slashed his sword across the scarlet-skinned creature's sword arm, drawing black blood from a vicious cut across its bicep.

"Dionne, you fool!" The demon yelled as he planted a broad hand against the wound. "It's me! It's Teynne!"

"I know what you are!" Dionne spat, fixing his glare on the monster's dark eyes and bringing his blade up and ready for another attack.

"Then stop this madness and listen to me!" Teynne snapped. "I'm your friend! I've stood by your side for a year now! I show you my true form, and this is how you repay me?"

Letting out a cry of anger and frustration, Dionne lunged forward and lashed out with his blade again. Teynne was forced back against the cave wall, parrying three of Dionne's strikes before creating an opening of his own and backhanding Dionne across the face with enough force to knock him to the ground. The demon quickly stepped over Dionne as he struggled back to his feet, standing between him and the cave entrance. Teynne held out a clenched fist and a wall of fire shot up from the rocks between them, trapping Dionne against the wall.

"Listen to me!" the demon pleaded again. "We are on the same side! We always have been! You've been duped! Lied to and fooled! You're judging me on my appearance, and I thought better of you!"

"You're a demon!" Dionne snarled as he looked down at the flames in front of him, assessing his chances of charging through them to continue the fight. "You're Abyssal scum, the embodiment of all that is evil in the world!"

"According to who?" Teynne demanded. "You're just quoting the nonsense that your Hegemon has forced on your people! The lies that corrupt leaders have controlled the masses with for centuries! Yes, my form is intimidating, and for good reason! But what you see before you is honest; I am a warrior of the Abyss and I stand by my principles and my code! Yet you try to hack me down because liars and corrupt men of unworldly wealth tell you what is 'good'?"

Dionne exhaled but kept his sword raised and ready to strike.

"Lies," he hissed, "you're trying to deceive me! I'm no fool!"

"You're acting like one!" Teynne sighed, his monstrous face appearing almost human as he closed his eyes in disappointment. "I'd heard of you. I'd heard that you stood up to the Hegemon because you wanted to do what you thought was right instead of blindly obeying bad orders. That is the Abyssal code! That is what we stand for! Yes, we have our hierarchy and yes there are those who live like kings at the top, but we do so at the expense of sinners and murderers, not innocent peasants whose only crime is being born poor! So you tell me, Dionne, whose system is more corrupt – yours or mine?"

Dionne eyed the demon cautiously, tightening his grip on his sword.

"It's not my system!" He seethed. "You know that! You know I've lost everything to stand against the Hegemon's corruption and selfishness!"

"So what do you want," the towering devil demanded, "to waste your time and skills living in the mountains as a simple bandit, or will you continue to work with me?"

"I'm not working with you! You're everything I'm fighting to defend people against! You and the filth spewing from the Abyss are the entire reason I'm here!"

The demon shook his horned head in despair.

"Are you so naïve? Is Basilea the same realm and the same people as the elves, the dwarves, the naiads, all the others? No! You even go to war against some of them, your principles differ so much! Do you not think it is the same in the Abyss? Yes, the orcs are murdering bastards who must be stopped! Yes, there are demons whose souls are pitiless and corrupt! But there is more going on in the Abyss than you know of! We, too, war over our principles! And your principles are identical to mine, identical!"

Dionne fought to control his breathing, his mind racing as conflict tore his thoughts in two. All physical evidence before him told him to leap to attack again, but Teynne's words made sense. Enough to make him question.

"In the Abyss, we too are at war," Teynne said, more calmly, "I won't lie to you, there are differences between what you fight for here and what lies within the scar to the north. But we have a common goal, and I can bring you enough power to achieve what you want. You can't make a difference with a band of a few dozen disgruntled farmers and miners! I can give you an army! An army with which to smash the orcs off this very mountain, to force back the Abyssal hordes that oppose what my side stands for!"

"Then why do you need me?" Dionne demanded, a voice within his head screaming furiously at him for even engaging in conversation with a demon. "If you've got your own army, then use it!"

"You're a far better tactician than me, you know that," Teynne forced a slight smile. "Now I can get an army for you, but you know best how to use it. But there's more to it than that. There are... limits to how long I can spend outside the Abyss. That is why I have disappeared on occasion for the past year we have been friends. Just lower that sword, show me enough trust for me to lower these flames, and let us talk it through. That force that has come here to stop you is moving ever closer and time is short."

Dionne paused. He thought his options through, considering the threat of the army sent by the Duma and the trust and dependability Teynne had always demonstrated. He nodded slowly. Teynne had never let him down. The Hegemon, the Duma, the legion, all had betrayed him. But over thirty years of fighting anything the Abyss threw at him would not be overridden by one conversation, no matter how convincing. The Abyss was the enemy. It opposed everything good in Mantica.

"We're not partners," Dionne said as he lowered his sword. "I won't fight for your wicked masters. Not now, not ever. But you have earned my respect and my trust. And I will listen to what you have to say."

"Good," Teynne nodded slowly, "because this expedition sent by the Duma to bring you in for trial must be stopped. I've already taken measures. Even as we speak, your warriors are amassing. I've sent out orders to amass all of your soldiers. Every encampment, every patrol, every man loyal to you. They're all on their way. But we must leave, you and I. We must leave immediately."

"You've ordered my men here?! Without consulting me?! I don't give a damn if you're a bastard demonic lord of the Abyss itself! That's my army!"

"You would have done the same!" Teynne retorted with almost equal force. "It is the only logical choice! Look me in the eyes and tell me otherwise if you disagree!"

Dionne stared up at the Abyssal Champion, his teeth clenched in rage. The demon's monstrous form represented the very figure of nightmares, everything he had ever been taught was evil in the world, the very servants of the Wicked Ones themselves. But the one thing the demon had uttered that had rung completely true was that all of his education and assumption about the Abyss came from the Hegemony, the very corruption and core of lies that he now stood against. He looked into Teynne's eyes and somehow saw past the monster he faced, just for a moment, and saw the eyes of the man who had loyally stood by his side through thick and thin for over a year.

"Why must we leave?" Dionne demanded. "If there is a detachment from the legion on the way here now, we should face it. And I should lead my men from front and center."

"It is just a rear guard action," Teynne said, "a delaying skirmish to buy us time. Vassia is a good soldier; a capable leader. He can hamper the progress of the legion detachment and then get your men to safety. That will buy us time to get to the north."

"To what end?" Dionne snapped.

The towering demon smiled, his harsh face almost warm in the friendliness of the action.

"I am going to get you an army, my friend. A proper one. So you can do what you came here to do, and do it well. And I will stay by your side to help you."

*****

The slow, almost mournful ballad emanating from Hayden's lute drowned out any sounds from the town of Emalitos. The force had set up camp at the top of the small hill to the south of the town, and the normal array of tents and campfires broke the skyline as the last embers of daylight tucked themselves away below the orange horizon to the east. One leg tucked beneath her, Constance sat with a handful of her mercenaries by a large fire at the western end of the encampment, staring into the crackling flames as she took a small swig from a bottle of wine that was being passed around. They had, of course, heard all about the Dictator-Prefect's rampage through the town and his use of the men-at-arms to beat the local population into a pulp. Constance was left wondering whether, as a young legion soldier herself, she would have blindly followed such brutal and absurd orders. But that issue had never presented itself as her captain had always placed the safety of civilians before the lives of even his own soldiers. Her captain was a man she had once greatly respected, admired, perhaps even idolized. And now she found herself here accepting payment to be a part of the force that was hunting that same man down.

"What a bastard," Wulf remarked dryly from where he sat atop a barrel next to Constance, "what an absolute bastard. I can see now why you all hate him so much."

"You don't know the half of it," Jaque spat, staring past the flames and up toward the north.

Hayden flashed a forced smile as he continued to play his lute, swaying gently back and forth in time to the music.

"At least the paladins stopped him," Wulf said. "At least they're doing their job."

"I heard it was only one of them," Mallius added, "that huge one we saw fighting the other night. I heard he faced down twenty of them single-handed."

66

"Don't spout nonsense!" Wulf sneered. "Paladin or not, no man can face twenty men-at-arms and live. They might be vicious bastards, but the legion is the finest fighting force in Mantica."

A brief lull in the conversation allowed Constance to appreciate Hayden's lute playing for another few moments before Jaque stood up and dusted himself off.

"Right," the thin man declared, "I'm off to thank him."

"What?" Constance looked up. "Who?"

"That paladin. The big bearded one who stopped Hugh the Bastard from massacring that town. I'm off to thank him."

"Jaque, wait!"

Constance jumped to her feet and dashed to catch up with Jaque as he walked purposefully off toward the eastern end of the encampment. The men-at-arms had set up in the center and were also separated into small groups around fires, gambling or exchanging stories. Jaque marched straight past them toward where the Ark Knights were camped near the road.

"Jaque, I'm not so sure this is a good idea," Constance said as she caught up with him.

"Why?"

"Well... it's a nice sentiment, but paladins are still nobility, even if only in a minor way. We're commoners. We can't go barging in and demanding an audience."

"I'm not demanding anything," Jaque said as he threaded his way through the smaller tents of the paladins' area, attracting a few curious looks from young squires who sharpened blades and serviced armor in the light of the fires. "I'm just going to pay my respects."

At the very edge of the encampment, Jaque and Constance found the man they were looking for. The huge paladin sat on a tree trunk, sharpening both edges of a broad, two-handed sword as a shaven headed squire of perhaps fourteen or fifteen years of age sat a few paces away, oiling the links of his master's mail armor. Both looked up as Jaque approached. The thin mercenary opened his mouth to speak, remained silent, and then closed it again as the bearded paladin regarded him with an intense stare.

"My lord," Constance gave a respectful nod of the head, "we wanted to pay our respects. And gratitude. For your intervention in the town today."

The paladin placed his sharpening stone to one side and looked down at the edges of the huge sword.

"That is enough for today, Kell," he glanced coolly across at the squire. "Go and see to your studies and prayer."

The squire smiled nervously and carefully packed away the mail hauberk before disappearing off into the small maze of tents. The paladin sheathed the two handed sword and switched his piercing gaze back to Jaque and Constance.

"My lord..." Jaque began.

The paladin held up a hand to silence him.

"Orion. My name is Orion. While we are away from the commanders of this expedition, we do not need to stand on formality. We all take the same risks. We are all equals here."

"It is a pleasure to meet you, Orion," Constance said, walking over to stand opposite him. "My name is Constance and this is Jaque."

The paladin gestured for them to sit before taking a waterskin that lay next to him and offering it across.

"Did you really face down twenty men-at-arms today?" Jaque suddenly blurted out.

Constance shot him an admonishing glare.

"No, that has been exaggerated," Orion replied quietly. "It was only nineteen of them, and in two separate encounters, so no more than thirteen at once. And it did not escalate to a fight at any point; only words."

"Nonetheless," Constance said, "it was a great thing you did. We should not have come here to beat on innocent townsfolk. We are not supposed to be the villains of this piece."

"That is a rare stance for a sword for hire to take," Orion said, "if you do not mind me being so bold to observe."

"Being a mercenary is not the same as a hired thug or assassin," Constance replied, a little hurt by the accusation. "I can never claim much of a moral pedestal in my profession but I can – and do – choose who I work for and why."

Orion kept his eyes fixed on the two, seemingly unconvinced. Laughter erupted from one of the closer groups of legion men-at-arms.

"You are both ex-legion?" Orion asked.

"Yes," Jaque nodded, "a few years back now, but me an' Constance used to be with that lot. Well, the 78th Legion at least. We've spent a good few years traveling all over Mantica now."

"You parted company with the legion?" Orion asked.

Jaque rolled up one sleeve to reply to the paladin's question. His right shoulder bore the feint remnants of the Primovantorian numerals of the number '78', the standard tattoo worn proudly by men-at-arms to show their allegiance to their own legion. A vicious cross was branded into his flesh, the scar tissue blotting out the badge of honor. Constance bore the same scar on her own shoulder but did not feel the need to show it. Orion nodded.

"What manner of crime saw you ejected from the legion and branded for the rest of your days?"

"Our captain disobeyed his orders and struck out on his own," Constance answered on Jaque's behalf. "We were Dionne's soldiers. Some of his soldiers sided with him. We did not. We remained loyal to the Hegemony, despite the loyalty we felt for our captain. But we were guilty by association nonetheless. We were discharged, branded, and imprisoned."

Orion's features softened. He closed his eyes and shook his shaven head briefly.

"I am sorry," he whispered, "Basilean justice is so often unfair. I am so sorry. Did you know Dionne well?"

"Not really," Jaque answered, "we were just two faces in the crowd. He was responsible for a couple of hundred soldiers. But he treated us all well and he made every effort to get to know us. He knew all of our names, I never knew a commander who took the time to do that. The thing I remember about him most was that he did everything to protect innocent people caught up in the battles we fought in. He... was a great commander and we certainly respected and admired him."

"Leaving the legion under such circumstances was tragic," Constance added, painful memories flooding to the fore as in a handful of seconds she revisited the most traumatic year of her life, "but the... have you ever... have you ever seen one of our prisons?"

The paladin shook his head.

"Twenty three of us went in," Jaque explained, "we were there for just over six months before we were released. Nine of us were left alive by then. That tells you all you need to know about Basilean prisons."

Constance swallowed and shuddered as she remembered the screams of torment from her comrades, choking on the stale air in the pitch black of the cell she was left to rot in, little more than a gap in the stone walls of the prison – too low for her to stand and too narrow for her to even turn around in. At the time, she was sixteen years of age and with only a few weeks soldiering experience under her belt. It was a miracle that she was one of the survivors. Bile rose in her throat and she quickly repressed the mental images.

"But we endured," she forced a smile, "by the grace of the Shining Ones. Despite Hugh's judgment."

Orion's brow raised.

"This Hugh? It was Dictator-Prefect Hugh of Athelle who passed judgment on you and had you branded and imprisoned?"

"Certainly makes a tale!" Jaque smiled bitterly. "Here we are, hired by the bastard who tried to have us rot to death to bring in the man we once would have followed into the very depths of the Abyss."

Orion raised a lightly clenched fist to his closed mouth thoughtfully.

"I am sorry for you both. I cannot even begin to comprehend the turmoil and confliction you must both be facing."

"There is no confliction," Constance shrugged. "Captain Dionne was a good man. I think he still is. Hopefully the Duma will see that when we bring him in. At least the captain will face a fair trial rather than the sham we suffered at the hands of Hugh the Bastard."

Orion's response was cut off as another series of bellowed laughter echoed from the legion men gathered around the largest of the encampment's fires. Constance felt Jaque's hand on her shoulder, giving a gentle but reassuring squeeze. She flashed him an appreciative smile, although it did little to nullify the feelings that the conversation had rekindled following its uncomfortable change of direction.

"We've taken up enough of your time," Constance declared as she stood. "I'm sorry the conversation took on a rather somber turn, but thank you for listening and thank you for what you did today."

Orion stood and bowed his head slightly.

"I am sorry to hear your story," he said, "I hope it does not sound trite, but I will pray for you both. And your departed comrades. I hope we will speak again soon."

Jaque held out a hand to the towering paladin. Orion shook it warmly.

"Good night," he gave a slight smile.

*****

A stifled laugh was quickly hushed in the far corner of the inn, and four figures huddled around a small, circular wooden table glanced nervously across to where Tancred sat alone near the door. He had initially agreed with Hugh's decision to billet the detachment's more senior members in the comfort of the town's inn, but having finished his meal, Tancred now felt that at best, he was surrounded by people who despised him; at worst, his life was under threat.

The inn itself was not dissimilar to any other that Tancred had seen in rural Basilea. A low, timbered ceiling separated a seating area with the lodgings above, and a large, open fire cast shimmering shadows across the planked floor. A long bar ran along the far wall from the door, acting as a serving area for both food and drink. Aside from Tancred, only three other tables were occupied, and the atmosphere was understandably tense given the events of the day.

Heavy footsteps thudded along the staircase leading to the lodgings. Tancred looked across and saw Hugh emerge from the alcove by the fireplace, dressed in fine clothes of embroidered black suede. Conversation at the other tables died away the instant the Dictator-Prefect appeared. Tancred felt his pulse quicken as the nobleman walked over toward him, the wooden boards creaking beneath his heavy boots. While Tancred knew that he had done the *right* thing and he certainly did not regret his actions, he still bitterly regretted the very fact that the scenario had developed, and he had now gravely offended the only man in the detachment who could have a real influence on his career and advancement. Swallowing his pride, Tancred stood and forced a smile and a courteous bow as Hugh approached.

"Please, don't," the Dictator-Prefect raised a hand, his green eyes narrowing uncomfortably. "I have come to apologize."

Tancred was instantly aware that he was eyeing the older man warily, and so issued a slight smile so as not to show his suspicion.

"May I?" Hugh gestured to a chair opposite Tancred.

"Of course."

Both men sat down. The Dictator-Prefect leaned forward and placed the tips of his fingers together, leaning his elbows on the dark wood table.

"I tend to be rather passionate about our cause," he began, "perhaps sometimes too much so. I want to see Dionne answer for his crimes. I want to see justice served. I want to see the man who was responsible for the deaths of so many, due to his own inactivity, pay for his incompetence and lack of foresight."

"There are many who still see him as a hero," Tancred leaned back in his chair.

"They are fools," Hugh replied with a regretful shake of his head, "so easily duped by this egotistical bastard's lies. He is no hero. He was entrusted with his part of the defense of the Hegemony, and he failed Basilea and her people. There is nothing to idolize about the man. That is why I was so angry with the people here for defending him, for refusing to help us do the right thing and bring him to justice!"

Tancred watched the nobleman carefully, analyzing his words, gestures, and facial expressions. Tancred's father had taught him a great deal about social interactions, and he was confident that in most cases he could spot a liar. Hugh certainly seemed to believe what he was saying, but something about the conversation still did not sit quite right with Tancred.

"I am glad you intervened when you did," Hugh continued, breaking eye contact and covering his mouth with one hand for a brief moment. "I think these people are harboring a traitor. But perhaps you are right and perhaps they do know nothing. They deserve the benefit of the doubt. That is the difference between a man like Dionne and somebody such as myself."

"Then there will not be a repeat of today's incident," Tancred declared rather than asked.

"Of course. And we need not speak of it again."

There it was. Tancred suppressed a bitter smile. Hugh had not come to apologize; he had come to charm Tancred into silence in an attempt to ensure his actions were not spoken of in the capital. For a brief moment, Tancred considered the possibilities of the leverage he now possessed over such a powerful and influential figure.

"You will go far, Tancred," Hugh smiled as he stood. "Thank you for your time and your understanding. A lesser man would see things in extremes, in simple black and white. But a wiser man has the ability to see past these oversimplifications, to look deeper at what is going on beneath the surface. I am glad you are such a man."

Tancred nodded curtly. Hugh looked at him expectantly, but Tancred remained silent, folding his arms. The Dictator-Prefect's eyes narrowed, a moment of real concern painted across his handsome face before the anxiety was replaced by a broad smile. Tancred was satisfied to see that his silence had unnerved the man. It was very much intentional.

"I shall bid you good night," Hugh said.

"Good night, sir," Tancred replied, standing up respectfully as the nobleman walked back to the alcove leading up to the second floor.

Tancred finished his drink and gazed out of the inn at the clear night sky, thinking through the possible courses of action that had now presented themselves to him. This was a situation that had played into his hand, and one that could be subtly manipulated to his advantage. Still pondering over possibilities, Tancred walked passed the bar and paid for his evening meal before walking up to his room.

After washing and saying his prayers, Tancred settled into a light, disturbed sleep. He awoke several times throughout the night, feeling isolated and vulnerable in his room, even with a sword resting against the bed next to him. It was dawn when he awoke properly, suddenly finding himself sat bolt upright in bed and reaching for his blade as his eyes focused on an armed man in his room.

"Tancred!" Hugh shouted, "Tancred! Get up! There are warriors crossing the fields to the north! Two hundred of them!"

Seven

The beating of drums echoed across the small copses of trees to either side of the road as the soldiers marched north toward the open fields outside the town of Emalitos. The early morning sun cast long shadows across the dusty road and burnt sienna grass that ran alongside, and a thin haze muddied the horizon below an otherwise clear sky. The legion men-at-arms marched at the front of the column in three ranks, their Dictator-Prefect and his ever-present bodyguards riding at the head with their captain, while the paladins of the Order of the Sacred Ark rode protectively along the flanks. Behind them all, Constance trudged on at the head of her band of thirty mercenaries.

A series of orders were barked out from the front of the column as the first ranks of soldiers reached the precipice of a shallow hill. The men-at-arms immediately formed into a tight rectangle, five ranks of ten soldiers, and marched off to the east to the beating of drums. The Dictator-Prefect and his two bodyguards galloped back down the road to Constance and her mercenaries. She looked up into the face of the man she despised more than anybody she had crossed paths with as he hauled in the reins of his horse next to her. It was clear to her that the nobleman had no recollection of her whatsoever as he looked down at her from his saddle.

"Crossbowmen!" he yelled. "Move north! Take position to the right side of this road and await my orders!"

The mercenaries continued to march forward, heedless of the commands of the Dictator-Prefect. Constance suppressed a proud smirk.

"Company!" she shouted. "Form three ranks, standard intervals! Take position on my command!"

To emphasize the command to any of the mercenaries who could not hear her, Hayden gave three short blasts on his horn, followed by one steady tone. With well-drilled precision, the mercenaries immediately arranged themselves in three columns, a shoulder width separating each row of ten men and women, and followed Constance as she continued along the road. They crested the precipice of the hill and she let out an anxious breath as she looked down into the shallow valley below.

The road curved off to the left, around the back of a small hill to the northwest. To the right of the road, a wooded area of ruddy brown trees extended up to the horizon. Waiting to either side of the road, a few hundred yards ahead, stood two blocks of fifty soldiers carrying swords and shields of the same pattern as legion men-at-arms. The hundred warriors also wore the same armor, but without tabards or feathers in their steel helmets. To the left, west of the professional soldiers were two smaller groups; some twenty men armed with crossbows and perhaps thirty carrying crude spears and pitchforks, all without armor, stood atop the small hill overlooking the valley that separated the two forces. Off on the right flank, another group of some forty peasants with crude weapons waited by the treeline. The better part of two hundred soldiers, half of them well-armed and trained professionals. They were outnumbered two-to-one.

As directed, Constance trudged off the road and positioned herself to the east of the track at the crest of a gentle plateau. She held up her hand and Hayden blew another blast from the horn to signal that the crossbowmen were in position. The thirty mercenaries quickly came to a halt, turning in ranks to face their enemy. To the east of the plateau, the fifty men-at-arms reformed their square and waited in place. Constance walked out in front of her soldiers and turned to face them.

"Company! Load!"

*****

Tancred hauled in his reins as he reached Hugh and his aides, dragging his warhorse to a stop by the nobleman and his bodyguard. The three riders sat atop their horses in a central position, between the mercenary crossbowmen and the pristine block of men-at-arms spearmen. The Dictator-Prefect looked to the north where the shouts of commands to the units of soldiers could be heard across the gentle morning breeze as the opposing force fanned out to face them. Hugh looked up at Tancred as he arrived, flashing him a confident smile.

"Good morning again, Lord Paladin!" he beamed. "Nice of you to join us. We're outnumbered two to one, but half of their numbers are untrained peasants with sticks, and I've got your heavy cavalry. We need to whittle down their two core units of men-at-arms and then these farmers will run. I'll chip away at the unit on the left with the crossbows, and then move our men-at-arms up to fight the unit on the right."

"Understood," Tancred nodded as he scanned his eyes across the horizon to assess the strength of the enemy. "What do you want from me?"

"Get your main strength on the right flank. As soon as I move the men-at-arms up to tackle the soldiers to the east of center, you sweep in and attack their flank. Get a few of your knights on the left flank to deal with their crossbowmen; I want to be the only one here who can shoot."

Tancred looked to the west flank where a small group of scruffy crossbowmen were visible atop a small hillock, next to an equally amateur looking unit of men with spears and pitchforks. The concern was the fifty professionally armed and armored men stood just to the east of them, near the center of the enemy force.

"I can get ten knights positioned on the west flank to act as a deterrent, but if I give them the order to charge that hill, they will be outnumbered by those fifty swordsmen near the center. They will not stand a chance."

Hugh looked at Tancred and then regarded the left flank again.

"Alright," he nodded slowly, "you are my expert with heavy cavalry. Get ten knights on the left flank and the bulk of your men on the right. Be ready to charge in when the men-at-arms are in combat. Wait for my signal."

"Understood," Tancred replied, dragging his horse back around and digging his spurs into the animal's flanks to gallop back to the south of the plateau. His warriors waited patiently atop their armored steeds, their polished plate armor and gold trim sparkling in the early morning sunlight, the gentle breeze tugging at the light blue of their surcoats and cloaks.

Tancred looked for his second in command. Orion sat atop his huge, powerful looking warhorse toward the left of the group, his blue eyes set in a frown. Tancred would not have chosen Orion to be his second - that honor would have fallen to Xavier as his most experienced paladin, or perhaps Jeneveve with her head for tactics and the respect she clearly held with the other knights – but while Orion was no leader of men, he was undoubtedly Tancred's best man in a fight. By a considerable margin. But that, unfortunately, was all he brought with him.

"Brother Orion, take nine knights to the left flank, stand ready to defend our crossbowmen and hold position until the Dictator-Prefect orders. Do not charge unless you believe the attack to be tenable, or unless I am the one giving you a direct command. The rest of you, follow me."

Orion barked out orders to detail off his nine knights and then led them in a canter over to his designated position. Tancred turned again to lead the bulk of his command over to the east flank. The whistle of crossbow bolts in the air to the north of the plateau announced that the battle had begun.

*****

"Front rank," Constance shouted, an outstretched hand held high above her head as she faced her soldiers, "take aim!"

The ten mercenaries of the front rank brought their heavy crossbows up to their shoulders, the deadly weapons pointed toward the further of the two units of fifty armored swordsmen who advanced steadily across the fields to the staccato beating of drums. Constance brought her hand down.

"Loose!"

The sound of twanging strings rippled along the front rank as each crossbowman squeezed his trigger, sending a volley of deadly bolts up into the air and slicing down through the ranks of enemy swordsmen. Even from some three hundred yards away, Constance saw the effect of the shooting – the volley struck home with commendable accuracy, some bolts slipping between the enemy soldiers while others impacted with shields. Still, two or three figures from the unit sagged and dropped to the ground. The group of swordsman continued, more slowly, their shields locked in a defensive shell ahead and above them.

"Front rank," Constance yelled, "reload! Center rank, take aim! Loose!"

Another volley of bolts was away, arcing up across the hazy blue sky and falling down with deadly accuracy. Almost simultaneously, a salvo of bolts shot from the crossbowmen on the hill to the north descended down to fall around the mercenaries. The scatter of the shots was wide, giving a good indication of the low levels of skill of the enemy crossbowmen. Their shooting was ineffectual; now was not the time to respond.

"Center rank! Reload!" Constance bellowed.

The ten mercenaries of the center rank dropped to one knee, each man and woman unclipping their pulley from their belts and putting one foot in the stirrup at the front of their weapon, holding it perpendicular to the ground and attaching the pulley to the string mechanism, before frantically winding the devices to drag the heavy string back to sit in the weapon's nut.

"Rear rank, take aim! Loose!"

Another two soldiers dropped from the flanks of the enemy unit from the continuous assault from Constance's crossbowmen. Content that the rhythm of her orders was being followed, Constance took her own arbalest from her back and paced over to stand by the front rank to add her own shots to their output.

"Rear rank, reload! Front rank, take aim! Loose!" she called.

Hugging the tiller of her crossbow against her right shoulder, Constance squeezed the trigger and felt the string slide along the weapon's table, propelling the bolt up into the air. Her shot met its mark and fell down into the armored bulk of the advancing enemy infantry, but whether it found a target or not, she could not tell at this range.

"Pick your targets!" she shouted as she put her foot into the crossbow's stirrup and attached her pulley to draw the heavy string back. "Independent shooting!"

Well aware that rate of shot was nearly as important as accuracy, Constance pumped her toned arms and rapidly wound her pulley to reload the crossbow. Another volley of bolts fell down from the enemy shooters on the hill. This time, she heard two pained cries from the rear rank. Without a word, Hayden sprang from her side and dashed to the rear rank, dragging his medical bag around to open it as he did so. The rebel swordsmen were drawing nearer. Pulling her crossbow back to her shoulder, Constance let loose again.

*****

"Come on! Come on!" Orion seethed, his armored fingers clenching and unclenching on the reins of his warhorse as the bulky animal mimicked the sentiments of the rider, grunting and shuffling in agitation.

76

Orion looked to his right, off to the east and along the lines of soldiers of the Dictator-Prefect's force. Next along was the mercenary crossbowmen, pouring out an impressive rate of shooting as they pelted one of the advancing columns of enemy swordsmen with bolts. Next sat the Dictator-Prefect himself with his two aides and a trumpeter for signaling his orders, commanding the force from a central position. On the far side of their leader, the fifty men-at-arms under the command of Captain Georgis waited smartly in position. At the right flank, twenty paladin-knights waited in two ranks of ten, Lord Paladin Tancred a few paces in front.

Orion brought his gaze back to Hugh and his small entourage, looking for any sign that he might be ordered to charge. Ahead of them, the rebel crossbowmen continued a sporadic and ill disciplined volley of shots aimed at the mercenary crossbowmen – while it highlighted the poor level of skill when compared to the professional mercenaries, Orion could still see the big musician from the mercenary band quickly moving along the ranks, assisting with medical aid wherever he could to the wounded. Two of the crossbowmen were already beyond help. Some of Orion's paladin knights were skilled enough with divinity magic that they could use their powers of healing on others, but Orion knew that dismounting and leaving his position would leave the entire left flank of the force completely exposed.

Swearing under his breath, he looked north again. Next to the rebel crossbowmen were thirty or so poorly equipped peasants; Orion's opposite number in guarding the west flank. A lance charge against them would have them scattered, and then he could sweep around and take on the crossbowmen. That being said, the peasants were just ordinary people who had been duped by Dionne's lies – they did not deserve to be remorselessly put down like the traitors who had knowingly followed Dionne into exile – but that was easily solved by attacking with the flat of a sword blade until the farmers panicked and ran. However, such a charge would leave the professional swordsmen free to sweep through the center of the Basilean force. Orion looked right again and saw another volley of bolts cut through the mercenary crossbowmen, sending another three falling to the dusty ground.

"Troop!" he shouted to the nine horsemen who accompanied him. "Form up!"

The knights nudged their horses forward to take position to either side of him, forming two ranks of five.

"Couch lances!" Orion bellowed.

Each knight brought their lance up into position under the arm, aiming the deadly tips at the enemy. Immediately a horn blasted from the center position of the enemy ranks. Orion smiled grimly. They had seen his posturing. Following the command, the twenty enemy crossbowmen pivoted slightly to face Orion's paladin knights. He might not be able to charge the enemy until ordered, but he could at least offer himself as a more resilient target to allow the mercenaries a better chance of doing their job.

*****

Sweat stinging her eyes, Constance fought through the cramp in her arms as she hurriedly wound the pulley of her crossbow, bringing the string back to the nut in preparation for another shot. The drums of the enemy swordsmen grew louder with each passing moment; the veteran warriors now close enough for her to hear their shouts and taunts. The unit on the right, those who had weathered the storm of her mercenaries' shooting, continued to limp on despite their steadily growing casualties. However, the closer unit on the left marched forward boldly, still at full strength and only moments away from being within charging distance of her mercenaries.

Bringing her crossbow up to her shoulder, Constance took aim at a soldier on the front rank – close enough now to begin to make out his facial features – and pulled the trigger. The string twanged and the bolt flew out, slicing through the hot air and impacting into the soldier's neck, sending him screaming to his knees. Her breathing labored, Constance lowered her crossbow, placed her foot in the stirrup, and then stopped as she realized that blood was dripping down into her eyes. Confused, she wearily raised a hand to her head and found it sticky with blood. She did not remember being hit. It made no difference. Gritting her teeth, she reattached the pulley and set about preparing for another shot as a steady stream of projectiles continued to pour from the ranks of her soldiers.

Looking up, she saw bolts falling down from the blue skies toward her unit. The enemy crossbowmen had clearly tired of targeting the paladins to her left – a respite she was thankful for – and had now returned to their original target. Her focus a little blurred, Constance looked up and watched with weary curiosity as the bolts arced down toward her. She knew effective shooting when she saw it, and these peasants had finally got their eyes in. Nonetheless, it still came as a surprise when a bolt struck her, burying itself into her thigh and sending pain shooting along her entire leg.

Suppressing the steadily intensifying agony with a cry that narrowly escaped through her gritted teeth, Constance labored on. It made no difference. Hauling her heavy crossbow up again, she let lose another accurate shot that only succeeded in burying itself in the shield of a swordsman in the second rank of advancing soldiers.

"Constance!" Jaque shouted from next to her. "They're close! They're damn close!"

"Don't run!" Constance yelled, limping around on the spot to face her soldiers. "If you run, they'll cut you down! Stand your ground and finish the job!"

Wiping blood from her eyes again, Constance turned back to face the enemy. To her right, the beating of drums became frantic and a combined roar emanated from the legion men-at-arms as they charged out to attack the rebel swordsmen ahead of them. That left the fresh unit directly ahead of Constance and her soldiers, but it was too late to whittle them down now and too late to run. Constance dropped her crossbow and drew her sword.

"Keep shooting!" she screamed. "As fast as you can!"

The rebel soldiers, better trained and equipped and outnumbering her own men and women two-to-one, broke into a charge. Her shaking hands holding onto her sword, Constance stood her ground with determination as the yelling horde of soldiers ran at her mercenaries. For a brief moment, she thought of her mother and her siblings, and she regretted the fact that she would die so needlessly for a cause she had no belief in, in a battle with no consequence. Ignoring the pain in her wounded leg, she limped forward to meet the enemy soldiers.

*****

The impatient whining and spluttering of warhorses behind him was still audible as Tancred watched the square of rebel soldiers break into a charge against the mercenary crossbowmen on the far side of the battlefield. Closer to him, the legion men-at-arms under the command of Captain Georgis were now engaged in bitter fighting against the second square of rebel soldiers who had been mauled by the continuous shooting from Constance's mercenaries. Even without any assistance from cavalry, the loyalist legion men would soon overpower them. Oblivious to this, the peasant infantry directly opposite Tancred's twenty paladin knights were now boldly advancing toward him and their doom.

To the left, in the center of the line, Tancred heard the blast of a horn, three times to signify the right flank, followed by the two tone order to charge. The signal he had been waiting for. He looked across and saw Dictator-Prefect Hugh pointing his sword toward the unit of enemy swordsmen engaged in fighting with the legion spearmen – Tancred's paladins were to ignore the advancing peasants and charge the flanks of the near decimated unit of professional soldiers. Tancred looked to his right and nodded to Brother Paladin Kharius, his unit's own musician. The slim paladin raised his horn to his lips and repeated the order. Tancred dug his spurs into Desiree's flanks and the majestic animal sprung forward at the order, accelerating to a quick canter as to either side his paladins advanced in two neat lines. To his left, Brother Paladin Xavier held the unit's blue banner aloft, fluttering in the wind created by the accelerating mass of armored horses and riders, the Order's white phoenix flying proudly.

Another blast of the horn from Hugh's command group caused Orion to lead his ten paladins into a charge from the left flank, rapidly wheeling around to face the exposed side of the unit of swordsmen who charged at Constance and her crossbowmen. Through the narrow slits in his helmet, Tancred watched as the ten mounted paladins lined up for the attack, their lances lowered for the charge. Even thundering into the flanks, ten paladins would only slow the professional soldiers rather than stop them dead. Conversely, Tancred's twenty knights were all but wasted against their half beaten target. He leaned over in his saddle and bellowed a command to Kharius over the thundering of hooves on the dry earth.

"Brother Kharius! Sound my orders!"

*****

An ineffectual volley of crossbow bolts whistled off somewhere behind Orion and his knights as the ten horsemen charged from their position out to face the charging swordsmen rapidly bearing down on the scattered mercenaries. Gritting his teeth and leaning forward in his saddle, Orion lowered his lance and tucked the haft of the weapon firmly beneath his right arm, settling into the couched position and ready for attack. Taking his lead, the horsemen to either side took his signal and lowered their own weapons.

To their right, a handful of the mercenaries had already broken and were fleeing the battlefield in disarray, while at the front and center of the unit, Orion made out the hazy figure of Constance in the dusty confusion, shouting out commands to her troops as she limped forward to face the charging swordsmen. The rebel swordsmen had seen Orion and his knights wheeling around for attack and had now stopped, quickly turning in place and closing up tight as their leader shouted out commands to form a shield wall, ready for the lance charge.

From further right, Orion heard the unmistakable blast of a cavalry horn followed by a familiar, descending pitch command. Looking right, he saw Tancred leading his knights in a charge, perpendicular to the line of battle and straight toward the two units of enemy swordsmen. The order had come from Tancred, not the Dictator-Prefect. The order was to break off his attack. Orion hauled in his reins and raised his lance again, slowing his horse and feeling a sickening remorse as he recognized Jaque standing on the front line of mercenaries. The thin man turned to face him, his ecstatic smile of relief turning into a mask of bewilderment and betrayal as their salvation peeled away from the fight.

*****

Constance allowed herself the briefest of smiles as the exchange of horn blasts echoed from the center of the force, the right flank and then the left. The thunder of heavy cavalry rumbled from the east as twenty knights, their polished armor shining and twinkling in the early morning sun, rode rapidly but with grace and poise toward the enemy. To the left she saw Orion, conspicuous by his height and immense, lumbering warhorse lead his group of ten heavily armored warriors across to line up their blue lances at the very rebel swordsmen who threatened her life and that of her comrades.

Aware of the horsemen lining up to smash into their exposed flanks, the rebel swordsmen charging at her were called to a rapid halt and their captain quickly barked out orders to bring them around to face the threat from the mounted paladins. The swordsmen rapidly reformed, locking their shields together to form a protective shell against the deadly lances of the Basilean paladins. Now their flank faced Constance.

"Shoot!" she yelled hoarsely as she unslung her crossbow from her back. "Quickly! Shoot the bastards!"

Her blurred vision swimming in and out of focus, she forced a numb foot into the stirrup of her crossbow and clumsily attached her pulley to the back of the weapon. Blood and sweat dripped down from her head in equal measure as she blinked dirt out of her eyes; the sun's rays shone through the dust in the air around her.

"Come on! Come on!" she urged herself as her tired arms pumped the pulley to draw the heavy string back.

Swaying on her feet, Constance raised the weapon to her shoulder and took the extra few vital seconds to compose herself before squeezing the trigger and sending a deadly bolt straight into the ribs of an enemy swordsman in the tightly packed block of men ahead of her. More bolts shot out from her comrades, hacking into the side of the unit as Orion led his horsemen down to face them.

The adrenaline that surged through her suddenly dissipated as another series of horn blasts was exchanged between the two converging units of mounted paladins, and she watched in horror as Orion and his knights raised their lances again and peeled off to the north and away from the enemy swordsmen. Shouts of anguish were issued from the mercenaries as the realization hit them that the paladins were not riding to their aid. Constance had seen it a dozen times before – low value units sometimes had to be sacrificed on the battlefield. She was being left to die. Her energy seemingly leaking out of her sweat covered, bleeding limbs, she forced her arms to cock her crossbow for one last time. Shaking her head in despair and frustration, she watched with bitter anguish as the swordsmen again turned in place to face her as the paladins continued off behind them.

That was the moment that Tancred's twenty paladins of the main force smashed into the side of the swordsmen. With an almost inhuman roar, the paladins struck; their lances shattered on impact, sending splinters of broken wood twirling up into the dusty, sun-streaked air as sprinkles of blood fountained up from the first rank to stand against their onslaught. The tidal wave of armored horses cut a great swath into the midst of the armored swordsmen, trampling men to death under their hooves and splitting the unit in two.

Constance watched, fixated. The elegant, sky blue clad warriors of the stories of her youth were transformed before her very eyes into yelling, snarling, blood covered butchers who hacked and maimed with brutal fury at the panic stricken enemies at their feet. The veteran swordsmen turned to run but stood no chance against the speed and ferocity of the heavy cavalry, chasing them down and executing them with well-drilled, brutal precision.

*****

Shifting his weight in his saddle, Orion leaned into the turn as he guided his knights away from Tancred's headlong charge ahead of him. The two units of knights flashed by each other, close enough to feel the disturbed flow of air from the twenty paladins who hurtled past in the opposite direction, impacting into the enemy infantry behind Orion with a deafening clatter. Orion continued heedless, lowering his lance again and sinking into his saddle to prepare for the impact of the charge.

Ahead of him, the easterly of the two units of rebel swordsmen were locked in a swirling melee with Captain Georgis' men-at-arms; the legion men advanced steadily against their foes, their shields still locked and their spears jabbing out viciously ahead as the two units moved back and forth over a growing carpet of dead and dying soldiers from both sides. Orion fixed his glare on an enemy soldier on the edge of the unit, lined up his lance, and let out a yell.

"Charge!"

The cry was taken up by the knights to either side as Orion dug his spurs into his warhorse with renewed vigor, urging the frenzied animal into a full gallop. All surrounding sounds replaced with the thunder of hooves and the cries of his comrades, Orion gritted his teeth and leaned forward with his couched lance, lining the deadly tip up as the enemy soldiers juddered closer and closer with every passing moment. An enemy swordsman looked up and saw Orion at the last instant, a bitter moment frozen in time as the panic-stricken man fixed his eyes on those of his killer in his last second of life. The lance tip plunged through the man's torso with ease, penetrating the armor before the lance shattered, sending slivers of wood flying up into the air. The mortally wounded swordsman disappeared in an instant, trampled beneath the hooves of the charging horses as Orion continued into the midst of the rebel unit.

Throwing aside his shattered lance and unsheathing his longsword, Orion raised his shield of gold and blue up to protect his left side as he hacked down at an enemy soldier trapped in between his own horse and that of a second paladin. The man had lost his helmet in the fight, allowing Orion to hack off half of his head with one precise swipe. A heavy blow clanged against the metal of his shield, shifting him in his saddle as the mass of bodies surged back and forth in a tide of blood and the agonized cries of the dying. Struggling to move his sword arm in the tightly packed swarm of soldiers, Orion pushed back with his shield against a second enemy soldier before capitalizing on the brief opening to lean over in his saddle and plunge the tip of his sword through the man's chest, sending him disappearing down into the sea of struggling bodies.

Orion looked around frantically, his blood covered blade held high and ready to strike, but he could see only mounted paladins and legion men-at-arms. To the north, on the other side of a rank of spearmen, perhaps a dozen enemy soldiers ran desperately for the woods at the edge of the battlefield, their swords and shields abandoned in their panic. On both flanks, the peasant soldiers employed by the rebels had already turned and run. The battle was won. Cheering had already started from the legion men. But Orion knew from bitter experience that a fleeing enemy could come back in force, and quickly.

"Form up!" he yelled to his knights above the cheers from the infantrymen. "Two ranks! Do not let them get away! Charge!"

*****

Tancred muttered the Rites for the Departed Souls under his breath, again and again, as his eyes moved across the lines and heaps of dead bodies scattered haphazardly across the fields. Over one hundred rebel soldiers and peasants lay motionless where they fell in battle; next to the road lay twenty-one dead of his own force in two neat rows, including three of his paladins who had been killed in the final charges. The numbers suggested a decisive victory against a numerically superior opposition, but to Tancred, it simply spelled out a tragic waste of life – on both sides – that was utterly avoidable. All down to the ambition and stupidity of one man.

Two lines of injured mercenaries and men-at-arms lay at the bottom of the plateau to the south of the battlefield; paladins moved among the wounded, those who were trained and able using their divinity magic to heal. Tancred watched them from atop his horse, a welcome sliver of pride forcing its way into the midst of his sorrow and despair.

"Lord Paladin?"

Tancred's attention was dragged away from the macabre result of the morning's confrontation to the voice that addressed him. Sat on top of her own horse, Sister Jeneveve regarded him with concerned eyes. Her hair was matted to her face with sweat from the exertions of the charge, and blood speckled her armor and blue surcoat.

"Sister," Tancred forced a smile, "what is it?"

"The Dictator-Prefect sends his compliments and requests your company."

Tancred nodded and spurred his horse into a slow trot toward where Hugh waited atop the plateau with a small gathering of other soldiers. Jeneveve rode silently next to Tancred as his horse trudged through the dusty, dry earth in the ferocity of the high, midday sun. Tancred tried to summon up the energy to create small talk with his subordinate, but he failed.

Hugh sat tall and proud atop his impressive white charger, his red cape falling over one shoulder in the fashion that was popular in the capital. Next to him were his two ever present aides, his musician, Captain Georgis, and Orion.

"My Lord Paladin!" Hugh beamed as Tancred and Jeneveve approached. "What a spectacular result! What a victory!"

"Yes," Tancred failed to muster a smile, "the day went our way. Congratulations on your victory, Dictator-Prefect."

"Nonsense," Hugh issued a dismissive gesture, "your flexibility, cool-headedness, and decision making prowess was what won this day. I issued my orders to both of your units, and it was your decision to revoke my orders and change targets for you charges."

"My apologies," Tancred erred on the side of caution, in case the nobleman's smile was hiding a seething rage at Tancred's decision, "I saw an opportunity and..."

"No apology necessary at all. A man can never be a leader if he just blindly follows the orders he is given without thought of the consequences. You were in a position to see parts of the battlefield that I could not. Likewise, you know the capabilities and limitations of heavy cavalry better than I. Rest assured, you made the right decision and I will ensure the Duma hears of this upon my return."

Tancred found himself smiling at last, sitting higher and prouder in his saddle.

"Thank you, my lord," he nodded his head politely.

Captain Georgis, mounted on his speckled horse beside Hugh's aides, cleared his throat and raised his brow. The Dictator-Prefect looked over.

"My lord, while I certainly agree that the cavalry charges directed by the Lord Paladin were instrumental, it was not lances that saved my men-at-arms from the worst the enemy could throw at us. It was crossbow bolts. Without the steadfast support provided by the mercenaries to our left, we would have been defeated. I think that is worthy of credit."

The Dictator-Prefect nodded slowly.

"Of course, you are absolutely correct. That show of spirit and professionalism should be rewarded. Platus, go and fetch the leader of the mercenary band and bring him here."

Platus, the taller of the two aides, nodded an acknowledgement and spurred his horse into a gentle canter down from the slope to where the surviving mercenaries were gathered in small groups of fours and fives. Still proud and emboldened by the Dictator-Prefect's words, and the promise of recognition within the Duma itself, Tancred turned in his saddle to smile at Jeneveve. The young woman stared down at the lines of dead bodies at the foot of the plateau, watching in silence as a small group of men-at-arms began the unenviable task of digging graves. Tancred felt his smile fade.

"It was worthwhile," he offered gently, "our mission here is vital. Dionne's influence must be stopped."

"Must it?" Jeneveve asked, her hazel eyes still fixed on the corpses below. "Must we stop a man who tried to do the right thing?"

Tancred opened his mouth to voice the obvious response, but upon realizing how bad it sounded when he ran the words through his mind, he remained silent. Jeneveve turned to fix her eyes on his.

"The Dictator-Prefect says you are to be commended for using your initiative. Because you did not just blindly follow orders. Is that not what Captain Dionne did? Yet here we are, fighting and dying so that we may drag him in for conviction and execution?"

Tancred met her accusing stare for a few minutes before looking away. A gnawing in his gut urged him to apologize to her, but he was not sure what for; and so he elected to remain silent. At the foot of the hill, Platus returned and spurred his horse back up to take his place by Hugh's side. Tancred recognized the hunched figure of Constance, the unremarkable looking woman who led the mercenaries. She limped to the base of the hill, supported on one side by a towering, middle aged man who held onto one of her arms at the elbow. Constance was covered in dirt, and blood seeped through bandages around her forehead and across one thigh.

Tancred witnessed a brief altercation between the two – judging from their gestures at least, as he was not close enough to overhear the exchange of words – before Constance gestured to her comrade to leave her be.

The stubborn woman limped slowly up the hill, pain registering on her features with each alternate step as weight rested on her wounded leg. Finally arriving to stand before the assembled semi-circle of horsemen, she looked up at the Dictator-Prefect with narrowed eyes.

"You are the leader of this mercenary band?" Hugh asked, gesturing to the crossbowmen at the foot of the plateau.

"What of it?" Constance said, her tone betraying irritation.

Hugh leaned back, confusion on his face. He looked to either side at the assembled warriors.

"You will address the Dictator-Prefect with the correct marks of respect!" Platus snapped. "And stand up straight when you speak to him!"

Constance wearily dragged her gaze across to fix Platus with a look of utter contempt, before glaring back at Hugh and folding her arms silently.

"I have summoned you here to commend you on your bravery, and to complement the skill of your men," Hugh said gently, one hand gripping the reins of his steed while the other was passively open.

"And what form is this commendation to take?" Constance replied petulantly.

"Are my words not enough for you?" Hugh exclaimed.

"I couldn't give two shits for your words," Constance hissed through gritted teeth.

His face a mask of fury, Platus leaned over in his saddle and raised his armored hand high up above his head to strike her. With a sound like a clap of thunder, Orion's hand shot out and grabbed the master duelist by the wrist. Platus, himself a warrior of imposing size, was dwarfed by the huge paladin who glared down at him. Platus attempted to overpower the bearded, blood-stained paladin, but within moments, he was crying out in pain as Orion bent his arm backward at an unnatural angle.

"If you ever try to strike any soldier in this force again, I will break you!" Orion growled. "Do you understand me, little man? I will *break* you!"

"Brother Orion!" Tancred yelled.

The shaven-headed paladin responded instantly, throwing Platus' arm aside and dragging his warhorse away from the two aides. Constance failed to suppress a smirk.

"Go!" Hugh gestured at the young woman. "Begone from my sight!"

Tancred watched as Constance turned and limped back down the slope, seemingly with more difficulty than the ascent, until her tall comrade jogged up to assist her again. Hugh turned to face his aides.

"By the Shining Ones, what just happened?" he exclaimed, looking in utter bewilderment at the assembled riders. "In what world does a peasant woman throw gratitude back in the face of a Dictator?"

"It's disgusting, my lord," sneered Trennio, his second aide. "Utterly unforgiveable."

"It has spoiled my mood entirely," Hugh declared as he sunk lower into his saddle. "Go, all of you."

The nobleman kicked his horse into a sullen trot and headed back south, away from the site of the battle. Trennio allowed a few seconds for a respectable distance before following his master. Platus looked up at Orion, saw a snarling mask of fury, and immediately looked away again before following on. Jeneveve was already halfway to catching up with Constance, leaving Tancred alone. Weary and confused by the hollow feeling inside, Tancred dragged his tired warhorse around and trotted off to the east, toward the coast that lay only a stone throw away on the other side of a line of gentle foothills. Within moments, he was aware of another rider catching up with him. He was surprised to see it was Orion.

"Lord Paladin," the huge man bowed his head, "please allow me to apologize for my outburst. I…"

"Tancred. Just call me Tancred. You are my second, and I glean nothing by putting this wall up between us."

Orion's surprise echoed the feeling Tancred felt at his own words. The two regarded each other in silence for a few moments before Tancred found himself blurting out his own sentiments the instant they formed in his mind.

"I am struggling, Orion. I find command more difficult than I expected. I do not respect the man we follow, and I cannot quite understand why that is. Yes, he is brutal, but there are times that is needed. If our armies are commanded by men of great sentimentality, we will be crushed. The Hegemony needs men like Hugh. Yet I find myself resenting him. I find myself wishing I was more like you."

Orion raised his brow and exhaled, and for a moment, he looked like the young man in his late twenties who so successfully hid behind the terrifying facade.

"We all have our strengths and weaknesses, Tancred," he smiled softly. "Yes, the world sadly needs men and women who can make difficult decisions, but not like this. I believe you are right to trust your instinct. We would be wise to distance ourselves from the Dictator-Prefect. He readily crosses lines that good men would not even consider approaching."

"And the mercenary woman knows this too?" Tancred asked.

"That is her story to tell, not mine," Orion gave a slight shrug, "but yes, they have a history, even if the Dictator-Prefect does not recall it."

Tancred let out a breath and closed his eyes for a few moments. He opened them to see the glorious sun and clear blue skies that were at such odds with his mood.

"I am sorry," he said to Orion, unable to look him in the eyes as he did so, "I have not treated you well since we met."

"I have not made it easy. I apologize for that. But I am ready to follow your orders and give you my full assistance in whatever difficulties we face."

Tancred looked across at the tall knight. Orion held his hand out and looked down at him expectantly. Tancred shook his hand.

"I shall see how our brothers and sisters fare after this morning," Orion said.

Tancred nodded and watched him leave before turning to look eastward toward the sea again. He felt much better for the exchange with Orion, as if a small victory had been pulled from a scenario that left him feeling growingly nauseous with each passing day. Reaching for his Eloicon, he dismounted his warhorse and dropped to one knee to offer his prayers to the Shining Ones and seek guidance in his time of plight.

*****

The crackling of the small campfire broke the silence as Dionne looked across the flames at the human form of the Abyssal Champion. The black sky above the hilltop was relatively clear, showing a starry night broken only by a handful of clouds that appeared as black smears across a deep, blue panorama. The demon, now back in the human form of a slightly built man in red robes with flowing hair of blond, sat on his backpack and gnawed distastefully at a well-cooked rabbit leg skewered on a rusty tent peg. Dionne kept his eyes fixed on the man. It was the second night since their confrontation at the cave, and Dionne had not taken his eyes off 'Teynne' since seeing his true form; the previous night had been spent in his bedroll, feigning sleep while he waited to spring into a fight, sword held at the ready under his blanket.

"You needn't look at me like that," Teynne said calmly.

"Like what?" Dionne demanded, well aware that the complete lack of sleep was making his temper even more volatile; a temper he was well aware of.

Teynne looked up.

"I need to eat, just the same as you. I think this rabbit tastes like shit because I have preferences and emotions, just like you. I'm the same man you've known and trusted for a year. Nothing has changed."

Dionne let out a growl of frustration and leapt to his feet, looking around for something to kick at.

"Everything has changed!" he snapped. "You lied to me!"

"I never lied to you," Teynne said passively, looking up from where he remained seated. "I chose to withhold information from you. Look at you now. Can you blame me?"

"So I am in the wrong here?" Dionne grunted through gritted teeth.

"Must I always be in the wrong, simply because I am an Abyssal?" Teynne countered. "You persist in judging me based solely on the mis-education forced upon you by a regime you yourself have come to the conclusion is corrupt and dishonest. That is your argument against me?"

"Do you expect anything less from me?" Dionne shouted. "I've spent my entire life fighting against your kind!"

"And I've spent my entire life fighting against you and people like you!" Teynne countered, his eyes narrowing in anger. "Yet here I am, willing to look past that to work with somebody I have faith in toward a common goal! Somebody I looked at as a friend!"

Dionne turned his back, unable to keep his eyes fixed on the enigma sat on the other side of the fire. He looked up toward Mount Kolosu, once a spectacular sight and a source of inspiration. Now, finally realizing that his entire life was fuelled by lies, it only made his rage grow deeper. His mind flew back to the very day he discovered the Duma had declared him a traitor. The feelings of betrayal, the wounds that only seemed to grow with each passing year after he was cast aside after giving his life in loyal service, all of the hatred and resentment bubbled up to the surface again. He took a breath in an attempt to calm his anger and stepped away from the fire.

A few moments of silence passed as Teynne remained seated. He finally spoke.

"I fought my way up to where I am," he said quietly, "just the same as you. We have a hierarchy; we reward the brave and the loyal. We have some idiots in positions of authority. We're just the same in that respect."

Dionne turned to face him again but remained silent. Teynne continued.

"I find many human women beautiful," Teynne smiled, "and some of the elves, too. But not dwarf women. They're hideous. It's the beards. So you see, we're actually quite similar."

Dionne burst into a fit of laughter. The combination of the stress, the lack of sleep, the lunacy of the situation where he found himself sharing a joke with a demon, all of it added up to make the situation all the more hilarious. After several moments of rare and appreciated mirth, Dionne sank back down to sit opposite Teynne.

"So now what?" he asked. "Where are we getting these men from?"

"What men?"

"The army you promised me?"

"I never said the army was made up of men," Teynne frowned. "We are going to the Abyss."

Dionne's eyes widened in amazement.

"What?" he snarled. "When did I ever agree to going to the Abyss?"

"What did you think?" Teynne sighed, resting his head in one hand in frustration.

"You said we were going north! The most obvious conclusion to draw is that we were heading to the border forts! I assumed that you knew of some legion men who were similarly minded!"

"You assumed wrong! What, an entire army of legion soldiers just waiting for the right man to follow against their masters? That was your assumption? Of course we are headed to the Abyss! Where else do you think I will find an army for you?"

Dionne sprang to his feet and set about gathering up his belongings.

"The deal is off! I was an idiot to ever trust you! Consider yourself lucky that I have enough respect for you not to strike you down here and now! Go! Go back to your Abyss!"

Dionne was surprised when Teynne stood and, without a word, packed up his belongings and slung his pack onto his back.

"I've had enough of you. I've had enough of your bickering, your whining, your lack of trust in me, and your idiotic close mindedness. I offer you my loyalty, my friendship, and an entire army to go to war against the regime that stabbed you in the back after a life of service! And what do I ask? One thing. To see past my form and the lies the Hegemon forced on you. And you couldn't even do that. Then piss off, Centurion, you are not the man I thought you were. I've wasted a year on you, and I'm not wasting any more time."

Dionne watched as the false image of the demon turned his back and walked off to the north, soon disappearing into the shadows. He stood alone, staring down into the fire, confused by how in the world he had been left feeling as if he were the one in the wrong. He had turned his back on an offer made by a creature of the Abyss, and every tale he had ever heard about offers from demons always ended in misery. But then again, they were just that: tales. Myths. Stories conjured up as Basilean folklore. Lies.

What if Teynne really was telling the truth? Certainly, Dionne had never seen any evidence of dishonesty from him. Was it fair to judge somebody based on their form, no matter how terrifying? He had trusted many soldiers in his time whose perfect uniforms made them out to be the stuff of legend, stalwart, dependable heroes who fought for the honor of Basilea and the Shining Ones above. Yet, when the Hegemon betrayed Dionne, when the Duma had the audacity to pronounce him a traitor, all of these heroic soldiers turned their backs on him. Only the rank and file, the mud and blood covered men with their broken noses, scars and tattoos, they were the only ones who loyally stood by their captain. Appearances meant nothing. Loyalty was everything.

"Wait!" Dionne called out into the night. "Just wait a damn moment!"

He ran off to the north where he saw Teynne stood impatiently on the pathway ahead of him, his arms folded defiantly.

Eight

A fine drizzle cascaded down from an iron-gray sky above as Dionne willed his aching legs to continue the climb. On the narrow mountain path ahead, Teynne continued to lead the way at a solid pace, just as he had done for the past week now. After taking a boat across the Anerian Wash, the two had traveled up through the Mountains of Tarkis along the east coast of the Province of Solios, closing with the very northern boundary of the entire Hegemony. Days of travel with little food or rest had left even Dionne weary, but it was a weariness he was well accustomed to after years of traveling, a weariness that returned to him like an old friend even though his body did not welcome that friend as readily as it might have a decade earlier.

Up on the path ahead, Teynne stopped and turned to face Dionne with a smile.

"Do you feel that?" the devil masquerading as a man smiled.

Dionne shook his head. Teynne closed his eyes and inhaled deeply, his smile growing broader. Dionne looked out to the east and over the Low Sea of Suan where the first few miles of the familiar seascape were visible through the misty line of moisture that blotted out the clean line of the horizon. The island of Ge was just visible, although its characteristic coastal fishing villages were hidden behind the midmorning mist atop the jagged mountains, the uniform cold gray punctuated only periodically by the dull green of vegetation. Dionne turned to look to the northwest where, penetrating up through the fog somewhere ahead, was the Mountain of Kolosu, the spiritual home of the entire Hegemony.

Up on that very mountain peak was the home of the Shining Ones themselves, the gods of all that was right and just in the world of Mantica. When Dionne had first turned and run from the accusations that were leveled against him following the disaster of the Defence of Samirik, his plan had been to climb that very mountain. Whether it was to seek redemption or vindication, he had never really decided, as a series of unexpected events had stalled his progress until his band of loyal soldiers had set up camp not far from the spot he stood at now with Teynne. They were only a stone throw from where the two paladins had found him years earlier, and where the next disaster that punctuated that phase of his life had unfolded. He had never even gotten close to finding his redemption. Dionne gritted

91

his teeth. There was no way that all of these events could have passed by the Shining Ones without their notice; not so close to Kolosu. Perhaps everything Teynne had told him was true. Perhaps the faith of the Shining Ones was a fallacy. It certainly seemed that way as he looked up into the fog that hid the home of these so-called gods.

"We're here," Teynne said as Dionne approached, "this is close enough."

"Close enough for what?"

"To go home," Teynne smiled, his red eyes twinkling with something between a friendly warmth and a simmering danger. "I can feel the pull of the Abyss from here. It is not much, but it is enough to get home."

"You can open... a portal?" Dionne asked.

"Of sorts."

"Then why wait this long? In fact, if you have such powers then why wait for anything? You say this world is corrupt and you wish to cleanse it, so why not open your portal right into the very heart of the City of the Golden Horn and pour your armies forth?"

The man-demon grinned broadly and let out a long laugh, his lithe arms folded across his chest.

"If only it were that easy, friend! If it were so, it would be done by now, I assure you! But sadly no, that is not how the transference of energy works. Portals require much power, and that power depends on the size of the portal, the duration it must be opened for, and the distance it must cover. Indeed, to move from the Abyss to a gateway in the mortal world, we also need somebody with a portal stone to establish the gateway at the other end of the tunnel. Normally we rely on loyal servants hidden across the mortal world to achieve this, but today it is I who carries such a stone. There are limits to even the powers of the Wicked Ones and those who serve them. If it were not so, then the portals could be used to crush any opposition in exactly the manner you describe."

Dionne nodded slowly as his labored breathing returned to normal, the musty smells of the mountainside moss filling his nostrils.

"So what is the reality of it all?" He asked as Teynne took a small, smooth stone of obsidian black from a pouch on his belt.

"The reality is that I am now at the very fringe of my connection to the Abyss with a portal stone so small. From here, I will open a gateway for the two of us to travel to the Abyss. If I wanted something bigger, grander, able to bring forth an army or even travel much further from the Abyss, I would need a larger portal stone or greater assistance from the Abyss itself. The ritual to activate such a stone is also significantly longer and more complex. But from here I can get you to your new home."

"Remember that this is temporary," Dionne warned, his eyes narrowing.

"Of course," the demon nodded. "Come, time for us to go."

Dionne had not stopped to consider what he was expecting in the summoning of a gateway, but whatever it was, he found himself disappointed by the normality of the process. Without ritual or theatrics, Teynne held one hand out and a small, dull spark appeared at head height a few paces ahead of him. The spark moved down to touch the rocky ground, drawing a straight line in space ahead. The line opened into a yawn, creating an oval with a shimmering outline; through the oval, Dionne saw a land that had been seemingly crafted from the worst nightmares of his childhood.

A landscape of ugly, black rocks was punctuated by rivers of glowing red lava, while immense chains of black iron held masses of rocky land in place. The skies were blood red, partially blotted out with thick clouds of sulfurous black. Winged demons with skin of vivid scarlet flew across the skies, while bulbous land-based counterparts stood watch on the mountains of black below as lines of screaming men and women, clad in rags and chains, blistered and burned, were whipped and forced to stagger and limp in line toward the tallest mountain in the distance.

Without a word, Teynne stepped through the gateway and instantly transformed back into his true form of a towering, red-skinned Abyssal Champion. He looked back through the portal at Dionne and grinned a saw toothed smile that somehow seemed friendly to him, even trustworthy.

"Follow me, friend," Teynne said, "all is well now."

Drawing himself up to his full height, one hand by his sword, Dionne stepped through the portal and into the Abyss.

The searing heat of the cutting winds and the stench of sulfur immediately hit him. Looking over his shoulder, Dionne saw the now comparatively idyllic vision of the drizzle-covered Mountains of Tarkis disappear as the portal sealed itself before disappearing altogether. From his vantage point atop a jagged precipice, as far as the eye could see, the land was made up of the same blackened mountains protruding through lakes of burning lava, populated by the lines of damned, tortured victims in chains who trudged painfully and aimlessly toward the central mountain on the horizon, while red-skinned Abyssals of differing shapes and sizes patrolled their flanks.

The dreadful moaning of the tortured victims was occasionally drowned out as walls of fire shot up from the lakes of lava with a roar, falling back down again to spit yellow-hot rocks scattering across the blackened shorelines of the jagged islands. Horned creatures clad in scraps of armor took turns to drag men and women out of line, seemingly at random, to stab at them with pitchforks or flay their skin raw with vicious, barbed whips. Three-headed dogs, nearly as tall as a man, were let loose by their demonic owners to violently maul and tear at victims in the line.

Dionne looked up at the towering figure of Teynne who watched with a grim smile of pride, his arms folded across his muscular chest and his wings tucked in behind his back.

"Who are they?" Dionne demanded, pointing at the endless lines of the amassed hundreds of suffering victims.

"Sinners," Dionne spat, "larvae, fleshlings, the eternally damned. They are the murderers, rapists, corrupt leaders, and cheats of a thousand years. They deserve their fate, every one of them. You have heard stories, no doubt, of Abyssals taking the innocent from their beds at night and dragging them here into the depths of the Abyss?"

Dionne nodded.

"Nonsense and lies!" Teynne growled. "This is the order of Mantica! This is the unsigned pact between the Shining Ones and the Wicked Ones! There must be a place for the sinners, they must answer for their deeds. And we, we are the guardians of this place, and we are chosen to ensure justice is served. There is only one way for a good man to enter the Abyss – he must willingly choose to do so, as you have just done. This is not a place of nightmares for the undeserving, there is no hell for those who do not deserve it! Only the cruelest, foulest sinners end up here!"

Dionne cast his eyes over the lines of defeated, dejected, and vacant-eyed slaves who continued to trudge on mechanically as they were beaten and whipped. He searched for sympathy for them and found none.

"This is the First Circle," Teynne continued, "the uppermost of the Seven Circles of the Abyss. This is the place that straddles the path to the other circles from your mortal world; this is the tear across the mortal world of Mantica. But it is also much more, for the Abyss is both a physical place but also a spiritual and incorporeal one. You look around and you see hell; that is as it should be. This is the nightmare for those who deserve it. But there is more to the Abyss, so much more than your priests will have taught you as a child. The Abyss is agony and fire to those who deserve it, but it is also beauty and warmth to those who earn it. If time permits, I might choose to show you a different Circle of the Abyss."

Dionne looked down from the rocky precipice and watched in silence as the denizens of lower Abyssal continued to torture the endless lines of the damned. A hunchback with a mouthful of viciously sharp teeth and horns sprouting from its head suddenly turned to look up at where Teynne and Dionne stood. The creature let out a yell and pointed. The cry of alarm instantly attracted the attention of dozens of other red-skinned creatures who abruptly stopped their activities and sprinted over lakes of fire and razor edged rocks to form a mass of hellish monsters at the foot of the raised ground. Dionne instinctively reached for his sword as the wall of creatures formed below him, but Teynne held out a hand to stop him.

As one, the Abyssals dropped to their knees and bowed their heads. Teynne nodded in approval.

"Arise," he commanded, his tone more regal. "Your lord and master has returned."

The ranks of clawed, horned creatures silently stood; a few flickering fork tongues or shifting tails were the only signs of movement from the otherwise surprisingly disciplined mob. A spark of shimmering light suddenly appeared to Teynne's right and another gateway was opened. Dionne had a moment to glance through and saw a confused landscape of unearthly beauty, with skies of rich turquoise atop a shifting landscape of green and blue vegetation unlike anything he had seen in his years of travel. A being stepped through the gateway and instantly dropped to one knee in front of the Abyssal Champion as the portal closed.

The being was undoubtedly female, her appealing physique accentuated by scant armor of spiked metal that barely covered her red-skinned form. Her seductive appearance and facial beauty was marred by curved horns sprouting from her forehead and leathery wings folded at her back. Dionne recognized her as a temptress; a high ranking and powerful succubus, an Abyssal that was conjured into being by the base and deprived thoughts of evil, lustful men. At least, that is what he had been taught in a version of events that he now doubted more with every passing day.

"My Lord Champion," the temptress said, her voice hushed and respectful, "I answer your summons."

"Arise," Teynne gave a curt nod.

The figure of twisted beauty stood and shifted her black eyes over to regard Dionne with interest.

"Dionne, this is Am'Bira. She will attend to your every need as we find a way to work together."

Dionne looked at the temptress, his base thoughts stopping his answer from leaving his mouth. The temptress paced forward with a seductive swing of her hips, leaning in to regard Dionne.

"He finds my form... upsetting," she smirked.

"Then find something more normal to him," Teynne barked. "Dionne, I have chosen Am'Bira for you because she is much like you. She, too, began her life as a mortal under the iron rule of the Hegemon. She saw sense and is now one of us."

"But I am not one of you," Dionne said carefully, concerned for causing offense to a sea of hellish creatures who had somehow demonstrated more respect to him than his own commanders in the legion. "We have but a temporary alliance."

"My friend, I think we are past that now," Teynne smiled. "Am'Bira, a more settling form for our new brother."

Before Dionne's eyes, the temptress's bright red skin faded to a pale, conventional hue while her wings and horns faded away to disappear. Her jagged, revealing armor was replaced by tall boots of black suede, with matching gloves and a tight corset, a cloak of black falling from one shoulder. Her black hair framed the striking face of an eye-catching woman in her mid to late thirties. But that was not the part that stood out to Dionne. The woman's belt buckle was a large metal block fashioned into the emblem of a blazing sun, but now defaced with a deep scratch across its surface. Dionne's eyes widened. She had once been a nun of the Basilean Sisterhood. A sister who had fallen into damnation. He looked up at her to find her still watching him with interest.

"We've met before, haven't we?" The dark haired woman issued a slight smile.

"We have?"

"Only briefly, some years ago now," she confirmed. "You might not remember me, but I remember you."

Dionne looked back across to Teynne. The towering champion looked down impassively, his arms still folded.

"Am'Bira will act as your guide," Teynne declared, "for I have my own lords to converse with. Am'Bira will introduce you to your new soldiers."

Dionne shook his head.

"This was not our agreement," he said sternly, "we have a temporary alliance. I have not spoken to my men regarding this, and I owe them that much. Without me talking to them, they will judge you on your appearance, and attack you on sight. First, I must..."

"Dionne, my friend," Teynne held up a hand to silence him, "sadly none of this will be necessary. All of your men are dead."

"What?" Dionne demanded, his fists clenched as he took a stride toward the demon. "What did you do?"

"I did nothing," Teynne said sympathetically, "they were killed by the forces of the Hegemony. Men of the legion and the paladin orders. Your men were all killed in battle near Emalitos, a week ago now. They stood fast, resolute, against a much greater force. They fought bravely to the last, for you."

Dionne took a step back, his vision swimming in the hot, stifling winds of the First Circle of the Abyss. Losing his footing on the jagged rocks, he stumbled and dropped to one knee. Am'Bira stepped across and offered a hand to him. With a snarl of rage, he batted it away. Teynne drifted over and towered above him.

"Your loyal, brave soldiers were killed by the true villains in this sorry saga," the winged devil said with sincerity. "The Hegemon's deluded killers. For centuries now, since the mirror shattered and our world was torn asunder, the Shining Ones have deluded all mortals with deceit, twisted lies that paint us within the Abyss as mindless animals, things to be feared. Only the evil and the damned should fear us! We bring order and balance to the world where the followers of the Shining Ones bring only riches to the corrupt!"

Fighting to control his breath, Dionne looked up at Teynne as the Abyssal Champion's outline was silhouetted by a wall of fire shooting up from the lakes of lava behind him.

"Your world is not fair, my friend!" Teynne snarled. "You know that! You tried to do the right thing many years ago, and you have lived as a criminal ever since as a reward for your integrity! Listen to the voice of reason, man! Your whole life is a lie, pedaled by the very bastards who dare to judge you and call you a criminal! They've taken your honor, they've killed the men who looked up to you as a father! You have nothing back there, nothing! But here? Here you belong! Here you will have respect *and* loyalty!"

Whether the hordes of lower Abyssals had moved up to form a circle around him or whether the land itself had lowered to meet them, Dionne did not know, but he found himself now surrounded by a sea of fanged, horned faces of red that somehow did not seem to pose a threat.

"For years I have watched you from afar!" Teynne continued, his voice filled with passion and sincerity. "For a year I traveled by your side to know and understand who you truly are! I have chosen you, my friend! You belong here, with us! Your men are gone, but you have a new family now! You belong here! Trust me! Take my hand, and trust me!"

Dionne looked up as the demon loomed over him, a clawed hand extended toward him in friendship. Dionne reached out and took it.

*****

The outskirts of the town of Torgias seemed little more than a dreary continuation of the drab, rock strewn road that led north from the shores of the Anerian Wash; the gaping inlet of water that cut west inland from the Low Sea of Suan. Ramshackle huts and rickety wooden buildings flanked the broad road, growing in regularity as the two paladins continued the ride north toward the Mountains of Tarkis. Grime covered children played in the path leading up to the town as aging miners watched the riders suspiciously from doorways. A heavy cloud of black hung over the western edge of the town, drifting down from the smelting yard just outside the town boundary. To the east, a motley collection of sails was visible above the high ground from merchant ships that had traveled upriver to trade the precious, valuable wares from the sprawling mining community at the foot of the mountains.

Tancred looked up at the sky and saw a welcome flash of clear blue through a tear in the drizzly, gray clouds that had followed them for nearly a week now. The detachment had continued to track north after defeating Dionne's forces, and having paid off a few of the locals, they had even succeeded in finding out that there had been several sighting of Dionne himself, fleeing to the north with a mysterious stranger. Hugh made the decision to send Tancred on ahead to stay on the trail and keep tracking their mark, while the remainder of the force carried out the long, laborious crossing of the Anerian Wash by boat. Accompanied by Orion, just in case they caught up with their man, the two paladins had managed to stay two days ahead of the force until a flood from a collapsed dam had forced them to divert further inland.

As they rounded a corner in the road, Tancred saw the town wall up ahead; a simple but sturdy construct consisting of a tall wooden wall punctuated with four towers, joining the natural rock walls at either side of a valley. Two guards stood by the gates, both of them standing to attention as the paladins approached.

"Good evening, Sir Paladin," the older of the two guards called out, bowing his head respectfully.

Tancred ignored the titular error he had been addressed with and swung himself down from his saddle.

"Good evening," he replied, "we are here on the Hegemon's business. Go and fetch your guard commander."

The aging guard nodded wordlessly before turning on his heel and dashing off through the gates, leaving a tall, lanky guard with a vacant expression alone with the two paladins. Orion vaulted down from his warhorse and led the animal by the reins to stand by Tancred.

"Now what?" he asked, surveying the surroundings. "This place will be good to resupply our force, at least."

"We need to stay on Dionne's trail," Tancred replied, "but my concern is getting information. These miners are cut off from the rest of the Hegemony, all the way up here. I think it likely they will see Dionne as a hero rather than a criminal. I doubt we will obtain much assistance here. We need to tread carefully."

After a few moments, the guard returned, accompanied by a rotund, middle aged man with a waxed mustache and beard, dressed in a shining breastplate and hurriedly attaching a thick cloak of rich, red velvet as he approached.

"Welcome to Torgias," the man said as he approached, the tone of his voice failing to marry up with the sentiments of his words. "I am Vendis, the guard commander. What brings you here?"

"My name is Tancred of Effisus, Lord Paladin of the Order of the Sacred Ark," Tancred drew himself up to his full height, content that he was marginally taller than Vendis, "and this is my second, Brother Paladin Orion of Suda. We are tracking a fugitive, under orders from the Duma, sanctioned by the Hegemon himself."

Vendis' brows raised.

"A certain ex-captain of the legion, one assumes?" he said in a hushed tone, leaning closer. "Be careful in this town, gentlemen. Your quarry is considered quite the hero of the people in these parts. That being said, he has not been to Torgias recently. So, Dionne's name has reached the ears of the Hegemon?"

Tancred exchanged a glance with Orion but elected not to follow up on the commander's query.

"Our man might not be here, but we believe he is close. Certainly in this area. He is heading north, that much we know for sure. What help can you offer us?"

"If he is heading north, he will be further inland," Vendis replied with confidence, "unless he is looking to flee altogether, in which case he would already have made for the coast and will be on a merchant ship by now. You'll never find him if that is the case. Given his history in the area, however, my prediction would be that he will take to the mountains with his bandits. He seems quite settled here. You would need an army to go up there and dislodge him, though, and there I cannot help you. I can't spare the men. I have problems of my own."

"We are not looking for soldiers, we have enough of those only a day or so behind us," Tancred continued, "but if we are heading up into the Mountains of Tarkis, we shall need some assistance. Can you spare one man with a good knowledge of the mountain trail?"

The commander shook his head.

"I cannot spare a single man, unless you produce documentation giving you the authority to override my authority in this post. But there are other options, better ones, dare I say. Go into town and, if you have the money, I would recommend you hire the service of a woman named Aestelle. She is one of these... adventurers."

Vendis practically spat the last word before continuing.

"There are caves up in those mountains, dozens of networks of old tunnels from centuries past. We get these adventurers turn up here from time to time to make their fortune. They nearly all fail to return quite quickly. But not Aestelle. She has been in this area for about a year now. She's the best of the lot."

"How do I find her?" Tancred asked.

"She lives quite an extravagant existence in the Trade Wind Inn near the center of town. You'll know her as soon as you see her. If not, follow the trail of lovesick men trying to catch her attention. Now, obviously, a paladin would never be so base as to be motivated by lust, so I will not insult your integrity by daring to give you advice, but for your soldiers when they do arrive – I strongly recommend treating her with the upmost respect. She is far, far more dangerous than she looks."

*****

The clouds continued to disperse as the sun dipped to touch the horizon, leaving only a scattering of thin sheets of orange-tinted cloud stretched across a sky of darkening azure. Tancred flipped a coin to the stable boy who rushed out excitedly to see the two paladins as they led their horses into the large courtyard in the center of the Trade Wind Inn's collection of neat buildings.

"Take good care of these two," Tancred nodded to the blond haired boy.

"Thank you, Shining Ones bless you," Orion smiled warmly to the boy, eliciting an excited nod before he led their warhorses away.

The inn itself was surrounded by a tall stone wall, curiously of more modern and solid construct than the town walls. The main inn building was two stories high, its upper floor swelling out to overhang the lower floor. The windows to the lower floor glowed a faint orange from the hearth inside, and the sound of laughter and music drifted across the warm evening air. Tancred walked over and hauled open one of the heavy double doors leading in, stepping back as a powerfully built salamander pushed past him, the reptilian creature eyeing the paladins suspiciously before pulling a dark hood up over its long face and walking off toward the stables.

The interior of the inn was furnished with pristine, expensive looking furniture of oiled, light wood. A series of alcoves were built around a central bar where the landlord and two women busily served fine wines and exotic ales. Two bards played an intricate duel on their lutes in a far corner by a large, open fire. Perhaps thirty people were crammed into the inn, all dressed in fine clothes and engaged in friendly conversations in small groups. The few nearest the main entrance eyed Tancred warily as he entered; when his bearded, shaven headed comrade walked into the room, it caused half the patrons to fall completely silent.

Tancred looked over to a trio of merchants on the nearest table who were sharing a bottle of red wine. The three middle-aged men looked back at him nervously.

"I'm looking for Aestelle," Tancred said.

A tall man with a thick, red beard pointed to an alcove on the far side of the bar. Tancred pushed his way through the assembled patrons. The sight of Aestelle caught his breath, despite the warning.

Five men in the garb of affluent merchant sailors sat in a semi-circle around a single young woman, who leaned back in her chair with one booted foot up on the table in front of her. Noticeably tall and slim, she wore tall boots of black leather over tight leggings of the same material, and a white shirt of rich silk with slits cut along the sleeves to display toned arms. Her face – the most beautiful Tancred had ever seen in his life – was half hidden by cascading hair of platinum blonde, decorated with a few sparse rows of interwoven pearls and exquisitely carved miniature wooden beads of a dozen colors, and intricately woven plats. She fixed Tancred with a sultry stare from her pale blue, almost silver eyes as he approached and held a hand up to silence one of the men opposite her.

"Can I help you gentlemen?" she asked, her clipped accent betraying an expensive education.

"Aestelle?" Tancred asked, finding his confidence rapidly eroding as he addressed the beautiful young woman.

"That's right."

"The… guard commander pointed us in your direction. He said you might be able to assist us with a task we have in this area."

Aestelle took her foot off the table and crossed her legs, leaning forward to pick up a glass of sparkling, white wine.

"Go on," she nodded to the men crowded around her, "business calls."

With grunts of frustration, the assembled merchants quickly bid their farewells and left the table. Aestelle nodded to the empty seats opposite her and poured two fresh glasses of wine before sliding them across. Tancred sat down and leaned across the table. Still intoxicated by her beauty, he made the decision to alter the course of the conversation to try to put her on the defensive and gain some amount of control.

"You are not exactly what I was expecting when I was told to look here for a mountain guide," he said, his tone deliberately dismissive.

"I'm terribly sorry to disappoint," the blonde woman smirked and narrowed her eyes, "but the two of you are equally something of a surprise to me. I grew up on stories of paladins being handsome, dashing sorts. How many times have you had your nose broken?"

"I have fought in many battles," Tancred retorted defensively, folding his arms as he felt his face redden.

"As have I," the tall woman said dismissively, idly picking at the plaster on the wall behind her, "but I've never been hit in the face. That's just careless. And your ogre? Does it speak?"

"I speak well enough," Orion answered gruffly, "and I have been in enough fights to spot an individual who is all talk. Now that we have the insults done and dusted, perhaps you would care to listen to my Brother Paladin?"

Aestelle winced briefly at Orion's accusation but recovered her composure so rapidly that Tancred doubted the tall man would have detected the impact of his words.

"Go on," Aestelle said, "I am listening."

Tancred leaned back and paused for a moment to consider how much the woman needed to know. The musicians on the other side of the room shifted pace to a gentler ballad, immediately changing the atmosphere.

"We are chasing a fugitive. We are currently scouting ahead of our main force which is a day behind us. Our man has apparently fled to the Mountains of Tarkis. We need to track him and we need a pathway through the mountains for a hundred men, with horses and supplies."

"Is that all?" Aestelle laughed sarcastically. "You only want to track a single man across an entire mountain range and move a small army?"

"Can you do it or not?" Orion snapped.

"Easy, Ogre," Aestelle held up one hand with a flash of annoyance in her silvery blue eyes. "You need me more than I need you, so I suggest you keep a lid on those little tantrums."

"Can you help us?" Tancred asked.

Aestelle sat back and took a drink from her wine glass, tapping a clenched fist on her chin pensively.

"Tracking one man across those mountains is impossible, for anybody," she finally replied. "I can take you on the route I would go, the fastest across. But there is very little to travel to if one is heading north. Tmoskai, perhaps? Unless your man is on a pilgrimage to Kolosu itself. Perhaps I could assist you better if I knew more about the individual you are looking to bring to justice."

Tancred looked across at Orion. The big man shrugged.

"Dionne," Tancred said quietly, "we are looking to bring Dionne in to face charges with the Duma."

Aestelle's eyes widened a little at the mention of the name.

"He's a dangerous man," she said seriously, "and he is loved in these lands. Most people in this region would hide him from the Duma's soldiers rather than turn him in."

"And you?" Orion demanded. "Would you help him?"

"Depends on who is paying me the most. I have no loyalty to him, just as I have no loyalty to you. But money talks. Now put up your money and I shall help you track your man. I may even know of a way to get your little army over those mountains without having to spend days diverting east to the coast."

Tancred took a sample sip from the wine. It tasted good; expensive.

"What is your plan for getting our force over the mountains?"

"Money first," Aestelle said coldly.

"Five bezals," Tancred countered.

"Do not waste my time, Paladin," Aestelle scowled. "These boots cost half that much. Fifty."

"Fifty?" Tancred exclaimed. "I could hire a whole troop of mercenaries for that!"

"A troop of mercenaries can't get your army across a mountain range," Aestelle replied. "I can. There are few people here who know these mountains once you deviate from the paths to the mines. Of those few, I am the only one who will keep you alive long enough to cross them. That is worth fifty."

"Thirty," Tancred countered, "and we both know that is well in excess of what any single mercenary is worth."

Aestelle finished her wine, stood up, and recovered a sword belt from the back of her chair. Carrying the scabbarded blade casually over one shoulder, she turned on her heel.

"Then we are done here. Good evening, gentlemen."

Tancred looked in astonishment at the detail on the quillions and pommel of the exquisite greatsword. The blade itself was nearly the height of Aestelle, and the silver and gems inlaid on the weapon's handle and pommel spoke of a woman who was well used to refinement.

"Forty!" Tancred said as he shot to his feet, noting with discomfort that Aestelle was noticeably taller than him. "All upfront! It's all I can offer!"

The beautiful blonde woman stopped, regarded him over one shoulder before turning to face him again.

"Very well," she finally said. "As soon as your soldiers arrive, come and find me. Make sure they are all ready to move fast."

Nine

Intrusive beams of sunlight crept in through the slits between the wooden shutters over the windows, highlighting the dust that swirled around the room. Aestelle opened one eye and groaned in pain, immediately reaching for the waterskin she kept hanging from the bedpost. Instead, she found an empty bottle of wine on the small table by the bedside and let out a follow up moan of discomfort from the pounding at her temples. Her vision refusing to clear or even stay stationary, she forced herself to sit up.

Outside the inn, the chirping of birds in the morning sun seemed loud enough to cut through glass. Slumping off the bed, Aestelle cursed herself for another night of alcohol-based indulgence. She checked the saddlebag hung on the bedpost next to the waterskin. Recovering a small, velvet pouch she counted her money. This elicited a third groan. The facade of wealth would not continue any longer, especially if she carried on wasting her money on over indulgent inns and fine wines. At least the two paladins she had encountered seemed serious about paying her a very good wage for leading them across some stubby mountains for a few days.

Aestelle staggered over to the clear area of her inn room by the end of her bed and sank down to carry out her morning regime of press-ups. Gritting her teeth in pain as her head flared up in protest and her stomach churned with each repetition of the exercise, she focused her mind and refused to be beaten by the nausea. After a mere fifty press-ups, her stomach won the fight and forced her to launch herself for the small chamber adjoining her bedroom where she was sick into a bucket. Feeling slightly better for the ordeal, Aestelle washed herself meticulously from her washbasin before dashing dark, powdered make up over her already dark, hungover eyes. Tying her braided hair back and spending the extra time in front of a brass framed mirror to stylishly arrange the beads which danged from one side of her forehead, she hauled her leather armor on and buckled her pistol and knife belt around her waist.

The irony of the contrary activities was not lost on her as she applied a few slaps of criminally expensive perfume, before recovering her greatsword and buckling it to her back to leave the handle accessible over her right shoulder. Finally, she slung her bow along with a quiver of arrows to protrude over her left shoulder.

Prepared to face the outside world, she left her room to buy a drink powerful enough to freshen the foul taste in her mouth before finding the two paladins so she could remedy her worryingly low level of funds.

*****

The Dictator-Prefect, clearly in a foul mood, had ordered a stop to the marching drums not long after the detachment began its march north at sunrise. Footsteps from sixty soldiers echoed across the wet cobbles underfoot, the clipping of hooves from the knights and their squires not far behind. Constance glanced around at the town of Torgias as she marched to the right of her mercenaries, pain still flaring up in her injured thigh despite the healing magic of the paladins and two weeks to recover.

The town seemed to be an odd mixture of poverty and affluence with not much in between. The outskirts of the town were littered with cramped, shoddily constructed huts for the scores of miners, while the center of the settlement surrounded an impressive town hall and square, complete with an ornate fountain and a small collection of marble statues of well-dressed merchants, perhaps the town founders. A large church sat opposite the town hall on the other side of the square, complete with a tall, open steeple boasting some new looking brass bells. A dozen black birds fluttered up into the air with a noisy caw as the soldiers marched into the town square, their movements silently followed by the eyes of every man, woman, and child they passed.

Atop his impressive steed at the head of the column, Hugh held up a gloved hand to signify a halt. An indistinguishable order was immediately barked out by Captain Georgis, and the men-at-arms of the 32nd Legion immediately snapped to a standstill.

"Company... halt!" Constance ordered, smiling proudly as her ex-military men and women came to a stop with exactly the same precision and smartness as their legion counterparts.

Three horses waited by the church steeple; only two with riders. Constance made out the familiar figures of Tancred and Orion. Hugh immediately rode over to them, flanked by Platus and Trennio. The foot soldiers and knights waited in silence as their leader spoke with the two paladins. It occurred to Constance that there was absolutely no need to stand on ceremony, not when her soldiers could be enjoying some lunch or a drink.

"Company... fall out," she shouted, before adding, "don't go far."

Ignoring the disapproving glares of the legion men, the mercenaries broke off into smaller groups and walked away amidst the buzz of casual conversation. Only Hayden and Jaque remained behind to walk over to Constance.

"You coming for a drink?" Hayden offered with a smile.

"Yeah, I think so," Constance winced as she massaged her thumbs into her injured leg. "Let's go find someplace we can afford, though."

"Shall we see if Orion wants to come?" Jaque offered. "We haven't seen him in a couple of weeks."

"Sure," Constance shrugged, remembering her few conversations with the tall knight with some affection, "why not?"

The three walked across the square toward where Hugh and his aides faced Tancred, Orion, and the riderless horse. Orion saw them, jumped down from his saddle, and walked out to meet them.

"Hello," he greeted with a slight smile, "welcome to Torgias. Not much of a place, I am afraid."

Jaque stepped forward and shook the huge paladin's hand.

"Glad you're still in one piece," Constance offered. "I fancy you and your leader there might have gotten into trouble if you'd met Dionne alone."

"Maybe," Orion gave a slight shrug, "maybe not. How is your leg?"

"Yeah, nearly there."

"I am honestly sorry," Orion bowed his head. "I led that charge away from you with a very heavy heart. But I saw what Lord Paladin Tancred was trying to achieve, and my job was to support his plan."

Constance furrowed her brow as she tried to pick apart the meaning of his words.

"Sorry, you've lost me."

"The battle," the bearded knight explained, "outside Emalitos. The Dictator-Prefect ordered me to lead a charge against the rebels attacking you, but then the order was countered by the Lord Paladin. It pained me greatly to turn away from helping you all."

Constance glanced across at her two comrades. Jaque appeared confused, even amused by the sentiment. Hayden folded his arms and frowned.

"Just orders, Orion," Constance laughed, "it's never personal. None of us expected you to break the line and make up your own plan just because we've enjoyed a conversation of two. I wouldn't worry."

"Besides," Jaque grinned, "we all heard about you nearly breaking the arm of one of Hugh's little lap dogs afterward! That would make up for anything!"
Constance remembered Orion's hand shooting out to defend her from Platus' attack.

"Likewise, that was nothing personal," Orion confessed. "There is a special area in the darkest recesses of my heart that is reserved for bullies."

"Well, it made me laugh!" Jaque smiled. "We're off to find a tavern for lunch and a drink. Would you like to join us?"

The tall knight took a step back, his brow lowering as his dark eyes flickered from man to woman in suspicion. After a moment of silence, his mood seemed to lighten just as quickly.

"I would like that very much," Orion answered, "but I fear we will not have the time. We are awaiting our new guide for our move up into the mountains. Once she arrives, we will be off again."

"I'd best round up our lot again, before they get drunk and start fighting," Hayden exhaled. "Excuse me."

Constance watched the big man walk off in the direction of her mercenaries. She turned to look up at the spectacular church above them, taking in the intricate details of the small stone arches carved atop the walls, just beneath its terracotta roof tiles. A stiff breeze swept across the open town square, adding a bitter chill to the air.

"Why do you shave your head?" Jaque suddenly demanded.

"Pardon?" Orion asked quizzically.

"Why do you shave your head?" the thin man repeated. "I thought only paladin's squires had to do that. All the other paladins here prance around sporting all sorts of fancy hair, and you go out of your way to look like a squire. Or to look intimidating, whichever. I was just wondering why you do it."

"Jaque!" Constance snapped uncomfortably. "Don't you think you're being a bit intrusive?"

"It is alright," Orion said impassively, "it is a reasonable question. I... suppose it is rather petulant, even self indulgent of me. All of my childhood there was always such pressure to succeed as a squire and to become a paladin. So many failed. My father expected, no, demanded that I succeed. But I was a terrible squire, and I should have failed a dozen times over."

The tall knight paused, as if unsure whether to open up about his past any further, but continued tentatively.

"But one day... something happened and it gave me the anger and drive to change who I was. And when I was knighted, I suppose I rather resented the implication that I was suddenly a better person and accepted in this elite group. So I continued to shave my head to show them all that I was the same person, and I did not care for their acceptance."

"Is it to look scary?" Jaque grinned his gap toothed grin. "Because we were all terrified of you when we first met you!"

"Jaque!" Constance snapped again.

Orion's face cracked into a broad grin.

"In my vocation, an intimidating appearance has its advantages," he admitted.

Jaque laughed, a well natured but silly sounding laugh. After a few moments, Orion joined him. Constance watched them both until they stopped, her mind racing as she considered the deeper implications of a pointless tradition that must have lasted for years.

"You should stop shaving your head," she suddenly found herself declaring. "You don't need to look intimidating, and you don't have any point to prove to anybody. Besides, it scares people away from trying to get to know you. And that's their loss, as well as yours."

Orion regarded Constance with serious eyes. His features softened.

"Thank you," he said sincerely, "that is a nice thing to say. Fine, I will stop."

The moment was ruined as Jaque let out a crass expletive. Constance glared admonishingly at him, but found his attention diverted to something over her shoulder. She turned and saw a tall, slender woman of staggering beauty striding confidently across the square. The blonde woman wore skin-tight armor of black leather, her arms left bare, save for a series of leather straps which crossed up to her elbows. In one hand she carried an exquisitely jeweled greatsword while in the other she carried a bow; a dwarven flintlock pistol dangled from her belt alongside a pair of throwing knives. The eyes of every man in the detachment followed the beautiful woman as she walked over to the horse next to Tancred and buckled the two weapons to the saddle before elegantly swinging herself up to a seated position.

"That is our guide," Orion explained wearily.

"Where did you find that?" Jaque exclaimed.

"Never mind that," Constance grimaced as she saw Hayden returning with her disappointed looking contingent of mercenaries, "our lot are back. Come on, looks like we're moving again."

*****

The unsettling marriage of ethereal beauty with rampant breaches of the laws of nature left Dionne simultaneously astounded and uneasy. He lay back on a hill of purple grass, looking up at a lime green sky as thin wisps of cloud rapidly shot over him, linking, forming, growing into elegant shapes, and then silently dying all in the space of a few seconds. The hill he lay on was at the center of a small island that floated steadily through the sky; many others of similar dimensions drifted gently around him, each with a picturesque waterfall that bubbled up out of the middle of the island to then meander down over gently sloping rocks, to then fall over the lip of each island and plunge down into the abyss of nothingness that lay somewhere in the darkness, miles below.

"You seem to prefer this scenery to the First Circle," Am'Bira remarked casually from where she sat to Dionne's side, still in her human form.

"I'm not sure how anybody could ever feel settled in that place," Dionne replied as he gazed up at the dancing clouds.

"That is why it is as it is," Am'Bira shrugged, her fingers idly playing with Dionne's hair. "It is the place where sinners are punished. It is but one Circle – there is much more to the Abyss than that."

Dionne exhaled slowly, consciously fighting to defeat the clawing discomfort in his gut. The warm wind blew gently over him, the soothing sounds of the waterfalls pleasantly accompanied the rustling of the long grass, yet he remained far from contented.

"How did you end up here?" he asked the dark-haired woman.

"You know that already," she replied. "I saw you looking at my belt buckle earlier."

"But how did you come to leave the Basilean sisterhood and... well... end

107

up here?"

The temptress let out a short laugh.

"I took the sixth step," she replied nonchalantly, "I was expelled from my order. Ironic, really. As a fighting order of nuns, we were charged with keeping Basilea safe from evil; and yet when I did so, I was charged with being... too extreme. The problem with Basilea is that it is all well and good preaching, but when it comes to making tough decisions, one needs tough people. People like you and I. People who realize that there are some in this world who do not need forgiveness and a chance to repent, they require punishing. They need to know the error of their ways and pay a price for their actions."

"So how did you end up in the Abyss?" Dionne looked up at her.

Am'Bira looked down and narrowed her red eyes quizzically.

"Why, I was drawn to it. Just as you have been. We belong here."

Dionne met her captivating gaze for a few moments before continuing.

"You said earlier that we've met before. When was that?"

Am'Bira smiled slyly.

"It was only the briefest of encounters," she smiled. "You may not have noticed me, but I certainly remember you."

Before she could continue, a small portal tore itself in the air in front of the hill. The tall, imposing form of Teynne stepped through to tower over the two. He folded his powerful arms and smiled a sharp-toothed grin. Am'Bira immediately sprang up to drop to one knee and bow her head.

"My lord."

Dionne stood up. Teynne looked at him expectantly for a moment before turning to the temptress.

"Go, Am'Bira, leave us for a while."

The dark haired woman obliged, leaving Dionne alone with the Abyssal Champion. The demon looked out across the green skies at the skyscape of floating islands.

"It would be more appropriate if you were to pay me the correct marks of respects from now on," he said sternly. "Particularly in the presence of others."

"I didn't ask to be brought here," Dionne countered assertively.

"My friend, my rank and status in this place is far higher than yours ever was in Basilea. Yet in your realm, I had the courtesy to submit to your authority and address you with respect as a subordinate. I'd have thought that after all we've been through and all I have offered to you, you could extend me the same simple courtesy."

Dionne sighed and nodded, feeling shame welling up from his proud outburst.

"My apologies, my lord," he muttered.

"Not here, not now," Teynne gave a dismissive gesture. "Just in front of others. How are you doing? Is Am'Bira looking after you?"

"Yes... yes," Dionne stammered uncomfortably.

The demon turned to regard him with a knowing smile.

"You needn't feel any guilt, my friend," he frowned, "she is a temptress. It is one of the things she is there for. But more importantly, I have spoken to my lords and masters about you. You are to return to Basilea."

"I'm no longer welcome here?" Dionne planted his fists on his hips.

"No, no, far from it," Teynne replied evenly. "A man of your ability and reputation is most welcome within our fold. But you are being hunted by the same men who killed your friends and comrades. It will send a powerful statement to the Hegemony when you defeat their force, and that is what you must do."

Dionne turned away to consider his situation. He certainly had no love of the Hegemony, but killing legion men and paladins was another thing entirely. He took a few deep breaths and looked across at the next purple island drifting through the warm sky. These were the men who had killed all those who remained loyal to him for years of exile and hiding. They had given him no chance to explain his actions. They were there to bring him in and execute him before their corrupt masters for the simple sin of trying to save women and children from the ravages of war. He owed them nothing. Dionne stopped to think of the faces of the men who had resolutely stood by his side for years of running, leaving all to fight alongside him. His mind listed their names as he thought of them lying dead in a forgotten field in the foothills of northern Basilea, massacred in a small battle that would already have been forgotten by all.

He fought to control his breathing. Even if he knew he was being used as a pawn to make a statement in the great strategic game between Basilea and the Abyss, he felt no turmoil. Only anger.

"I shall need an army if you wish me to defeat paladins and legion men," Dionne said as he turned back to face Teynne.

The tall demon smiled broadly.

"Dionne, my friend, you needn't worry about that."

*****

The wind had whipped up enough to audibly whistle across the jagged rocks that punctured up through the lush green vegetation covering the mountainside. A thin pathway cut through two gentle peaks of rock, meandering lazily northward toward the very boundaries of Basilea and the tallest mountains in the Tarkis range. With the approach of the fall, the mountains ahead already glistened white with snow at their very peaks, although the temperature of the lower ranges was moderate, at least without the wind chill to contend with. Off to the east was the ever-present sparkle of the Low Sea of Suan, its deep azure waters starkly contrasting the gentle blue of the sky above.

Settling lower in his saddle in a fruitless attempt to guard himself from the wind, Tancred turned his attention from the gentle sea on the eastern horizon to the line of soldiers struggling up the steep slope ahead. The ever changing gradient of the path over the last three days of travel had forced a frustrating change of pace and a tedious necessity to dismount almost on the hour, every hour, to guide the horses by the reins. He dreaded to think how the baggage train was faring behind him.

A mild commotion began amidst the ranks of men-at-arms up ahead as a lone soldier struggled to move against the flow, fighting his way back down the slopes, much to the frustration of his comrades. The young soldier looked up to make eye contact with Tancred and then changed direction, waving a hand above his head in an attempt to gain the paladin's attention. Tancred swung himself down from his saddle and moved to the head of the line of cavalry to meet him.

"My lord," the soldier exhaled breathlessly, "we have encountered a problem at the head of the column. The Dictator-Prefect requests your presence."

Tancred nodded, handing the reins of his warhorse to Jeneveve.

"Have our knights dismount and rest," he ordered. "I will be back as quickly as I can."

Tancred followed the soldier back up the slope, the crammed ranks of men-at-arms wordlessly parting to either side of the muddy track to allow him through. His thighs burning with the exertion of continuing up the ever-increasing slope, Tancred reached the top of the peak and let out a groan of despair as he saw the delay up ahead. The track stopped at a sheer drop, leaving a gaping chasm between the end of the track and where it started again at the next peak north; significantly higher, lying across a gap of perhaps a hundred feet. At each side of the gaping yawn, attached to the ground at the edges of the pathway, were the broken remnants of the wood and rope bridge that once crossed the gap.

Suppressing a string of curses, Tancred made his way over to the edge of the chasm where Hugh and his aides waited with Georgis and Aestelle.

"What are our options?" Tancred asked as he approached.

"We can't throw a line across, not from this distance and uphill so far," Hugh grimaced as he looked up at the edge of the shattered bridge on the far peak, "and we will lose too much time in building an entire new bridge."

"We could find another way north," Georgis offered, his face reddened from the exertion of the march. "This can't be the only way through the peaks."

"You'll lose two days heading east to the coast, even more to the west," Aestelle shrugged nonchalantly, her blonde hair whipped out to one side by the wind. "This bridge has been just fine for the last five years. Somebody doesn't want you following them."

"Yes, I can see that!" Hugh snapped, turning his back on her and the sight of the impassable obstacle.

Platus immediately flashed what Tancred assumed was supposed to be a dashing and apologetic smile to the tall woman. She returned the gesture with a brief frown of contempt before suppressing a yawn. Tancred shook his head. He found Platus' sycophancy disappointing, but not surprising. Many, if not most, men would be influenced in their actions by a woman of such incomparable beauty, but not Tancred. Rather than be seduced by something as base as aesthetic appeal, Tancred was confident that his parents would be able to arrange a suitable marriage for him based on wealth and social status, when the time was right.

"You've got one other option," Aestelle continued. "There's a cave entrance only a stone throw from here. Very cramped, very unstable, but it leads up to the path on the other side of this chasm. It will take a little over an hour to get there."

"We can't move an entire force, with horses and wagons, through a cramped cave!" Hugh seethed. "Especially if the damn thing might collapse on us!"

"It is a good thing that was not my suggestion, then!" Aestelle snapped irritably with a fire that clearly surprised the Dictator-Prefect. "But if you get a man with a good throwing arm up on the other side of this chasm, he could get a couple of lines down to you. Then you could repair that bridge."

Hugh glared at Aestelle and then turned to face his aides.

"Trennio, thoughts?"

"We're weighing up the risk of losing a few hours and one man, versus losing days. I can't see a better option, my lord."

"Platus?"

"Likewise," the tall man nodded slowly.

"I shall go," Tancred took a step forward. "I can find my way to the other side."

"No," Hugh held up a gloved hand, "if those caves collapse, I lose one of my best men and your paladins lose their leader. You're not going. However, your bull of a man who insists on beating up my soldiers. How about him? He's got a good throwing arm, I'm sure."

Tancred felt his temper rising as his eyes shifted from face to face among the four men stood in front of him, all of whom smirked while they waited for his reaction. The fractious nature of their group had so far been nothing more than a severe irritation; now there was talk of endangering the life of one of his men with calculated deliberation.

"He is my right hand man," Tancred argued. "He is not the best choice."

"A moment ago you were willing to go yourself," Georgis countered.

"And the folly of my offer was immediately pointed out to me! The same logic applies to the safety of my second!"

The legion captain opened his mouth to speak again but was silenced as Aestelle walked to stand between them.

"I'll look after your man," the blonde woman said coolly, her face serious as if discussing a business transaction. "As long as he does exactly what I tell him to, we shall be fine. I'll go with him."

Faced with the victorious smiles of Hugh and his lackeys, Tancred could only turn on his heel and stomp back to the peak to the south, down to where the knights and men-at-arms rested on the grassy slopes in the early afternoon sun. He quickly found Orion, alone on a small plateau to the east of the path, reading his Eloicon. The huge man had trimmed his beard neatly back which, combined with

111

the few days hair growth atop his head, had completely altered his appearance. His features softened considerably, he now looked a decade younger and far closer to the handsome and heroic image often associated with paladins. He turned to face Tancred as he approached, putting his book carefully back by his side and offering a warm smile.

"There's a problem up ahead, Orion," Tancred winced.

"How can I help?" the big man asked.

"The bridge is down. We need somebody to get over to the other side to throw lines down so we can repair it and keep moving. There is a tunnel leading over to the other side."

"Alright," Orion nodded.

"We cannot all take it, as it is too cramped. And unstable. Dangerously unstable," Tancred explained quietly.

"Ah."

"The Dictator-Prefect asked for you personally. Said you would be the best man for the task."

"I'll bet he did," Orion laughed quietly to himself, looking down at his feet momentarily. "Alright then. Best go get this done."

Ten

The cave leading to the higher peak was less of a tunnel and more of a sheer drop, at least to start with. Orion peered warily over the lip of the cave entrance into the dimness below, estimating how far down it was as he did so. The cave mouth itself was surrounded by a handful of skeletal, wind-bent trees and moss-covered rocks. Tancred stood by Orion with a lit torch while Aestelle carefully coiled the ropes they would need to take through the caves. Hugh and his aides looked on from the top of the hill, a few dozen yards away.

"If we have not heard anything from you after an hour, I shall come down and find you myself," Tancred said. "I will bring a couple of our best with me, just in case you are in any trouble."

"I am sure it will be simple enough," Orion said as he heaved the heavy rope up over his head and shoulder to sit diagonally across his chest. "Our guide believes we should not have any difficulty in negotiating a path through."

"Be careful, nonetheless," Tancred urged as he looked down into the darkness below. "I will ensure no stupid decisions are made in your absence. Like moving on without you."

"Yes," Orion nodded, appreciative of the sentiment but now worried about an eventuality he had not yet considered, "that would be good."

Aestelle walked over to the two paladins, the various weapons on her back and around her waist chinking with each step.

"All ready?" she asked.

Orion nodded.

"Right," she gave a slight smile, "after you, then."

Tancred tossed the torch down into the darkness. Its flames danced off the cave walls as it fell, coming to an abrupt halt on a platform after only a short drop. Orion sat on the edge of the cave mouth, turned, and lowered himself down before letting go of the lip. The first second of plummeting through darkness was expected, but after only the briefest of moments, he felt fear surging through him as the fall lasted longer than he had anticipated. Then the world came to a stop with a jar, and he suppressed a yell as pain flared up through his left ankle. Struggling up onto one knee, he pressed a hand against the injured area and quickly healed the affliction with his meager grasp of divinity magic.

A light thud echoed from the cave walls, and Orion turned to see where Aestelle had landed effortlessly next to him. She picked up the torch and turned to face toward the higher peaks, looking up at where a small gap in the rocks led to another cave.

"This way," she commanded, tossing the torch through the gap and then planting one foot on a natural ledge in the rock face to vault up and through to the next cave.

Orion followed her example, dragging himself up to the opening easily enough, but then finding it considerably harder work to squeeze his armored bulk through the same gap. Finally arriving in the next cave, he looked around at the almost unearthly sight of stalagmites and stalactites stretching up from the cave floor and down from the rocks above, pushing up through a milky colored lake of perfectly still water.

"Watch your footing, Ogre," Aestelle warned. "Step where I step. Put a foot wrong, and we're both in trouble."

Orion followed the tall woman tentatively through the cave, working slowly toward the far side where a gentle slope of jagged rocks led back uphill toward their destination. He watched in interest as the blonde woman alternated between small steps and long strides, trying in vain to work out any discernible pattern to her progress.

Without any warning, the rocks below Orion gave way. He felt the ground crumble and fall, leaving him tumbling down into the blackness, bouncing painfully from hidden obstacles as all light was snubbed out of his world. It all stopped almost as quickly as it started, leaving him in silence and darkness. His head throbbed with pain and his hands felt numbly around in the murkiness as he realized he had no idea how much time had passed since he fell; whether it was a brief few seconds or even hours. His face felt cold as it pressed against the rocks, and as his thoughts began to clear, a rising panic forced its way into his mind as the thought of being buried alive leapt to the fore. A dull but welcome yellow flare of light appeared in the corner of his vision.

"Down below! Are you there?" A familiar voice called out from what sounded like a long way away.

"H…here…" he managed weakly as he struggled up to his hands and knees, the sound of rock falling on rock echoing around him as a great weight lifted from his back. The stale air felt thick and close.

"Can you hear me?" He heard Tancred's voice call distantly again.

"We're down here," Aestelle replied from somewhere close by, "we're fine."

The yellow light became something more discernible, transforming into neat squares of dark red. Orion felt a firm hand on one shoulder.

"Hold still," Aestelle said, "you've taken a knock to the head. Let me have a look."

Orion's vision sharpened back into focus and he saw his own hands planted on the ground ahead of him. The red squares were tiles on the floor, cracked and ancient with weeds growing up between them. He stifled a grunt of pain as he felt a bandage being wrapped around his head.

"Stay there," Tancred's voice echoed down again, "I'll get help."

"We're fine," Aestelle called up, "we can still make it through. Wait by the bridge. We're carrying on." |

"I am sorry," Orion managed as the bandage was tied around his head, "I did not mean to…"

"Not your fault," Aestelle cut him off coolly, "don't worry about it."

Another wave of small rocks fell from Orion as he slowly stood, one hand pressed to the wound on the side of his head as he looked around. Pyramids of stones, waist high, were scattered across the chamber around him where they had plunged through the ceiling. Aestelle's torch cast a circle of flickering, yellow light around them, illuminating a semi-sphere in the darkness for only a few paces. All that Orion could see was the detail on the carefully constructed tiles on the floor beneath him. Wherever they were, it was a place that had not been disturbed for many years.

A single knock echoed in the darkness and two tongues of orange fire leapt up from torches secured to the walls to either side of Orion and Aestelle. A second knock sounded and another pair of torches burst into flame, followed by another and another every second until a line of a dozen torches along the walls to either side of them illuminated the chamber. An ancient set of tall, double doors barred their way at the far end of the chamber. Lining the walls, between the torches, tall alcoves were cut into the rock. In each alcove stood the figure of an armored, long dead warrior. Their skeletal remains stood obediently to attention, their rusty coats of mail covering their bony torsos while their hands clung to circular shields and pitted, notched longswords.

Aestelle drew the huge greatsword from her back.

"They're going to move," she warned.

Orion opened his mouth to chastise her for letting her imagination run away.

Before he could speak, small orbs of red glowed to life in the eye sockets of each of the twelve skeletal guards, and the undead soldiers stepped casually down from their alcoves. Much to Orion's surprise, they began to walk right toward them.

Aestelle dashed out to meet the first skeleton, bashing its shield to one side with a heavy swing of her sword before hacking the undead warrior down with three vicious strikes to the torso. Galvanized into action, Orion drew his own heavy greatsword and stepped out to meet the skeletons advancing from their right, swinging his blade in a great arc around him to decapitate the first warrior before advancing to cut a second adversary in half at the waist.

Sensing a strike coming in from his left, Orion pivoted on the spot and deflected a series of well-placed attacks by another of the skeletal horde before jumping back to dodge a swing at his head from a second undead warrior advancing from his right. The skeleton lurched forward under the weight of its own blade, giving Orion a fraction of a second to capitalize on the opening; he brought a fist around to smash into the skeleton's face with a crunching of bone, sending it sprawling to the ground. Orion brought an armored boot stamping down on the undead soldier's head, crushing the skull underfoot.

Deflecting another well-aimed blow from the undead swordsman to his left, Orion saw the skull skittering across the floor from the warrior he had beheaded. It joined up with the prone form of the rest of its body, and the reanimated corpse staggered back up to its feet to rejoin the fight.

"Get that door open!" Aestelle shouted from his side as she ducked beneath an attack aimed at her head before kicking an undead warrior back against one of the dusty walls. "We can't hold them off forever!"

"You go!" Orion answered. "I will keep them back!"

With an angry yell, Aestelle slid beneath the attacks of one of the five skeletons that surrounded her, batted aside a strike by a second, and then shoulder barged her way through a third and fourth undead warrior to sprint for the door at the far end of the chamber.

Bringing his own blade slicing down from above his head, Orion cleaved another of the skeletons in two from crown to groin and then dashed through the opening he had created, turning his back on Aestelle and the door to face the remaining skeletons. He felt a strike clang off his breastplate from a skeletal swordsman who had come around to the right; he turned to face his attacker just in time to see an arrow whistle through the air and smash straight through the skeleton's nasal cavities, lodging itself firmly in the undead creature's face. The skeleton staggered in confusion for a few moments before crumpling to the ground. Orion looked over his shoulder and saw Aestelle stood by the open door, notching another arrow to her bow.

"Hurry up, for the Ones' sake!" she shouted from the far end of the chamber.

Orion turned to run and immediately felt a strike on his back, again impacting harmlessly off his breastplate. Accelerating to a sprint, he winced as Aestelle loosed an arrow that shot straight past his face and over his shoulder, resulting in the clattering of bones behind him. Orion kept the pace for the remainder of the chamber, hurtling through the open doorway and into the darkness beyond. The doors closed with a heavy, echoing thud behind him, and he turned to see Aestelle positioning a heavy wooden beam across the doors to lock them in place.

The tall woman picked up the blazing torch from where she had discarded it near her feet and turned to look at Orion, fixing him with a narrow-eyed stare of disapproval and accompanying smirk that he somehow found simultaneously patronizing and charming.

"We're in a burial chamber," she explained as she paced past him, holding up the torch to examine the room they had entered as the dull, distant echo of hammering sounded from the far side of the thick doors. "I am going to assume that you have not found yourself in a location such as this before."

"Well, I have been to a few funerals," Orion offered, straight-faced.

Aestelle suppressed a smile and raised her brow.

"Funny," she continued, taking a few tentative paces around the narrow tunnel they had entered, "but the dead don't walk at funerals, Ogre. You're heavy cavalry, you dominate the battlefield, I understand that well enough. But this isn't the battlefield; you're in my world now, and this is how I make a living. This mountain range is littered with places like this, most of them from The Time of Ice. They tend to follow a certain pattern."

Orion looked along the tunnel ahead, his eyes slowly adjusting to the darkness but still failing to see any ending to the passageway. The same red tiles continued underfoot but far less effort had been put into the bland tunnel walls.

"I do have a name," Orion offered to Aestelle.

"You are 'Ogre'. I don't need to know your name. Consider yourself honored that I have given you a nickname. In my experience, which is extensive, your skills are even a touch above mediocrity. Now be a good fellow and do exactly what I say from here on in."

Orion let out a sigh of exasperation and turned again to make his way down the tunnel. He had taken only a single step when Aestelle grabbed him by the back of his breastplate's neck seam with surprising strength, jolting him into motionlessness.

"I said, 'do exactly what I say'," Aestelle hissed through gritted teeth, drawing her blade and pointing the tip of the weapon down near Orion's feet. Through the darkness, he made out a thin line suspended at ankle height lying just over his toes.

"Trip wire," Aestelle said, before planting a fingertip on his chin and guiding his head to look down at a tiny, rusted metal box at the foot of the wall and then up at a slit built into the brickwork at head height. "Trigger mechanism, decapitating blade."

Orion shivered involuntarily as he realized how close to death he had just found himself. He stared, fixated on the slit in the wall and the blade that lay hidden within.

"Now, I appreciate that you're far too proud to say you want me to save you," Aestelle leaned in and smiled dangerously, "but nonetheless, I'm here for you, to stop you killing yourself. I'll go first, shall I?"

The tall woman walked along the tunnel with a cocky swagger, pointing casually at various pressure plates, trip wires, and other booby traps at irregular intervals as they proceeded. The chill Orion felt failed to dissipate as he realized just how out of his depth he was. As a soldier, he had always scoffed at the term 'adventurer' as a description of selfish, glory seeking idiots who wasted their time wandering around abandoned mines. Now, just a few minutes in Aestelle's company was quickly demonstrating the expertise required to survive in this environment.

"We arrived in the outer chamber," Aestelle explained as they approached the end of the corridor, "that is traditionally where the deceased would place their outer guard; normally loyal soldiers who died in battle alongside their master, or sometimes even men who were willing to die by their own hand just to be buried as guards. This, where we are now, is the chamber of procession, where the body was ceremonially carried by clergy to be laid in their final resting place. That's up ahead somewhere."

"So if we're going deeper into this crypt," Orion queried, "should we not turn around and try to find our way back out?"

"These things rarely have a single entrance," Aestelle replied as they reached another large, double door at the end of the tunnel. "This should be the burial chamber itself. There may be another tunnel leading in from the far side."

Aestelle heaved the heavy wooden bar off the doorway, and the double doors swung noisily open on their creaky, rusted hinges. Orion followed Aestelle into the next chamber. The ubiquitous red tiles continued underfoot into a large, circular room. A huge, uneven pile lay in the center of the room, only a few paces ahead. Orion looked around for evidence of a sarcophagus or anything similar but found nothing. He turned to look at Aestelle and found her cocky smirk replaced with a look of concern, bordering on fear.

"What is wrong?"

"This is not a burial chamber," she replied in a hoarse whisper, "this was no ordinary nobleman."

"What does that mean?"

"Two things," Aestelle whispered, taking a careful step forward. "First, there is somebody important buried here."

Orion cast his eyes around the darkened chamber but found nothing of note in the flickering shadows that were semi-illuminated by Aestelle's torch. No other exit was obvious; all that was visible was the shadowy pile a few paces away.

"And the second?"

"This person was important enough to have an inner guard chamber," Aestelle replied nervously, "and that's where we are right now. I think there's something in here with us."

The pile moved. With an earsplitting, raspy roar, the pile shot up toward the ceiling, growing in size at a spectacular rate. It turned in place, and Orion let out a gasp as he realized that it was in fact a being, roughly humanoid in shape but twice the height and width. The huge creature spread out its thick arms and leaned forward, the torchlight capturing its grotesque form. Great rends in its gray skin showed rotting flesh and bone beneath, entrails were visible through tears in its abdomen, and two void black holes sunk into a hideous face where its eyes had once been. A rusted, bronze nose ring emerged from the creature's nostrils and a tatty loincloth fell from beneath its swollen, corpulent belly.

The huge, zombified creature took a pace forward and leaned over to shove its head within an inch of Aestelle's face. It opened its mouth and let out a deafening roar that echoed and reverberated through the dark cavern. Aestelle grabbed the creature by its nose ring, yanked its face closer and brought her own forehead crashing down to connect audibly with the monster's head. The huge creature let out a cry and reeled back; Aestelle whipped her pistol up from her side and shot the beast in the neck.

With a chocking gasp, the zombie monster reeled back and dropped to one knee. Aestelle twirled the smoking pistol around on one finger and looked across at Orion, flashing him a cocky smile and a wink. The undead monster sprang back to its feet and lashed out with an immense, clenched fist, smacking into Aestelle and sending her tumbling through the air like a discarded child's toy. She landed untidily on a pile of rocks at the far end of the chamber and lay still. Orion brought his greatsword up and ran forward to attack.

*****

Her breathing labored, Aestelle struggled to force herself up onto one elbow. She saw spatters of crimson blood sprinkle across the tiles below her from her open mouth as she forced herself up onto one knee, one arm instinctively wrapped around her ribs as her breath wheezed in and out of her damaged respiratory system. She looked up at where the paladin was locked in combat with the zombie troll, the big man now dwarfed by the undead monstrosity who flailed powerful limbs around in an attempt to swat at the knight.

"Alright, you bastard," Aestelle laughed, "you want to play rough..."

Struggling up to her feet, she immediately let out a cry of pain as she felt her broken ribs cave in and restrict her lung. Collapsing back down again, she spat out another mouthful of blood and swore viciously as she realized with disappointment that it was time to use the very limited control she had over magic. Placing a hand against the damaged area, she concentrated hard and summoned the energies of divinity magic that, even with her long dwindled faith in the Shining Ones, still always somehow obeyed her call. Her ribs clicked back into place and fused, allowing her breathing to return to normal.

Springing back to her feet, Aestelle discarded her bow and quiver and recovered her greatsword. Up ahead, the paladin was holding his own against the undead monstrosity – if anything, he even had the upper hand. She had never seen anyone able to force such an opponent back single-handed. She paused for a fraction of a second to watch him, something about him reminding her of a distant memory that somehow did not wish to be recalled. It did not matter.

With a yell, Aestelle sprinted forward to join the fight.

*****

Orion ducked quickly under another unstoppable blow from the rotten fists of the macabre monster he faced, darting to one side to try to create an opening to attack. The monster's fist slammed into the wall a few inches from where he had stood, plunging through the crumbling stonework and causing a small landslide of earth and broken stones to flow down across the flooring. With a roar, the monster yanked its fist clear again and turned to face Orion, tirelessly returning to the offensive and swinging its deadly hands back in his direction.

Taking a step back, Orion allowed the lumbering monster to overextend and lean too far into its attacks. Losing its footing, the monster stumbled forward, and Orion had his opening. Hacking down in between the creature's flailing limbs, he tore open a vicious wound in the monster's gut that spilled its rotten entrails across the dusty floor. Orion followed up with a lancing attack to the monstrosity's chest, puncturing his greatsword through the creature's ribcage and twisting the blade to create a larger wound before retracting it. He continued the offensive with a series of cuts and thrusts aimed at the head and torso, forcing the monster to fall back toward the far end of the cavern.

Out of nowhere, a hammer blow caught his shoulder and span him around, dropping him helplessly to one knee in full sight of the undead creature. He felt a light blow behind him as Aestelle appeared from the shadows, leaping up to plant a foot on his back and propel herself up into the air to meet the monster. Her blade whipped up and severed one of the creature's arms; she landed to one side and immediately hacked out to drag her blade viciously against the back of the creature's knee, severing tendons and ligaments and leaving the limb useless. The creature collapsed on its wounded leg and held up its severed stump of an arm, howling in pain and rage.

Seizing the opportunity, Orion leapt back into the attack and swung his heavy blade around to tear the sharp tip through the creature's throat, hacking open a gaping wound. Bringing the blade up again and again, he repeated the attack to hack at the widening wound, ripping open the tear until the head detached completely and the monster finally fell down at his feet.

Wiping sweat from his eyes, he walked over to where Aestelle was recovering her pistol and bow.

"How are you... alright?" he managed. "I saw that thing nearly kill you with one punch!"

"That?" the blonde woman scoffed. "Barely felt it. I once went head to head with Skullface for nearly half an hour. In comparison, this was nothing."

Orion narrowed his eyes in disbelief at the young woman's claim of survival at the hands of Mantica's most notorious orc warlord, but he quickly dismissed the thought.

"What was that?" he asked, pointing his sword at the defeated monster.

"A zombified troll, a very large one, too. That thing was the inner guard of whoever is buried here. Spells and incantations keep creatures like this frozen for hundreds of years until idiots like you come blundering in here and trigger the spell that wakes them up. The magic is never perfect, that's why the troll was rotting."

"It still begs the question," Orion said as he glanced cautiously around the cavern, "who is all of this for the benefit of?"

"Oh, the fellow who is buried here?" Aestelle flashed a dashing smile. "Fear not, Ogre, we'll meet him soon enough. The fact that those skeletons were reforming suggests you've woken their master up, too. Skeletons rarely do that by themselves. Somebody is watching us."

"A necromancer, then? That is who we have stirred?"

"No, that is whom you have stirred," Aestelle tossed her beaded blonde hair over one shoulder. "But that shouldn't concern you. You paladins have all got your little book of faith to keep the dark denizens at bay."

With her reference to the Eloicon, Aestelle moved to dismissively backhand the sacred book that was chained to Orion's waist. He swiftly reached out to grab her wrist and drag it up away from the holy text. His anger flaring up instantly, he fixed his eyes on hers.

"Do not ever disrespect the word of the Shining Ones or their prophets again!" he snarled. "Not in my presence! Disrespect their word, and lady or not, I will put you down!"

Aestelle stood her ground and showed no obvious fear but met his stare with a neutral expression. It was the first time he had seen her without her arrogant exterior. He released her wrist and turned away.

"You're right," she said softly, "I overstepped the line. It's your faith and I have to respect that. I'm sorry."

Inhaling deeply, Orion took a few paces, but then remembered the traps in the previous tunnel and remained still. He lifted his Eloicon up and unlatched the book, opening it on a random page to search for clarity and inspiration. He saw a few notes written in the margin, questions for a priest that would never be answered. It was his uncle's writing.

"Stay here," Aestelle said, "give me a few minutes to look around. I'll find a way out."

Orion nodded. He dropped to one knee and closed the tome, placing a palm over the case and silently reciting a few prayers from the Book of Salvation. His anger subsided as the minutes passed. Orion had taken the book from Jahus' side the day he had died, and his uncle's Eloicon was what drove him to excel, to be the best warrior he could be. To never let anybody down again. Lost in his own thoughts, he fought to display mastery over his own mind by dispelling the memories of his uncle's loss and replacing them with focus on the words of his prayers. He failed.

"Got it, I think," Aestelle's voice propelled him back to the present.

Orion looked over to see Aestelle running a finger along the edges of a rock that looked the same as any of the others that surrounded it on the chamber wall. She spent another few moments examining the nondescript stone before pushing one edge of it. The rock clicked into place in the wall, and a few paces down, an entire section of the wall rotated in place to reveal another passageway. Aestelle looked across to Orion and grinned broadly. Orion walked to catch her up as she peered tentatively into the newly revealed tunnel.

The passageway itself was short and covered in cobwebs. At one end, a spiral staircase had been carved into the corridor leading up toward the surface. At the other end, a similarly fashioned stairway led further down.

"Perfect," Aestelle said, nodding at the second staircase, "that'll lead to the main burial chamber, I'd wager."

Orion looked across at her incredulously.

"That does not matter now," he said sternly, "there is a way leading back to the surface. There are people waiting for us. Depending on us."

"The burial chamber is where the riches are!" Aestelle snapped. "We have not fought off skeletons, traps, and trolls to walk away now! Do you have any idea how much we are likely to find down there?"

"You were paid to do a job!" Orion thundered, his temper flaring up again. "There is an entire army stranded up there, waiting for us to do our part! We carry on with the plan!"

"Just think for a second, you fool!" Aestelle met his anger with equal ferocity. "We've done most of the job already! How often do you think an opportunity like this just falls into one's lap? I know these mountains, and I know burial chambers like these! There is one chamber left at the foot of those stairs – one! If we go in there and return whatever aberration is waiting for us to the grave, we'll both walk away rich! I'll split it with you straight down the middle, and that is generous considering how the workload has been split between us!"

"I do not want your treasure!" Orion snarled. "You have clearly misjudged me!"

"Don't be so high and mighty!" Aestelle leaned in closer to point a finger in accusation at him. "Take your half of the money and do something good with it if you must! Go and pay for better beds in an orphanage or whatever paladins do, I don't care! But we will finish the damn job! Unless you are content to leave some undead shit free to roam?"

"The job is to get back to the surface and fix the bridge so the force can bring in that bastard we are hunting down!" Orion growled. "That is the job! There is not a shred of proof that we have woken up anything, so do not try to use my morals against me just so that you can rob a tomb! I am going to carry out our task, with or without you!"

Orion barged his way past the tall woman and began to ascend the spiral staircase.

"Wait! If you blunder your way up there without my help, you're dead! Do you understand? You will die without me!"

Orion stopped and looked back down the stairs at Aestelle.

"My comrades are relying on me to help them. Basilea is relying on us all to bring in a dangerous and evil man. They are my principles, and I am willing to die for them. Your principles are just money. There is nothing more to you than that. You go and die for your principles and allow me to die for mine."

Orion continued to climb the staircase, leaving an ominous silence behind him for a few moments. Then he heard Aestelle growl a string of words he never thought he would hear uttered from a woman.

"Fine!" she snapped at last as she nimbly ascended the staircase behind him. "I'll look after you! Again! You pig-headed, narrow-minded, clumsy f..."

*****

The wind had picked up considerably over the course of the last hour. The majority of the soldiers had moved to take cover on the leeward side of the slope, huddled in against the rock face as the chilling wind whipped around and brought biting waves of drizzle with it. The moisture in the air settled into a thin mist, obscuring the horizons in all directions.

Tancred stood alone by the fallen bridge, shielding his streaming eyes to look up at the peak on the far side of the chasm. Still nothing. He paced up and down along the chasm lip, looking down at the half of the bridge that had been recovered by a handful of the men-at-arms. All useless without a line to attach it to.

"Your man has been two hours now," Hugh said as he walked across, his rich cloak flying out to one side in the wind. "We cannot afford to wait!"

"What is the alternative?" Tancred retorted, throwing his hands to either side. "We either repair this bridge or admit defeat! If we head back to the coast, then the trail is lost, and Dionne is so far ahead we might as well start from scratch!"

"I'd rather that than sit on a mountainside overnight, watching the weather close in when we have inadequate shelter!" the Dictator-Prefect countered. "We need to get off this peak and find some decent natural shelter to set up camp for the night!"

"Then go!" Tancred exclaimed. "But I shall wait here for my soldier!"

Hugh shook his head in despair and turned to leave.

"Such a waste," he muttered.

"He will come through yet."

"I didn't mean your thug," Hugh replied. "I couldn't care less if he's been crushed under a rock fall. I meant the girl."

Tancred repressed an angry retort, turning away, and rested a hand on his Eloicon for comfort as the Dictator-Prefect walked back down the slope.

A thick, snaking rope flew through the gray sky to land on the lip of the chasm before falling to disappear into the darkness below. Tancred's eyes widened.

"Over here!" he yelled back down the slope. "They've made it! They're up there!"

Hugh immediately set about barking orders to his men. Ten men-at-arms were sprinting up the slope within seconds as Tancred looked up through the chill wind to see two hazy figures standing on the far side of the chasm. The taller of the two hauled the rope back in for a second attempt at bridging the gap between them.

"Here!" Tancred yelled. "Over here!"

Whether there was a reply or not, Tancred could not tell over the whistling of the wind through the chasm. He waited for a second attempt at a throw and saw Orion spin the end of the rope around before letting it fly through the air again.

123

This time, Tancred was ready and caught the rope before it could disappear back into the chasm. He quickly set about tying it to one of the posts driven into the earth by the start of the bridge. Within moments, the second line was successfully across, and Hugh's men carefully set about securing the first half of the bridge to its new lines. In less than an hour, the bridge was fully repaired, and Tancred followed Hugh and his aides across to the other side.

Tancred made his way quickly over to Orion who stood soaked in the drizzle, his armor dulled by the damp, with blood leaking from a bandage wrapped around his head. Tancred shot him a smile and tapped him on the shoulder before placing his hand on the head injury and healing the wound.

"Good job," he grinned. "Glad you have made it through in one piece."

"Sorry we are late," Orion winced, "it turned out to be a little more problematic than first anticipated. I shall tell all after I have cleaned myself up a little."

"Not to worry. We are back on track now."

Tancred watched as small groups of men-at-arms carefully made their way across the bridge, careful to keep the weight of each group to a reasonable minimum. Constance's mercenaries were next across, with the paladins and their warhorses waiting behind before the baggage train and squires. Tancred saw the mesmerizing figure of Aestelle walk over to him, her blonde hair pasted to her face and her wet leathers glistening in the drizzle. She stopped by Tancred and glowered down at him.

"That's the last time I'm working with your pet ogre," she snapped. "Tell your Dictator that I shall be scouting ahead again."

Tancred watched the young woman turn on her heel and stride off upslope again before looking across at Orion.

"You certainly have a way with the beautiful women," he remarked casually.

"Do not even jest," Orion grumbled. "I am off to ensure my idiot of a squire has not cooked my horse yet."

Eleven

Sat on a smooth rock on a rare sunny morning, Constance regarded the apple she had received from the quartermaster with disinterest. It was the fourth day of chasing Dionne across the Tarkis Mountains, and the fourth day of long uphill marches and nothing to pass the time other than watch the ever changeable mountain weather. Their path had moved further to the east, tantalizingly close to the gentler terrain and climate of the coastline; close enough for Constance to wonder why they did not divert to the coastal road to increase the pace of their path northward. Thankful for small mercies, Constance was at least appreciative of the gentler gradient to the mountain path and the occasional breathtaking glimpse of the Low Sea of Suan to the east, when the mountains saw fit to allow such a glimpse in between their majestic peaks. The detachment had stopped, again, and now sat or lay in small groups to either side of the mountain path as they awaited news of the latest delay from up ahead.

"Uh oh," Jaque remarked from where he lay sprawled in the long grass next to her, a trio of colorful butterflies dancing in the air above him. "It looks like your opinions are required again, Constance."

Constance looked over her shoulder from her place in the small semi-circle of mercenaries and saw Tancred picking his way through the groups of soldiers toward her. His armor was still shining and resplendent, despite days on the road, and his surcoat still held its bold blue; a testament to the effort of his squires rather than his own hard work. Constance furrowed her brow as the Lord Paladin approached; it was normally one of Hugh's aides sent to bring her in for the periodic and highly unnecessary command chats. Tancred's presence was possibly indicative of an actual problem, for once.

"Come on," she urged her mercenaries as she stood up, "on your feet. Let's show the proper marks of respect, we're not letting our standards slip."

Her ten mercenaries immediately followed her lead, more out of respect for her than the paladin, she figured. Tancred nodded a silent acknowledgement of their respect to his status and walked directly to address Constance.

"There is an issue up ahead," he said seriously, "the Dictator-Prefect has requested your input."

"Requested?" Constance scoffed. "Well, given how polite the invitation is,

I'd hate to seem rude by disappointing him."

The assembled mercenaries unsuccessfully stifled sniggers at the comment, causing Constance to smile at the infectious mirth. Tancred's face twisted into a scowl.

"Stand up straight," he snapped formally.

Her old military training kicking in instinctively, Constance obliged.

"You have made your feelings toward the Dictator-Prefect well known throughout this entire force," the redheaded paladin said sternly, "and, for that matter, your history with him. Whether you believe that is a mature and professional approach is down to you, but both you and I are working under his command, and I will not stand idly by and watch you disrespect a leader appointed directly by the Duma. Consider this a final warning before I take action against you. Is that clear?"

Constance looked across into the serious eyes of the young paladin. She bore no animosity to him and was surprised to find deep feelings of disappointment welling up over the fact that she had incurred his disapproval.

"Perfectly clear, my lord," she replied with a curt bow of the head.

"The same applies to the rest of you," Tancred raised his voice a little as he turned to face the others.

A few despondent mumbles of acquiescence greeted the challenge. Constance exchanged a wince with Hayden and tossed her apple to the big man before jogging to catch up with the paladin. She followed Tancred along the pathway toward where it wound right to face eastward around another shallow peak.

"Are your soldiers fairing well?" Tancred asked, a moment after she had dismissed the idea of conversation.

"They are well, my lord," she replied, grateful of his clear attempt to move past their earlier disagreement. "Just eager to finish the task at hand."

The two trudged along the path, past the dismounted paladins and men-at-arms, until they finally arrived at the head of the column of soldiers. Hugh sat atop his horse, looking out to the east. His two aides stood by his side, along with Captain Georgis and Aestelle, the mercenary guide they had picked up a few days before.

Constance exhaled in frustration at the sight of the other woman. The sun seemed to follow the beautiful adventurer, lighting up her perfect face and blonde hair. Constance prided herself in being better than succumbing to jealousy over something as trivial as good looks, but she had spent a decade of her life struggling to succeed in a man's military by virtue of skill and hard work alone. Women fighting in the Hegemony's army was still new, and she felt privileged to be one of the very first; but it would take years, decades, even centuries for culture to change, and she still found daily hurdles to overcome based on her treatment by men who refused to acknowledge her ability based solely on her gender. She took pride in facing these challenges with grace and integrity.

But Constance was willing to bet all she had that Aestelle did not face these same challenges. Constance's eyes narrowed in contempt as she regarded the young woman basking in the sunlight, her flawless features accentuated by makeup even when scouting a mountain, and her perfect figure arrogantly displayed by her impractical and needlessly form fitting leathers. Second only to this was the woman's accent, which spoke of a rich education and a noble upbringing. Constance shook her head and tutted. No doubt a spoiled rich girl lashing out at her parents by dipping into the world of soldiering before returning to a castle and an estate when she grew bored of it.

"Your thoughts?"

"Hmm?" Constance looked across to the voice addressing her.

The assembled men were all staring at her expectantly. Hugh pointed at a thick pillar of smoke rising from the coastline down to the east.

"That," he snapped, "I want to know your thoughts about that."

Constance focused her eyes on the eastern horizon. The column of smoke wafting up into the air was broad, far too thick to be anything minor. She surveyed the surrounding landscape. There were no forests, nothing obviously combustible. The smoke originated from the coast itself, which led to only one conclusion.

"It's a fishing village, isn't it?" she said quietly. "It couldn't be anything else."

"Just as I said," Hugh gestured irritably with one hand.

"It changes nothing, my lord," Platus offered.

"It changes everything!" Hugh snapped. "There is an entire village burning down there! Villages do not just burn!"

"It could be the work of Dionne," Georgis offered.

"Nonsense!" Constance snapped. "We are here hunting the man down because he disobeyed his orders to save civilians, not because he burned them! I served under him; he is not capable of ordering something like this!"

"Irrespective of who or what has caused it, I believe we are duty bound to go to investigate and offer what help we can," Tancred said.

"We can't go getting distracted from our task by every sorrowful story we encounter on the way!" Platus exclaimed. "So what if it is a burning village? You want us to abandon our entire hunt just because some idiot hasn't been careful enough with his hearth?"

"This is more than a mere 'sorrowful story'!" Tancred retorted. "This is hundreds of the Hegemon's citizens in peril! So yes, that is more important than our core task!"

The assembled group fell silent for a few moments, each staring at the rising smoke on the eastern horizon.

"I could be down there before nightfall," Aestelle offered, "and back with you before sunrise. You can continue north without hindrance. These slopes are gentle enough for a horse, and I can ride through the night. I'll find out what has happened, and you can make a decision tomorrow morning."

"I'll go with her," Platus offered eagerly.

"Not now, man!" Hugh sighed irritably. "Tancred, I do respect your concerns and I do see why you worry, but the Duma has ordered us to track down a dangerous man, not scour the countryside looking for people who need help. We must continue north. Unless there is evidence that Dionne is behind this."

"He is not behind this," Constance interjected.

Hugh looked down from atop his horse and fixed her with a dangerous glare.

"I show you respect by inviting you here so that I may benefit from your extensive experience," he glowered at her, "so at least do me the courtesy of addressing me properly and allowing me to finish when I am speaking!"

Constance bit her lip and turned away. She took in a deep breath silently, fighting to clam her temper. It was incredulous to her that any of them could possibly believe Dionne was responsible for burning an entire village. He was loved by the people, he had spent years fighting the evil spewing forth from the Abyss and protecting these very lands.

"Go," Hugh nodded to Aestelle, "get down there and back to me as fast as you can. We will proceed north."

"You can take my best horse," Tancred offered. "Desiree is the finest..."

"I don't need your magic horse," Aestelle rolled her eyes as she turned to leave. "I will see you all at sunrise."

*****

Having spent several years in the area, Aestelle already had her suspicions that the pillar of smoke to the east originated from Peleura, a large and prosperous fishing village she had visited on several occasions. Within an hour of her journey, she could see enough ahead to sadly confirm this. The eastern edge of the mountain range quickly gave way to gentler foothills, and with the change of terrain, Aestelle picked up her pace considerably. Galloping her horse across gently undulating pastures and through sparse, scenic woods, the picturesque surroundings did nothing to ease the rising feeling of apprehension as she drew closer to the burning village with each hour.

By midafternoon, she encountered the first survivors fleeing from Peleura; a trio of grime covered peasants who limped along the small road leading from the village, just outside a neat orchard that basked in the midafternoon sun.

"I couldn't stop and fight them!" a ragged fisherman in his early thirties called out to Aestelle as she hailed him, holding onto a sobbing wife and young daughter. "I had to get my family out! You understand, don't you? I had to look after my family!"

"What happened?" Aestelle demanded.

"Demons! They just appeared! They came down from the mountains! They killed everyone! They were just... tearing people apart!"

Aestelle's eyes widened in surprise. Bandits she expected, even an orc raiding party. But Abyssals? This far from the great scar of the Abyss?

"Keep moving," Aestelle urged the family, "don't stop for anything."

Spurring her horse back into a gallop, she continued eastward toward the coast. A few similar encounters with small groups of disheveled fishermen and their families confirmed the claims made by the first she had met. By late afternoon, she approached the boundaries of the village, the smell of burning now pungent in her nostrils. Her horse whined and reared up, twisting and shaking as she drew closer. The outline of the village came into view as she reached the crest of the last of the hills to the west.

The fires had stopped now, leaving only blackened, charred remains of houses, shops, jetties, and other buildings. Posts had been driven into the ground to line the road leading up to the village, and each one supported an irregular shape; Aestelle was too far away for her eyes to discern exactly what the shapes were, but from having faced demons before, she had a good idea. The entire village was silent; there was no sign of further survivors, and even the cawing of seabirds was noticeable in its absence, leaving only the gentle cascading of waves against the shore.

Aestelle dismounted from her horse and tied the reins of the terrified animal to a nearby tree before taking her pistol from her belt and cocking the hammer with her thumb. After only a few paces, she sensed the evil presence of forces of the Abyss; even with her new path in life, her old training and the abilities that came with it had not abandoned her.

The line of posts leading up to the village entrance were exactly what she feared; skewered men and women atop long spears, their faces twisted in such utter agony that they must have been alive when they were run through. A sickening feeling clawed at Aestelle's stomach as she heard a weak whimper from one survivor atop a spear. After ascertaining that no medicine or magic in the world could save the man, Aestelle swiftly said a prayer for the dying fisherman before ending his misery as quickly and painlessly as she could.

Calling on old powers, half forgotten and long left neglected, Aestelle sensed the most powerful source of darkness within reach. There were many sources of evil and malevolence scattered around the burned out village – most likely lower Abyssals – but there was one presence that pulsated like a beacon of darkness and depravity in a sea of light. Aestelle continued striding along the road, now well aware that malicious eyes were watching her from the shadows of the burnt out buildings to either side. Following the primary source of darkness in a manner akin to a wolf hunting its prey, Aestelle continued on toward the center of the village. She rounded a corner and let out a breath.

Ahead of her, piles of burnt corpses lay scattered and dismembered in the streets; the stench of death was overpowering. On the wooden steps leading up to a burnt tavern sat a striking woman with dark hair and black clothes, her legs crossed and a half empty bottle of wine in one hand. The aura of darkness surrounding her was like a stench. She was the beacon Aestelle had hunted. Around her were perhaps twenty red skinned demons; lower Abyssals, made up of knotted muscle, each standing the height of a man and adorned in spiked, savage armor to accompany their curved horns and sharp teeth.

The closest two Abyssals turned to stare at Aestelle as she approached. Both looked her up and down with cruel and hungry eyes, smiling lecherously and then sprinting toward her. Without slowing her pace, Aestelle allowed the two demons to reach her. As both savage creatures attempted to wrap their clawed hands around her, Aestelle pressed the muzzle of her pistol up into the chin of the first devil and pulled the trigger, blowing the contents of its skull through the top of its head. Simultaneously, she pulled a throwing knife from her belt and stabbed it down through the top of the second demon's head, puncturing its skull and forcing a choked, gurgling noise to emit from its fanged mouth before it too dropped dead at her feet.

Replacing both weapons in her belt, Aestelle unsheathed her greatsword with one hand and rested it over her shoulders, stopping by the steps leading up to the burnt tavern as the remainder of the red skinned monsters moved toward her cautiously. Aestelle knew she could not stand a chance against so many, but intimidating them into keeping their distance allowed her to at least run for her horse at any time. The dark haired woman looked up at her and smiled. A moment's silence passed, broken only by the waves on the shoreline and the rustling of dead, autumn leaves in the light breeze.

"Well, well," the woman raised her brow, "aren't you a sight?"

The woman stood, and Aestelle's eyes were instantly drawn to her belt buckle; a blazing sun marred with a deep scratch across its surface. The symbol of the Basilean sisterhood, now defaced. The woman looked at Aestelle and smiled again.

"Welcome, Sister," she offered the bottle of wine to Aestelle. "They may kick us out of their convents, but the aura always remains, does it not? I can still smell the sisterhood on you."

Aestelle took the bottle of wine and dug her sword into the ground by the smoldering steps before sitting down and taking a swig. The dark haired woman sat next to her as the assembled throng of demonic Abyssals watched them both with narrowed eyes and gritted teeth. The woman's skin turned to a fiery red while horns emerged from her head and leathery, bat-like wings from her shoulder blades. Her clothing was replaced with scant scraps of studded leather and chains that barely covered her. A temptress – one of the elite of the ranks of succubi. Aestelle glanced across as the transformation took place before her eyes but gave no response other than taking another swig from the bottle of wine. The temptress narrowed her eyes just a little – a barely perceptible indication of her disappointment with Aestelle's lack of reaction. The surrounding circle of lower Abyssals grunted and growled, holding their place uneasily as they waited for orders from their mistress.

"You're right," Aestelle nodded, casting her eyes casually over the simple label on the wine bottle, "I was once a Basilean nun, just as you were. And given your powers, I imagine you're also aware that my apprenticeship was as a demon hunter."

Aestelle averted her eyes from the temptress, in case her hatred of the being was too obvious. She knew well that succubi were, in general, created by the energies of dark magic to take on the forms of whatever their foes desired, to lull them in close enough for the kill. For a mortal woman to gain the favor of the lords of the underworld to advance within the circles of the Abyss to become a succubi, let alone a temptress, would require the very depths of cruelty and depravity.

"And you think that gives you the power to take me on, along with my slaves here?" the temptress asked in a husky voice as she leaned closer.

"I'm confident I could take your head," Aestelle answered honestly, "and then they'd run. But I'm not going to do that."

"And why, pray, are you extending such mercy my way?" the horned temptress purred, running a hand along Aestelle's thigh.

Again, Aestelle chose not to react, knowing the frustration it would cause, despite the rising anger and hatred she felt welling up within her.

"If you wanted me dead, you would have attacked me already," Aestelle shrugged as she finished the wine. "So clearly you have something in mind for me. My guess is that you're here to make a statement for your masters. You want me to take a message somewhere."

"That's quite a gamble," the temptress hissed.

"The odds are in my favor."

The temptress leaned back and grinned.

"I like you. I'm glad I decided to let you live. For now. Go back to your masters. Tell them that Captain Dionne sends his regards."

This time, Aestelle could not hide her surprise.

"Dionne? He ordered this?"

"He has returned to Basilea," the temptress whispered, "at the head of an Abyssal legion that will crush all who stand before him."

"Well, that's not true, is it?" Aestelle flashed a smile as she placed the empty bottle down by her side and rose to her feet. "Because you're all a long way from the Abyss, and that means you've used portals, and the amount of power required to move a sizeable army through a portal would need to come from the depths of the Abyss itself. And if that had happened, I wouldn't be talking to a mere temptress."

The red-skinned demon woman finally stopped smiling. She stood and faced Aestelle with folded arms. Aestelle met her glare. Much of her indoctrination at the hands of the sisterhood left her feeling bitter and in contempt of that institution, but not when it came to their teachings regarding the Abyss and its denizens. Aestelle hated them all to her core for everything she had seen them do. The dead villagers that surrounded her only cemented those feelings.

"And to answer your earlier question properly, why am I showing you mercy?" Aestelle walked back over to her sword and heaved it back over one shoulder.

"Why indeed?"

"Because I know enough about your kind to know that if you fall in the mortal realm while in the service of your masters, you will be rewarded with power in the Abyss. So slaying you is the last thing I want to do with you. You see, this, all this around us? Dead innocents, needlessly killed to make your petty point and try to intimidate? All you've done is make me a little bit angry."

Aestelle paused and fixed the temptress with a steady stare.

"So here's my promise to you. I'll take your message back. But next time we meet, I will cut you down. I won't kill you. For the sake of these people you have murdered, I will hurt you. I will take a limb, maybe two, maybe your eyes and tongue, I don't know yet. But I will leave you as a simpering, quivering wreck whom will have to spend the next few years dragging itself on its knees over those frozen mountains to arrive in shame, failure, and agony back to the Abyss. That's my promise."

The temptress burst out laughing gleefully.

"You think you can morally judge me? You were ejected from the sisterhood, the same as I! You took the Sixth Step! You failed the steps to deliverance! All that separates you and I is one bad day! So make your ludicrous threats and speeches all you want, because there are only two eventualities from our next meeting. Either I will kill you, or you will join me in my new sisterhood. I'll even let you choose. Now go, you bore me."

Aestelle backed away, keeping her eyes fixed on the black orbs in the temptress' face. She pointed the tip of her greatsword at the demon as she departed.

"Remember my promise, *sister*," she hissed through gritted teeth.

*****

The embers of the fires scattered across the campsite glowed a dull orange to match the sun as it rose above the horizon. The hushed tones of quiet conversation across the encampment were steadily replaced with louder discussions as the camp awoke. Squires brushed their master's horses, tents were carefully collapsed and packed, soldiers washed and shaved with water warmed by the night fires. The view to the east was spectacular from the low mountains on the edge of the Tarkis range; the sun's rays painted the sparkling waters of the Low Sea of Suan in glittering shades of yellow and orange beneath a cloudless sky that boasted every shade of blue, from the lightest at the horizon to fade up into the dark dawn sky above.

Constance pulled her mail coat on over her padded, cotton under jacket, sighing as her limbs complained of days of marching over inhospitable terrain. She buckled her sword belt around her waist and heaved her heavy pack onto her shoulders. Around her, her mercenaries completed their final preparations for another day of marching. She cast her eyes across her comrades - Wulf scrounged the leftovers of breakfast as he did every morning, somehow putting all of the food away and maintaining his thin frame; Mallius finished shaving and used the water to plaster his dark hair back into a tight ponytail before carefully arranging his long fringe in a small mirror, ignoring the teasing of his vanity from his friends; Jaque hurriedly rolled up his bedding and shoved his possessions untidily into his pack, late to prepare as always; Hayden sat on a smooth rock and scribbled a few words onto a battered piece of parchment as he looked pensively off to the south.

"Who are you writing to?" Constance asked as she walked over to Hayden, keeping her voice low so as not to attract attention to what was most likely a personal letter.

"My daughter," the big man replied. "I'm letting her know what this is all like, warts and all."

"How old is Maya now? Fifteen?"

"Sixteen in spring," Hayden replied with a fond smile, "and she is desperate to find her own way in the world. A lot of her friends seem content to tide life over with a simple job until they are married. Not my Maya. She wants to... how did she phrase it... 'set the world alight, even if it's only my little corner of the world'."

Constance sat down next to her old friend, resting her elbows on her knees and her chin in her hands as she watched the paladins kneel in morning prayer together on the far side of the camp.

"Is that so bad? Setting a little part of the world alight?"

"It depends what she means," Hayden shrugged. "I don't think even she knows what she means. But I've spent years hiding the truth from her, and now she seems to think that life on campaign is something glamorous. She doesn't see this for what it is."

"Perhaps she wants to set the world alight with her music," Constance flashed an optimistic smile. "That talent comes from you."

"Nice of you to say," Hayden gave a short chuckle, "and maybe you're even right. But I can't help but wonder whether I wasted a gift given to me by the Shining Ones on blowing a few simple notes on a battlefield. Maybe I could have done more. Hopefully that's what Maya means to do. I don't know. If you could have your time again, Constance, would you do it all the same?"

Constance paused to contemplate the question. Her instant reaction was negative, thinking about the effect her imprisonment had on her life. She thought of the friends she had lost and the atrocities she had witnessed, and how much misery and pain had surrounded her vocation at seemingly every turn. But she had always prided herself on her optimism and switched focus to think on the happy times, on the camaraderie and the bonds of friendship she had forged over the years, of the places she had seen from the frozen peaks of the Dragon Teeth Mountains, across to the breathtaking plains of Ardovikian, and even as far south as the Twilight Glades themselves, far away and across the seas. But was it worth it? If she could do it all again, was soldiering really the life she would choose? Or should she have heeded her father's advice and followed him into a comfortable existence as a successful merchant?

She opened her mouth to voice her thoughts, but her attention was dragged away from her introspection by the pounding of hooves on the southern slope. A lone rider, cloaked in black, sped up the slope in a gallop toward the encampment. Two sentries rushed out to confront the rider, but after a short exchange, they

133

quickly allowed admission.

"She's back," Constance exhaled, "I had best go report to our friend Hugh and see what we're up to next."

Constance trudged up the hill to where the Dictator-Prefect's impressive tent was in the process of being collapsed and packed by his entourage of servants, under the aggressive guidance of Trennio. Tancred also clearly had a similar idea to Constance, as he too made his way over from the paladins' area of the encampment. They both arrived only moments after Aestelle had dismounted to deliver her report to the Dictator-Prefect and Captain Georgis.

"This far south?" Hugh exclaimed.

"It is rare, but not unheard of," Aestelle said, her tone serious and concern showing in her eyes. "How many there are remains to be seen."

"What was it?" Tancred asked as he arrived. "What did you find?"

"Abyssals," Aestelle replied.

Constance let out an audible breath as the familiar sensation of anxiety took an immediate and violent clutch at her gut.

"You are sure?" Tancred demanded.

"Yes, I'm sure!" Aestelle snapped. "I killed two of them and spoke at length to another! They burned a fishing village, killed nearly everyone! That place is full of bodies if you'd care to go and look, and what they've done to those bodies? Not even orcs treat their captured so badly."

"How many of them?" Hugh asked sternly as he beckoned for Trennio and Platus to approach.

"I saw a couple of dozen," Aestelle said, "nearly all lower Abyssals. They were led by a temptress. She claimed there were many more that were already further south. I don't know how many."

"What now?" Georgis exclaimed. "We can't keep chasing Dionne! We're duty bound to stop these monstrosities!"

"They're one and the same!" Aestelle growled breathlessly. "The temptress said that Dionne sent his regards. She claimed he was leading an entire Abyssal legion."

"Nonsense!" Constance intervened. "There is not a shred of evidence that Dionne would do such a thing! Disobeying orders and going rogue from the legion is an entire world away from selling a soul to demons and turning to the Abyss!"

"I'm telling you exactly what I was told," Aestelle said, "I heard…"

"Then you are a fool! An idiot!" Constance yelled, her fists clenched. "You believed the words of a demon? They lie, how could you not know that? They seduce with lies! Perhaps if you'd spent more time in the field, actually fighting, and less time worrying about your damn make up then you would realize that!"

Aestelle drew herself up to her full height and towered over Constance, leaning forward to fix her blue eyes dangerously on Constance's.

"I know demons," she seethed, "more than you can know. I'm well aware of how they operate and I'm well aware of…"

"I'm well aware of the man we are hunting down!" Constance cut her off angrily, again. "I marched under Captain Dionne's banner for long enough to know that he is not the sort of piece of shit who sells his soul to devils! He would never do that! Ask any of my men who served under him!"

The tall adventurer folded her arms and flipped her beaded locks over one shoulder.

"Then if you think your beloved former commander is some sort of deity with enough willpower to resist the temptations of the Abyss, it is you that is the fool. The idiot. Now is the time to take action, not simper and cry like some sycophantic puppy."

Constance lunged forward and swung a fist for Aestelle's jaw. Before she could connect, she was shoved back with enough force to make her stumble a few steps. Tancred stood between Constance and Aestelle, both of his arms extended as he pushed the two women apart.

"Enough!" the red headed paladin commanded. "This is getting us nowhere! The situation is dire and now is not the time for petty bickering!"

Aestelle looked down at the short paladin incredulously.

"If you ever lay a finger on me again, little man, I'll take it off."

"Listen to him!" Hugh bellowed. "I don't have time for your squabbles! I have made up my mind. We are heading south. We are chasing down that Abyssal horde. I think it will lead us to Dionne. It might not. But there is no way in all seven circles of that hell they've come from that I am allowing those monsters to proceed through Basilea! Get your soldiers ready to move, we are heading south immediately."

Constance swore and turned away, struggling to contain her anger and frustration at such a poor decision. Hugh turned back to Aestelle.

"You, mercenary," he said, "how confident are you that there are indeed any more of them than the mere two dozen you saw?"

"I'm all but certain," Aestelle replied coolly. "It is almost impossible that any Abyssals could have made it so far south into Basilea on foot, so they would have used a portal. Portals take a phenomenal amount of power to open and somebody with the arcane skills and loyalty to the Abyss to activate a portal stone at the destination. Such effort would not be wasted on a force so small. There are more of them, I'm fairly sure." ·

"Then go," Hugh ordered, "get back on your horse and ride south as fast as you can, get past them. You must get word back to the Duma that there are Abyssals within our borders. The Duma must know."

"This is not what I agreed to," Aestelle shrugged. "This is more than you paid me to do. Much more."

"You have just seen innocent people slaughtered," Captain Georgis whispered, "men and women with families. And you really think that now is the time to negotiate more payment?"

Aestelle looked down at the tubby legion captain. For a brief moment, her features softened. Wordlessly, the tall woman swung herself back up into her saddle and dragged her horse around to the south before spurring the animal back into a gallop.

Twelve

One foot tapping restlessly on the marble floor of the waiting chamber, Valletto fixed his eyes anxiously on the tall, highly polished doors on the far side of the lavishly decorated room. The midafternoon sun poured light in through the balcony to his right, still ferocious in its heat despite summer begrudgingly giving way to the fall. He glanced down at the length and angle of the shadows to calculate the time; he would be late to walk his son home from school. His wife would not be happy if the message did not get through to her.

"Stop looking so worried, Val. You'll get me started."

Valletto looked across to where Saffus sat on a long bench opposite him, his arms spread out lazily along the back of the carved, ornate furniture. Saffus fixed him with a look combining concern, deep concentration, and mild irritation. Valletto knew from years of experience that it did not pay to anger the sorcerer; his mood swings were the stuff of legend amidst the gossip of trainee mages. The tall mage gave an almost sinister smile, his thick, black eyebrows marring with the pure white of his receding hair.

"How long will they leave us waiting here?" Valletto asked, half to himself, as he stood and resumed his restless pacing in front of the grand doors.

"As long as it takes!" Saffus exclaimed. "This is the Duma! The democratically elected representatives of the most powerful nation in Mantica! They'll take as long as they want to!"

Valletto let out a frustrated sigh and walked out to the balcony, leaning on the rails running around the small platform as he looked down on the city below. The Quarter of Governance sprawled out beneath him, basking in the warmth of the sun. Rows of buildings in white marble and dull terracotta housed countless government offices and officials, all supporting the decisions and policy of the Duma as it enacted the will of the Hegemon. The Plaza of Exchange, the largest and most prosperous marketplace in the entire world, lay a mere stone throw from the extravagant entrance to the Duma complex. Merchants hurriedly prepared their wares outside their shops or, for the less successful, in smaller temporary stalls. Tomorrow would be another market day, as was one in three, where anything could be purchased from sandals and bread up to the deeds for mansion complexes outside the city. Even after six years of living in the City of the Golden Horn with his family, Valletto still marveled at the luxury and power that was displayed in even the smallest of details around him.

Valletto turned around as the double doors opened behind him to admit a short official of the Duma, clothed in a toga of white with a purple sash denoting his rank and position.

"Their Lordships will hear you now," he announced.

His heart pounding in his chest, Valletto jogged over to catch up with Saffus before walking in with the taller man. The chamber was breathtaking. A huge, circular room with tall pillars of pure white marble supporting an extravagant ceiling where a huge mural, said to have taken two generations to paint, weaved in and out of beautifully crafted skylights above. The huge painting depicted the epic victory of Bolisean and his legions during the Battle of Antovar, with a blood red sky dominated by the winged, angelic Elohi sent by the Shining Ones to assist the faithful mortals below. Valletto had only heard about the painting before; its beauty stirred his soul with faith and patriotism as he gazed up at its majesty.

"Keep up," Saffus grumbled under his breath.

Valletto quickened his pace and kept his eyes down at ground level. The cavernous, white room was not dissimilar to an auditorium; a central, circular speaking platform dominated the middle of the room surrounded on all sides of rows of long, curved benches, escalating in steps up to the grand doors at each of the cardinal compass points. A low buzz of conversation echoed around the room from its two hundred or so occupants; the senators – born into nobility, they nonetheless each had to be democratically elected into the Duma for a period of three years. If a senator was, however, successful enough to be re-elected to serve three consecutive terms, he was rewarded with lifetime status and would not stand for election again.

"Sit here," Saffus ordered curtly, pointing to a seat at the end of a row of curved marble benches, about halfway down from the double doors to the speaking platform below. Valletto obeyed wordlessly and watched as his former teacher continued fearlessly down to address the most powerful body of men – and, very recently, women – in the world. Each senator had their own bench, complete with a small entourage of clerks, guards, and slaves. Valletto knew from the people he worked with that he should know the names of many of these politicians, but politics had never interested him. Still, he was fascinated by the myriad of different approaches in displaying power. The senator sat closest to him was a tall, muscular man in his late forties with a legion sword at his belt; his two guards and two clerks likewise all wore some evidence of previous military service. Conversely, the next man along was obese, bald, and lounged back on his bench while two beautiful, blonde slave girls in short togas that bordered on obscene fed him grapes and wine.

Conversation began to die down as Saffus was escorted onto the platform in the middle of the room. The official who had escorted them in turned to face the assembled senators.

"My lords and ladies," he bellowed out, his voice traveling to the back of the chamber, "may I present to you Grand Mage Saffus of Aigina, Advisor Primus of the Arcane to the Duma."

Valletto leaned forward on his bench, resting his chin pensively in his hands as he watched Saffus prepare to address the Duma. Valletto felt the bristles of his short beard prickle at his hands; flecks of white had recently began to show on his chin and at the temples of his short hair, reminding him that his fortieth birthday was only a few seasons away.

"My lords and ladies," Saffus announced boldly, his words now taking on far greater articulation than in normal conversation, "I come to you today with grave news. It has been brought to my attention that the dark forces of the Abyss have succeeded in polluting the noble soil of Basilea with their presence."

The low buzz of conversation wound up again. Valletto looked around him and saw a variety of responses; younger senators were engaged in animated, even panicked discussion at the news, while more veteran politicians smirked in amusement or even yawned. Saffus held up his hands to appeal for silence.

"Our lands are no stranger to the threat of the Abyss, we all know," the ageing mage continued, "for it is our Hegemony that keeps the dark threat of these demons at bay for the rest of the world. It is both our honor and our curse. But the news that has been brought before me is not of skirmishes along our borders to the north. It is not of isolated warbands amidst the peaks of the mountains north of Kolosu. It is of Abyssals on our very soil, our own sacred earth, well inside our borders!"

"How far inside our borders?" an unseen senator demanded from the north stand.

"On the eastern coast, perhaps a day north of the Anerian wash," Saffus replied.

Conversation again erupted along the stands but was silenced as another question was shouted out.

"How many of them, Saffus?"

"I do not know," the mage replied, "but even the smallest force that far south is enough to concern me."

"If you do not know how many there are, how are you even positive that this threat exists at all?" demanded the corpulent bald man from Valletto's row. "How has this news come to your ears?"

"One of my colleagues brought it to my attention. He was contacted by a previous student who has settled in the area. That mage was in turn contacted by a messenger sent by Dictator-Prefect Hugh of Athelle, leading the expedition to apprehend Captain Dionne. The expedition ordered by this very assembly."

The cacophony of responses drowned out Saffus' attempt to continue in his explanation. Some seemed alarmed by the mention of Hugh's expedition; others seemed overtly amused by the explanation. The fat senator stood to raise his voice over all others.

"Saffus!" he demanded. "You come here to raise panic and you are honestly telling us that your sole evidence is that a mysterious, lone messenger told a man who told another man who told you that there is some demonic invasion? Really? That is what you come here to tell us?"

Again, laughter and fear reigned in equilibrium as the senators argued, shouted, and laughed among themselves. Saffus looked over to Valletto and gestured for him to join him on the platform. Valletto hesitated. Saffus nodded slowly and deliberately, pointing at the platform next to him. Valletto stood, straightened his tunic, and made his way down the broad steps to join his former mentor on the stage. He turned to face the assembled crowd, now all the more intimidating as he looked up at the sea of faces in the stands surrounding him, the sunlight pouring in through the skylights to dazzle and half blind him as sweat began to form on his brow.

Saffus spoke again to silence the crowds.

"Senators, I present to you the 'man who told me'."

The crowds silenced. All eyes were fixed on Valletto. He took a tentative step forward and cleared his throat.

"My lords and ladies," he repeated the formal introduction he had heard twice before, "my name is Valletto of Auron. I was contacted via the arcane plains by a former…"

Valletto was yanked a step back by the powerful, vice like grip of Saffus. The taller mage stepped forward to speak again.

"My friend here is too modest!" He shouted out, a tinge of anger clear in his tone. "Allow me to introduce him properly so that there can be *no doubt* – no doubt – as to his authority and integrity. *Captain* Valleto of Auron is the Deputy Senior Battle Mage of the 2nd Legion. He has served you, the Duma, in your legion for sixteen years. He is a veteran of the Plains Wars, where he served with distinction and was wounded. Unwilling to be pensioned out of the legion, this hero of your legion continued to serve as an instructor to legion battle mages for three years while he recovered. After this, he was appointed as the Senior Arcane Advisor to Legion Command, such is the respect for this man's experience and authority. That is the caliber of man who now addresses you!"

Valletto shuddered at the silence he faced. All conversation, be it in panic or mirth, had now stopped for him. He was deeply uncomfortable with being referred to as a captain – Saffus knew well that this was an honorary rank only, given to experienced battle mages as a mark of respect so that they would be taken more seriously by the soldiers they worked alongside. Valletto did not consider himself a legion captain; although he was fully trained as a soldier and could use a sword and spear, he was not trained or experienced in leading men in the field. He also resented the reference to his time at war, and certainly being referred to as a 'hero'. Valletto had never even faced a man in combat. His role in the war was to cast protective spells to look after soldiers on the field of battle. He had been attacked and faced death several times, but he had never struck down an opponent. He was no hero.

He was being used as a political pawn in this grand arena, and Saffus' words offended him. Worst of all was the reference to his wounds and years of recovery. He had never suffered a single physical wound. Exhausted by his time on campaign, deeply saddened by the death and misery that surrounded him on a daily basis for months on end, it did not take much to snap his weakening mind when he was assaulted by an enemy sorcerer. After coming home, his friends and family were quick to notice the change in him. He argued, fought, drank heavily, and cast all his friends aside. Only Clera, his wife, stood by him. Day after day as the months, and then years, slowly passed, she supported him with love until together they overcame all he had faced. The legion did nothing for his recovery. It was all from his wife.

A hand again clamped on Valletto's shoulder. He turned around and looked up at Saffus. The elderly mage smiled encouragingly. Valletto realized he was shaking. He had tears in his eyes. Taking a few deep breaths to compose himself, Valletto turned to face the senators again.

"A former student of mine contacted me through the arcane plains," Valletto explained. "It is a way that mages can converse over long distances. He lives in Dennec, just north of the Anerian Wash. He was contacted by a woman who has been taken into the employ of Dictator-Prefect Hugh of Athelle. The Dictator-Prefect ordered this woman to bring news to the Duma of an Abyssal incursion into the area. She also claimed that it was led by Captain Dionne, who has now turned to the Abyss."

That was enough to generate the cacophony of debate again. Within seconds, senators were up on their feet, arguing passionately with others around them, shouting out questions and demands to Saffus and Valletto on the platform, wading out onto the stairways between stands to physically confront other senators. Long moments, perhaps a full minute, passed until a senior Duma official shot out onto the stage to bang a huge gong in the center. The room fell silent.

"Gentlemen, ladies," the official called out, "need I remind you all of Rule Twelve? I beg of you to conduct yourselves in accordance with your position."

There was a brief pause until the bald man who had challenged Saffus again stood up.

"Captain Valletto," he gave a respectful nod of the head, "I am confident that I speak for all here when I say that your credentials and your honor are beyond question. But what of this man who contacted you? And what of this mysterious woman claiming to be the agent of Dictator-Prefect Hugh?"

"I trust my former pupil," Valletto said honestly. "I taught him for a year and we have remained in contact periodically since. His service to the legion was without fault, and he left with full honors. I appreciate, sir, that you trust me; but put simply, that trust you describe is exactly how I feel about Perrio. As for the woman who contacted him, I have no idea who she is, but Perrio told me that he has worked with her before, and he believes her."

"I thank you, Captain," the senator continued. "You were contacted with this news and you have acted appropriately, in good faith, by bringing this to the attention of your superiors. You have done the right thing. But I think this should go no further."

The lumbering man held up his hands to appeal for quiet as soon as shouts and jeers were issued from other stands around him.

"The flow of this information is simply too long!" he urged as he continued. "Are we children playing Elvish Whispers? Let us assume for a moment that Dictator-Prefect Hugh is indeed the originator of this message; in itself a foolish assumption. But taking that as truth, the message has had ample opportunity to be distorted beyond its original meaning by the plethora of channels it has been through in reaching us!"

"The message is clear!" a woman shouted from the south stand. "The essence of a message so important would never be distorted so easily!"

"Our military is stretched to the point of breaking!" another senator yelled. "We do not have the resources to respond to every last rumor that reaches us!"

"We would be fools to ignore this threat!" the military man who had sat near Valletto stood and declared. "At the very least, it should be investigated! I call for a formal debate and vote to decide on whether military action is appropriate!"

"Seconded!" the female senator from the south stand stood and called. Valletto could now see the woman – a regal looking lady of advanced years with an impressive mane of gray hair. While he had no interest in politics, everybody in Basilea knew of Senator Agorea of Vecci, the leader of the successful campaign lobbying for women to be allowed to serve as soldiers in the legion.

The room again descended into anarchy and arguments. Saffus leaned in to shout over the noise into Valletto's ear.

"We have done all we can, Val. Now is the time for us to leave."

*****

It was nearly sunset by the time Valletto tied up his horse and walked through the small courtyard of his house just outside the city's perimeter. His heart heavy, he dragged his feet wearily up to the door to his home, a two-story house sitting inside an acre of land. The door was opened by Hustas, his loyal servant of five years.

"Good evening, sir," the short man smiled politely.

"Is it?" Valletto murmured. "I'm afraid I don't think it is a good evening, on this occasion."

The middle-aged servant's face fell.

"Oh dear," he said quietly, "let me take your cloak and I'll fetch you a drink."

"Thank you," Valletto managed a warm and sincere smile as he carefully folded his dusty cloak and handed it across to the older man.

As soon as he walked in to the hallway of his house, his six-year-old son, Lyius, sprinted out to embrace his legs in a tight hug.

"Daddy!" he grinned. "You're home!"

Valletto glanced up and saw Clera, his wife, walking carefully down the stairs carrying their daughter, Jullia, herself only a year old.

Valletto tried to force a smile for Clera. Three years his junior, she was still the most beautiful woman he had ever met. It confused him sometimes, even frustrated him, when men talked about other women's beauty but did not mention Clera. No other woman had ever so much as turned his head. If love truly was blindness, then he was truly happy in his blindness, for he needed nothing else. But she knew him well, and instantly, her welcoming smile faded as she sensed his unease.

"Give your father a moment, Lyius," she said to their son gently. "Be a good boy and go and help Hustas with the drinks."

The small, frail boy clung desperately to Valletto's legs for another few moments before disappearing off toward the kitchen with decidedly less enthusiasm. Valletto watched him go and then brought his eyes back to Clera.

"They're sending you away, aren't they," she said, a declaration rather than a question.

No words came to mind, so Valletto remained silent. Jullia looked around the hallway blankly while dangling in her mother's arms.

"How long are you going for?" Clera asked.

"They say a month," Valletto replied. "I think it will be perhaps double that. Still, not nearly as long as a proper campaign with the legion."

His wife nodded slowly, her face as rigid as stone.

"Well, we knew it was coming," she forced a weak smile, "we knew it was our turn again when they moved you on from teaching. We'll get through. We always do. Is it dangerous?"

"Oh no," Valletto shook his head, "I really don't think so."

That was a lie. But a worthwhile lie; a good one to stop his family from worrying. Valletto looked across to where his son stood in the kitchen doorway with Hustas, holding up a glass of water for him. The boy blinked in confusion.

"Where are you going?" he asked timidly.

"Up north, near the Mountains of Tarkis," Valletto dropped to one knee to face his thin son. "Not for too long."

"How long?"

"I'll be back in time for your birthday."

"My birthday is three months away."

Again, Valletto had no answers. He watched helplessly as Lyius slowly lowered the glass of water to his side and burst into tears. Hustas diplomatically stepped back into the kitchen. Valletto dashed forward to tightly embrace his son, hoping it would make the tears stop. The wailing that would have infuriated any other man in the world was different to him; it was his child and his fault, and it brought tears to his own eyes. Clera gently put Jullia down and picked up Lyius, carrying him up the stairs.

"He'll be alright in a moment," she urged Valletto, "I'll get him happy again."

Valletto closed his eyes and fell back against the wall as the sound receded up the staircase. He sank down to his knees and then found himself lying on the floor in the entrance hall, his hands pressed against his face as he struggled to pick through the crippling range of emotions racing through his mind. He was vaguely aware of gentle movement next to his head. He opened his eyes, expecting to see one of the family cats brushing past him. Instead he saw Jullia stood over him, looking down at him silently. Unable to muster a smile even for her, he looked back up into her curious eyes in silence. She slowly leaned over, kissed him on the cheek, and then turned to totter off and clumsily climb the stairs after her mother and brother.

After a sleepless night, he said his farewells to his family. At dawn, two paladins from the Order of the Blades of Onzyan arrived at his home to escort him on the long ride north.

Thirteen

Tancred sat bolt upright on his bedroll. His head was dull, as if the air inside his tent was too close and humid. Exhaling, he crawled to the entrance of his tent and peeled back the flap of fabric to look up at the night sky. The full moon sat high, slightly obscured by a few strands of thin, wispy cloud. It was perhaps a little after midnight and around him the encampment was all but silent. A few fires still crackled and two sentries on the camp perimeter were engaged in a hushed conversation, but nothing more. For three days they had tracked the Abyssal forces as they meandered south, twisting and turning in their progress as if the demons were unsure whether to close with the big cities of Basilea. A gut churning path of death, dismemberment, and destruction was left in their wake as another two villages fell to the merciless onslaught of the Abyssals. Yet still there was no sign of them.

Turning to crawl back to his bedroll, Tancred stopped. A little more awake now, he was more focused, more aware that the dullness in his head was not from the humid environment. There was something close by, something malevolent. Tancred hauled his padded underarmor jacket on over his shoulders and crept out of his tent. Standing up in the cool night air, he glanced around at the woods at the foot of the plateau the force had made its camp atop. There was nothing. No rustle of movement, no indication of disturbance of any kind. Still uncomfortable, Tancred returned to his tent and pulled on his coat of mail and buckled his breastplate on top before securing his sword belt around his waist to give him a bare minimum of weaponry and protection. Spending a few minutes silently pacing around the camp perimeter, he again failed to see anything of concern. But the feeling, the sensation of peril closing in from all sides, would not leave him. Closing his eyes and focusing his thoughts, Tancred delved into the core of his control over the spiritual powers of divinity magic in an attempt to discern whether this was merely a bad feeling, or his senses alerting him to danger.

His eyes shot open. Silently, his bare feet padding on the dry earth below, he dashed over to Jeneveve's tent. Creeping inside, he found her asleep on her side in her bedroll. Clamping a hand over her mouth, he shook her awake. She opened her eyes and a dagger appeared at Tancred's throat. Realizing who had awoken her, she lowered the weapon.

"Jeneveve!" Tancred whispered desperately. "The camp is being surrounded! I need you to go and wake up two other knights and then come back here to get into your armor. Tell them all to do exactly the same. And prepare torches, too. But keep it down! We must not alert whatever is out there!"

"W...what is going on?" Jeneveve whispered as Tancred removed his hand from her mouth.

"Can you not sense it?" Tancred asked anxiously.

The dark haired woman closed her eyes in concentration but shook her head.

"No, Lord Paladin," she admitted, "but surely better to exercise caution and prepare for the worst? I will wake the others and prepare for battle."

Tancred clumsily extricated himself from the tent and watched as Jeneveve darted off to wake up Brother Paladin Xavier in the next tent along. Tancred headed over to the two guards who were talking by the edge of the encampment. By the time he arrived, the feeling of darkness was overwhelming, threatening to envelop his senses and leaving him utterly convinced that an attack was imminent.

"Guards," he said in a low voice as he approached, "we are being surrounded by the forces of the Abyss. You – go and awake the Dictator-Prefect and tell him to prepare his men for battle, but do it silently. Do not make a single noise. You – stay here and keep your eyes fixed on the woods below. If you see or hear anything untoward, raise the alarm."

Both guards nodded, the first man sprinting off toward Hugh's grand tent in the center of the encampment while the second soldier looked down at the dark trees fifty yards downslope at the foot of the hill, one hand clamped around the handle of his sword. Tancred rushed back to his own tent and silently awoke his squires to help him complete the process of putting on his armor.

Tancred returned to the perimeter as soon as he was fully armored, arriving just ahead of Jeneveve and Xavier. The three paladins stood with the lone guard and looked out to the south.

"I can sense it now," Jeneveve said in a hushed tone, "not just from the south. All around us. Why are they attacking us here? They must know we can sense their presence? We have the advantage of high ground and a defendable position."

"We are tired and do not see well in the dark," Tancred replied uneasily. "They feel no fatigue and see better in the darkness. I have ordered the squires to prepare torches to light this hilltop up like it is the Feast of the Life."

"Our supplies," Xavier said, "we are also half crippled by having to defend our caravan and supplymen."

"I will tell them they need to take up arms tonight," Jeneveve said. "All must carry swords if we are to hold our ground here."

Tancred watched as Jeneveve made her way over to the supply tents while the first few men-at-arms and mercenaries emerged from their own tents, fully armed and armored. Hugh was the next to arrive at the edge of the camp, his eyes red with weariness as he clipped his extravagant black cloak around his neck.

"What is it, Tancred? Where is the threat coming from?"

"All around us," Tancred replied, "we are surrounded. I can sense it. Our advantage now is that they are unaware we are expecting them. We need to keep the noise down for as long as possible. We should let them attack thinking they have us caught completely unaware."

Hugh nodded as he cast his eyes around the surrounding terrain.

"We shall set up the mercenaries to the east to take advantage of the most open terrain. Captain Georgis can take the north and west. Can you charge down this slope to meet them from the south? This seems the most gentle slope for horses."

"If we rouse the horses, they will make a lot of noise," Tancred replied.

"Understood," Hugh said, "tell your squires to get the horses prepared as soon as the fighting begins. Pick your best mounted warriors and tell them to fall back to the horses. The rest of your paladins must hold here. I will have a defensive position prepared in the center of camp, but you need to buy time for it to be constructed. Are you content?"

"Yes, content," Tancred nodded, feeling slightly better as another three of his paladins approached the southern slope, fully armored and prepared for battle.

*****

Moving swiftly along the line of prone crossbowmen, Constance arrived at the far end by Jaque. The thin man lay down by a small bush, staring out toward the plains to the east. He was the end of her line, marking the limits of her company's area of responsibility; a few yards away to the left saw the beginning of the area held by the legion men-at-arms.

"Anything?" Constance whispered as she crouched down next to her comrade.

"Oh yeah," Jaque nodded, his eyes fixed ahead, "I can't see them yet, but if you listen you can hear the bastards chittering occasionally. They're there, alright."

"Good," Constance gave his bony shoulder an encouraging squeeze, "if anybody is going to remain hidden, it's us. We've got heavy cavalry and infantry with us, we're the only ones who ever do the scouting. None of these others have the first idea about staying hidden, so it's down to us to hold this open plain until just the right moment. I'm trusting you to make that decision and start shooting if you think it's necessary, alright?"

"Got it, Constance," Jaque whispered. "Don't worry, I'll wait until we can't miss them."

Staying low and silent, cursing her mail armor for its chinking in the darkness, Constance dashed back to take her place in the center of the line. The last few of her soldiers to be awoken were now taking their places, accepting unlit torches from the paladins' squires as they arrived. Twenty-two men and women remained in Constance's company. Discounting the squires and supplymen, only about ninety soldiers lay in wait for whatever was approaching from the darkness. Constance hoped it would be enough.

Then she saw them. Just a single figure at first, man-sized and hunched over as it sprinted low and fast across the open plain ahead of her. The light of the full moon reflected off its metal armor and bare skin, highlighting the silhouette of a muscular frame, bent over almost double as it ran. A second, then a third, came into view. Then it was a whole line.

"Wait for my command to loose!" Constance whispered.

The order was hurriedly passed along the line. Constance turned and frantically beckoned for one of the squires to run over to her from the pile of torches.

"Go and tell the Dictator-Prefect that we are being attacked from the east," she said quickly. "Get the horses ready for the cavalry and be ready to light the torches! Go!"

When Constance turned back to face the east, the entire plain was a living, writhing mass of advancing bodies. Lumbering, muscular figures with curved horns sprouting from their heads and spiked, battered armor glinting in the moonlight moved rapidly toward her position. Fear rose sharply in the form of bile rising to her throat. She feared death as much as any other, but that fear she had overcome many times. But this was not death. This was the threat of being dragged to hell itself for an eternity of torture unlike anything in the mortal world.

The sea of burly bodies was within range now, but a few seconds more would guarantee accuracy from some of her weaker shooters. Constance drew herself up to one knee and brought her crossbow to her shoulder. Her action was mimicked along the line as her mercenaries clambered up to either side. They were close now, close enough to hear their animalistic huffing and grunting as they ran across the dry plain on their cloven hooves. Any closer and there would not be enough time to load for a second salvo. Now was the time.

"Loose!" Constance shouted, picking out a target in the shadowy demonic mass rushing at the encampment.

The twang of crossbow strings reverberated down the line as twenty-two bolts shot out and whistled through the cool night air, thudding into the advancing wall of hellish flesh. Snarls of pain and rage emanated from the demonic line as Abyssals dropped to the earth, dead or grievously wounded, trampled underfoot by the continuing surge of their remorseless fellow demons.

Hurriedly drawing the string of her weapon back, Constance let out a breath as the night sky was lit up by dozens of torches on a command from the center of the camp. The closest of the devils were visible in the light now; red-skinned, muscular, near naked with only isolated clumps of armor strapped to their powerful bodies, the horned lower Abyssals continued to run up the gentle slope with their viciously serrated swords and curved axes held high above their horned heads. Constance reckoned there were perhaps fifty or sixty of them on the east slope, let alone whatever was charging up the other sides of the hill. They had time for one more shot before the demonic horde would be on them. Constance realized then they did not stand a chance. Loading her bolt onto the crossbow, she prepared to face her end with courage.

*****

The wall of demons surged up the slope, weapons brandished high above their heads and snarling, animalistic cries echoing through the night. Standing front and center of the twenty paladins, Tancred tightened his grip around the handle of his greatsword and held it ready to one side. He could make out the details of his opponents now – three ranks of lower Abyssals numbering at least fifty; ornate, brass trimmed armor over their red skin marking them out as elite Abyssal guards; the very best and bloodiest warriors of their circle of the pit.

"Wait for my command!" Tancred yelled as he looked to either side at the line of paladins who stood steady behind the wall of lit torches. "Make every strike count!"

The lines of Abyssal guards lumbered closer, the plates of their armor clanking and the darkness emanating from their core surrounding and enveloping Tancred like a black shroud.

"Charge!" Tancred yelled, sprinting out at the head of his ranks of warriors.

Timed to perfection, Tancred had just enough space to accelerate to a full sprint before he brought his sword up high and hacked down with all of his might as the two opposing ranks of warriors clashed together. His first strike cleaved through an Abyssal guard on the front row, tearing open a great rent in the demon from shoulder across to midriff. Trying to capitalize on his momentum, Tancred surged forward into the second rank and swiped out at the next monstrosity he faced, but his attack was batted aside with a well-executed block from the horned devil he faced.

The two opposing warriors stood facing each other, their weapons locked together as they stared into each other's eyes with gritted teeth. The Abyssal guard hauled its axe back and swung it around in a rapid strike aimed at Tancred's neck; the paladin ducked beneath and twisted in place to thrust his sword toward the demon's face, but this too was batted aside by the skillful warrior. Tancred was forced to take two steps back as the Abyssal advanced on him with a flurry of blows executed with precision and inhuman speed; then, out of nowhere, Jeneveve appeared at his side and decapitated the horned demon with one fluid blow.

Less than a second later, another Abyssal guard leapt forward and smashed a warhammer into Jeneveve's head, sending her sprawling down into the dirt with blood leaking out from a great rend torn in her helmet. With a cry of rage, Tancred hurled himself forward and barged his shoulder into Jeneveve's victor, knocking the demon to the ground. Tancred planted an armored foot onto the demon's chest to pin it in place and then brought his own sword hacking down again and again, butchering the Abyssal until little remained intact.

A blow thundered into Tancred and he was smashed down to the ground, locked in a fierce grapple against another of the red-skinned horde as the two rolled over each other amidst the growing sea of dead and dying that covered the earth around them. The horned Abyssal overpowered Tancred and rolled on top of him, fixing him with a black-eyed stare of hatred before sinking its razor sharp fangs into Tancred's neck. Tancred let out a howl of pain and smashed an elbow into the side of the monster's head, dislodging the demonic creature for long enough to grab his sword and bring the hilt thudding down into the Abyssal's face to obliterate its nose. Yelling, Tancred brought the handle down again and again, changing his aiming point from the face to the side of the head until the creature's skull gave way and brain matter was exposed.

Staggering back to his feet, Tancred brought up his sword and launched himself back into the attack with renewed vigor.

*****

A barricade had been hastily assembled in the center of the camp, predominantly made up of a circle of overturned wagons. The quartermaster remained within with his supplymen, alongside Hugh and his two aides. A few bows had been distributed to the quartermaster's stevedores, but Orion knew these would be useless given how long it took to teach a man to use a bow effectively. Seeing the seven paladins approaching, one of the wagons was quickly pushed to one side to allow a small opening in the defenses for the men to dash through. Hugh ran over to intercept them as the defenses were shut behind them.

"Where's the rest of you?" he demanded breathlessly, raising his voice over the panicked shouts around them.

"Tancred attacked with all of the others," Orion replied. "We are all that remains. Are the horses ready?"

"Yes, ten of them," the Dictator-Prefect said. "Go and support Tancred to the south. Captain Georgis is holding at the north and west. I fear the mercenaries are about to fall to the east, and seven horsemen won't stop that."

Orion nodded, immediately forcing the painful thoughts of the inevitable demise of his friends within the mercenary company to the back of his mind. The din of battle echoed from all around, drawing ever closer with each passing moment.

"Come on!" he urged the six paladins accompanying him. "Mount up, get a lance!"

Orion was met in the very middle of the final defensive position by Kell. The boy walked to him, his shaking hands wrapped around the reins of Orion's warhorse. Six similarly armored warhorses were dragged over by other squires as alarmed shouts increased in intensity from the other side of the wagon barricade. Orion tore the reins of the horse from his squire and put his foot into one of the stirrups to drag himself up into the saddle.

"Lance, boy! Go and fetch me a lance!"

Within seconds, Kell had returned with a lance and a shield. He handed both up to Orion and then took a step back, panic wrinkling his freckled, youthful features as the screams of the dying and wounded drew closer from the other side of the barricade. Orion looked down at him as he buckled his shield to his arm.

"Arm yourself, boy!" he growled. "Remember everything I have taught you! Give them hell!"

The youth nodded mutely, tears forming in his eyes. Orion stopped. The world seemed to pause for the briefest of moments. He stared down at the boy who had faithfully served him for two years, always with the greatest of effort and always without a single complaint. Kell was not a born fighter. He did not stand a chance. Orion saw something of himself in the frail youth who stood loyally by his side, shaking in the terror of the inevitable. Orion cursed himself for his failure. He had been a poor master and mentor. He had never taken the time to talk to Kell, to get to know him, to get the best out of him and bring him on as a potential knight. It was too late for all of that now. Orion felt his head loll forward in shame at his failure.

"This will be over soon," he forced a smile for the young squire. "You will either live through it or you will be with the Elohi in the afterlife. Either way, you will be fine."

"Y... yes, sir," Kell nodded.

His shaking hand drew the short sword from his belt and immediately dropped it. Orion's mind was instantly cast back over a decade, to the moment he dropped his sword on the mountainside when his uncle needed his help.

"Kell!" he shouted down to the boy as he scrabbled in the dirt for his weapon.

The squire stood up again with his sword, looking timidly up at his master.

"I am so proud of the man you have become," Orion said sincerely, "and I am so, so sorry I have let you down. Please forgive me."

Murmuring a prayer for Kell, Orion spurred his horse forward to the edge of the barricade as the quartermaster's men dragged a wagon around to create an opening. Glancing over his shoulders, Orion confirmed that the other knights were ready. He held his lance high to attract their attention.

"On me," he yelled above the rising din of battle, "one rank!"

The cavalrymen quickly cantered through the opening in the wagon barricade and formed up in the open ground beyond. To the north, Orion saw heavily armored riders atop black warhorses with eyes of burning red; the Abyssal horsemen smashed their way through the already battered ranks of men-at-arms, trampling men underfoot and cutting them down as they came. Within seconds, they were at the defensive barrier in the center of the camp, hacking at the wall of wagons. To the east, ranks of lower Abyssals charged across from the lip of the hill, all signs of the mercenaries who had faced them now gone. To the south, of the twenty paladins Orion had left with Tancred, perhaps half a dozen remained, surrounded on all sides by some thirty Abyssal guards who fought atop a mountain of dead from both sides.

Orion lowered his lance.

"Charge!"

Digging his spurs into the flanks of his warhorse, the huge animal accelerated into a full gallop beneath him for what Orion realized would be his final charge. The thudding of hooves echoed to either side from his comrades as the line of knights hurtled toward the Abyssal guards hacking and slashing at their beleaguered brethren on the slopes ahead. Smiling grimly as he aimed the tip of his lance at the back of one of the creatures, Orion tensed his muscles and waited for the impact. His lance pierced the breastplate of the infernal creature, plunging through its torso and snapping a moment after the impact.

Spurring his steed over the top of the dead demon, Orion threw the haft of the lance aside and unsheathed his sword, leaning over in his saddle to hack at the back of a second Abyssal, killing it with two heavy blows before his horse was surrounded with a sea of snarling red skinned warriors slicing and slashing up at him. One of the paladins to his left was slain in his saddle with a sword strike to the gut; to his right, a second knight was dragged to the ground and butchered in the dirt by a chittering horde of devils. Deflecting a succession of blows with his shield, Orion twisted in his saddle and struck down another of the demons before clawed hands clutched at his legs and he was dragged from his own saddle into the dirt and the dead.

Yelling for all he was worth, Orion hauled himself back up to his feet and swung a series of rapid, heavy attacks at perhaps four of the demons who surrounded him, forcing them to back away. Screaming in rage, Orion flung his shield at the closest of the Abyssals to allow him to wrap both hands around the hilt of his greatsword.

"Come on!" he screamed. "Come on, you bastards! Face me, you cowards!"

With an inhuman shriek, the closest of the demons hurtled forward to attack, its warhammer held high. Orion darted forward and slammed a clenched fist into the creature's face, smashing its nose and sending it staggering back, stunned. Orion dug his sword into the ground next to him and towered over the demon, grabbing it tightly by the neck and one leg before lifting the creature high over his head.

With a bellow of rage, Orion brought the struggling Abyssal guard down with all his might, slamming his armored knee up into the creature's back to break its spine. The crippled devil sagged to the ground, giving Orion just enough time to raise his metal clad foot and plunge it down to smash the Abyssal's skull. Recovering his sword, Orion looked up at the loose circle of demons surrounding him. Words escaping him, Orion could only let out a thunderous roar of unadulterated aggression before fixing his opponents with a determined grin of clenched teeth as they rushed to attack him where he stood.

*****

His feet bumping over corpses as he was dragged slowly by the armpits, Tancred looked hazily up at the moonlit sky as a hellish flock of winged demons swooped down above him, their blue-gray skin illuminated by the blazing torches below as they fell. Looking frantically around him, the pain in his wounded neck flaring up to overpower the detached feeling of numbness, Tancred let out a sigh of relief as he saw his shaking, blood drenched fingers still clung to the handle of his sword. He tried to lift his arm as he was dragged, desperately willing his body to twist and turn to face whatever was hauling him away, but his limbs stubbornly refused to heed his commands.

The night grew lighter, flickering sporadically around him in shades of orange and yellow as lines of lit torches swam passed him. Still refusing to yield, Tancred tried in vain once more to twist around to face the creature dragging him off to his doom. It was then that he saw two overturned wooden wagons drift slowly past, and it occurred to him that he was back in the center of the encampment - he was not being dragged off by the Abyssals; he was being carried to safety.

Tancred was laid down and his rescuer moved around to lean over him. He looked up and saw Jeneveve's face fill his vision – crimson blood leaked down to cover one side of her face from a vicious wound on her crown. He could tell by her expression that she was shouting at him, but it had taken this long to realize that his hearing had been replaced by an incessant, high pitched whine. He remembered nothing before the initial charge against the attacking Abyssals.

The wizened lines of Brother Paladin Xavier appeared next to Jeneveve. The veteran paladin reached down toward Tancred with hands awash with the pale, blue light of spiritual sorcery. The powers of divinity magic flowed from Xavier to Tancred, and within seconds, his hearing faded back to normality and the dull aching across his entire body quickly transformed into sharp pains, causing him to cry out in shock.

"Lord Paladin!" Jeneveve shouted over the chaotic clash of battle around them. "Can you hear me?"

"Get me up!" Tancred spat, the bitter taste of blood in his mouth. "Help me back up!"

"Wait there, Lord Paladin!" Xavier said, the silver haired knight cautiously checking around them for the next attack. "You are badly wounded!"

"To blazes with that!" Tancred spat out a mouthful of blood and forced himself up onto one knee, his head swimming unsteadily as soon as he did so. "We need to get back to the fight!"

Gritting his teeth as a sharp pain flared up in his ribs, Tancred staggered unsteadily back to his feet. Looking around him, he quickly ascertained that he was one of only six paladins who had reached the relative safety of the inner defenses. Perhaps ten supplymen cowered in the very center with a similar number of squires, along with a dozen warhorses. Only Hugh, Platus, and Trennio looked capable of carrying out any sort of attack. There was no sign of any of the legion men-at-arms or the mercenaries.

"Is this it?" Tancred managed weakly, coughing up another mouthful of blood.

There was no answer. His paladins looked out to the south. Tancred staggered over to the wagons for support, and his eyes instantly focused on the object of the other paladins' attention.

The battlefield on the southern slope was a carpet of red; maimed demons lay dead by the score, punctuated occasionally by the shining silver armor and noble blue surcoats of their paladin vanquishers. Tancred let out a gasp of despair as he saw at least a dozen of his knights torn to shreds amidst the hideous bodies of the Abyssals they had slain.

But the fight still raged. A swarm of lower Abyssals were crowded in a circle around a lone survivor, a single paladin who still fought on. His face pale from loss of blood, his blue surcoat washed red in the blood of his foes, Orion towered over the devils rushing at him, still slicing and slashing at the endless horde of evil. Five of the fanged creatures dived on him simultaneously, and Orion was momentarily lost under the pulsating sea of demons before he threw them off him with a roar, his sword arcing down to decapitate one of the Abyssal guards before he stepped forward and pierced the gut of a second opponent.

"Come on!" Tancred hissed hoarsely. "We have to help him!"

Tancred limped a step forward before Jeneveve's hand shot out to stop him.

"We can't save him!" she urged. "He saved *us!* That is how we were able to escape! If we go back for him now, then it was all for naught!"

Three of the winged, blue skinned demons soared down from the skies toward the lone paladin. Gargoyles – hideous, shrieking creatures with feminine bodies, bat-like wings, and curved horns crowning a pair of glowing red eyes – flapped and fluttered around Orion, tearing at his face with their talons. Orion swept his sword out at one and cleaved it in half at the waist; its hips and legs dropped to the ground while the body continued to flap in frantic agony for a moment before falling.

A second strike clipped the wing of another demon, felling it, while the third Abyssal backed off in terror. Orion reached down and grabbed the she-demon by the neck, lifting it up off its feet, and then grabbing the maimed wing with his other hand, tearing it clean off the howling demon. The gargoyle dropped to the ground and Orion brought his sword down on top of its head, cleaving straight through the Abyssal until his sword became lodged in its hipbone. He planted a foot on the gargoyle's torso and wrenched his sword clear just in time to face the next wave of assaulting demons. Orion cut down the first foe to reach him but then disappeared beneath a red wave of lower Abyssals. This time he did not reappear.

Tancred let out a weak cry of despair, but his attention was dragged around to the north as eight legion men-at-arms sprinted frantically for the wagon barrier, a line of two dozen Abyssals surging forward at their heels. The first soldier was hacked down from behind, reaching out desperately to his comrades as he was dragged back into the jeering, chittering crowd of scarlet demons. The wailing man was held high above their heads and then torn in half before the Abyssals fell on the parts of his body, feasting on his bloodied flesh.

The first three men-at-arms reached the wagons and hauled themselves over. Two of the squires bravely ran over to assist the remaining men. Tancred recognized the bulky frame of Captain Georgis at the rear of the group of men. Inexplicably, he stopped in place and turned back to face the devils.

"Captain!" the closest of his men screamed. "Captain! What are you doing?"

"She needs help!" Georgis cried. "Quickly! Get back here!"

"No!" Xavier yelled. "It is a deception! Quickly, drag him to safety!"

Tancred looked across to the front rank of the advancing demons. Backing away, a terrified look across her face, was a beautiful young peasant woman, her blonde hair braided and her hands held up pathetically as if to keep the demons at bay. But for Tancred, trained and skilled in the powers of divinity magic, he could see straight through the lie. Behind the faded falsity of the pretty peasant girl was a tall, seductively feminine demon with a pointed tail flickering behind her, along with folded wings and fanged teeth.

Georgis never heard the shouts behind him. Bravely ignoring the danger and the wounds he had already suffered, he reached the apparition of the peasant girl and held out a hand for her. She looked up at him, eternal gratitude lighting up her emerald green eyes before the facade faded to nothing, and the temptress that stood in her place grabbed him with her clawed hands to pull him into a vicious embrace, sinking her teeth into his throat while puncturing his gut with her tail. Blood flowing from his wounds, Georgis staggered back from the temptress as she laughed hysterically at his expression of utter bewilderment. Georgis dropped to his knees and was almost instantly dragged into the baying mob of Abyssals, suffering the same fate as the last of his soldiers to fall as his limbs were wrenched out of their sockets.

Then, just as quickly as the battle had started, the howls and cries of the Abyssal horde faded to nothing. Showing something akin to discipline, the ragged mob of hellish devils stood still in their ranks, surrounding the wagon barricade in silence. The crackle of flames and the moaning of the dying was all that broke the silence. From the north, the crowd of demons silently parted to allow a single figure to walk forward toward the barricade.

A tall, broad shouldered warrior clad in dull, iron gray plates walked boldly out to the front of the Abyssal mob. His fingers, armored with spike-backed plates of steel, reached up to remove his helmet. The man, for he certainly appeared to be human, was middle-aged with gray flecks in his short, dark hair, and red rings rimming his dark eyes. A darkness emanated from the warrior; nothing like the evil that flowed from the Abyssal horde, but a distinct and detectable darkness nonetheless. Although Tancred had never laid eyes on him before, he knew the warrior must logically be the man he was looking for.

"You have come all the way out here to find me," Dionne called out to the wounded warriors cowering behind the barricade, "well, here I am. You killed men who stood by my side for over a decade. I am here to collect your debt."

"Traitor!" Xavier yelled back over the barricade.

Dionne did not respond to the challenge, but merely kept his glowering eyes fixed ahead on the barricade. Tancred heard a commotion behind him and turned to see Platus and Trennio engaged in a hushed debate while the squires continued to buckle armored barding onto the remaining warhorses. His eyes closed, Hugh nodded slowly a few times before walking out to the edge of the barricade.

"You have betrayed all of Basilea," he said coldly to the armored man stood before the horde of Abyssals. "Whatever your perceived motivation, whatever excuses you have told yourself, whatever lies you use to convince those around you, you are nothing more than a coward, a liar, and a traitor. And while I have failed to stop you, others will not. You will fall."

Trennio grabbed Tancred by the elbow.

"Get on your horse and get the Dictator-Prefect to safety!" he hissed under his breath.

Tancred turned to question the aide, but the blur of the events of the next few seconds caught him off guard.

"We will all fall, one way or another," Dionne replied to Hugh, "but tonight is your turn. Come out and face it with some courage."

Their yells combined, Platus and Trennio sprinted up to the barrier, vaulted over, and swung their swords down to attack Dionne in the open ground in front of his army of demons.

"No!" Hugh yelled, unsheathing his own sword. "Stop!"

Xavier grabbed the Dictator-Prefect by the arms and dragged him away. Jeneveve was already on her warhorse, a terrified squire sat behind her and clutching desperately to her waist. Supplymen and squires hauled themselves up onto horses as Trennio's first attack met Dionne's guard with a dull clang. Platus was quick to step up with an expertly timed sword thrust toward Dionne's neck. This too was batted away with ease by their demonic adversary. Fighting to ignore the cramp and dizziness from loss of blood, Tancred found Desiree and struggled up into the saddle. He spent the extra few seconds in tying the reins of his second horse, Estree, to his saddle.

Ahead of him, Dionne stood his ground with flawless precision, changing stance and guard with the speed normally associated with a short sword rather than the heavy longsword he carried. His face set in determination, almost appearing bored and unchallenged, he fended off the flurry of lightning fast and expertly coordinated attacks conducted by Trennio and Platus. Hugh was dragged up into the saddle of his horse under Xavier's supervision. Every last survivor was saddled and ready. All except for the Dictator-Prefect's two valiant aides.

"Now!" Jeneveve shouted. "Go!"

The stampede of hooves echoed across the top of the hill as the armored warhorses charged to the east, barging their way through the wagon barricade. Tancred looked over his shoulder and saw Dionne's eyes widen in surprise. He batted aside an attack from Trennio and then plunged his sword straight through the man's belly, lifting the screaming swordsman bodily off the ground before throwing him down and slicing off his head. With a cry of rage, Platus ran forward to avenge his friend; Dionne neatly side stepped the attack and slashed down into Platus' back as he ran past, cutting him open and sending him skidding to the ground.

The galloping group of warhorses battered their way through the ranks of lower Abyssals on the southern slope of the plateau – Tancred's last view of the torch lit plateau peak was Dionne stepping over to drive his sword through Platus' chest as he lay helplessly at his feet. Behind them, on the southern slope where Tancred had led his charge, a momentary flash of purest white lit the sky, its warmth washing over him with a welcome feeling of optimism and tranquility before it was gone.

Looking ahead, Tancred wearily dug his spurs into Desiree's side and urged every last measure of speed he could out of his loyal steed, driving ahead of the other riders as they escaped into the night. Behind them, a dozen armored Abyssal warriors atop flame-eyed warhorses thundered after them. Panicked cries were exchanged from the squires, supplymen, and men-at-arms at the sight of their pursuers.

"Keep going!" Tancred urged. "Do not look back! Keep going!"

The horses continued down the slope and into a flat plain of open ground leading toward the coast. Behind them, the Abyssal cavalry continued the chase, failing to close the gap but never easing off the hunt. For what seemed like hours, the chase continued, the thunder of hooves echoing across the plains, woods, and hills into the early morning hours.

By the time the sun rose, Tancred realized that they had escaped; but looking around him, only a handful of the very last survivors remained with him.

Fourteen

The agonized screaming from her dreams merged seamlessly into consciousness as Constance wearily opened her eyes. The morning sky above her was blood red, broken only by wispy clouds hued in pink by the sunrise. Her temples throbbing in pain, she forced herself to sit up to take in her surroundings. The broken walls of a small farm building surrounded her, the wooden beams of its roof having long collapsed to leave an unobstructed view of the sky up above. Sitting despondently against one of the walls were Jaque and Hayden, both battered, bloodied, and weary. Chains bound their wrists and ankles, leaving dirty bloodstains where they broke the skin. Constance looked down to find herself similarly bound.

An ear piercing, high-pitched scream from somewhere outside the farm building opened her eyes wide in terror. She looked across at her two comrades, but neither reacted.

"Wh… where are we?" she whispered. "What happened?"

"We lost," Hayden replied dejectedly, "they brought the prisoners here. We're all that is left."

"Wulf and Carmen were with us to begin with," Jaque added, his voice choked, "they took Carmen out first. Then they took Wulf with one of the legion men and a squire. That's who you can hear now. We're next."

"Then we need to escape," Constance urged her two friends. "Come on! We need to find a way out of these chains!"

"And then what?" Jaque finally turned to fix his red-rimmed eyes on her. "This hut is surrounded by a hundred of those demons! There is no escape!"

"Then we die fighting!" Constance snarled, frantically looking around for something she could use to try to force open her restraints. "Don't give up now!"

Struggling up to her feet, Constance let out a cry as pain flared up in her midriff, and sagged back to her knees. Looking down, she saw crimson leaking through her garments, and memories of being cut down by the vicious, serrated blade of an Abyssal flooded back to her. It made no difference. She opened her mouth to urge Hayden and Jaque into action, but she saw both of them looking over her shoulder. She turned and saw a figure of nightmare standing at the doorway of the hut, smiling down at her.

The woman, if the demon could be called a woman, had the same vivid red skin as the rest of her devilish kin, but her black, cruel eyes shone with a deep and malicious intelligence. She wore scant scraps of spiked leather, leaving most of her slender form exposed as if in an attempt to allure. Black-skinned wings emerged from her back and a long, arrow headed tail flickered from the base of her spine. Four lower Abyssals flanked her, waiting deferentially a step behind her.

"What a speech," the hellish woman hissed as she leered down at Constance. "Let us hope that you retain some of that spirit for your demise! I'm getting tired of the wailing and pleading from your friends I am killing."

Constance met the demon's stare and spat out a brief challenge using some choice language.

"Good!" the demon grinned. "That is exactly what I'm looking for! Come on, bring them out!"

The muscular lower Abyssals stomped forward, one grabbing Constance by her hair and dragging her painfully out of the building before throwing her down on her knees. The building stood alone atop a small hill, looking down at an expanse of farmland in every direction. All around were groups of the seemingly endless scarlet skinned demons, over a hundred of the monstrosities. Some fought each other viciously in small groups, others argued over hunks of meat that could have been farm animals, villagers, or even the dead from the previous night's battle.

Prostrate on the ground in front of her was Wulf, the lower half of his body burnt back to bare, charred bone, his face twisted in utter agony from the moment of his death. Ignoring the pain from her wounds, Constance drew herself back to her feet and attempted to rush at the demon woman. She had taken only a single step when her Abyssal guard clamped a clawed hand around her throat and slammed a fist into her face, knocking her back to the ground and leaving her to spit out blood and a broken tooth. She looked across at Wulf's body again, her fists clenched in anger.

Hayden was thrown down beside her. The big man waited for a moment and then reached across to hold her hand tightly.

"I wish I'd met your father," he whispered to her. "I'd bet he'd be proud of you now."

The comment diffused her anger, the thought of her father and the affection of her old friend replacing her rage with a hollow sense of loss and hopelessness. Fighting to rise above it, she forced a smile for Hayden.

"He would have liked you," she said quietly.

Constance struggled up to her feet again. Two of the lower Abyssals dragged Jaque out toward the leather-clad demon. Constance watched in tormented agony as her friend broke down in tears, sobbing and wailing as he awaited his fate.

"See it through, Jaque!" Constance urged, hobbling after him. "Let them do their worst, and then the three of us will be together in paradise, with the Elohi!"

Her comment resulted in a hideous, unearthly laugh from the leader of the demons. It paced over to Constance and towered over her.

"What folly!" The devil smirked, tracing a finger across Constance's cheek.

"You cannot believe that, surely? You're mercenaries! You kill indiscriminately for money! No scruples, no morals, nothing! You take anybody's coins to kill anyone! Even by your own twisted morality, the three of you are nothing short of utter villains!"

"No!" Jaque cried, collapsing to his knees. "No! Tell her she is wrong!"

"You ignore this piece of shit, Jaque!" Constance growled. "We did the right thing! Just a few moments of pain and then heaven awaits!"

The hideous, shrieking laughter came again. The devilish woman paced back to Jaque and stroked his hair softly.

"This one is already broken! I think I'll have more fun torturing your soul than your body! But let me leave you in no doubt, you are going to the fires of the Abyss! You are a murdering mercenary who cast all of your society's rules aside for money, and now I own you! You are going to burn! An eternity of slow, agonizing pain as you die a thousand times over! You, all of you, your souls are going to burn in the pit! And I'll be there to stoke the fires!"

Tears welled in Constance's eyes as Jaque collapsed to the ground, his body convulsing in tears. She tried to stagger over to him again but was held in place by one of her guards.

The sudden sound of bounding hooves drummed up the side of the hill, and Constance turned to see an armored rider gallop across to the ruined farm building atop a blazing eyed horse clad in rusted barding. The rider stopped by the demonic guards and dismounted. His plate armor was tinged a dark blue-black and adorned with studs across the tall pauldrons. She recognized him instantly, despite his aged face and red eyes.

"What is going on here?" Dionne demanded as he paced over.

"This is how I deal with prisoners," the demonic woman replied evenly.

Dionne smashed the back of an armored hand across her face, causing her to yelp in delight.

"I gave orders to have the prisoners executed," Dionne snarled, "quickly and cleanly. They fought well. They deserve that much. Now stop this nonsense and carry out my orders!"

"Captain Dionne!" Constance yelled.

Dionne's head whipped around to stare at her. His eyes moved across to the other survivors.

"Constance? Hayden? Jaque? Why are you here?"

"You remember us?" Constance stammered.

"I would never forget the name of any soldier who served me," Dionne said as he walked over to her, "but why are you here? Why are you opposing me?"

"We… had to bring you in, sir," Hayden managed. "The Duma ordered it."

"The Duma?" Dionne spat. "Come, old friend! You are branded as a criminal! You oppose me to defend the ideals of such a corrupt and rotten institution?"

"But you… you ride with demons of the Abyss!" Hayden exclaimed.

Dionne's face fell for a moment and then twisted in anger.

"I was driven to this! This isn't what I wanted! But if this is what I must do to end the corruption of the Hegemon, then it is a small sacrifice to make!"

"It's your soul, sir!" Constance pleaded. "That is no small price! Is there no other way?"

The aging warrior's face softened once more. He turned to face the hellish torturer.

"Am'Bira, go," he ordered, "leave us."

The demonic woman bowed her head in obedience and walked away. Dionne turned back to Constance.

"I respect you as a soldier, so please do not judge me for treating you differently, but I am too old fashioned to allow a helpless woman to be killed at my hands," Dionne said quietly before turning to the closest of the lower Abyssals. "Release her."

The horned demon stared at Dionne incredulously, a low growl of confusion questioning the command. In one smooth and accurate motion, Dionne unsheathed his sword and sliced the Abyssal's head off. The monster remained upright for a moment, blood fountaining from its neck stump before it crumpled to one side. Dionne turned to the remaining three Abyssals.

"When I give an order, you carry it out!" he bellowed. "Instantly, and without question!"

A second demon seized the initiative and dashed forward to remove the restraints from Constance's wrists and ankles.

"Now go," Dionne said as he turned away. "I'll end the suffering for your friends quickly and painlessly."

"No, stop!" Constance pleaded. "Look at them both! They were your soldiers! They deserve better than this! Hayden will be too old to fight any season now, let him go home to his daughter! And look at what your creatures have done to Jaque! He's done! Let him go! If you must strike somebody down to prove something to your monsters, then exchange me for the two of them! Let them go and I'll stay!"

Hayden cried out a protest but was silenced as Dionne held up one hand. He looked into Constance's eyes and smiled sadly.

"If Basilea were run by the likes of you, Constance, then none of this would ever have to happen," he said despondently.

He nodded to two of the Abyssals who instantly carried out his orders, freeing Hayden and Jaque.

"Go," he said, "all of you. This land will fall. Head west, go to the Kingdoms. You will be safe there. But never return to Basilea. We will take this entire, rotten nation. And if you come back, I will kill you."

Constance opened her mouth to plead again with Dionne, to ask him to turn his back on all of it and come with them, but Jaque collapsed into her arms, still sobbing. She clutched her friend close to her, taking a moment to settle him until the three of them walked slowly and painfully away from the hilltop, through the terrifying spectacle of a hundred demons watching them in silence as they left.

The sun continued to rise and replace the red of the skies with a hazy blue as they stumbled on in silence for hours, clinging desperately to each other as they wearily paced through fields, forests, and streams. Eventually Hayden called a stop.

"This is where it ends for me," the tall man said with a sad smile.

"What do you mean?" Constance coughed, one hand pressed against the bleeding wound at her side. "We're away from them now! We just need to find somewhere to rest and recover, and then…"

"And then what?" Hayden interrupted. "You said it yourself, I'm too old for this now. I'm not carrying on anymore. I'm going to find my daughter. I'm going to settle down near her, and I'm going to see out the rest of my days playing a lute in a tavern. I'm done with this, Constance. I should have died back there, but the devil himself gave me one last chance to spend my days with my daughter. I'm done soldiering."

Jaque finally spoke.

"When this is over, we will come and find you," he muttered. "Enjoy your retirement, Hayden. The Shining Ones know, you deserve it more than anybody."

Hayden accepted Jaque's outstretched hand and shook it firmly, forcing a slight smile. Constance stepped forward to embrace him.

"Thank you, Hayden," she said softly, "for everything. Thank you so much."

The tall man kissed the top of her head and walked slowly off toward the south. Constance watched him until his familiar, stooped form disappeared into the trees ahead. She closed her eyes, exhausted and dismayed with the horrific turn of events that had brought her to stand with only one friend by her side, still bleeding from her wounds, and lost in the wilderness of a nation that abandoned her long ago. But Dionne had not abandoned them. Hayden now traveled off to what she hoped would be a happy retirement, near his daughter and with his music, safe away from the fields of battle. And it was Dionne that gave him that opportunity. It was Dionne that had let them all live in the face of the hellish monstrosities that would have been their agonizing demise. Constance opened her eyes again and turned to face Jaque.

"I'm going back," she said apologetically.

"What?"

"That is our captain back there, alone with those creatures. I'm going back for him."

"Constance! That is not our captain! That is not the same man who led us at Farr Ridge and across the Estraitees River! Captain Dionne is dead! That… thing back there is just another demon!"

"No," Constance shook her head, "he let us go, Jaque! He saved us! He is still in there, and if there is any chance that I can save him, I have to try!"

"Constance, no!" Jaque yelled, clamping his hands against her shoulders

163

and looking her in the eyes. "You've always been the clever one! I've always trusted you and I've always followed you, you're my leader and you're my captain now! And my friend! Please, just once, listen to me! This is a bad idea, a huge mistake! Dionne is no more, there is just an Abyssal monster waiting back there! Don't go!"

"I have to," Constance whispered, "I can't abandon him. Everybody else has."

"If you go, I can't go with you," Jaque said desperately. "I can't go back."

Constance gently took his hands from her shoulders, gave them a reassuring squeeze, and took a step back away from him.

"I know, Jaque," she forced a weary smile. "I know. I never would have asked you to. Get yourself home. Get yourself safe."

Leaving her friend looking hopelessly lost, confused, and despairing, Constance took a few further steps back away from him before turning around to head back to the north.

*****

Dawn brought with it a welcome but ominous sky of blood red, deteriorating by midmorning to a leaden gray, heavy with rainclouds. The rumble of thunder could be heard to the east as the line of weary horses and their riders arrived at a small logging village somewhere southeast of the Tarkis Mountains. The entire village was deserted, save for a few small farm animals that paced and clucked around the village grounds, oblivious to the disaster unfolding around them.

Tancred led the exhausted procession to the village's tavern, where he slowly and painfully dismounted before limping over toward the door. A squire immediately dashed across to take his two horses away.

"As soon as you are done with them, get in the tavern," he ordered the boy. "We all stay together from now on."

The tavern door was locked shut. Wincing in pain with each step, Tancred limped around the back to look for another entrance, but within only a few paces, one of the men-at-arms had kicked the door open to break the lock. Hugh led the survivors inside where the handful of soldiers and supplymen quickly set about lighting candles and searching the building for food and drink. The tavern looked to Tancred like any other, with a long bar separating a seating area from a small kitchen, and stairs leading up to rooms and down to a wine cellar. Tancred sank down into a bench seat in the far corner away from the door where within moments one of the men-at-arms came across to re-bandage his wounds.

The Dictator-Prefect slumped down alone at the far side of the room, holding a hand up to refuse any assistance from another of the men-at-arms. Tancred sat in silence and watched the nobleman for a few moments. Hugh stared dejectedly at the rough, wood paneled floor, his eyes occasionally flickering as if he were replaying conversations in his mind. Tancred waited until the soldier had finished bandaging the wounds across his gut and on his thigh, mumbled a thank you, and then limped over to Hugh.

"What now?" he asked.

The Dictator-Prefect stared silently at the floor.

"Dictator-Prefect?" Tancred asked.

"I don't know!" the older man snapped. "Do what you want."

Tancred suppressed a yawn and turned to face the other survivors. Bottles of wine had been recovered from the cellar, and loaves of bread and cheese were being handed out from the kitchen. He counted five paladins including himself, five legion men-at-arms, seven squires, three supplymen, and the Dictator-Prefect who had survived the previous night's ordeal. Twenty-one survivors from a force that had left the City of the Golden Horn with some one hundred and fifty.

"Listen to me, all of you," Tancred announced, turning all heads to regard him. "We will stop here for rest and shelter, but not for long. Those demons will no doubt be heading south toward the larger settlements, and we lie in their path. Once we are rested, we must keep moving."

"Where to, my lord?" one of the legion men asked. "What is our plan now?"

"I sent word to the Duma," Hugh said quietly from his dark corner of the room. "A relief force will be marching north. We can join up with them. They will no doubt take the main coastal road."

"Do we know that for certain?" Jeneveve demanded, her normally placid tone replaced with hostility. "Have you had any confirmation that the message ever reached the Duma? Or that a decision has even been made to send another force up here?"

"What would you rather we do?" Hugh murmured. "Just give up? We keep going. Just as Tancred says."

"Twenty-one of us and twelve horses," Jeneveve continued, "how long do you think…"

"We keep going!" Tancred snapped. "As the Dictator-Prefect has decreed! Nobody said it will be easy, but we have things a lot better than our comrades we left behind!"

Jeneveve stood, her face thunderous with anger, and walked over to the main door to head back outside where a light rainfall announced the onset of worse weather to come. Tancred limped over to the five legion men.

"Go and see if there are any beds upstairs. Go and get some rest. I shall take the first watch."

*****

Nightmare images slowly faded away; an endless sea of devils, cascading down in the night to claw, hack, bite, and maim. Orion sat up in the bed, his heart pounding as he looked frantically around to ascertain where he was and how he had ended up there. Rain pounded against a window to his left, thunder rumbled outside the building, and a flash of lightning illuminated an otherwise black, night sky. He lay in a narrow, simple bed in a small room with a single door, furnished only with a wardrobe, a cracked mirror, and a washbasin. He felt suddenly calm, safe, even loved and cherished. A warm wave of affection washed over him, tangible enough for him to realize that he was in the presence of something good, something pure. Something completely opposite to the darkness he felt when fighting for his life against the Abyssal horde. It was then that he realized there was a chair to his left, in a dark corner of the room, and the chair was occupied.

"Lie down and rest," a hushed, female voice said softly, the tone unearthly in its kindness and care. "You must recover."

Orion turned to face the woman and briefly saw a tall figure, taller even than himself, clothed in a white hood and cloak.

"Avert your eyes," the woman commanded, "for your own good."

Orion obeyed, swinging his legs around to sit on the edge of the bed with his back to the woman. It quickly made sense. His last memories were of impending death, knocked to the ground by countless demons that hacked and clawed at him, breaking his body and overriding his senses with pain as his life ebbed away. Yet now he found himself alive, rescued, in the presence of something holy and divine – a woman of inhuman grace who thought it best for him not to gaze upon her.

"You are an Elohi," Orion said quietly, "an angel of the Shining Ones."

"Yes," the angelic woman replied simply.

"You rescued me," Orion continued.

"That is correct."

"Thank you," Orion said humbly, "I... do not see why I am worthy of such treatment. I have seen your brethren on the battlefield before from afar, but I have never had the honor of talking to an Elohi."

"It is rare," the angel agreed, her voice soft and agreeable in every way, "but the Wicked Ones have intruded the sacred earth of the Shining Ones' chosen people. It was time to act."

"Then why did you not help us in battle?" Orion said, fighting the temptation to turn to look at the Elohi. "I do not wish to sound confrontational, but why did you not help us if it is the time to act?"

"If only it were so simple," Orion detected something akin to a slight laugh in the woman's voice, a laugh that was sympathetic rather than abrasive or patronizing, "but for the same reasons that the Wicked Ones cannot send their demons to the mortal world without limitation, we too are limited in our ability to intervene. Saving you was the best I could do."

"How were you able to do that?"

"I flew down and picked you up," the Elohi replied simply. "I healed many of your wounds and I brought you here. No, do not turn around, Orion."

Orion stopped himself from turning to face the Elohi. He had heard that to make eye contact with one of the angelic host was to risk instantly and obsessively falling in love, to the cost of all else.

"Thank you," Orion managed again, staring at the simple rug covering the floorboards at his feet.

"I must leave soon," the angel continued. "You are safe, but even with my powers, your wounds will require more time to heal."

"But… what now?" Orion asked. "Everybody is dead! Demons invade Basilea! What now?"

"All is far from lost," the Elohi said with a tone emanating an inspirational determination. "There is… one of our kind. She will know what to do. And you must protect her. That is why I chose to save you."

"Because I was the best warrior?"

The comment met silence. Orion felt a wave of disappointment hit him, wounding him to the core of his very soul. He felt tears well in his eyes for causing such disappointment and found himself uncontrollably mumbling apologies.

"Jahus worries about you," the Elohi finally said.

Orion's eyes opened wide in surprise.

"Uncle Jahus? He is watching me?"

"It is not like that," the angel explained, "it is… better than that. To try to explain it to you would not fit in with mortal comprehension. It is not so linear. To understand paradise is to see it, and that time will come for you. But not now."

"But… Uncle Jahus… Why does he worry?"

"He feels you have strayed from what he taught you. With each passing season you stray further still."

"How? I let him down on that mountain! I let him die! Since that day, I have never let anybody down on the field of battle, I have never made a mistake that has caused comrades to lose their lives! I have stood my ground and fought hard!"

"You have spent every waking hour perfecting your swordsmanship to the cost of all else. To the cost of friendship, spirituality, worship, devotion to the Shining Ones. You have challenged every warrior you have met to further your own feeling of self-worth. You hide behind a facade of dishonesty by telling yourself that it is for your comrades on the field of battle. But it is not."

Orion felt the tears flow freely as he heard the disappointment in the Elohi's softly spoken words.

"Your uncle taught you to be a good man, to choose the hard road if it helps others. Instead, you make your road easier with constant training for war, and then you choose a road filled with violence. Even if you do not need to. When you realized that I was an Elohi, you even considered challenging me to fight. Only for a moment, but I felt it."

Orion leaned forward and planted his face in his hands, fighting to control his breathing as the tears continued to flow. He felt the depth of the angel's words penetrate his core, find the root of his intentions and his deepest motivations. He saw himself in a new light, as if darkness had been lifted from all around him. He did not like what he saw.

"I am sorry," he whispered, "I am so sorry. Tell my uncle that I am sorry I let him down."

He felt a soft hand rest carefully on his shoulder, the warmth of the angel's touch immediately filling him with hope.

"Your uncle loves you," she said kindly, "I have faith that I made a wise choice in you."

With those words, the presence was gone. Orion remained alone, analyzing his words, deeds, thoughts, and very core deeper than he had ever done before. Minutes became hours as the night drew on, lightning continuing to flash in the window behind him. The loss of the Elohi's very presence left him feeling hollow and saddened, but the warmth of her touch and the inspiration of her final, simple words left him renewed and reinvigorated. Orion thought hard on how to change for the better.

*****

The flow of blood from Constance's injured abdomen had at least stemmed by the time she found her way back to the ruined farmhouse that had been her prison the night before. In the long shadows of the cool evening, she had found the bodies of the unfortunate souls tortured by the Abyssals, but no evidence of the demons themselves. She spent a pair of hours using a sharp rock to dig a shallow grave before dragging the bodies in and burying them, muttering a few brief prayers for the departed before spending the night huddled in the corner of the ruined farm building. The next morning, she found an orchard and recovered some of her strength with consuming as many apples as she could manage, but of Dionne and his army there was no sign.

As she continued her search, Constance noticed that her ragged clothes were coming apart at the seams and streaked with blood and dirt. Her wounds showed signs of infection and her forehead felt as if it were ablaze. She found a small farmstead at midday, but it was abandoned. She helped herself to food and water and found a kitchen knife that was at least usable as a weapon. Constance continued her search throughout the afternoon, her hopes fading as she realized that without any idea of where the Abyssal horde had gone, she had no plan and no way ahead. Then, at sunset, the northern horizon glowed a gentle amber-red, as if the sun, too, was lost and had chosen to set on the wrong compass heading.

As Constance walked north, her suspicions were confirmed when it became evident that the flickering red was fire; columns of smoke wafted up into the air from atop a blazing forest that lay in a shallow valley between the gentle, rolling hills that lay inshore of the Basilean coastal road. The wind rushed over her shoulders as she approached the blazing forest, sucked into the fiery maelstrom to fuel the rising flames. Trudging wearily through waist-high grass down the gentle slope toward the forest, she saw the figures ahead before she heard them, their screams carried away from her in the winds rushing toward the heart of the fire.

Men ran in panic away from a small logging camp at the edge of the burning forest, frantically trying to claw their way to safety away from the fires behind them and the flame-skinned demons that chased them remorselessly down. The loggers, perhaps as many as twenty, were hunted down by packs of lower Abyssals, five or six of the demons for each helpless logger, and were then dragged screaming back to the encampment. Powerless to intervene, Constance felt her soul grow heavier as she lumbered hypnotically toward the scene of the carnage, watching helplessly as the men were brutally tortured to death under the cruel supervision of the same temptress that had threatened to kill Constance and her friends. Of Dionne, there was no sign.

Gritting her teeth as pain flared up in her abdomen, Constance bent over double to hide herself in the long grass as she skirted around the scene of the brutal massacre, heading to the west of the forest. Keeping her distance, she spent the better part of an hour threading her way through copses of trees to sneak slowly closer to the Abyssal force, her eyes scanning the groups of demons for her former captain as the natural light faded, leaving only the eerie illumination of the blazing forest to silhouette the monstrous Abyssals.

Then, walking away from the blazing trees alone to the north, she saw the familiar figure of the man she once followed into battle for the Hegemon. Dionne, still encased in his imposing suit of plate armor, walked slowly away from the blaze and the Abyssals scrabbling and squabbling over the corpses of the loggers. Careful to remain hidden from the demons ahead of her, Constance patiently bided her time and crept slowly closer to Dionne as he continued to distance himself from the massacre behind him. Seeing her opportunity, she rushed out to face him once he was clear away from his devilish horde.

"Captain!" she called out.

Dionne stopped and slowly turned his head to face her. His features were darkened to blackness, shadowed by the raging fire behind him, but his eyes glowed burning red within the darkness. Constance limped over toward him.

"Captain!" she said again. "I've come back to talk to you! To plead with you to see reason!"

"Constance," Dionne said quietly, but firmly, "I gave you your chance. I honored my commitment to you as one of my former soldiers. I told you what would happen if you came back."

"I know that," Constance said desperately, her arms held passively out to either side as she approached him, "but I owe you more than that. You are my captain, and I won't abandon you. I've come to ask you to walk away from this madness, before it is too late!"

Dionne took a pace to stand in front of her, slipping an armored hand over her shoulder to gently grab the back of her neck. He leaned over to look into her eyes. Constance watched helplessly, aware of the events unfolding but somehow unable to will her limbs into stopping them as Dionne took the kitchen knife tucked into her belt and drove it into her gut, to the hilt. The pain in her body did not compare to the pain of betrayal that wracked her soul as she looked into the cold,

Fifteen

The dark rainclouds had all but disappeared over the western horizon, forced up by the mountains and leaving a clear morning with a crisp, autumn wind blowing in from the coast. Aestelle poured the very last of her water into her parched throat before swearing violently. Her horse's hooves kicked lazily along the path north as the muddy ground soaked by the previous night's downpour already rapidly warmed and dried in the morning sun. Her task to send the Dictator-Prefect's message to the Duma had been simple enough, especially when utilizing the arcane powers of an old friend to convey the message directly to the city of the Golden Horn, saving her days of travel on the road. Now she was left on the road back north, searching for the Basilean force she had left so that she could renegotiate her pay. But first she needed fresh water, and that meant stopping at the next of the many small villages that punctuated the northern trade road.

Within an hour, she found a small collection of farmhouses a few yards off the track, on the horizon ahead of her. Three houses and a few small barns and stables; definitely enough to require its own source of water. Aestelle's mind drifted to what she might spend her money on once this debacle was over – perhaps some new clothes or armor, maybe even an excursion to the city of the Golden Horn itself, but in all likelihood she figured she would do what she normally did and spend most of it on a few weeks extravagant accommodation and fine wine. The thought of a long bath and a good bottle of white wine drew a long groan from her lips.

A high-pitched scream from the farm buildings ahead immediately brought Aestelle's attention back to the here and now. She looked up and saw a small girl, perhaps four or five years old, sprint clumsily out from the far side of the buildings and hurtle a few steps across the field beyond, tears streaming from her face. Aestelle's eyes widened in alarm as a red-skinned Abyssal warrior ran after her, grabbing her by one muscular arm and lifting her off the ground before stomping back over toward the houses, snarling viciously at the petrified girl.

Aestelle quickly dismounted her horse and ran through the long grass of the field to the east of the road, crouching low. In only a few paces, she had reached a vantage point where she could see the courtyard in between the three houses. Six lower Abyssals formed a semi-circle around the same number of farmers; a family consisting of a young man and woman, two small children, and, judging by their attire, two farm workers. The woman was shrieking and crying, held back and overpowered by one of the demons as their kin dragged the little girl back over to the courtyard. The man, presumably the husband and father, lay motionless in the courtyard in front of a large well.

Fighting to control her anger, Aestelle rapidly formulated a plan. She had faced worse odds. It was all about speed and surprise. She took her bow from her back as she stood, notched an arrow into place, and drew the string back whist she took aim. Letting the arrow fly, she allowed herself a grim smile as the projectile met its mark, impacting the side of the head of one of the demons. The creature staggered a few steps, looking around in almost comic confusion before dropping down dead. Angry screeches and growls were exchanged between the five remaining Abyssals as they drew their swords and axes, looking frantically around for the source of the attack.

"I'm up here, you bastards!" Aestelle shouted.

With a roar, the five devils hurtled toward her through the long grass. Aestelle lined up another shot, drew her bow, and planted an arrow straight into the chest of another. Throwing her bow aside, she walked out to meet the remaining four, drawing her greatsword from her back. One of the Abyssals was foolish enough to run out ahead of the others; Aestelle met the creature head on, swinging her greatsword up to rip open the monster's guts before slicing back down and opening a great, bloody welt on its back as its momentum carried it past her. The demon fell down dead. Aestelle brought her pistol up from her side and shot the next lower Abyssal in the face before throwing the smoking gun aside and returning both hands to the handle of her sword, standing in place to face the final two demons.

The two hulking Abyssals stood their ground, fixing their black eyes on her. The first of the two seemed to arrive at a sudden realization and turned to sprint away from her in terror. Realizing it stood alone, the second Abyssal also turned to run. Aestelle unsheathed one of the pair of throwing knives at the small of her back and flung it after the closer of the two fleeing demons, striking it squarely between its shoulder blades. The Abyssal let out a roar of pain and slowed to an awkward stumble, reaching pathetically behind it with both clawed hands to try to remove the offending blade. Aestelle caught up in a few paces and plunged the tip of her greatsword through the creature's back. The thin blade emerged from the demon's chest with a great spurt of blood, eliciting another howling roar before the creature fell silent and slipped off the sword to crumple motionless into the long grass. The final Abyssal ran across the courtyard in terror and disappeared into a wooded area behind the buildings.

Slinging her blood drenched blade up over both of her shoulders, Aestelle walked casually onto the courtyard, careful not to break into a run after the final demon, for fear of ruining appearances in front of the farmers she had just rescued from a terrible fate. The closest of the six was one of the farmhands, a thin boy in his late teens, who stared at Aestelle wide-eyed and jaw open. She momentarily transposed herself into his position to see things from his viewpoint; he had faced a slow and agonizing death at the hands of the stuff of nightmares, but now found himself safe and well after the intervention of a beautiful, powerful woman that was most likely the stuff of his wildest dreams. Aestelle shot him a wink as she walked past him, the smug feeling of leaving men helpless in her wake still being one of the highlights in her life.

The young woman she had rescued knelt by the side of the bleeding man by the well, wailing in despair and holding tightly onto his hand. Aestelle dropped to one knee by the farmer, quickly checking over his wounds. All superficial from the beating he had received. She placed a hand on his chest and focused her powers of divinity to accelerate his healing.

"He'll be fine," she said coolly to the woman before nodding toward the tree line where the final Abyssal had run to. "But that bastard won't be."

Aestelle walked purposefully into the trees, easily able to follow the dark aura left behind by the fleeing demon. She whistled a tune she remembered from her childhood, a simple song she had sung in one of the rare moments she had been allowed to play during her education by the sisterhood.

"*Don't hide, don't hide, don't hide from me*," she sang softly as her eyes scanned the shadows around her.

Sensing the Abyssal ahead, she felt the attack coming moments before the demon leapt from behind a tree ahead of her, a double headed axe held above its horned head in both powerful hands. Aestelle was quicker, stepping forward to skewer the demon with her greatsword, puncturing its chest and pinning it to the thick tree behind it. The lower Abyssal howled, grunted, and thrashed about frantically in place; its clawed hands grasping at the blade, frantically trying to pull it out of its chest and free itself from the tree. Aestelle took a step back, thrusting her hips to one side and folding her arms in a pose somewhere between haughty and seductive as she watched her prey writhe in place. The demon finally stopped, fixing its glowering eyes on hers before grunting and rasping a sequence of syllables in its own guttural language. Aestelle was years out of practice, but remembered enough to grasp the gist of what the demon was trying to communicate.

"Language, language!" she admonished with a smirk. "That is no way to talk to a lady."

The Abyssal attempted to lean forward, angrily spitting its accursed language at her and reaching out its huge hands toward her neck.

"This encounter has not gone quite the way you seem to think," Aestelle said as she unsheathed her second knife from her back. "Now, there is a little girl over there who will probably have nightmares for the rest of her life because of you. The problem with your lot is that you think fear to be a one-way process. You rarely feel fear, so you don't know the effect you have."

The wounded demon stared at her with hate filled eyes.

"Allow me to remedy that," Aestelle said, stepping forward with her knife.

*****

Aestelle emerged from the woods a few minutes later, drenched in the cold blood of the final devil. The farmers and the two children were gathered around the well, the woman and one of the farmhands seeing to the injured man's wounds with bandages, while the last farm worker nervously eyed the fields of long grass on the other side of the courtyard. All of them stopped to stare at Aestelle as she approached them.

"Don't worry," she shrugged, "none of this is my blood."

She took a bucket of water from the well and emptied it over her head, washing the majority of the blood off her skin and leather armor.

"Th… thank you!" the redheaded woman tending to her husband said, her voice shaking with emotion. "Thank you so much!"

"I'm a professional, not some traveling hero of legend," Aestelle said, "I expect to be paid."

"Anything!" the woman said. "Anything we can give you for saving our family!"

"Your best bottle of wine would be a good start," Aestelle replied.

"Justin," the woman turned to the love-struck farm hand she had winked to earlier. "Go and fetch some wine!"

"And be a good fellow and go and find my pistol, knife, and bow," Aestelle added, "they're somewhere off in that field."

Justin the farmhand looked across to the field of long grass with horror.

"What if they're… not dead?"

"I'm rather good at what I do," Aestelle snapped irritably. "Believe me, they're dead. Now go and fetch my weapons and get me that wine. Chop, chop."

The terrified boy stumbled off toward the field, then changed his mind and ambled off toward the farmhouses. Aestelle was surprised when a significant force thudded into one of her legs, knocking her back a step. She looked down and saw the little girl who had momentarily escaped from the demons, her arms wrapped tightly around Aestelle's leg. While a part of her appreciated the gratitude, Aestelle had never been particularly fond of children. Then the little girl looked up at her with pure admiration in her deep, brown eyes and the biggest smile Aestelle had ever seen. Aestelle fought to stop the smile from becoming infectious, and failed. Her opinion of children changing in what seemed like an instant, Aestelle found herself involuntarily returning the smile back down to the little girl.

Her father, color returning to his pain-wracked face, limped over to place an affectionate hand on top of the girl's head.

"Hello," Aestelle said quietly.

The girl stared up mutely, still smiling. Aestelle found herself thinking on her own childhood, on the loss of her parents at a similar age, and how it led to her induction and education at the hands of the sisterhood. She found herself pitying the little girl and all of the trials that life had ahead. Being captured and nearly eaten by demons was one experience that a child definitely should never have had.

"Don't you ever worry about what you saw today," Aestelle said seriously.

"These monsters, they scare people. But I scare the monsters even more."

"You're funny!" the little girl laughed.

Aestelle paused for a moment to consider how to interpret the unexpected response.

"I shall take that," she flashed a smile.

"I like your hair!" the girl continued, pointing up at the lines of beads and pearls woven into the strands of blonde hair that fell down from one temple.

Aestelle reached up and slid one of the colored beads off.

"I take them from all of the monsters I kill," she winked, handing it over, "but this one is yours now."

"Go on," the girl's father forced a smile, looking nervously around him at the horizon in each direction. "Go inside."

Aestelle watched the girl go and looked to the house, wondering what was taking so long with her wine.

"Those Abyssals," she said to the father, "how many of them are there around here?"

"We'd heard all about them," the pale-skinned man said, "but they're the first we've seen. All the folk for leagues have said they've seen them. That's why we were heading south. This isn't my farm, this belongs to my brother. We were just staying here overnight, and then... well, then they were here. Are you one of the survivors from the force sent from the capital?"

"Yes," Aestelle replied, "well, sort of. I'm attached to... wait! What do you mean, 'survivors'?"

"The battle," the farmer said, "there was a battle between the legion and these demons, some nights ago now, to the north. A friend of mine said he saw the battlefield the next day. He said there was over a hundred dead from each side."

Aestelle turned away, taking a deep breath and fighting to compose herself at the news. If that was true, then the Dictator-Prefect's entire force was dead and gone. The last barrier between the demonic incursion and the helpless people of the rural north, away from the major military bastions and barricades, was now also gone.

"Are you sure?" Aestelle demanded.

"It is only what I have heard," the man said nervously, "but you've seen the evidence for yourself. There are demons here! Walking our lands! In broad daylight!"

"And the entire force sent from the capital?" Aestelle asked again. "You say they're all dead?"

"That is what I have heard," the farmer exhaled, his breathing still labored from his beating. "My cousin says he has a survivor at his tavern. But he drinks a lot. He says the soldier was brought to him in the night by an Elohi. But he..."

Aestelle's eyes widened.

"Where is your cousin's tavern?" she demanded.

*****

175

Sat on the rough, wooden windowsill of the latest in a procession of taverns, Tancred looked out at the evening sky apprehensively. Their progression south had been slow but steady, and now that they were back on the coastal road, there was at least a greater chance of running into a legion patrol or some sort of military presence between the great cities of the south and the strongholds of the northern borders. The surviving paladins had regained their strength during the move south, to the point that after their own recovery, those who were trained were able to use their powers to heal the wounds of the other party members. Now, the twenty strong group of soldiers, squires, and supplymen continued on toward the origin point of their journey in the hope of meeting up with a military force that may or may not have been assembled to reinforce them.

Eager for the opportunity to rest, most of the bedraggled party had already retired for the night, some sleeping in the tavern rooms while others took to the stables or used tents they had been able to acquire on the journey. Only Tancred, Hugh, Jeneveve, and Xavier remained in the tavern along with a small number of travelers and merchants. His other two surviving paladins, Reynaud and Tantus, had retreated to a small chapel not far away for evening prayers. Now, several days away from the demonic incursion, the number of fleeing refugees had thinned out to next to nothing, and this far south, many of the locals dismissed the Abyssal attacks as nothing more than fanciful rumors.

Tancred looked over to the other side of the tavern where Hugh sat alone, a serving girl bringing him his evening meal as he stared despondently at the facing wall. Tancred wondered which of the many things it was that had silenced the outspoken nobleman for the last few days; whether it was his perception of personal failure, the guilt of being one of a very small number of survivors, or the loss of his two aides who had died bravely to allow the others to escape. Perhaps it was a combination of all of this and more, but Tancred wondered if Hugh was even capable of feeling guilt or loss. He looked back out of the window, hoping and praying that other survivors would suddenly appear; a column of disheveled paladins and men-at-arms, exhausted but relieved to find their leaders again. Tancred remembered seeing Orion fight, without a shadow of a doubt the finest display of swordsmanship he had seen in his life as the huge knight cut down demon after demon surrounding him. It felt like even the Wicked Ones themselves could not slay Orion and, not having seen him fall with his own eyes, Tancred clung to the hope that the big man had somehow survived and escaped. But deep down, he knew it to be all but impossible.

"You look thoughtful, Lord Paladin," Jeneveve's voice came from over his shoulder.

He turned briefly to glance at her, saw her venture a gentle smile, and then looked back out at the surrounding fields darkening under the enveloping evening sky.

"Just wondering whether anybody else escaped after all. Maybe Orion managed to fight his way out."

"Brother Orion is dead," Jeneveve replied, perhaps a little more forcefully than necessary, Tancred felt, "the same as all the others."

"But did you see him fight!" Tancred smiled fondly. "He took down so many of them before he fell! Like something out of an epic song! When we get back, I shall ensure his final stand is made known to the entire Order! He deserves that much."

"He deserves no more than any of our other fallen brothers and sisters," Jeneveve countered. "Yes, he could fight, but that was all there was to him. He was a bully. A course, rough, bully. He did not join us in prayer, he gave no alms to the poor, he served nobody and nothing other than his own obsession with besting every warrior he met in single combat. He was my brother in the Order and I certainly wished no harm onto him, but I do not think he deserves to be immortalized in legend. He had his flaws, the same as the rest of us. Perhaps more so."

"*...and Gideus declared to all, 'mortal man should not judge, for the final judgment shall be cast onto all by the Celestials themselves at the sunset of time'*," Tancred quoted. "Chapter Three, Daven's Letter to Cortisians."

"I do not need lecturing from the Eloicon," Jeneveve said defensively, "I know it well enough."

"Then perhaps you should spend more time contemplating its words," Tancred said as he stood and turned to face her, "and less time casting shadow over the memory of our Brother."

Tancred left Jeneveve and walked over to stand by Hugh. The Dictator-Prefect continued to stare silently at the far wall for some moments, his food growing cold on the table before him. He eventually looked across at Tancred.

"Yes?"

"Just seeing if there was anything to discuss, Dictator-Prefect," Tancred offered quietly.

Hugh took a long swig from a broad, wooden mug of wine.

"No, nothing I can think of."

"I shall leave you in peace," Tancred said as he took a step back, nodding his head respectfully.

"No, no, please sit," Hugh replied, coughing and thumping a clenched fist against his chest, "I...I..."

The coughing intensified, and within moments, Tancred met the dark realization that this was something more than simply a disagreeable cup of wine.

"Hugh?" Tancred darted forward, thumping the man on the back as he struggled to his feet, his face red with the violence of his coughing and choking.

By the tavern's bar, the serving girl began to scream hysterically. Xavier and Jeneveve dashed over as Tancred placed his hands on Hugh's torso, frantically looking for the source of an injury he could use his powers to heal.

"He made me do it!" the serving girl yelled, her eyes screwed tightly shut and her hands clamped over her ears. "He made me serve that wine!"

Even over Hugh's coughing, Tancred could hear a struggle and commotion outside in the courtyard. He quickly assessed the scenario that was unfolding around him. His eyes opened wide.

"Jeneveve! Go and get that man! He's outside! Get him before he escapes! Xavier, help me!"

Jeneveve bounded across the tavern, her heavy footsteps creaking the floorboards until she barged her way through the door and out into the night. Xavier took Hugh by the armpits, gently guiding him down to lie across the tavern floor as a trio of legion soldiers sprinted down from the rooms on the first floor, hurriedly pulling on their mail coats and sword belts in response to the commotion from the ground floor. Tancred looked down desperately at the Dictator-Prefect as thin streams of blood trickled from both sides of his mouth. Xavier's fingers glowed blue with magic as he moved his hands over Hugh's torso, but to no avail. Hugh looked up at Tancred desperately as the coughing died away.

"I'm so sorry," he managed hoarsely, "I made such a mess of things... I'm so sorry..."

Realizing that nothing could be done, Tancred dropped to one knee next to the dying man and held his hand, quickly quoting the Litany of the Soul's Transition.

"*Shining Ones, accept your son Hugh into your hearts, prepare a place for him at the peak of The Mountain, let his soul transition to you to rest in a place of love and holiness...*"

"Thank you," Hugh coughed weakly, tears streaming down his face as his hand gripped onto Tancred's tightly. Halfway through the litany, Hugh died. Tancred continued to recite the verses to the very end, determined to complete the litany for the fallen Dictator-Prefect. The three soldiers dragged the crying serving girl across as Jeneveve reappeared at the doorway, dragging a tall, thin man in his forties dressed in a dark cloak and hood.

Tancred leaned over to respectfully straighten Hugh's arms and legs, tilting his head to stare directly up at the ceiling. He turned to look up at the serving girl.

"She had no idea," the silver haired man in the dark hood said coldly. "Let her go."

Tancred nodded to the soldiers who released the crying serving girl, and then he walked over to stand before the man in the dark hood, looking up into his emotionless eyes. He felt a darkness emanating from the thin, stone faced man, similar to the malice and blackness he had felt in the moments leading up to the Abyssal attack on the hilltop encampment. He glanced over at Xavier. The veteran paladin nodded. He felt it too. Tancred turned back to the captive.

"Why did you poison him?" Tancred demanded.

The hooded man said nothing and stared straight ahead. Tancred's fraying temper snapped. He slammed a fist into the man's stomach, causing him to bend over double and cough painfully, dropping to one knee. Tancred grabbed him by the neck and dragged him off toward one of the tavern's back rooms.

"Wait!" Jeneveve demanded. "What are you going to do?"

"I am going to find out who this bastard is, and why he murdered the

Dictator-Prefect," Tancred replied evenly.

"You cannot do that! This is the magistrate's jurisdiction! You have no right to beat information out of this man!"

"There is not time for that nonsense!" Tancred bellowed. "This man is in league with the forces of the Abyss, he has forsaken his legal rights!"

"You do not know that!" Jeneveve pointed an armored finger at Tancred in accusation. "We do not choose which laws we like and do not like! We uphold all the laws of the land!"

"Not when it comes to demonology!" Tancred exclaimed.

"Orion would tell you the same!" Jeneveve spat with venom. "He would stand against you!"

"Then draw your sword, as he would have!" Tancred hissed. "But Orion would have stopped me, because he was the better swordsman! You are not! I am your senior in our Order, and you will follow my commands!"

"Not if those commands are not legal!" Jeneveve slammed an open palm into the table next to her.

The assembled soldiers and tavern patrons stared on in astounded silence.

"Then try to stop me," Tancred decided, "for I am taking this man into that room, and I intend to beat the truth out of him even if it kills him, as The Ones are my witness!"

Jeneveve looked across at Xavier pleadingly.

"Xavier?"

The older paladin shook his head slowly.

"I am sorry, Sister," he said quietly, "we know what is coming from the north. There are bigger things afoot than the rights of a single man. I support the Lord Paladin's decision."

"Then may The Ones have mercy on you both!" Jeneveve shook her head before turning on her heel and storming out of the tavern.

Tancred dragged the smiling man in the hood toward the door at the other end of the tavern. A hand fell on his shoulder.

"I am coming with you," Xavier murmured under his breath, "but do not kill this man, Tancred. Do not sacrifice your soul only to become the very man we are pursuing. This wretch is not worth it."

"Understood," Tancred nodded.

*****

"Wait!" the innkeeper called as he dashed after Aestelle. "You can't just come barging in here like this! These people are my guests!"

Aestelle paced up the stairs to the second floor, the center of each wooden step giving a little and creaking even under her light weight. The innkeeper, a short man approaching middle age with a balding head and ratty features, scrambled after her up the stairs.

"Where is he?" Aestelle demanded as she reached the first floor hallway. "You have a soldier staying here with you. Which room is he in?"

The innkeeper winced as Aestelle walked along the corridor, slamming a fist on the door of every room she passed. The walls and floor were, like the rest of the building, made up of simple planks of wood with no paint or decoration, warped in places and faded by exposure to sunlight in others.

"Stop that!" the short man demanded. "These people don't deserve to be intimidated by you!"

"Then tell me where the soldier is!" Aestelle insisted. "The one you claim was brought here by an Elohi."

"Shh… keep your voice down!" the innkeeper whispered desperately as Aestelle reached the end of the corridor. "People will think I am mad! Business is bad enough with devils roaming the hills without you scaring off what few paying customers I have left!"

Aestelle stopped at the end of the corridor. The sharp intake of breath the innkeeper made told her all she needed to know.

"He is in here, then," she nodded to the last room, "open the door."

"I don't think he wants to be disturbed."

"Open the door or you shall see me properly disturb your place of business."

Sighing, the short man took a small, brass key chained to his belt and unlocked the door ahead of them. Swearing under his breath, he turned and scuttled quickly away down the corridor. Aestelle opened the door and walked inside. She immediately winced from the brightness of the late morning sunlight streaming in through the only window at the far side of the small room. A neat bed took up most of the room, with its only other furnishings being made up of a chair and a small wardrobe with a cracked mirror to one side.

A familiar, tall and muscular man sat in the chair, looking up at Aestelle as she entered the room. Clean shaven, blue eyed and with short, blond hair, Aestelle found herself taken off guard by the young soldier's handsome face. He wore only the padded trousers usually worn as a protective layer beneath armor and had clean bandages around his abdomen and along one shoulder. He carefully closed a book, the Eloicon, and stood up. It was only when she saw his full height that the familiarity she had felt developed into full recognition.

"Ogre?" she exclaimed.

"Orion," the paladin corrected patiently, "I have a name. It is Orion."

Aestelle let out an audible breath and took a step back as clear memories flooded to the fore of her thoughts.

The two bandits sprinted headlong at Aestelle, the closest clumsily swinging a hammer at her head while the second man lunged at her midriff with a small axe. Aestelle slipped easily beneath the first attack and brought her flail up to ensnare the wrist of the axe wielding bandit and forced him over near the edge of the mountain path before bringing her knee up into his gut and swinging an elbow around to break his nose. In an instant, the first, taller bandit was on the attack again, but Aestelle was faster, despite the bruises on her back from the ordeal of the past few days. She swung her flail around to connect the ball into the man's chest with a cracking of bone, dropping him wheezing to his knees.

Realizing the skill of the woman he faced, the shorter bandit turned to run. Aestelle took her knife from her belt and slit the first man's throat and then flung it after the second bandit, striking him in the center of the back. He fell to his knees and called out weakly for help. Aestelle silenced his pleas, bringing her flail down to crush his skull.

Up ahead, the two paladins she had seen earlier were sheathing their swords after a successful confrontation with their adversaries. Aestelle turned to face their hapless squire; a boy, perhaps four years her junior, who would probably grow up to be handsome if he bothered to bulk up with some muscle. Her breathing labored through the blue cotton scarf she was forced to wear around her mouth and nose, Aestelle folded her arms and looked down at the quivering squire with disgust.

"You, boy!" she demanded. "You're armed! You shouldn't need me to save you! What were you thinking? Well, boy, speak!"

The squire looked up at her pathetically.

"I...I..."

She took a pace closer.

"How old are you?" she demanded, standing in front of him.

"Fif... sixteen," the boy managed.

"Sixteen?" she forced a healthy amount of disgust into her words, although that was the age she had guessed earlier. "You should be wearing spurs by now, not groveling around as a squire! When I was your age, I'd already fought a full campaign against the orcs!"

"Orion?" the older of the two paladins called as he made his way back down the winding mountain path. "Are you hurt?"

"Orion?" Aestelle laughed at how ill-suited the useless squire's name was, "Your parents named you after the patron of courage and hunting? I hope the irony isn't lost on you."

"And your name?" the younger of the two paladins demanded as he followed his senior along the path back to their squire.

"My name is unimportant, Paladin," Aestelle replied, eager to spend as little time with their little expedition as possible so she could return to her own ordeal on the mountain. "I'm a sister, you will refer to me as that."

"You were the boy on the mountain all those years ago," Aestelle whispered, half to herself, "the one I saved."

Orion leaned back against the wall behind him and folded his powerful arms.

"I do not know what you mean," he said suspiciously.

"The mountain!" Aestelle repeated. "What... ten, eleven years ago? Tarkis! You were a squire with two paladins. One was your uncle. I was the nun who met you the day your uncle died."

Orion's eyes slowly widened.

181

"You... cannot have been!" he exclaimed. "You are not old enough!"

"I was twenty years old the day we met," Aestelle recalled.

"But you kept calling me 'boy'!" Orion shook his head, the incredulity of the situation still clearly baffling him.

"When you are twenty, a sixteen year old is just a boy, if you can remember back that far," Aestelle gave him a slight smile.

Orion returned the smirk, his striking features lighting up with his smile.

"This is just incredible," he muttered, sinking back down into the rickety chair by the window.

Aestelle took her bow, arrows, and greatsword from her aching back and carefully laid them down by the wardrobe, shutting the door behind her.

"We have a lot to discuss," she said, walking over to the bed and sinking down on it with a creak of leather.

Placing her hands behind her head, she stared up at the dull ceiling above her and the patterns in the shadows created by the bright sunlight pouring in through the window. She looked across at the paladin.

"You don't mind me taking your bed for a few minutes?"

"Be my guest."

Aestelle exhaled.

"I have one question before I start," she said. "Rumors reached me that you were brought here by an Elohi. Is that true?"

"Yes," Orion nodded, "I was gravely wounded in battle when the forces of the Abyss ambushed us at our encampment, not long after you left. I was as good as dead. I fought as long as I could, but I was overwhelmed. I do not remember much after that. I woke up here. There was an Elohi, a tall woman clothed in white, sat in this very chair. She said she brought me here."

"What did she tell you?" Aestelle turned her head on the pillow and looked over at him, crossing one tired ankle over another at the foot of the bed.

Orion let out a contemplative breath.

"She said... that she had done all she could for my wounds and that I would heal in time. That is why I have waited here, I..."

"What else did she tell you?" Aestelle insisted, familiar enough with the tales of visits from Elohi to know that there were always messages in their words.

"She said my uncle – one of the men who died that day on the mountain when you were with us – feels... disappointed in me. That I need to change. And that I need to find another Elohi. When I find her, she will know what to do. I was saved to protect her."

Aestelle nodded slowly, her mind racing with each new piece of information.

"You've found her," she said, "that's me. I'm the Elohi."

"Impossible," Orion shook his head, "I have seen Elohi before, on the battlefield. You... share traits with them, but you are not one of them."

"Half," Aestelle continued, "my mother was mortal, but my father was an Elohi. He was wounded in battle and unable to return to the Mount. My mother nursed him back to health and they fell in love. Two things happened on the night they consummated that love – one was what happens whenever an Elohi and a mortal spend a night of passion together. The Elohi becomes mortal. My father awoke as but a normal man, of normal height, without his wings. The second result was, well, me. It is my blessing and my curse. I am faster, stronger, more intelligent and more beautiful than normal mortals. I am harder to kill, I age slower. But as a half breed, I am still very much mortal."

"So how did you end up in the Sisterhood? And for that matter, how did you end up leaving?"

Aestelle propped herself up on her elbows and looked across at him again.

"My parents passed away in the Great Blight Plague, when I was five years old. My mother's brother thought it best to entrust my upbringing to the Sisterhood. One assumes that decision was taken out of love, or at least one hopes so, but it… did not end well for me."

"How so?"

"Long story," Aestelle sank back onto the bed, "suffice to say, I've never done well at accepting authority. And then there are adolescent girls. Horrible at the best of times, but when jealousy rears its ugly head when a half-angel is in their midst, trouble is bound to follow. I never fitted in, I was never accepted, and every time I was provoked, my reaction was always somewhat explosive. That is why I was on the mountain the day I met you. I was taking the fifth step. My last chance for deliverance before damnation."

Aestelle remembered her conversation with the temptress and the comparisons the demon woman had made.

"You cannot be damned," Orion said, "I cannot sense it."

"I succeeded in the fifth step," Aestelle replied, "but I did not accept it. I left the Sisterhood of my own volition; I was not expelled. But enough of me. What happened with you?"

Aestelle leaned forward, bringing one knee up to wrap both arms around her leg and rest her chin on her knee, her blonde hair falling over one eye as she glanced across at the paladin.

"There is not much else to say," Orion leaned forward, his folded arms resting on his lap. "My older brother took the family estate. My father paid a lot of money for me to join the Order to train as a paladin. It was not what I wanted, and it hurt me deeply as a young boy to leave. Now? I do not know. Perhaps it was for the best. Either way, I became my uncle's squire. Jahus was a great man. He never held much rank, he was not the greatest warrior, but respect? Everybody respected him. I think that came from his kindness. He was wonderful with people of all walks of life; he had a way."

Aestelle listened in silence, seeing the paladin sat next to her in a completely new light.

"The day he died, everything changed," Orion continued. "You saw what happened. Dionne's men killed him and I did not stop them."

"You could not have stopped them," Aestelle said softly. "I was there, remember. Neither of us could."

"I could now," Orion countered, "if you put me on that mountaintop with the skills I have now, I could have stopped that happening. That was what made that day so important. It changed my life. I promised I would never let anybody else down again. I trained harder than every other squire, every other paladin; any warrior I found that I could learn anything from, I fought them. I have known nothing else since the day my uncle died. Just the sword. And now I do not let people down. Or, at least that is what I thought until the Elohi spoke to me."

"What did she say?"

"As I said, Jahus is disappointed in me. I have lost my way. I have sat here for days, reading this Eloicon, the very book I took from my uncle's body on the mountainside. I have been searching the scriptures for guidance, looking for whatever direction my life is supposed to take me. And of all places, I realized that the answer lay with my squire. Kell, his name is, or was. I was responsible for his training and his mentorship. He did everything right, spent years cleaning my armor and weapons, shoeing a warhorse I did not even have the common courtesy to give a name to. He stood steady on the night the Abyssals attacked our encampment. He died more of a man than I ever was. My lot was not to roam the land, beating down warriors for my own pride. I was supposed to provide guidance to those who needed it. I was supposed to be there for Kell."

Aestelle swung her legs over the side of the bed and sat upright, facing the tall paladin. She took a few moments to reflect on his words, carefully weighing up her own before speaking again. She took one of his hands in hers.

"I am sorry for everything that happened to your comrades when you were attacked at the camp," she said quietly, "but you're my Kell, my equivalent. You wanted to know the reason I left the Sisterhood. Because of you. I let you down. It took a lot of reflection for me to realize that, but it is true. Do you remember the last thing I said to you before I left you on that mountainside with your uncle's body? I told you that you needed to grow up. Those words have haunted me for ten years. When I knelt at the altar, ready to receive my absolution and acceptance back into the Sisterhood, that was all I could think of. I thought about what the Sisterhood meant, that it was about a life of selflessness and sacrifice, of protecting those who needed it. I was unworthy. I still am. That was why I left. I could never match the expectation of what it meant to be a Sister."

Orion's face broke into a sad, sympathetic smile.

"I forgive you," he offered meekly, "for what it is worth, I forgive you."

The words meant more to Aestelle than she was prepared for. She felt a smile spread across her lips, threatening to escalate to a relieved laugh.

"Thank you," she said genuinely, "I am sure Kell would say the same to you."

"Let us hope so," Orion looked down at the floor again.

"But this, all of this, is part of something bigger, don't you see?" Aestelle continued. "It cannot be a coincidence that we met on that mountainside. Not just you and I, but Dionne was there, too. The Shining Ones trade in fate, and I believe it was our fate to meet. It is our fate to be on the same stage again now. Old tales claim that the offspring of Elohi are destined for a higher calling, so maybe this is mine. So enough talk, let's do this."

Orion's eyes widened in confusion.

"Do what?"

Aestelle stood up.

"Fight," she smirked, with a wink, "throw these bastards back out of Basilea."

"We are but two," Orion sighed, "they number in the hundreds."

"And if I understand their plan correctly, they will number in their thousands if we do not stop them," Aestelle said as she slung her weapons back over her shoulders. "I was a demon hunter in the Order. The first rule of hunting a demon is the understanding that they thrive on fear. Both their physical manifestation and their non-corporeal presence. So to become a demon hunter is about the attitude with which you face the devil. You don't fear them. They fear you. And I'll teach you how to become a thing of fear to them. Are your wounds healed enough for you to ride?"

"I can ride alright," Orion said, "but I have no horse."

"I shall fix that," Aestelle said.

She stopped for a few moments, looking at the boy she had left on the mountaintop a decade before.

"I won't let you down again," she said seriously, "if you ever need me, just say you want me to save you, and I'll be there for you."

She offered the paladin her hand. He closed his fingers around her forearm.

"Then you and I are now our own Order," Aestelle said, feeling determination smoldering into life within her soul, "so let's go show these bastards what fear really means."

Sixteen

Yet another dawn sun, and another aching ride north along the coastal trade road. Valletto looked to the northwest and the Mountains of Tarkis, desperate to see a glimpse of The Mount itself, Kolosu, but the holy site was still many miles over the jagged horizon. The two paladins riding with Valletto were certainly polite, but not the most talkative. The older of the two, a knight named Silus, bore the scars of a veteran of many campaigns beneath his flowing but faded locks of blond hair. Valletto had heard him make reference to being present during the disaster at the Forest of Galahir alongside Dictator Trence Andorset, but beyond that, the aging soldier had let very little slip about his past. The younger paladin, Lyen, spoke even less and, given his subservient nature, Valletto guessed he had only recently been elevated from squire to full paladin.

Days of traveling left Valletto bitterly unhappy, resenting every minute spent away from his family. He spent his nights alone in tavern rooms, writing letters home that he knew had a less than even chance of reaching his wife before his own return. He remembered his life on campaign as a far younger man, newly married but with no other commitments left behind him at home. It had all seemed so exciting when he was in his mid-twenties; he felt as if he was part of something heroic and important, looking forward to returning home as a hero, the center of conversation at family events, seen in a new light as a figure of respect and admiration. Then the battles began and very quickly Valletto realized the folly of his immature expectations.

Now, over a decade later and with his children occupying the core of his entire existence, he had absolutely no interest in heading north to find a missing detachment of soldiers and ascertain that there was indeed no major and imminent threat from the Abyss. That being said, they had in the last day confirmed positive evidence that something was afoot. Three separate encounters on the road with dirty, disheveled farmers and laborers, fleeing south on overloading carts with their families and few possessions. All of them believed there were demons in the hills to the north, sweeping down to drag innocent people off to the fires of the Abyss. Yet none of them had seen a single Abyssal with their own eyes.

"There," Lyen alerted the other two riders, "up ahead, another one of them."

His mind brought back to the present, Valletto looked ahead on the road and saw a lone horse wandering slowly toward them, saddled but without a rider.

"It's just a horse," Valletto shrugged.

"No," Silus said gruffly, "I can sense something else."

The aging knight kicked his horse into a fast canter, quickly covering the distance across to the horse. Lyen and Valletto followed up, riding over to see what Silus had detected. As Valletto approached, he saw the rider, slumped forward over the horse's neck. The animal had an eye catching, sandy colored coat that unfortunately was light enough to highlight the tremendous amount of blood that had leaked from the rider, down the horse's flank.

"He's dead," Lyen exhaled sadly. "Do we stop to bury him?"

"She's not dead," Silus said sternly as he swung down from his warhorse. "Not yet, at least."

Valletto dismounted and rushed over to the rider, grabbing his staff from where he had secured it to his saddlebag. The woman appeared to be in her twenties, of average height and build with brown hair. Her eyes were closed and her clothing, little more than dirty and bloodied rags, marked her out as a peasant; although what a peasant was doing traveling on horseback remained to be seen. Silus pressed a hand against her stomach and Valletto sensed the build up of magical powers, the veteran paladin's manipulation of the arcane energies ebbing and flowing in strands around the three magic users. Of course, to the two paladins, this was the limit of their mastery of the divinity plains of power; but to Valletto who lived and breathed the arcane, it was a second sight, an ability to see an entire world around him that those without training and ability could not.

Silus drew power from the streams of arcane around him, perhaps not even aware that that was how he was doing it, and drew them into his very core before pushing them out along one arm and into his fingertips. His hand glowed blue as the energy reached the edge of the knight's very soul and then shot out of his hand to connect with the dying woman to race its way through her body to search for pain and damage to heal. Valletto had seen it done a thousand times before, but it always brought a smile to his face. It was the perfect demonstration of the arcane, using the gift to help people who needed it. It was what magic was for.

A breath escaped the woman's cracked and bloodied lips, and her eyes flickered behind their lids. Lyen stepped over and pressed his hand against her, drawing on the same energies. Valletto sensed the young paladin's coarser, almost clumsy manipulation of the arcane, but the power and purity of his spirit – the essence of divinity magic – sent another wave of healing energy into the woman. Her eyes half opened.

"Help me get her down," Silus commanded, "carefully."

The two knights gently carried the woman over to the side of the road and laid her down in the grass. Valletto knelt next to her and took his waterskin from his belt, using it to carefully clean her face and apply some moisture to her lips.

"Will she die?" Lyen asked quietly.

"Without proper care, yes, she will," Silus replied.

"Then we should take her to somebody who can help," Valletto decided. "She may be only a peasant in the eyes of most, but a life is a life to me, and our task can wait."

"She's not a peasant, she's a soldier," Silus retorted. "She is wearing legion issue boots and her neck is chaffed from poorly fitting armor. Her wound is from fighting; she has been run through with a blade."

The woman moaned weakly, a syllable forming on her lips, too quiet to decipher.

"Save your strength," Valletto gave her an encouraging smile. "We'll get help for you."

"Abyssals..." the woman whispered weakly.

"You saw them?" Silus demanded. "Did you see Abyssals yourself?"

The woman gave a barely perceptible nod.

Silus looked up at Valletto.

"There's the proof the Duma wanted."

"Will it be enough?" Lyen asked. "The word of one dying soldier?"

"How many of them?" Silus leaned in closer to her, his voice more animated. "How many?"

The woman opened her mouth to speak again, but her eyes lolled back and her eyelids drifted shut again.

"Give her a chance, man!" Valletto snapped. "We're not killing this woman to get information!"

"I saved her life, not you!" Silus growled. "And I know well enough how much she can take! We need to know what we are facing!"

Valletto sighed and took a step back, turning away from the paladins and the wounded soldier. He had never liked confrontation. Oddly, he had always been able to muster up his courage to face danger from the enemy or the elements, but crossing angry words was something Valletto hated. But the woman needed help, and that should be the priority. Knowing how many Abyssals lay ahead could wait; her life could not. Valletto turned back.

"The Duma placed me in charge, you are here to protect me," he said quietly, unable to meet the paladin's glare. "Now cease your interrogation of this woman. We are going to find help for her."

Silus stood up and folded his arms, regarding Valletto in silence. Valletto crouched down next to the woman and brought the waterskin to her lips carefully. She was still too weak to drink much, but she gave him the faintest smile of gratitude.

"I'm Val, what's your name?"

"Constance..." the soldier whispered, "I... I was... Dionne... with them..."

Valletto looked across at the paladins. Lyen appeared surprised while Silus nodded slowly. Valletto smiled his thanks to the woman and stood again.

"So that is that," Valletto said grimly. "Dionne has sided with the forces of the Abyss. Get her back on her horse, please. Take her south, back to the village we passed yesterday afternoon. There was a convent up on the hill there, the sisters are her best chance."

"And you?" Silus said.

"I am going to contact my seniors in the capital and let them know what we have found. Then I'll carry on north and see what else I can find out."

"Alone?" Silus demanded. "In the midst of Abyssals? Without our help?"

"I can take care of myself," Valletto smiled uncomfortably. "I'm a battle mage, that means I too am a soldier. Look, this message to the Duma cannot afford to wait. Not a single hour, let alone how long it will take to get back to the village. But her life cannot wait either. She needs to move now, and I need to convey this message now. Both need to happen concurrently, so you need to go."

Silus looked over his shoulder at his younger comrade.

"Do as he says, Lyen. Get her to the sisterhood."

"But…"

"Don't argue," the older knight said gently. "I know you came out here to fight the good fight, but that is not your task now. This soldier faced the forces of the Abyss. Do not let her die because you wanted tales of glory to go home with. Get her to help."

Chastened, the young knight's face fell.

"Yes, of course."

Silus turned back to Valletto.

"Send your message, Valletto. Then we carry on north."

*****

The magistrate was a tall, thin man clothed in black robes with flowing white hair beneath a black, wide brimmed hat; his receding gums giving him an unnerving smile as he drifted over to Tancred in the tavern courtyard. The wind was picking up again, bringing a bitter chill from the north and rustling the long grass in the silent fields around the small village. Tancred's motley collection of soldiers and supplymen waited in small groups around the courtyard, their hushed conversations fading to nothing as the pale magistrate approached Tancred.

"You did the right thing, sending for me, Lord Paladin," the old man smiled, his yellow tinged eyes narrowing as he did so. "'Tis best you leave the unpleasant business of extracting information to those of us who are used to getting our hands dirty in… disagreeable dealings. You save your strength for the battlefield, where you excel."

Tancred looked up at the tall magistrate, unsure whether the words were meant as a compliment or a thinly veiled slur. For that matter, he was uncertain whether he found the magistrate helpful or patronizing. The only feeling he was sure of was the unnerving presence of the man, who looked himself as if he were unsure whether to turn to the Abyss or a life of necromancy. But Tancred detected nothing malicious or hostile from him, just an aura of unease that no doubt came with the territory of deciding who lived and died on behalf of the Hegemon's law.

"What have your interrogators ascertained, Lord Magistrate?" Tancred asked.

"Your prisoner was looking for a portal stone," the thin man grinned. "Fortunately for us, it wasn't where he thought it would be. His task was to locate it and then guide Dionne and his Abyssal mongrels to it. Then he saw your Dictator-Prefect, the Shining Ones rest his soul, and realized that it was an opportunity too good to miss."

Tancred exhaled, walking in a small circle as a thousand thoughts, options, and plans raced through his head. Portal stones came in many sizes, and a lesser variant could be carried by an individual to transport themselves and a small group of accomplices to and from the Abyss. Then there were the static stones; huge boulders set into the very earth at sites of great significance that could be used to bring forth entire armies. It was how the forces of the Abyss were able to reach the far-flung corners of Mantica. But such an endeavor was far from simple. Activating a portal stone required the performance of a very specific ritual that very few knew. The ritual itself also required huge amounts of arcane power, far more than could be mustered from a mere mortal agent of the Abyss.

"We need to find that portal stone," Tancred muttered to himself.

"You no longer intend to head south to raise an army?" the magistrate queried.

Tancred shook his head.

"We cannot. There is no time. I need to find that stone and...and..."

"And what?" the magistrate leaned in closer, his thin lips twisting into an amused smile.

"I do not know yet!" Tancred snapped. "But I shall think of something!"

"You cannot move it, you cannot destroy it, you cannot face the force that seeks it," the magistrate said, "so I think your options are somewhat limited."

Tancred turned his back on the gaunt magistrate and waved for Xavier and Jeneveve to approach him. Both paladins quickly made their way over.

"It is a portal stone," Tancred said as they approached, "one of the huge ones. It is here, somewhere in this province. The Abyssal forces have twisted Dionne to their will and are using him to lead an advance force to find and activate the portal so that a proper army can come through. An army that could threaten the capital itself."

"Well... we have to stop them," Jeneveve spluttered, her eyes wide open.

"Then we will need more soldiers," Xavier offered, "and that means heading south."

"It will be too late by then," Jeneveve folded her arms.

Tancred looked back to the magistrate.

"We need soldiers. How many can you place under my command?"

The magistrate cackled a choked laugh that quickly transformed into a hacking cough. He dabbed at the corner of his thin lips with a handkerchief.

"My dear Lord Paladin! It is I who approach you for muscle when there is any risk of civil unrest! I do not have soldiers!"

"Town guards, militia, mercenaries, anything!" Tancred exclaimed. "Good Ones above, man, the nation may depend upon it!"

The magistrate moved his gaze from paladin to paladin, his eyes lingering on Jeneveve for longer than Tancred was comfortable with.

"I shall tell you what," the tall man leered. "You go find the portal stone. While you're gone, I shall raise the best force I can. I cannot promise much, but I will take manpower away from guarding the main trade routes, and I will hire any mercenaries I can find. The bill for those mercenaries will go to your Order, not the Duma, you understand. I am raising a force under your direction, Lord Paladin, not that of the Hegemon or the Duma. Now, I would suggest you get to work and find this stone. I have an army to raise and a man to hang. Excuse me, please."

Tancred watched the magistrate drift back toward the tavern, shuddering as the man left.

"I shall tell our men that we are going back north," Xavier said, "with your permission, Lord Paladin?"

Tancred nodded.

He looked up at the clear sky, at the thin lines of white cloud sweeping miles up ahead, beyond even where powerful birds of prey could reach. He felt exhausted, disillusioned with the past weeks, part of him aching to go home to the warm south while simultaneously he feared the reaction to his failures from the Order and his father. He shook his head at the thought. His father...

"Lord Paladin?"

Tancred looked back at Jeneveve, who stood in front of him, the slightest hint of a smile on her lips seeming at odds with the unease in her eyes.

"Thank you for bringing the magistrate in. I think it was the right thing to do."

Tancred looked down at the cobbled courtyard paving beneath his feet. He had found himself in a small room at the back of the tavern, dagger in hand, the Abyssal traitor tied to a chair in front of him. It was a moment he never wanted to re-live again.

"I knew the stakes," he said coolly to Jeneveve, "but I could not do it. With the fate of this part of our nation resting upon our shoulders, with the lives of hundreds if not thousands of women and children depending upon me to act, I could not harm a bound, helpless man. Even though he was a murderer, a traitor, and a consort of demons, I could not bring my blade to him when he was helpless. That is not a strength, Sister Jeneveve. That is a weakness."

Jeneveve's smile became a little warmer.

"That weakness is what proves you are the man we all hoped you were," she said quietly, briefly resting a hand on his forearm. "It is why we follow you. Thank you for doing the right thing, Lord Paladin."

No happier with the memory of his actions, and all the more uncomfortable with the conversation with Jeneveve, Tancred dismissed the complement with a wave of the hand and strode over to his warhorse to prepare for the ride north.

*****

"How sure are you?" Aestelle said seriously, her gloved hands planted on the flat, wooden planks at the back of the cart to either side of the hastily scrawled map.

Three men stood around her, also leaning over to regard the parchment spread out across the back of the cart – an elderly farmer, a disheveled huntsman, and a short, neat merchant. Behind them was gathered seemingly every survivor from the surrounding miles of farmland and villages who had not fled south. Perhaps thirty men, women, and children of varying trades and backgrounds, all from the less affluent areas of rural Basilean society, had come together at the tavern after hearing about the recovery of the soldier delivered by an Elohi, and the arrival of the woman who had single-handedly slain six demons.

"I saw nothing there myself," the little merchant said warily, "but my customers talk. They would have no reason to lie, surely? One of them told me that he had seen Abyssals at Fresh Creek."

"I'm not throwing accusations around," the dark haired huntsman said gruffly, "but in times of strife, people can very easily become hysterical. Looking at all the other sightings, it makes no sense that any of these monsters would be near Fresh Creek. It's too far out of the way of the other attacks."

"Not all of them," the old farmer said. "My brother escaped an attack here, near the old fort at outside Redwall. That's quite close."

Aestelle swore and shook her head, turning away from the map.

"There's no pattern to these attacks," she growled in frustration. "It's not obvious where they've come from or even where they're going!"

"Perhaps they're lost?" the merchant offered timidly. "Perhaps they're looking for something?"

"Don't be ridic..." Aestelle held up a hand to silence the huntsman's aggressive reply to the neat, little merchant.

Her eyes widened as the entire conundrum began to make sense.

"You wonderful, funny looking little man!" she exclaimed, planting a kiss on the merchant's cheek.

The merchant let out a high pitched wheeze of glee and looked around at the others, a huge grin plastered across his ruddy face. Aestelle turned and paced up and down in front of the cart, one fist pressed pensively against her lips as she thought through the options open to an Abyssal commander left exposed in the rural plains of northern Basilea. Her thoughts were interrupted as an excited gasp and whispered commotion rippled through the waiting crowd of villagers and farmers by the tavern behind her.

Aestelle looked over her shoulder. Orion had appeared at the tavern doorway. Standing a head taller than most men she had met, and nearly twice as broad shouldered, he was never a man to hide in a crowd. However, the shaven headed, bearded thug she had met at the beginning of this ordeal had now been replaced with a dashingly handsome, clean shaven knight with neat blond hair and sparkling blue eyes. His armor was polished to an almost mirrored finish, and his blue surcoat was cleaned as if for a parade. A few of the villagers closest to him, clearly unsure as to what his social status was, elected to err on the side of caution and bowed or curtseyed respectfully. At the back of the crowd, Aestelle saw a trio of young women whispering elatedly to each other as they watched him embarrassedly ask the villagers not to bow.

As Orion walked over to her, the gaps in the facade he had created became immediately apparent to Aestelle's experienced eyes. Fifteen years of fighting allowed her to see past the mirrored shine of the armor; ragged holes had been torn in his mail, great dents and smashes were evident in his breastplate, and the size of the tears in his surcoat he had stitched up were evidence of horrific injuries. There was proof enough before her that he had suffered enough wounds to die twice over; without the intervention of the Elohi, he would be dead and gone. She briefly wondered which of the Elohi had visited him, and if the huge significance of personal intervention by one of the angels of the Sacred Ones had actually registered in the paladin's mind. The thought of their complete lack of interest in her parentage did, however, leave a bitter taste.

"This all supposed to impress me?" Aestelle planted her hands on her hips as Orion approached her.

"You... actually think that the words and actions of everyone around you are for your benefit?" Orion asked wearily.

"Not all of it," Aestelle shrugged, "but certainly the overwhelming majority. I mean, look at me. Anyway, I've been busy. There's a horse on the way here for you and I've collated as much information as is available regarding where these bastards have been attacking. All accounts indicate that there's never more than a dozen or so of them attacking at once. These attacks are scattered and often simultaneous. I would guess that there are no more than a few hundred of them. Certainly not enough to mount a credible threat to a major settlement. This is nothing more than a large raid."

"So why are they even attacking the villagers?" Orion mused. "Why come and try to drag them off?"

Aestelle leaned in close to Orion.

"They still have to eat," she muttered quietly, keeping her voice low enough that none of the villagers could hear.

Orion let out a breath and nodded.

"To get a few hundred of them here would not take too much effort," Aestelle continued, "not in the grand scheme of things. Compared to the far corners of Mantica, we are quite close to the Abyssal scar. Sending a few hundred Abyssals a few hundred miles does not require world-shattering power. But it does require enough to make the effort worthwhile, so they are here with a very specific reason in mind. And based upon where they have been seen, they're circling. They're looking for something."

"That was me, I thought of that!" the little merchant piped up. "She kissed me for that!"

"Is that your normal approach for acquiring assistance?" Orion smirked.

Having spent her entire adult life constantly pursued by men, Aestelle recognized even the subtlest jealousy as soon as it presented itself to her. She suppressed a smug smile.

"Oh, I'll go a lot further than that," she said casually, jabbing a thumb at the jeweled greatsword on her back. "You should hear the story about what I did to get this sword. Back to the task in hand, you and I alone can't stop this army. But what we can do is hamper them until reinforcements get here from the south, or word reaches the border forts to the north. Either way, if we pester these bastards by killing any of them that dare to stray from the main pack, they'll stop straying. They'll be forced to stay together and that will seriously hinder their attempts to find whatever it is that they're looking for."

"What do you think that is?" Orion asked.

Aestelle bit her bottom lip.

"I have my suspicions. We can talk about that on the ride out of here. Ah, speaking of which."

The small crowd parted as a farmer led a broad, black horse with a neat, white stripe running down from the top of his head to his nose. Aestelle narrowed her eyes. She was no expert on horses, but it was clear that this particular specimen was well past his prime. Still, the animal looked strong and was saddled.

"I have the two things you asked for," the bearded farmer announced as he led the horse over. "One horse, one bottle of the best wine I could find."

"Good job," Aestelle said.

She snatched the bottle of wine, pulled the cork out with her teeth, and spat it out before draining half of its contents in one continuous gulp.

"And to think that you were a nun for nearly twenty years," Orion whispered under his breath.

Aestelle lowered the bottle and let out a gasp of contentment as the bitter liquid quenched her thirst.

"And now I'm making up for lost time with all the fun things in life they kept from me!" she smiled sarcastically at the paladin.

"Does that tie in to the story behind how you got that sword, too?" Orion asked with a sardonic smirk.

"Maybe," Aestelle returned the smirk.

"This is the best horse for a good few miles," the farmer cut in, handing the reins over to Orion. "He's a little long in the tooth, but as strong as an ox. He'll do you proud."

Taking Aestelle completely by surprise, a small boy of perhaps seven or eight years of age suddenly ran from the back of the crowd and yanked the reins out of Orion's hand, tears streaming down his cheeks.

"No!" the boy cried. "You can't have him!"

The farmer smiled uncomfortably, putting an arm around the boy's shoulders.

"My son, Davith," he said apologetically. "I'm afraid he loves this old horse."

"You can't take him!" the boy shouted again. "He'll get hurt!"

Aestelle held up a hand to stop Orion's response. She leaned over the distressed farm boy and laid a hand on his shoulder.

"Don't worry," she beamed. "He's old now! He's had a good run. This is a great way to go out!"

The boy's eyes widened in horror and his crying amplified in volume to hysterical wailing. Aestelle stood and took an uncomfortable step back. After years of finding nothing but annoyance in children, all of the bridges built by her heartfelt encounter with the little girl she had recently rescued were instantly torn down by the wailing farm boy.

"That is the best you could come up with?" Orion snapped incredulously.

Aestelle swore at him and returned to necking her bottle of wine. The paladin dropped down to one knee in front of the boy and smiled.

"What is your horse's name?" he asked gently.

"Henry!" the boy cried.

"I only need to borrow Henry. I just need his help for a few days. I shall bring him back to you. You see, he is a farm horse, not a knight's horse. He belongs here on a farm, with you."

The boy nodded, his cries dying down a little.

"Henry does not know how to be a knight's horse, so I cannot use him in battle," Orion explained. "I just need him to move around a little quicker. If things get dangerous, I shall not be taking Henry near the fighting."

The boy looked up at Orion, the hysterics continuing to die away.

"It is just for a few days," Orion said again, gently taking the reins, "and I promise you that if I am still fit enough to ride, I shall bring him back here to you before I go home. Is that alright?"

The farm boy nodded slowly before turning to bury his head in his father's chest as the farmer picked him up, nodding to Orion and Aestelle to leave. Aestelle walked over to her own horse and swung herself up into her saddle.

"Well, if you are quite done with yanking on the heartstrings of the simple folk, shall we go kill something?"

Orion jumped up into the saddle of the muscular farm horse. His face screwed up in confusion and he leaned forward over the animal.

"What's that, Henry?" he asked, perplexed, and then nodded and sat up again.

"Henry says you are dead inside and need to take yourself less seriously," Orion translated with a feined, uneasy smile.

Aestelle turned in her saddle to fix Orion with a dangerous glare.

"Tell Henry to go f…"

The small crowd of villagers cheered and waved as the two warriors rode at a fast canter off to the south.

Seventeen

Orion was not well suited to stealth. Trying to emulate Aestelle's silent, graceful movements, he clunked behind her as they dashed from tree to tree, closing the distance between themselves and the small group of Abyssals moving through the twilight lit undergrowth ahead. The wooded hill crested at an opening up ahead where, according to the information they had been given by locals, a stone circle had been set up in the Time of Light for worshipping the Celestials. After a few minutes of following the demons up the shallow slope, Orion saw the site up ahead; twelve rough obelisks standing tall at the top of the hill, silhouetted by the setting sun.

Aestelle crouched behind a tree trunk up ahead, a few feet back from the edge of the foliage. Orion walked carefully over to her again, wincing as every footstep resulted in the jingling of mail armor or the dull clunking of metal plate impacting metal plate at his elbow and knee joints. Aestelle fixed him with a warning glare as he knelt next to her. Orion shrugged an apology. Aestelle leaned against him and pressed her lips next to his ear, the scent of her expensive perfume washing over him.

"Did you have to polish that bloody armor? It's like sneaking next to a lighthouse."

Orion opened his mouth to point out their inability to attack from downwind due to her vanity, but Aestelle silenced him by holding a leather-clad finger up to her lips. She beckoned for him to wait where he was and then crept silently closer to the edge of the clearing at the top of the hill. Orion watched the Abyssals, ten in all, stomp purposefully around the ancient site of worship, their blazing eyes alternatively checking the trees around them and the obelisks themselves. It seemed surreal to Orion to watch them carry out the sort of activities one would expect from intelligent beings; to him, lower Abyssals were little more than wild animals, yet here they were checking over the tall stones ahead and even exchanging words in their guttural, vile language.

The last moments of his fight against the Abyssals at the campsite suddenly forced their way back to the fore of his mind. He remembered his feelings of rage and violence giving way to fear and despair as he succumbed to his wounds, surrounded by a neverending tide of demonic adversaries as his lifeblood flowed from his multiple injuries. He remembered the sight of the dead paladins who lay at his feet amidst the devils he had cut down, little more than names to him the day before the battle, but now they were dead brothers and sisters in arms who he bitterly regretted never taking the chance to befriend.

Above all, he again regretted his failure with Kell, the boy who had looked to him for guidance and found none. The dark humor he had briefly shared with Aestelle at the tavern now gave way to waves of despair as years of campaigns, killing, and dead comrades washed over him; horrific sights he would not wish upon anybody, wading their way from the back of his mind to dominate his thoughts. Orion let out a gasp, raising a hand to his head and closing his eyes. When he looked up, he saw Aestelle crouched in front of him. She placed a hand on his shoulder and looked directly at him, concern registering in her silver-blue eyes.

"You alright?" she mouthed silently.

Orion nodded.

She moved closer to whisper into his ear again.

"I couldn't understand much of what they were saying. They're looking for something, and it's not here. As I said on the ride across, I'm pretty sure it's a portal stone they're trying to find."

"I thought you spoke their tongue?!" Orion whispered. "You said you were a demon hunter!"

"*Apprentice!* A decade ago! So forgive me if I haven't been keeping on top of my demonic language studies! Listen, I'm going over to the far side of the clearing. Give me two minutes. Then I want you to do what you do; come out fighting and hack these bastards down. As soon as they turn to face you, I'll start putting arrows through their backs. Understood?"

Orion nodded. Her words triggered uncomfortable thoughts. '*What you do.*' Was there more to him than just killing? Had Jahus succeeded in guiding him into becoming a better man than that? Had the Elohi?

Aestelle fixed him with a serious expression.

"Keep it together, Paladin, I don't know what's going through your mind but if you lose it now, I'm in trouble. I won't stand for that. Just do what you do best."

Orion nodded again and watched her disappear into the rapidly darkening trees. He slowly and silently unsheathed his sword and looked down at the blade. When he was rescued by the Elohi, his helmet, longsword, and shield had been left behind. He still had his greatsword, but that was too heavy to effectively use on horseback if the situation called for it. The greatsword was meant to be used as a two-handed weapon, so the lack of a shield was not a problem; but fighting without a helmet to protect the most vulnerable part of the body was less than ideal. But fight he must, and the time had come. He rested a hand briefly on his uncle's Eloicon, muttered a quick prayer, and stood to stride to the edge of the clearing.

Without ceremony, Orion walked purposefully out toward the center of the stone circle. He felt calmer than normal before battle, less angry, but the clarity of mind also allowed him to realize the danger he faced. He felt fear. An angry, hateful phrase was growled from the first of the Abyssals to see him, and the ten red-skinned monsters immediately fanned out to encircle him, hissing and snarling as they stood with their swords and axes held ready.

Orion heard a thud and saw the head of one of the Abyssals loll. The hellish creature turned groggily to look behind, revealing an arrow lodged in the center of its back. A second arrow flew, catching the same Abyssal through the neck and dropping it down to the earth. Roars and snarls were quickly exchanged, and five of the lower Abyssals hurtled toward Orion while the others ran toward where Aestelle was no doubt loosing her arrows from the trees.

Rushing out to meet the first attacker, Orion flung his sword down in a powerful overhead attack. He was surprised to find his strike skillfully deflected by an agile defense from the creature, but the might of his attack threw the demon's guard aside. Orion took advantage of the opening by swinging a clenched fist into the Abyssal's face, feeling the crunch of bone as he dislodged the monster's jaw and knocked it dazed to its knees. The paladin quickly took off the demon's head with his sword and brought his guard back up as the remaining four demons stood in a loose circle around him, shouting out aggressively in their hideous tongue.

Orion lunged at the nearest devil, linking a flurry of blows that forced the Abyssal to step back as it desperately tried to defend itself from the vicious onslaught of strikes. The demon fell down on its back, but before Orion could finish the creature off, he was attacked on both sides by two more of his adversaries. His advantage was now completely reversed as he desperately brought his blade up to block attacks from all quarters, conscious that a third Abyssal was moving around behind him in an attempt to stab him in the back.

Deflecting a low blow aimed at his legs, Orion brought his sword swinging around in a long arc to connect the flat of the blade with the face of one of his Abyssal assailants, sending a torrent of blood and sharp teeth flying from its mouth. Continuing the sword's line of travel in a long, fluid arc, Orion brought the blade back up to sever the same creature's leg halfway up the thigh. The maimed demon fell to the ground, spraying black blood up from its stump as it writhed in agony. But the attack had left his right side exposed, and Orion knew the attack was coming moments before he felt an axe bite into his own leg, parting the links of his mail armor.

Letting out a cry of pain, Orion felt his leg give way beneath him. As he dropped to one knee, he saw the axe-wielding Abyssal responsible for his wound dart toward him, weapon held high in both clawed hands. Orion thrust his heavy sword out, piercing the creature's neck with the broad blade and sending it falling to one side, clutching at the fatal wound and gurgling in its own blood. Gritting his teeth, Orion forced himself back up to his feet and pressed a hand against his wound, summoning his meager knowledge of divinity magic to heal the injury.

The two remaining opponents advanced warily toward him, one of the creatures stopping briefly by the prone, screaming body of the demon missing its leg. The tall Abyssal brought the tip of its own blade down to pierce the chest of its injured fellow, killing it outright before remorselessly continuing toward Orion. Feeling drained from the simple act of one healing spell, Orion knew he needed to make the next few moments count, as he would not be healing the next wound he suffered.

Darting to his left, Orion bought himself a brief moment by lining his two adversaries up to deny them the opportunity to attack him simultaneously. He then flung himself forward to attack, slashing his blade at the closer demon's head and chest, and forcing it to bring its blade up to defend. Unable to counter Orion's superior speed and strength, the Abyssal took a step back, its guard still high. Orion lunged forward and thrust his sword through the demon's gut, sliding the blade all the way up to the hilt until he was eye to eye with the dying Abyssal.

The final demon brought its sword down to strike Orion's pauldron, failing to penetrate the thick armor. Orion planted a foot on the dying creature in front of him and yanked his sword free, but that gave his final opponent enough time for another strike. This time the demon aimed well, catching Orion in the upper arm and drawing a spray of blood from a deep gash across his bicep. Orion growled in pain, instinctively turning his uninjured side to face the maniacally grinning adversary. Unsure whether the wound would hinder his ability to wield his heavy sword, Orion flung himself at the final Abyssal and knocked it to the ground.

Both warriors wrestled to gain the upper hand against each other as they rolled through the grass, but the struggle was short lived, given Orion's size and strength. He rolled on top of the hissing, snapping demon and slammed a metal clad fist into its face, again and again and again, until the creature's struggles grew weaker and blood dripped from his fist. Orion looked around frantically for his sword but saw it discarded several feet away; his eyes picked a rock out in the darkness instead, so he lifted it high above his head and brought it crashing down on the Abyssal, time and time again until he felt the skull cave in.

His injured leg aching, blood dripping down his right arm from his open wound, and gore covering his left hand from beating the Abyssal to death, Orion wearily clambered back up to his feet, recovered his sword, and stumbled over toward Aestelle. The tall woman stood against two opponents, desperately defending herself in a furious melee against both fanged creatures; two more Abyssals lay dead at her feet. Orion let out a roar and quickened his pace toward them. Both Abyssals looked across at the blood-soaked paladin limping furiously over from killing five of their brethren and quickly sprinted off into the woods behind Aestelle.

"Take them down!" Orion yelled. "Shoot them!"

Sweat dripping from her brow, Aestelle shook her head.

"Let them go," she breathed heavily, "let them run back to their friends. I want those bastards to know all about us."

Orion exhaled and sheathed his greatsword, looking down at the Abyssals Aestelle had killed.

"What went wrong?" he demanded.

"I had it covered," Aestelle snapped, "I didn't need your help. Don't think for a second that you've rescued me or I owe you one. I can take care of myself."

"Yet the question remains," Orion continued, his blood still boiling from the fight. "You tell me you took on six of them single-handed, yet this has not gone as well."

"I have a way of dealing with these things," Aestelle said as she collapsed to sit on a felled tree trunk. "Get to a distance where you can fill the first enemy with arrows. That's the free one. Then they react. Shoot down the second, and by the time they reach you, they're already halfway to panicking. You only need to take down one or two more and the rest will run."

"So what went wrong?"

"I missed the second one," Aestelle said with evident frustration, "that never happens. Not normally. Anyway, you're in no position to judge. Look at your arm, you've caught one."

Orion nodded down to the torn mail at his leg.

"Two, actually."

Aestelle nodded, lifting her arm to show where three jagged, parallel tears ran through her armor to show exposed skin beneath from her armpit down across her midriff.

"I've already healed myself," she said. "I've got nothing left to help you, not until I've recovered."

"Never mind that," Orion said, "is this a portal stone? Did they find anything useful?"

"I have no idea, I wouldn't know a portal stone if I walked into one."

"What?! You said that Abyssals move using portal stones. If you're some great demon hunter, how come you know nothing about them?"

"I never said I was a great demon hunter!" Aestelle snarled. "Why do you expect so much from me?"

Orion shook his head and turned away. His healing powers had stopped the bleeding in his leg, but it still pained him greatly, and the wound in his arm throbbed from his fingertips to his shoulder.

"Sit down," Aestelle commanded curtly, producing a bandage from inside the top of one of her thigh boots. "I'll stop the bleeding until we can find some light, and then I can stitch that up for you."

Orion sat on the felled tree as Aestelle crouched next to him, unbuckling his pauldron and gauntlet to get a better look at the extent of his wound.

"Why do you expect so much from me?" she repeated, her tone now far less confrontational. "You expect me to know everything about what we face, you expect me to single-handedly slay every Abyssal in our path. Why do you put me on a pedestal?"

Orion winced as Aestelle pressed the bandage against his wound and set about wrapping it around his arm. He took a moment to attempt to find calm and clarity, to channel his words away from confrontation toward something more productive. Perhaps angered by the continual pain flaring up from his wounds, he decided that Aestelle did not have enough blunt honesty in her life. He could provide that.

"I do not put you on a pedestal," he said, "you do that yourself. Half of the words coming out of your mouth are self-praise and adoration. For most people who talk like you do, I would imagine it is a wall to shield their insecurities. But with you, I do not think that is the case. I think you really do think so much of yourself."

"Oh?" Aestelle stifled a laugh. "But you don't think so much of me."

"Not as much as you do, and I doubt there are enough people who stand up to you and tell you that, which is why you are so arrogant. A woman like you can go through life fluttering her eyelids, pouting, and shoving her chest out to get pretty much what she wants. But not from me. I shall tell you how it is even if others are too scared or enraptured by you to do so."

Orion gritted his teeth as the bandage was tied. He waited in silence for a sarcastic quip in response to his assertiveness, but nothing came. Confused, he stood and looked across at Aestelle. The tall woman picked up her bow and began walking down the hill, back toward where they had left their horses.

"We had better find somewhere to lay up for the night," she said quietly. "I'd imagine we'll be fighting them again tomorrow."

*****

Tancred inspected the blade handed back across to him from his surviving squire. The longsword was sharpened, oiled, and the intricacies of the decorative handle cleaned to an impressive shine. He looked up at where the squire stood nervously before him and smiled.

"Good job, Max," he said, "go and get some sleep. We shall be leaving early in the morning."

The young squire nodded silently and departed. Tancred sheathed the sword and stood up, stretching the aching muscles of his back. Their campsite was set up not far from the coastal road, to the north of the encampment massacre and sheltered from the elements in a shallow, natural ditch that remained dry in the unseasonably hot autumn. Jeneveve knelt by the group's campfire, leading the other paladins and a few of the men-at-arms and supplymen in prayer. Tancred picked up his Eloicon and paced over to join them but was stopped as the sound of hooves on the road grabbed his attention. Buckling his sword belt around his waist, he walked out to the road. His nerves settled as he saw Xavier galloping down from the north. The veteran paladin brought his horse to a halt by the encampment and jumped down from the saddle.

"There is something definitely afoot, Lord Paladin," he greeted Tancred. "More reports of the same sort of activity. There is a farm about two hours north of here. The workers there said the same thing. Two Elohi, riding out to do battle with the Abyssals."

The two days heading north, back toward the site of the original massacre where they had lost the majority of their soldiers, had resulted in many similar stories. Two riders, scouring the countryside to strike fear into the hearts of the invading demons. The story did not add up to Tancred, but he was confident that some of it would be based on some truth. They were not alone in their endeavors.

"Did you ask if any of them had seen the two?" Tancred asked. "How do they know they are Elohi?"

"I asked," Xavier nodded, "they said it was two Elohi, a man and a woman. Both were very tall, very powerful with blonde hair and blue eyes. Both were very beautiful."

"Yet they both rode horses," Tancred winced, "which would suggest they cannot fly and therefore do not have the wings possessed by all Elohi, without exception. This is, of course, moving past the obvious fact that an Elohi is twice the size of a man and would crush a horse by sitting on it."

"Do you wish to follow up these reports?" Xavier asked.

Tancred's thoughts were interrupted as, again, he heard the sound of galloping hooves. This time, the riders approached from the south. Xavier followed Tancred back to the road, both paladins with their swords ready at their sides. Two riders hurtled along the road, plumes of dust left in their wake in the early evening sunlight. Tancred could tell, even from some distance, that one of the riders was armored and rode a barded warhorse. Intrigued to see a military man approaching from the direction of the capital, Tancred hoped and prayed for the best, and he stepped out onto the road to attract their attention.

As the two riders approached, Tancred's face broke into a smile as he recognized the lead horseman as a paladin; wearing a lighter shade of blue than a knight of the Sacred Arc, but a paladin nonetheless. The two riders stopped by Tancred and Xavier. The second rider, a tall, lean man with short, dark hair and a neat beard, stepped down from his horse and offered a smile.

"Are you part of Dictator-Prefect Hugh's force, sent by the Duma?" the lead rider demanded, still sat atop his horse.

The paladin, a middle-aged warrior with a scarred face and long, blond-white hair, looked down at Tancred and Xavier expectantly. Tancred noticed a distinctive sword etched on the paladin's belt buckle, marking him out as from the Order of the Blades of Onzyan, another of the largest and most powerful paladin orders in the Hegemony.

"We are the force," Tancred replied, "at least, we are all that has survived. I am Lord Paladin Tancred of Effisus, 15th Cohort, Order of the Sacred Arc. This is Brother Xavier, my second."

"Brother Silus, 1st Cohort, Order of the Blades of Onzyan," the paladin replied, emphasizing the elite nature of his status as a knight of a 1st Cohort. "How many survivors do you have?"

Xavier stepped forward before Tancred could respond.

"I served with your lot sixteen years ago, at the Battle of Yattin Pass," Xavier said gruffly. "Fine Order. I would hate to think that standards have slipped so much that a rank and file paladin thinks it appropriate to address a senior officer of another order from atop his horse, without using the correct marks of respect."

Tancred stifled a smile at the touching mark of loyalty from his senior paladin. Silus lowered himself from his saddle.

"My apologies, Lord Paladin," he said in a tone that clearly indicated he was anything but remorseful. "May I enquire how many of the Dictator-Prefect's detachment have survived?"

Tancred pointed to the ragged group huddled around the fire in prayer.

"That is it. The others are all dead, including the Dictator-Prefect."

"Excuse me."

Tancred looked across to the second man, who moved across and offered his hand in greeting. Flecks of white in the man's beard and temples marked him out as either graying prematurely, or having a youthful face for a man of some forty years. He wore simple leggings of black with a blue jacket and matching cloak. He carried a legion pattern sword at his side, but was otherwise unremarkable.

"My name is Valletto," the man smiled as Tancred accepted his hand, "I was sent here by the Duma. Your message reached the senators and there is naturally much concern. I've been sent here to find out exactly what has happened so we can... cast any rumors aside and work out exactly what assistance you need."

Tancred's eyes widened as he fought to control his rising temper, his fatigue making the battle all the more difficult.

"We need assistance now!" he snapped. "We've over a hundred dead and Abyssals running amuck across the Hegemon's land! We do not need a Duma sponsored investigation, we need soldiers! An entire legion, for starters!"

"I need to get the information to the Duma for that to happen," Valletto said, his hands extended to either side. "Without knowing the extent of the threat, the Duma cannot respond appropriately. The Hegemon's forces are stretched thin from border to border, and beyond."

"And who are you to speak on behalf of the Duma?" Tancred insisted.

"I am the Deputy Senior Battle Mage of the 2nd Legion," Valletto replied. "I was selected to find you by Grand Mage Saffus of Aigina, Advisor Primus of the Arcane to the Duma."

Tancred closed his mouth immediately, exchanging an uncomfortable glance with Xavier. Saffus' reputation as a man never to be trifled with was notorious. Aside from Valletto's faultless credentials as an experienced battle mage, carrying the authority of Saffus of Aigina meant that respect was due.

"I understand, of course," Tancred said, mirroring the older man's use of a passive stance. "We all realize that this is but one threat to our beloved Hegemony. I would never expect the Duma to act on scant information. Just tell me what you need to know, and I will do all I can to provide you with the information you need."

"Thank you," Valletto smiled warmly. "But first, do you have a soldier named Constance?"

Again, Tancred and Xavier exchanged looks.

"You found Constance?" Tancred exclaimed.

"Yes, gravely wounded, sadly," Valletto said gently. "The knights escorting me did all they could to stabilize her injuries. She has been taken to a sisterhood convent where hopefully she will recover."

"What happened to her? Where did you find her?"

"Two days south of here. She had been stabbed. She could only say the name 'Dionne'. Did you find the former captain?"

"Oh, we found him," Tancred grimaced. "He is at the head of the entire Abyssal force."

"What force are we talking about?" Silus asked. "Everybody we have encountered on the ride north has only heard rumors or, at most, seen a mere handful of lower Abyssals."

"No, we saw them," Xavier explained. "They ambushed our encampment at night. They surrounded us on all sides. It was the dead of the night so giving you an accurate number is not possible, but I would estimate that the absolute minimum was two hundred. But double that number could have been hidden in the darkness behind the front ranks, if not more."

Valletto took in a slow breath.

"The Duma has already begun to assemble a force, assuming the worst," he explained, "but I must pass this information on immediately. It will take some time to send the message on to Saffus."

"Set up here for the night with us," Tancred said. "We are in the very midst of the lands polluted with their presence, and there is some safety in numbers."

*****

Valletto sat on a small rock at the edge of the encampment, his eyes drawn to the darkness of the wooded hill a few dozen yards ahead of him, and both hands wrapped around his staff. Leaves rustled in the foliage at the edge of the tree line, no doubt caused by something as harmless as a fox or a small deer. But, his senses on edge and enhanced by the darkness of the night, the disturbance was instantly warped into an army of Abyssals; their evil, malicious eyes fixed on him as they crept stealthily through the undergrowth, their blades held ready for the attack.

A soldier barked a short laugh in the small camp behind him, bringing his senses and imagination back to the real world. Set out on the ground in front of him was the arcane platform he needed to send his message to his master in the City of the Golden Horn. Three lines were drawn in the earth to form an irregular triangle, their measurements exact and precise. The required components were laid at each corner of the triangle; a blue soulgem, a pouch of ether dust, and a vial of marcani powder, again all measured out precisely. Valletto had drawn a circle inside the circle, its line touching two sides of the triangle at specific points. Any incorrect measurement would make the spell fail at best; at worst, he could inadvertently send information, thoughts, or emotions to a random corner of the world, or even into the Abyss itself. The preparations were simple enough; it was triple checking they were correct that took so much time.

Sighing, Valletto dragged himself up to his feet and paced over to take his place in the circle. He sat down untidily in the center, never one for unnecessary emotion. He had seen the spell turned into a theatrical ritual involving gratuitous candles, incantations, and all sorts of unnecessary additions to impress any that watched. But magic was simple enough to him, somewhere between the spiritual and science, and required followed procedures and nothing more. Closing his eyes and drawing a deep breath in through his nostrils, Valletto calmed his mind and focused on the task in hand. It was a spell he had used many times, a spell of the misleadingly named 'petty' school of magic; spells simple enough to be used by sorcerers of any discipline. But while the spell of transmission was simple enough over short distances, to send information across the length of an entire nation was something else entirely.

A mental image of Valletto's family forced its way to the fore of his mind. He let out a breath, smiling, holding onto that image for longer than he should as he savored every last detail of his wife's face, his son's smile, his daughter's eyes. With sadness clawing at his heart, Valletto pushed the image aside and set about mentally reciting the incantations required to push his presence into the arcane plains.

The dark red of his eyelids gave way to the wavy gray of the transition from his physical body as the spell took effect, the sound of his breathing faded away to be replaced by the whistling of the winds as his consciousness leapt up into the night sky above him, leaving the earth behind. There was no grand view, no sweeping panorama of the Basilean countryside below him, just the sensation of weightlessness and a dark, hazy, nauseous view of shimmering gray, patterns not quite identifiable in dull tones. Then he was in, intercepting the plains in the realm of the arcane. To describe them to a non magic user would be akin to describing color to the blind or music to the deaf; it was a sensation, something which surrounded the consciousness but not the physical body, something which permeated and cocooned, which could be tapped into but also could cause great harm if not respected.

"Saffus…" Valletto breathed.

The call went unanswered. Unless a sorcerer had pre-arranged a meeting in the plains, it always would. The simple action of sending a single word across over a hundred miles was draining enough, leaving Valletto feeling weary and fighting a desire to break off the spell. A presence hurtled past him as if he lay on a roadside as a horse and cart thundered by, leaving his mind buffeted and shimmied by the shockwaves of the passing. Another magic user sending his own message using the same spell. A timely reminder of how insecure the messages of the simple spell were, and how easy it was for unwelcome ears to intercept vital information, especially over long distances.

"Valletto."

Valletto felt instant relief as his master's familiar presence reached out to meet him across the plains. The connection was made, but time was of the essence.

"Dionne here, hundreds of Abyssals," Valletto said, his words echoing across the sweeping plains of shimmering gray, nausea again threatening to overwhelm him. At least he had said the most important words if the connection was severed, if his mind could not handle the impact of keeping the connection alive.

"Understood," came the simple reply.

"Dictator dead," Valletto continued, "few survivors."

The gray turned darker. He could hear his breathing again in the physical world, labored, wheezing. He felt pain, sickness, an overwhelming exhaustion from those last four words.

"Vanguard on way," Saffus' voice came back to him, "will push for main force..."

Valletto felt a hideous sensation, as if his head was suddenly yanked back with enough force to break his neck, his presence hauled back away from his master's at a sickening speed. The patterns of swirling gray around him instantly transformed into flicking lines, speeding past him to either side, above and below. He heard retching and realized it was his own body as his mind was yanked backward toward it.

"Easy!" an unfamiliar voice said to him, too distinct and clear to be anywhere but the physical world. "Easy does it!"

Valletto realized that he was on his hands and knees, his head pounding in pain, a vile puddle of his own vomit in the dirt beneath him. Something pressed against his forehead and he felt instant relief, a wave of calmness taking the pain away in a sensation that his arcane mind interpreted as a pale blue. His sight sharpening back into focus and his hearing becoming more distinct, he realized he was by the campfire a few yards from where he had set up the arcane platform, a wall of perhaps twenty men and women surrounding him.

"You will be alright," the voice said again.

Valletto struggled up to his knees and looked up to see Tancred knelt by his side. The red headed knight flashed him a warm smile, one of his hands still pressed against Valletto's head as the paladin's divinity magic continued to fight against the nausea and pain of his magical exertions.

"Thank you," Valletto gasped.

"Have you just tried to send a message all the way to the capital?" the young paladin asked.

Valletto nodded weakly.

"I might not be able to do that, but I do understand the connotations of such an endeavor," Tancred said. "So please be a good fellow and let me know next time you intend to try something like that! I did not realize that was what you meant! Get him some water, would you?"

"Stop staring!" a more authoritative voice ordered the encircling soldiers and paladins. "Give the man some privacy!"

The assembled men and women dispersed in muttered conversation as a female paladin with dark hair crouched down next to Valletto, offering him a tankard of water. Valletto took it with a grateful smile and washed the foul taste away from his mouth.

"I told them," he breathed, "they'll know now. I told them Dionne was here with an army of Abyssals. And that... the Dictator-Prefect is dead. There can be no confusion now. They know. They must act."

"When will we know?" the female paladin asked. "How long until they send us help?"

"It's already on the way," Valletto said after another swig of water. "I was told that a vanguard had already departed. My master said he would apply pressure to the Duma to hasten the departure of the main force."

Tancred looked across at the female paladin and then down at Valletto.

"Then we stay here and we keep them busy until help arrives. How many soldiers are on their way to aid us? How many in the vanguard and how many in the main force?"

Valletto shook his head, his body aching but the main impact of the exertions now beginning to lift noticeably.

"I don't know, I'm sorry. I could not get that level of detail, not from a spell of transmission over that distance. I don't know who is coming, or when."

"It changes nothing," the female paladin said, "we stand and fight them."

"With what?" Valletto breathed, forcing himself to his feet to stretch out his stiff muscles.

"There are a handful of us," Tancred said as he stood, "and the region's magistrate has promised us more men. There are also rumors of resistance in the area."

"What sort of rumors? Is it militia men? There is no garrison for miles."

"Elohi, if you believe that," Tancred smiled. "Two angels on a rampage across the countryside, slaying demons left and right. But there is no sight without light, as they say. I do not believe it is Elohi, but I believe something is going on to give the people hope. And the reports we have heard say it is all happening not far from here. Come, you get some sleep. We shall formulate our plan and inform you in the morning."

*****

Closing together the battered covers of his aged Eloicon, Orion sat up on his bedroll and looked up at the dawn sky. The thin clouds were parting to reveal a blood red heaven above, the horizon itself softened by the yellows and oranges of the rising sun. Orion and Aestelle had camped in the shelter of a small rock face of the leeward side of a wooded hill, shielded from the wind and occasional rain showers that passed through overnight.

Aestelle finished her normal morning routine of press-ups and sit-ups before she recovered a bottle of wine from her pack. She took a mouthful from the bottle before pacing over to Orion and holding out a map in front of him.

"That's where we are off to this morning," she declared, pointing at a cross drawn not far from their location, "there is a group of caves there that were used as a place of worship back during the God Wars. The pattern on Abyssal activity puts these caves in their path, so we shall try there this morning. We will leave as soon as you are ready."

Orion watched wordlessly as Aestelle walked away, taking another swig from her bottle of wine. As pure of heart as paladins were expected to be, he was only human and it was impossible for him not to notice and dwell on her aesthetic appeal. Still, the vocation that life and his father had chosen for him made romantic aspirations difficult at the best of times, even if there was any chance of reciprocation. Orion allowed himself a grim smile. He was hiding behind the vocation – he knew full well that his unapproachable nature was what led to his lonely path and lack of friends and companionship.

Orion stood and placed his Eloicon back in his pack. His eyes fell on the letter he had received from his mother some days ago, which he had still not properly read. He stared at the rolled up letter for a few contemplative moments before taking it and unrolling it. The kind, loving words on the page generated warmth within him, even during the recollections of largely trivial matters back home. Orion read the letter a second time before carefully folding it and placing it inside his Eloicon. He looked up and saw Aestelle waiting for him impatiently by her horse. The woes of the world could wait for five mintes for his mother. Orion took a small bottle of ink and quill from his pack and sat down to write to his mother.

Eighteen

"Well, that is fairly conclusive," Tancred remarked dryly as he looked down at the corpse by his feet, partially hidden in the long grass. From a distance, the dead body could have belonged to a man; the feet were clad in crude, armored boots and the body was liberally protected by rusted flecked plates of brutally spiked iron. It was the blood red skin, goat-like horns, and clawed hands that marked the dead creature out as a lower Abyssal. Flies buzzed noisily in a small, shifting cloud above the corpse.

It was Jeneveve, moving at the head of the small group, who had found the dead demon only a few paces from the small path. Tancred, following up on the latest rumor he had heard from local villagers claiming to have seen the two mysterious figures who traveled the countryside slaying demons, had assembled a small group to follow up on the lead. He, along with Jeneveve, Xavier, Silus, and Valletto had tracked west away from the coast on the advice of a small group of villagers who had remained behind to brave the incursion and stay with their lands.

"This was done by a small blade," Silus remarked as he crouched over the corpse, pointing at a vicious wound across the throat, "I doubt this bastard even knew it was dead before it hit the ground."

"Don't stray too close," Valletto remarked warily as he peered over at the dead Abyssal.

"This thing is dead," Silus fixed the mage with an admonishing glower. "It is not suddenly going to get up and attack. You have been listening to too many campfire tales."

"There's another one over here," Xavier called from a few paces away, half hidden within the dense foliage to the north of the winding path.

Tancred made his way over to his senior knight. Xavier stood over another body, again a lower Abyssal and similarly armed and armored, but killed in a very different way. Two enormous tears had been hacked into the demon's torso, the dimensions of the wounds being very familiar to Tancred.

"Looks like a greatsword," he remarked, "a very different kill to the stealth demonstrated on the other one."

He turned to address the other four warriors as they looked over the second dead Abyssal.

"Spread out, far enough to cover as much ground as you can, but make sure you can see at least two others. I will not have anybody being caught out. If anybody sees anything even vaguely threatening, shout out immediately. I shall take center; Xavier, Silus – left. Jeneveve, Valletto, to my right."

The five warriors began their traipse through the undergrowth as the morning sun continued its climb up into a cloud-streaked sky. Tall, ancient oak trees towered over Tancred as he advanced forward, their branches reaching out seemingly to hold hands with their ancient brethren to form a dense canopy of foliage above. Long, yellow grass sprouted up from the dusty earth to waist height, hiding a plethora of minor hazards ranging from rabbit holes that could cause painful slips and trips, to jagged rocks and sturdy tree roots.

Tancred glanced regularly to his left and right, ensuring he remained close enough to Silus and Valletto at all times in case of any danger. Perhaps a quarter of an hour dragged slowly by, heightened nerves and anxiety were quickly replaced with tedious boredom, until a shout was issued off from the west. Tancred looked over at Silus expectantly.

"It's Xavier," the aging knight called, "he has found something."

Tancred passed the message on to Valletto and Jeneveve, waiting for them to move across to him before they moved as a group over to find Xavier. The veteran knight stood by a broad cave entrance, the brown rock well hidden by weeds and tree roots. Two dead Abyssals lay by the cave entrance; one killed by an arrow to the head while the other had been brutally cut down by a large, bladed weapon.

"There is something in there," Valletto said nervously.

"I know," Tancred nodded.

He could sense the darkness of the Abyss, the maliciousness of the denizens of the Wicked Ones, something foul awaiting them inside.

"No," Valletto said, "something more than that. There is something arcane in there. Something emitting power. It is perhaps what they are looking for."

"Then we must proceed quickly," Xavier said grimly.

Tancred nodded in agreement, quickly formulating a plan in his head.

"Xavier, Silus, take the lead," he commanded, putting his two most experienced warriors at the fore. This allowed him to stay in the center of the group. While many a bard's tale spoke highly of heroes who led from the front, the less dramatic truth of the matter was that his job as the leader was to command from a central position wherever possible.

"Valletto, you stay with me. Jeneveve, protect the rear."

"This is hardly the time for courtliness!" Jeneveve protested bitterly. "I am more than capable of fighting on the front rank!"

"This is even less of a time for insubordination!" Tancred snapped back at her. "So do as I tell you and get to the back! Now!"

Her face twisted in anger, Jeneveve moved to stand behind Tancred and Valletto. Xavier and Silus advanced cautiously into the cave, their swords drawn and their shields raised and ready. Tancred followed close behind them, his own weapon held ready to strike. The cave opened out into a larger cavern, a small trickle of water cascading down between their feet as the warriors moved forward. The few rays of sun that had managed to penetrate the cave entrance were quickly left behind, plunging the group momentarily into darkness until Valletto held up his staff and a pool of pale red light flared up to illuminate the cave, casting long, flickering shadows from the fang-like stalagmites and stalactites jutting out from the surfaces around them.

The chinking of their mail echoing across the caverns, the small group advanced slowly forward to the end of the first cave and into a narrow tunnel, forcing them to move crouched low in single file. Tancred felt a tap on his shoulder.

"Just up ahead," Valletto whispered, "there is some source of power only a few yards away!"

Tancred's grasp of divinity magic did not allow him to experience the same sensation, but he could sense something other than the continual dull, invasive darkness of the Abyss that seemed to surround and envelop him. There was a small point of light in the darkness, a sensation of good up ahead that felt all but identical to the same feeling that emanated from the paladins around him.

"Lord Paladin!" Xavier whispered urgently from the head of the line of warriors. "I think there is one of ours, up ahead! Another survivor!"

"Be wary, Brother," Tancred replied quietly, eager not to let his excitement at the prospect build and overwhelm the anxiety he felt from the darkness he sensed around them.

The five emerged into another larger cavern, the center dominated with a single stone, an obelisk twice the size of a man, covered in detailed, runic carvings on all sides. Around the runic obelisk was a sea of bodies, perhaps a dozen, leaving the rocky floor to the cave awash in an inch of blood. The stench of darkness came from the bodies; all were the red-skinned, fang-toothed lower Abyssals. They lay in a macabre display of mutilation; some missing limbs while others had great wounds cutting their torsos open to expose their innards; one had even been cut clean in half at the waist.

Tancred heard a metallic click behind him and turned to look into the darkness to either side of the cavern entrance. Two figures emerged from the blackness. He immediately recognized Aestelle; the tall, extraordinary beautiful woman lowered her pistol when she showed the same recognition, the decorative beads woven into one side of her hair falling down past her blue eyes, a blood drenched greatsword held over one bare shoulder in a leather gloved hand. To her side was a colossal, muscular young paladin with neat, blond hair and the handsome features one would expect from a hero of the myths and legends of the God War. It took Tancred several moments before he recognized the man stood before him.

"Orion?"

"You are alive!" Orion's face lit up in an astonished smile. "You are all alive!"

The big paladin rushed over to seize Tancred's hand and shake it warmly, before changing his mind and pulling him in to embrace him. Astounded by the discovery, Tancred found himself dumbstruck as he watched Xavier warily shake hands with Orion, while Jeneveve greeted him only with a nod of her head.

"What happened?" Tancred finally managed, taking a step back to look Orion up and down in shock. "Where have you been?"

The tall paladin looked completely different to how Tancred remembered him. The shaven headed, bearded thug had been replaced with a clean cut, dashing knight with blue eyes matching his battered, blue surcoat which hung neatly above highly polished armor of silver and gold, its immaculate finish marred by the bloodstains of recent battle.

"Now is not the time," Jeneveve intervened, "there may be danger close by."

"I sense nothing," Silus said, "other than the filth of darkness around these corpses."

"There is this stone," Valletto said, walking over to place a hand on the obelisk in the center of the cavern. "I can sense the power emanating from this."

"A local huntsman told us of this place," Aestelle explained, "of this ancient stone. We thought it might be a portal stone."

"Clearly Dionne thought the same," Valletto said as he leaned in to examine the runic obelisk. "There would be no other reason to send his creatures here. But I'm afraid this is no portal stone. It is merely an arcane stone. These are far more common. They do little more other than tap into the arcane plains and act as a source of power for those who can summon it."

"Then there is no reason to remain here," Tancred said, "and this is not a safe place for us to discuss the past and the future. We should leave."

*****

The small encampment for the handful of survivors from the first Abyssal attack was not far from the caves, less than half an hour to the south. The ride was at some pace and so did not lend itself to much conversation, although Orion was desperate to hear more news from Tancred about what had happened in his absence. The seven riders reached the encampment; a collection of a few tents pitched in the grounds at the back of an abandoned farmhouse a few miles inland of the main coastal road.

The first thing which leapt out at Orion when he cast his eyes across the encampment was the group of warhorses penned in to a field adjoining the farmhouse. His eyes widened as his instantly recognized his own horse; the huge, lumbering animal plodded vacantly across the field, his tail swishing away at a small cloud of flies in his wake. Orion remembered the charge against the Abyssals from the hilltop, the animal bravely following his commands until he was dragged from the saddle to face the bloody melee below.

Orion jumped down from his saddle and quickly made his way across the field. He had never been the sort of person with a particular affinity for animals; to him, a warhorse was merely a weapon and a means of getting somewhere more quickly, but he felt a true warmth surge through him when the horse noticed him and immediately plodded over. Smiling broadly, Orion rested a hand on the horse's head, stroking the loyal animal with genuine affection.

"Hello, boy," he said quietly, "how in the world did you survive all that? It is good to see you again."

The warhorse nuzzled his snout into Orion's outstretched hand. He opened his mouth to continue talking to the animal but realized that the horse did not have a name. Having served him loyally for years, braving the bestial charges of orcs, the thunderous fire of Abyssal dwarves, and the hellish terror of the Abyssals themselves, Orion had never even bothered to give the poor animal a name.

"Kell," he breathed quietly, "it is a strong name."

He closed his eyes in regret, thinking of the commonalities in how he had let the two down; his warhorse and his squire, both of whom had quietly and obediently put up with him for years.

"Sir?"

Orion span around to face the voice behind him. He took a step back in shock when he saw his squire stood hesitantly at the edge of the field.

"Kell?" he exhaled. "I thought you dead!"

"Likewise, sir," the boy nodded, his face a confused mixture of surprise and anxiety.

Orion looked down at his squire, his heart heavy as he recognized the apprehension in the young man's eyes came from knowing that he must face his master again. The cold, unfeeling demands for perfection in preparation of weapons and armor, the fierce rebukes if service was anything less than perfect. Kell had weathered it all with quiet dignity.

Orion held out his hand. It was the best he could do, all he could think of. To shake hands with a squire was unthinkable, to acknowledge a subservient inferior as an equal with a handshake would be scorned by others. Orion kept his arm outstretched. Kell looked at him nervously.

"It is not a test," Orion said softly, "it is an apology."

Hesitantly, Kell shook his hand. Orion smiled, patting his shoulder and then taking a step back.

"I was just naming my horse after you," he said uncomfortably, "to remind me to appreciate those who help me."

"He already has a name, sir," Kell said. "If you pardon the liberty I took, sir. When you did not name him, I called him Star. After the pattern on his flanks."

Orion smiled again and nodded.

"Star it is, then. I have to talk to the Lord Paladin about our next steps. Come and find me in an hour or so and let me know what I can do to help you with your education. If you want to go through swordsmanship, riding, scripture, divinity, you have a think and let me know. I shall do the best I can to be a better teacher."

"Thank you, sir," Kell gave a slight smile before taking a step back, nodding his head politely and turning to make his leave.

Orion watched him go, wondering if he was overcompensating. Had he been such a bad master? He had never hit the boy, never resorted to name calling. But he could certainly do better.

"I suppose that's the end of the road for poor old Henry now you've got your proper warhorse back," Aestelle said as she walked over, leading her own horse by the reins into the paddock.

"I shall get Henry back to that farmer's boy," Orion replied. "I owe him that much."

"You're not going to leap upon the opportunity to make a joke?" Aestelle narrowed her eyes. "The opportunities for innuendo are plenty right now."

Orion eyed her in confusion.

"I have no idea what you mean."

"Nothing about having a powerful animal between your legs again, straining under the size of the thing, absolutely nothing?"

Orion met her inquisitive gaze for several long and uncomfortable moments in complete silence.

"I have absolutely no idea what you are talking about," he said in all honesty.

Aestelle exhaled and nodded, smiling at him sadly.

"Nevermind. I see you have taken to shaking hands with a squire. There are some who will think you have lost your mind."

"I am not after their approval," Orion replied, patting Star's head gently. "There are a lot of things about the way that I conduct myself that need to change."

"Oh, by the Ones," Aestelle sighed, rolling her eyes, "if I have to hear about your life changing visit by an Elohi one more time, I think I shall shoot myself."

Orion breathed out slowly through his nose in an attempt to counter the anger he felt rising in immediate response to her words as he watched her take a bottle of wine from the saddlebag of her horse and pull the cork out with her teeth.

"If you had been visited by an Elohi, maybe you would take the time to have a good, long look at yourself and try to change for the better. There is plenty I need to change about myself, so I am trying my best to do it. Perhaps you could start with something as simple as cutting down how much you drink."

Aestelle lowered the bottle from her lips and stared angrily at Orion.

"I don't need to be visited by Elohi," she hissed under her breath, her eyes checking to either side as she spoke. "My father was one of them! I have a close enough connection to your sacred angels, thank you very much!"

"Then why do you resent me so much for the visit I was honored with?" Orion demanded, turning to face her square on and folding his arms.

"Because they didn't visit me!" Aestelle snapped. "They never did! My father was one of them, and they never came! How many people do you think there are in Basilea, no, all of Mantica, who have an Elohi as a mother or father? Half a dozen, perhaps? Across the entire world? Your hero, Gnaeus Sallustis, is well known for having been born of an Elohi mother, and look where that's got him!"

Orion frowned, unsure at what had caused the pent up anger to overspill. Gnaeus Sallustis held the rank of Grand Master of Paladins, in charge of every individual paladin Order in all of Basilea. The great paladin was the shining example to all; devout, courageous, a peerless warrior, and a genius strategist, he was famed and loved across all of Basilea and rightfully feared across the rest of Mantica.

"The Grand Master earned his position at the head of our Orders," Orion said defensively. "I have never met him. I know some who have, and none have anything but respect for him. He is a great man who has worked tirelessly for the Hegemony."

"He is half Elohi!" Aestelle growled. "Just like me, and a tiny number of others! He is faster, stronger, and more intelligent than all of those around him! He was born with an unfair advantage! That is not the stuff of heroes! Just effortlessly dancing into a position of respect and authority while those around tire and toil with little or no reward for their efforts, neglected and ignored for the crime of being born normal!"

"And so you resent him," Orion nodded, her frustration now making more sense to him. "You hate him for his crime of being admired, respected, loved, and successful. You resent me because the Elohi saw fit to save my life, and my soul, and put me on the right track. You think you deserved that visit more than I. You think you deserve the love and admiration Basilea heaps upon Grand Master Sallustis."

Aestelle turned her head away from him but remained quiet. Content that he had hit the crux of the problem, Orion continued.

"But you do not deserve it. Because the Grand Master did one thing, one huge, pivotal, vital thing that you did not. He stuck it out. Training as a paladin is difficult, immeasurably difficult. Most fail. Some are even killed just in training. But the Grand Master stuck it out to the end. When he tired, he continued. When he fell, he stood back up again. But you? The moment you encountered difficulty in the sisterhood, you turned your back and fled. You ran away. If you had stuck it out, who knows what would have happened. You could be the Grand Abbess of the entire sisterhood by now, Sallustis' opposite. You could have achieved that with that unfair advantage you yourself admitted you were given. But you did not. You ran away. And now you dare to judge my Grand Master, and you dare to judge me."

The tall woman nodded slowly. She took another swig from her bottle of wine and looked at the ground for a few moments in silence. Orion almost immediately regretted his words. He opened his mouth to apologize, but pride immediately beat down humility and the words failed to materialize.

"There are so many things I could say to you," Aestelle said softly, "but you aren't worth it. You're just the same as they were, the women who I left the sisterhood to get away from. You have the last word, if that is what you want. I'm above this. I'm above you."

Aestelle slowly walked away, leading her horse by the reins with one hand

and swigging from the bottle of wine with the other. Orion watched her walk away helplessly, unable to find the courage to swallow his pride and run after her. He found himself dwelling on her words, on what she had said when she had first found him after the Elohi had visited him. She had told him that she would never let him down. She had been right.

In all of their encounters with the Abyssals over the days they had traveled across the region, in every fight they stood back to back, surrounded by greater numbers of the hellish demons, she had never let him down. She had always protected him. He had never once needed to worry about her having his back. He realized then how much he cared for her. Far more than he should after knowing her for only a few days.

Orion's attention was dragged away from gazing regretfully at the beautiful woman when he heard footsteps approaching him. He turned to see Tancred making his way over from the small, tented encampment.

"Come on," the shorter man said, "everyone is together. It is time for us to discuss exactly where we are and where we are going next."

Orion nodded.

"Can you go and get Aestelle?" Tancred asked.

"Probably best you do," Orion offered an uncomfortable smile.

"Oh."

Tancred returned the smile sympathetically and patted Orion on the shoulder as he walked past the older knight toward the brooding woman who walked alone at the far side of the paddock.

*****

In Tancred's mind, the clucking of hens and other assorted farmyard animal noises went a long way to detract from the severity of the situation as he unrolled the parchment map and spread it across the table in the farmhouse's small kitchen. The room itself was clean but austere, indicating that the family dwelling in the house were not particularly affluent and had not left the area long ago. Gathered around the table were the other five paladins from the Order of the Sacred Arc, Brother Paladin Silus of the Order of the Blades on Onzyan, Valletto, and Aestelle.

"These are the sightings we have of Abyssals in this area in the last few days," Tancred started, pointing to marks he had made on the map. "We have heard many rumors, but these are reported sightings that are most likely. You can all see that they congregate around Fresh Creek as a sort of central point."

Orion leaned over to point at the map.

"These are the four places that Aestelle and I fought against them. They tie in with what you have heard."

"Six," Aestelle corrected, "I fought them twice before I found you. Here… and here. While we are not sure entirely how many of these red-skinned bastards Dionne has with him, we've knocked that number down quite significantly by hacking away at them when they break off from the main group in small numbers."

"I'm afraid not," Valletto offered a regretful smile.

Aestelle glared across at the dark haired mage.

"What do you mean, 'I'm afraid not'?! We've killed enough of them to make a difference!"

"It doesn't work like that, I'm afraid," Valletto continued awkwardly, "not with this sort of army. The portal stone that Dionne or one of his lieutenants is carrying is the key. You see, if it was a simple case of this being a portal without much power, it could be opened periodically to keep trickling Abyssals through. Fortunately for us it does not work like that. It works on capacity."

Confused as to whether that was good news or bad news, Tancred leaned in closer. Valletto looked around the assembled paladins and, clearly convinced that a more in depth explanation was required, he continued.

"Abyssals do not belong in the mortal world. In the same way that a mortal could not survive within the Abyss, not for a protracted period of time at any rate; Abyssals will wither and die in our world. The portal stone not only allows them to physically travel to our world, it allows them to stay here. So, if you are killing lower Abyssals then it is, I'm afraid, simply a matter of replacing them. As long as the portal stone is still in the hands of somebody who can wield its power, it is easy enough to open another gateway to the Abyss and bring replacements through."

"So we've achieved nothing!" Aestelle slammed a gloved fist into the table. "All of that was for naught!"

"No," Orion said softly, shaking his head, "we showed the people here that they were protected. We gave them some hope, even if only a little. If forcing Dionne to waste time and effort to bring replacements across impeded his progress and saved a singe innocent life, then it was all worthwhile."

"That is the past," offered Reynauld, a tall paladin with plain features punctuated by a long scar running down to his chin. "What of the future? What now?"

"They are looking for a larger portal stone, that much we know from the magistrate," Tancred continued.

"Magistrate?" Aestelle asked. "What magistrate?"

"The magistrate of this region," Xavier replied, "we crossed paths a few days ago. His interrogators were able to… derive some information from an Abyssal agent we encountered, the same man who poisoned the Dictator-Prefect. He has also promised us some soldiers."

"Magistrate Turius?" Aestelle narrowed her eyes. "Tall, white hair, looks halfway to being undead already?"

"That sounds like the fellow," Tancred agreed.

Aestelle looked away, her eyes narrowed as a seemingly involuntary shiver pulsed through her for a brief moment. Tancred decided it was not prudent to query the reaction in front of the others and continued.

"If Dionne's portal stone is already at capacity, both for how far from the

Abyss he is and how many Abyssals he can keep sustained, it makes perfect sense that he is looking for a much larger stone – something far too heavy to move. He knows the rough area but is, I would wager, following up every tale, legend, and local folklore story he can torture out of anyone unfortunate enough to cross his path. But when he finds that stone, he can use it to bring a much larger force here?"

"Precisely," Valletto confirmed. "It is a long, complex and dangerous ritual to activate such a portal stone, but if it wields enough power, then Dionne could bring forth an entire army. Thousands, if not tens of thousands."

Tancred winced, a numb pain pounding at his temples. The only reason that an entire Abyssal invasion had not occurred was through luck rather than a well devised and prepared defense.

"Why?" Reynaud asked. "I understand that he is angry for the accusations leveled at him, but fully turning to the side of darkness? Carrying out actions that would bring about the fall of an entire nation?"

"Sadly, I do not think it matters why," Jeneveve said quietly. "It matters that it is so. But we have an army? Traveling north as we speak?"

"We have the vanguard of an army," Valletto said. "I could not keep the connection to my master for long enough to ascertain how many soldiers are heading this way. But they had already been dispatched. They could be very close. The main force will leave soon, Grand Mage Saffus will ensure that."

"And until then?" Silus said gruffly. "What do you propose?"

Tancred paused. He cast his eyes across the other warriors in the small kitchen. Orion appeared pensive, stonefaced; Silus and Aestelle both seemed angry and impatient; Jeneveve looked hopeful if anything, while Valletto's nervousness was obvious.

"We are not heading south, that much I am sure of," Tancred began, voicing his thoughts as they rushed through his mind. "Self preservation is tertiary at best, given the stakes. We will remain here. I see two options – we either find this stone first and do what we can to hide it or defend it, or we confront Dionne head on and attempt to slow his progress until reinforcements arrive."

"I say head on," Aestelle said immediately, "not across an open field of battle, his force is too powerful for that. But if we can find him, then instead of whittling away his Abyssal minions, there is a chance we can slay his lieutenants, perhaps even Dionne himself."

"Agreed," Xavier nodded.

"Aye," Silus nodded.

"No," Jeneveve shook her head, "we are all that stands in his way until the forces of the Hegemon arrive. A noble sacrifice is not what is called for. There is no guarantee of victory if that is the case. If we stop him getting to the portal stone, we stop the Abyssal invasion. In my mind it is that simple. We must find the stone first."

Tantus, the youngest of the assembled paladins, gave a curt nod of agreement.

"I also agree," Valletto said quietly. "That is the arcane solution rather than the soldier's play. Keep the stone and the demon apart and all are safe. The main force will arrive and then this entire problem is resolved."

"And how do we find the stone?" Silus snapped. "If Dionne cannot find it with a few hundred Abyssals scouring our lands, how will we?"

"I can find it," Valletto replied confidently. "The location of every known portal stone in Basilea is recorded in our archives. I can contact Saffus again and have him tell me where the stone is."

"Every known stone, you say," Aestelle planted her hands on the table and leaned forward, "and what if the stone they are searching for is not known to your arcane library?"

"I'm sorry, who are you, exactly, to be part of this decision making process?" Valletto demanded, his temper flaring a little for the first time Tancred had noticed since meeting the mage.

Aestelle stood again to her full, impressive height and folded her toned arms, looking across at Tancred expectantly.

"Aestelle was part of our force before the Abyssal attack at our encampment," Tancred said. "She had the Dictator-Prefect's trust and she has mine. She is the one who got the message through to you in the first place."

"Alright," Valletto held his hands up passively, "but the fact remains that a decision must still be made."

Tancred nodded, looking down at the map on the kitchen table again. For a moment, the severity of the situation hit him with full force. If Dionne was successful, if he managed to find the stone and activate a major gateway to the very Abyss itself, who knew what power would be behind the force which would spew forth. The very best outcome would be a rapid response from the Duma and the full might of the Hegemon's forces brought against the demonic invasion, resulting in the loss of life for thousands. At worst, it would very simply be the end of Basilea and a horrific expansion of the power of the Wicked Ones.

"Orion," Tancred looked up to the big knight stood at the back of the room, "you have been quiet. Even more so than normal."

"I shall follow your orders to the best of my ability, Lord Paladin," the blond knight nodded seriously.

"But what of your opinion?"

Orion's blue eyes darted from warrior to warrior as they each looked back at him expectantly.

"At the very least, I say we allow Valletto to contact his superiors," Orion finally said. "We lose nothing by gathering more information, especially if that information is unknown to our enemy."

"We lose nothing, except time!" Aestelle snapped. "Time we cannot afford to lose! For all we know, Dionne has found that portal stone while we have been procrastinating and debating our options here, and has already begun the ritual! We need to be out there, now, closing with our enemies and killing them!"

"Take the cleverer option, Lord Paladin," Jeneveve urged, eliciting a bitter curse from Aestelle.

Before Tancred could answer, the door to the farmhouse kitchen was flung open by an excited looking young squire.

"Lord Paladin!" he gasped. "Our reinforcements have arrived!"

Tancred exchanged a brief look of surprise with Orion before bounding for the door and barging past the squire, his spirits lifting with each step. Rushing out into the cool afternoon air, Tancred felt his optimism deflate just as quickly as it had arisen. Up ahead on the road, two ranks of men marched over the crest of the hill leading up to the farm. The men wore ill-fitting jerkins of studded leather and iron helmets; each carried a spear or halberd across one shoulder and had a short sword strapped to their waist.

"This is not the reinforcements," Tancred muttered to himself as he walked out to meet them.

With a barely comprehensible shout of command from an aging soldier at the front of the shabby procession, the forty men stopped on the road and then turned to face Tancred as he approached them. The aging soldier walked out and saluted Tancred by smartly placing one hand against the haft of his halberd.

"I'm Dorn, Lord Paladin," the man said, his tone respectful. "I'm the sergeant of the Fresh Creek Militia. Magistrate Turius sends his compliments and has instructed me to place these men under your direct command."

"Thank you, Sergeant," Tancred nodded, casting his eyes across the motley assortment of fighting men. "Fall your men out, please."

Dorn saluted again and turned sharply to bellow another unintelligible command to his men, resulting in them turning to the right and then walking off toward the farmhouse. Tancred watched them go; the majority were old men with a smattering of boys still in their teen years; a handful were possibly ex-legion judging by the higher standards evident in the personal maintenance of their weapons and equipment, but even those men carried limps or other evident injuries.

"It is better than nothing," Orion offered as he walked over to catch up with Tancred.

The Lord Paladin continued to watch the scruffy militiamen in silence, mentally weighing up his options for progressing with his small, barely trained force.

"Could you go and find Valletto, please?" he asked Orion. "Tell him to contact his master to find out the location of that stone. Then we shall pack up and go to find the wretched thing ourselves."

Nineteen

The seven squires looked up at Orion expectantly as he rolled out the map on the ground between them. With only two hours or so of daylight left, it was late for traveling, but every moment mattered, and Tancred had decided to move north overnight. Orion looked over the eager and anxious faces of the adolescent boys and girls who knelt around the map, their few belongings in small bags by their sides.

"No doubt you will have seen Valletto, the legion mage, over the past day or so. He has been in contact with another mage in the capital. We now think we know where the portal stone is."

"Where, sir?" asked Carolyn, a blonde haired girl of fifteen years of age.

"Right here," Orion said, pointing to a hill on the map, just a mile inland of the coastal town of Andro, "but you shall not be coming with us. I have another idea of how to better use the seven of you, and Lord Paladin Tancred has approved it."

A few of the squires looked disappointed, almost resentful at being left out of the move to Andro; a couple of the younger boys now seemed even more anxious.

"There is a relief force on the way north from the City of the Golden Horn," Orion continued, "Valletto has just heard that the vanguard is only a day or so to the south, while the main force will leave in the next two days. What we do not know is what route the vanguard will be taking, and they have no mage with them so we cannot communicate with them. That is where you come in."

The young squires hung on his words attentively.

"You will head south in three groups. The first group will take the coastal trade route, the second group will move through the hills toward Fort Rocke, while the last group will travel even further inland, down through Snake Pass. You all need to move fast. The further you get to the south, the safer you are. I trust you do not need me to emphasize to you just how disastrous it would be if the information you now know were to fall into the hands of the Abyssals."

"We cannot risk that," said Francis, the oldest of the squires, "and from what Sister Jeneveve has told us, even with the best will in the world, we would not weather the torture that would befall us if we were captured. So if we are surrounded, we know what we must do."

225

Orion exhaled uncomfortably at the young man's words. His implied choice of action was both wise and brave.

"It shall not come to that!" Orion forced optimism into his tone. "Because you are leaving now. You will be well ahead of anything that can harm you even by nightfall. Francis will split you into groups. Kell – I want you on the coastal road, I have another job for you. All of you, be sure you know exactly where the portal stone is, because our success depends on the accuracy of the report you issue to our relief force. We are relying on you. The defense of the Hegemony rests with you."

The seven youths exchanged excited looks at Orion's words. All except for Kell, who kept his impassive gaze fixed on Orion.

"So get to it!" Orion smiled as he folded up the map and stood up. "Ride fast, be ready with a strong sword arm if needed, and for whoever finds the relief force: make sure they know where to find us. Then get back to the capital. Shining Ones protect you all, I shall see you in a few days."

Orion watched Francis enthusiastically split his little team into three groups, excitedly responding to the menial task that Orion had assigned to them. Kell stood and walked over to Orion, giving him a short bow before addressing him.

"You said you had another job for me, sir," he said wearily.

"You do not seem particularly enthused with your task," Orion observed.

"I... I appreciate you sending us to safety, sir. But if I may, I think every sword arm available would be better employed here."

Orion smiled fondly and placed a hand on the boy's shoulder.

"You have seen right through me," he said honestly to his squire, his voice low to keep it from the other youths. "I should have known better. But keep it to yourself; faith and hope are powerful weapons. Yes, you are correct, I am sending you all to safety. We know the relief force is on the coastal road, but it is still vital that you direct them to the hills west of Andro, for that information they do not have."

"That is simple enough, sir," Kell said despondently, "but I would rather fight here."

"There will be plenty of time for that," Orion said, "and your next master will train you better than I ever did."

"Next master?" Kell's eyes lit up with concern. "You are not content with my service, sir?"

Orion raised his brow and smiled sadly.

"You are... not planning on returning to the capital," Kell nodded.

"It is out of my control," Orion said, "but sadly I would wager that the odds do not favor us. But it is our calling. It is what we are here to do. But enough of that! I said I had another job for you. I have marked a convent on your map. Do you remember Constance, the captain of the mercenary company? Valletto says she survived and is recovering there. Please send her my kindest regards and thank her for her friendship. That is important to me. Can you do that for me?"

"Yes, sir," Kell said, determination lighting his green eyes, "but... could I impose upon you to do something for me?"

"Of course," Orion replied, curious as to what the request might be.

"Sister Jeneveve," Kell said after a long and uncomfortable pause. "Please, as much as it is within your power to do so, please try to stop any harm befalling her."

Given the boy's age, a clandestine attraction to the pious, graceful Jeneveve made perfect sense. Orion barely knew the woman, but knew her well enough to know that she would not respond well to the thought of a squire being attracted to her. Nonetheless, he nodded his agreement to Kell.

"I shall do all I can," he said, glancing across as the squires mounted their horses behind Kell. "Now go. Get yourself away from this place."

Kell looked up at Orion, his face a mask of anxiety and apprehension.

"Thank you," he finally managed before turning to mount his horse.

Orion watched as the seven squires kicked their mounts into a trot and headed across the fields to the south. He turned and saw Aestelle watching him from where she leaned against the edge of the farmhouse, the sole of one foot planted on the wall behind her and her arms folded. Instantly, he remembered his last exchange of words with her, his accusations and criticisms of her leaving the sisterhood. He did not need to search his soul very deeply to realize how malicious and unfair his words had been. He walked straight over to her.

"I have come to apologize..."

Aestelle held a hand up to stop him.

"Don't worry," she shrugged nonchalantly, "I deserved it. People tend not to tell me what I need to hear. Most men just tell me what they think I want to hear. I suppose I'm not used to it."

Orion kept eye contact with her for a few moments.

"Are you coming with us?" he asked.

"Yes. Did you send the squires away to keep them from the fight?"

Orion nodded.

"Good. Probably for the best."

"I doubt they could have helped much," Orion said. "Even with all their heart, it takes more than fervor to kill demons."

"I was rather hoping to rely on fervor," Aestelle said as she stood up away from the wall. "I've spent too long fighting only for money. Might as well go out with a bang, doing something noble for once."

Orion opened his mouth to query her choice of words, but he stopped when Tancred approached.

"It is time," the small paladin said.

"Right," Orion replied quietly, looking off to the north and where the fate of Basilea lay just over the horizon.

*****

Valletto glanced around him as the small group of soldiers traveled north toward Andro. The sun sat on the horizon, trapped between a thick layer of cloud that painted the heavens in shades of dull gray and the jagged black teeth of the Mountains of Tarkis. A fine drizzle cascaded down from above to settle on the tanned leather of his horse's saddle and reins, glistening in the last of the day's rays of sunlight. Drizzle was more of a rarity in the City of the Golden Horn. In the south of Basilea, the norm was days of blistering sunshine punctuated with brief but torrential downpours; enough to keep the crops healthy and the forests alive in their lush greenery.

Valletto smiled as he fondly remembered his home, the cool shades of blue that painted a very different horizon with the rising sun, a sight he was far more familiar with in recent months due to disturbed nights and early mornings with his daughter, Jullia. Clera bore the vast majority of the sleepless nights with feeding their younger child, so Valletto figured the least he could do was look after their daughter at dawn and allow his wife a precious hour or two of sleep before he left home for his duties with the legion. What had begun as a chore had quickly morphed into his favorite time of the day, where he plonked his daughter up on his shoulders and took her for short walks around the fields by their home, gleefully responding to her confused commands as she pointed in her preferred direction of travel and yelped out unintelligible monosyllables.

The company he kept now could not have been any more different. Tancred rode at the head of the column of mounted paladins, men-at-arms, and militia infantry, his narrow eyes constantly flitting from feature to feature as they proceeded north. Even in the short time he had known Tancred, Valletto had failed to warm to him. Valletto prided himself on his ability to read another person, and while their few verbal exchanges had been relatively short, Tancred came across as a man with little depth beyond his blind personal ambition; a trait Valletto had seen many times in others he had worked with and had come to resent deeply over the years. Next to Tancred was Silus, another individual whose character traits were very typical of the military Valletto had come to know, including the dislike of magic users – even those on the same side. Behind them was Aestelle, the tall, beautiful woman whose form fitting and impractical leather armor revealed much of her vanity and need to be center of attention. Valletto could not deny the existence of her astounding beauty, but to him it merely placed her in the same league as his wife, but certainly not above his dear Clera.

The thought of his wife dragged his thoughts unwillingly back to the sunnier south and his home outside the capital, where his wife and children waited for his safe return. He allowed himself a short, grim chuckle as it occurred to him that the simple act of turning his horse around and riding back home to the only people he truly loved and cared for was actually outweighing the critical requirement to save his nation from being over swept by a horde of demons. Could somebody else not do his job? Was he really needed? Certainly, nobody else could be there for his family, that much had been made clear to him. Resisting the urge, Valletto sighed in frustration, angry with the Duma for sending him off to do a job which so many could have done in his stead. But, as Clera had said, it was their turn. It had been years since he had faced any danger and it was only fair. It was his turn.

Valletto's connection with Saffus had, at least, been a success. Before setting off for the north, Valletto had again carried out the procedure to contact his master and had ascertained the location of the portal stone near Andro. Luck was finally on their side – there was but one and it was large, atop a hill just to the south of the coastal mining town. They would reach the hill within only a few hours and, if their luck held out and they beat Dionne's horde to the discovery, their job was then simple – protect the hill until the force from the capital arrived. An elementary task in terms of complication, if not its actual achievement, and one that filled Valletto full of dread.

*****

Orion cast his eyes around him, turning in place to stare incredulously as his breath caught in his chest. It was a little past midnight and the black sky was lit up to the north by the burning buildings of Andro, the wooden houses and mining structures melting slowly away into the dancing orange flames that licked up toward the dark heavens. To the west, the seemingly endless procession of jagged peaks of the Tarkis range stepped up toward Kolosu; the tallest peak haloed in a dim aura of white light, punctuating the darkness and blurred in the mist and drizzle. To the east, the inky blackness of the Low Sea of Suan stretched out for miles, blending invisibly into the dark skies without any discernable horizon.

Jeneveve was the first to reach the crest of the hill. She cautiously approached the construct that sat atop the peak; the end of their journey and the reason for the Abyssal incursion into their lands. A trio of obelisk constructs sat at the crest of the peak, each made up of a further three massive and ancient stones. Each corner of the triangle consisted of two tall pillars of stone with a third balanced on top. Constructs such as these were rare but certainly not unheard of across Basilea; harking back from a simpler time before the God Wars, when all peoples worshipped the Celestials. While the stones themselves were still the subject of debate among many in scholastic circles, mainly regarding how such heavy objects could be moved by such primitive people, it occurred to Orion that the stones were very anticlimactic – there were no carvings, no glowing runes, nothing that would mark the stones out as magical or indeed anything other than ancient sites of religious significance.

"So this is it," Jeneveve said, turning back to her comrades, one side of her face illuminated by the flames of the burning mining town to the north, "this is where we stand and fight."

Orion walked past her and looked down from the hilltop to the town of Andro. The tall, wooden frames of the mine's pump houses and ventilation shafts were still visible amidst the raging flames. The road snaking through the town was well lit by the inferno, allowing Orion's eyes to pick out dozens of figures swarming toward the hill to the south; it took only the briefest of moments for him to realize that their red hue was no reflection from the flames, but their very skin. Dionne's army of Abyssals advanced rapidly toward them and the portal stone.

"We hold the high ground," Tancred said, his tone betraying his fear. "We stand our ground here and we knock them back down this hill. There is no room for them to use their numbers on this little hill – we must remain resolute, indefatigable. We trust in the Shining Ones and we hold this hill until help arrives."

"They are some way away yet," Jeneveve remarked. "There is time for prayer."

"Prayer?" Valletto exploded. "Look down there! You wish to spend your last few moments in prayer? We cannot win! We cannot hold this hill for anything more than a few moments! It is too late! We need to fall back and find the army traveling here from the capital!"

"You need to conquer your fear, Captain!" Tancred pointed a finger in accusation. "Coming apart at the seams now does no good!"

"Fear?!" Valletto yelled. "What do you know of fear? You've got nothing to lose! Nothing! To you, this is just an opportunity to either live or die as a hero! You'd gladly waste all of our lives for that!"

"And what is all of this to you?" Xavier demanded. "Why do you know fear more than any others?"

"Because I have responsibilities that you cannot understand!" the mage retorted. "I went to war when most of you were just boys, and afterward I saw what happened to children when their fathers never came home! I saw war tear families apart with grief, never to recover! I won't do that to my family!"

Tancred walked over and placed a hand gently on Valletto's shoulder.

"Valletto, there is no escape from the situation we find ourselves in," he said firmly, but with some compassion. "I would never wish ill on you or your family, but in my eyes, your family is no more important than any of the others we are here to defend. This portal we stand on right now is the gateway to the doom of all Basilea. If we run, the nation may fall. Thousands of children will lose their parents. Thousands more will die themselves. I cannot prioritize your family over all of them. We must all stand here and fight to the last."

The dark haired mage looked down at the short paladin. His face, twisted in rage, transitioned through sorrow, shame, and eventually came to rest at grim resolution.

"I am sorry," Valletto's head dropped forward. "I lost perspective. I am so very sorry. Of course, we must fight here to the last. We must do the right thing."

Tancred offered a brief, uncomfortable smile and nodded. He walked over to stand before the assembled paladins and militiamen, and unchained the Eloicon from his hip. Unclasping the sacred texts, he held the thick tome aloft to the heavens in a moment of symbolic reverence before opening the book at one of its many colored bookmarks. Orion joined his paladin brethren in dropping to one knee in front of Tancred, taking his sword and gently digging the tip of the blade into the soft earth in front of him. Resting both of his hands atop the upright pommel of the sword, he bowed his head in preparation for prayer. Tancred looked across, the surprise showing on his face quickly replaced with a grateful smile.

To his side, he saw Dorn usher the militiamen and the handful of surviving men-at-arms from the original force clear of the hilltop. Valletto, his features still wracked with apprehension, walked across to join the paladins in prayer. More surprising to Orion was when Aestelle knelt next to him. She followed the example set by the paladins and dug her own greatsword into the earth in front of her, one hand resting on the pommel while the other clutched an Eloicon to her heart. Orion looked across at the sacred tome and noticed the icon of the Sisterhood stamped into the brass of the clasp. Aestelle glanced across at Orion and offered a warm, encouraging smile.

"Julius' First Letter to the Suanites, chapter three, verse one," Tancred began.

Orion knew the letter well. They all did. Written in the days after The Mirror smashed and the God War began, Julius' writings to the Suanites spoke of courage and resolve in the face of overwhelming adversity in an attempt to bolster their will before help could arrive in facing the new terrors unleashed on the world by the rendering of the Celestians.

"We enter a new age," Tancred read from the Eloicon, *"we face new adversities as well as old. Our people must stand together and stand strong, for we are chosen for great things. Our people must maintain the will to fight, even when facing overwhelming opposition. Our people must defend the word and defend the faith, even when darkness threatens to envelop us from all around."*

His eyes closed, Orion's mind drifted from the familiar words to consider those around him. He briefly wondered how many of the militiamen wanted to join the paladins in prayer, having seen hundreds of men with scant faith suddenly becoming the most god-fearing individuals on the eve of their death. He thought on Valletto and Aestelle's faith, and whether they would have joined them in prayer had it not been for the tide of red-skinned demons cascading toward the foot of the hill at that very moment. Mentally chastising himself, Orion focused his mind again to think upon Julius' words and the plight faced by the ancestors of Basilea.

"Our people must remain devout, thankful with the burden of being the chosen, thankful in Grace."

Grace. A word that appeared again and again in sacred texts, homilies, and sermons. A word that held special meaning within the confines of faith, but one that Orion still felt he did not truly understand. Perhaps his meeting with the Elohi would start the path to Grace, if the hellish army rushing toward him would not end it on this night. Orion searched his soul for confidence, optimism, a belief that they could survive. He found none. It mattered little. He could not control the events around him, one man could not change the outcome of an entire battle. But he could control how he faced his end.

"Our people must..."

Tancred stopped. Orion opened his eyes and looked up. Dorn stood by

Tancred, his face apologetic as he leaned in to converse in a whisper, disturbing the prayers. Tancred's eyes widened in surprise at whatever news Dorn delivered. He dashed over to the south side of the hill. Jeneveve and Xavier exchanged quizzical glances and both stood to join their leader. Orion closed his eyes again, concluded his own prayer silently for a moment, and then stood. By the time he had reached the others at the far side of the hill's dark summit, the militiamen were cheering joyously.

"There!" Dorn pointed excitedly to the south, "on the coastal road, just to the east of Twin Barrows!"

Orion's eyes searched the darkness to the south, unfamiliar as they were with the reference point the local militiaman had mentioned. Then he saw the source of the commotion. A procession of twinkling torchlights moved slowly along the coastal road, heading north toward them. Snaking out from in between hills painted black by the night, the torches continued onward and provided just enough light to illuminate a tiny banner.

"The Vanguard!" Jeneveve exclaimed. "They are here!"

Orion allowed himself a brief smile as a feeling of relief and euphoria washed over him. The vanguard was closing. The cheering continued unabated. Quickly calculating the distance, he realized that the hill was nearly halfway between the Basilean vanguard and the Abyssal horde. They would not need to hold the hill for long before help arrived. They had a chance.

"Wait!" Aestelle yelled above the excitement. "Look!"

Orion's smile faded as the realization of Aestelle's alert quickly set in. The Basilean soldiers had reached a fork in the road. Inexplicably, against all reason, the force turned west and began to head inland away from Andro and the hilltop portal stones.

"No!" Jeneveve shouted. "No, you fools! Over here!"

Cries of frustration and angry expletives were roared from the militiamen as they watched their only hope for survival turn away, slowly disappearing behind the darkness of another of the low hills inland of the coastal road.

"Why?" Dorn shouted. "Why are they going west?"

"Dark sorcery and trickery? Navigational ineptitude?" Valletto offered quietly as he sank down in despair to sit on a smooth rock. "It matters not now."

"We're not giving up!" Aestelle snapped. "There! Look southwest, by the windmill! There is a tall hill, halfway between us and the vanguard. If I can get there in time, I can signal them. I'm going. There isn't a moment to spare."

"You are right," Tancred nodded, moving over to look across the dark hills to the tall peak between them, their salvation, and their only hope of keeping the portal closed. "Take my horse, she is the fastest…"

"Not now!" Aestelle interrupted in frustration and she quickly returned her greatsword to its scabbard on her back.

"I am not offering, I am ordering you!" Tancred growled. "Desiree is the fastest horse I have ever seen and every second counts! Tantus – take the barding

232

off her, quickly!"

The young paladin nodded and dashed over to Tancred's graceful warhorse where he quickly set about unbuckling her armor. Xavier paced purposefully over to Aestelle as she rapidly loaded her pistol and slung her bow and arrows over her shoulder.

"You shall need a proper signal for them to understand who we are," the aging knight said.

He walked over to his own horse and took the unit banner from where it was clipped to his saddle. Aestelle looked over to Tancred. The Lord Paladin nodded curtly in approval. Xavier handed over his banner and then raised his right hand to shoulder height in salute. Aestelle placed her right hand over her heart and bowed her head; the salute of the Sisterhood.

"I will guard your banner with my life, Brother Paladin," she said seriously.

Tantus brought Desiree over to Aestelle by the reins, the powerful warhorse now stripped of all armor. Orion felt a rising sickening in his gut as he watched the events unfold. She needed to leave, now, but he still found his feet moving beneath him, and in an instant he was by her side. Aestelle turned to face him. She flashed him a confident smile and rested one hand against his neck.

"Do what you do best, Ri," she said softly. "Kill 'em all. Stay safe. I'll be back as soon as I can."

Orion watched in silence as Aestelle vaulted up onto the warhorse, secured the banner to her saddle, and accepted a lit torch from Tantus. She nodded a final farewell and kicked the warhorse into a gallop, hurtling down the hillside and quickly disappearing into the night. Orion felt relieved that she had a safer task ahead of her than defending the hill, but he still felt a gnawing regret at her departure. There were things left unsaid, and he doubted they would meet again.

"Lord Paladin!" Silus shouted from the north side of the hilltop. "Scouts! At the foot of the hill! They are here!"

Tancred unsheathed his sword and paced over toward Silus.

"Form up the defense!" he shouted. "Stand strong! It begins now!"

Twenty

Trees rushed past Aestelle to either side in a blur, briefly illuminated by her lit torch as she urged every last shred of speed out of Tancred's warhorse. Aestelle was an experienced enough rider to appreciate the strengths and weaknesses of horses, but she remained astounded by the sheer speed and power of Desiree – a finer steed she had never seen. The horse's hooves crunched on the stones of the path beneath them as she reached the foot of the hill. Ahead of her was a narrow valley leading to the next hill, a shallow plateau which lay between her and the final destination; the peak overlooking the inland road and her only way of attracting the attention of the lost army.

"Come on," Aestelle urged, desperately digging her heels into the horse's flanks again, "faster!"

Drizzle impacted her face and wind rushed through her hair as the horse galloped at breakneck speed across the valley, responding to her pulls on the reins as she navigated her way through the skeletal trees ahead. Aestelle leaned forward in the saddle in an attempt to avoid the low branches of the trees, but at a full gallop in the darkness she could only respond so quickly; twigs that felt like knives scratched her face and bare arms.

Thundering through the far side of the woods, Aestelle reached the foot of the plateau and urged Desiree up the shallow incline toward the next area of high ground. The wind, channeled through the valley, howled past her as she kicked at the horse, fighting to maintain speed as the slope grew steeper. An inkling, an old instinct, suddenly washed over her and filled her with dread. Twisting in the saddle, Aestelle turned to look all around her as she sensed danger approaching.

Behind her, swooping down through the black clouds, a dozen winged demons rushed through the skies to pursue her from the north.

*****

Peering down into the darkness at the foot of the hill, Tancred could hear the Abyssal scouts before he could see them. The rapid and eclectic changes of their vicious chittering and guttural language was barely audible through the night air. The seven paladins stood shoulder to shoulder at the top of the hill, their swords held

235

ready as the cold drizzle sank through their robes and armor. Ten ragged militiamen stood in lines to either side of the paladins, securing their flanks from attack. Behind them, at the far side of the hill's crest, Dorn had assembled the other half of the forty militiamen and the five last men-at-arms to stand guard at the south side of the hill, in case their enemies attempted to attack from the rear.

Below them, in the darkness of the hillside, the foliage rustled. Tancred tightened the grip on his sword and fought to even his breathing. Every moment that passed was a moment closer to their reinforcements arriving.

"East!" Dorn yelled from behind him. "East side of the hill!"

Tancred spun in place and saw a trio of lower Abyssals scrambling over the lip of the hilltop, raising their jagged swords and axes high above their heads. Valletto stepped out from the midst of the militiamen and held out his staff in one hand. A second later, the hilltop became a deafening cacophony of wind as a violent and invisible hand picked up the three demonic warriors and threw them back down the slope. The warrior-mage stepped forward, directing the harsh winds onto the east slope and forcing back a wave of Abyssal warriors who attempted to trudge forward through the blast to the crest of the hill and the portal stones themselves.

"Let them come!" Silus growled angrily. "Let them fight!"

"We're delaying them, you fool!" Valletto yelled as he held his staff up before him, keeping his magic alive and preventing any of their enemies from progressing up the eastern slope. "We are not looking for a glorious death!"

Before Silus could answer, a ball of fire shot up from the undergrowth in the darkness of the northern slope, roaring through the air to impact into one of the militiamen and set him alight. The man tumbled down the northern slope, screaming as he fell, his entire body ablaze. Before Tancred could react, a second fireball shot up from the slope below and set another militiaman on fire, his screams of pain clear even above the howling wind created by Valletto's sorcery.

"Fall back!" Tancred ordered. "Get away from the edge of the slope!"

He knew the connotations of his order – the Abyssals, clearly advancing simultaneously up all sides of the slope, would now be able to reach the summit unopposed. Tancred's small force would lose the advantage of fighting downhill, but better that than have his soldiers picked off one by one from balls of hellfire.

Tancred heard the clash and din of battle behind him as Dorn and his militiamen were engaged in fighting at the top of the southern slope of the hill; a moment later, the first Abyssal warrior appeared atop the northern slope, and with a snarl, rushed forward to fight. Orion darted out to meet the demon, ducking beneath the Abyssal's first sword swing and bringing his own blade up to tear open the guts of the monster, sending it sprawling to the ground in its death throes. More fanged, horned faces appeared at the rim of the hilltop. Letting out a cry, Tancred held his sword aloft and led his paladins forward to attack.

*****

Checking over her shoulder again, Aestelle slammed her heels into the warhorse's flanks and yelled in desperation as they neared the top of the final hill. Her pursuers were close now, close enough for her to make out their lithe, iron-gray forms swooping through the sky behind her. Perhaps a dozen gargoyles, their flame red eyes glowing in the black sky, relentlessly kept pace with her as she urged her horse on to its final destination.

Rounding the crest of the hill, Aestelle let out a cry of relief as she saw the Basilean force advancing along the road beneath her. Quickly jumping down from her horse, she ran over to the nearest tree and held her torch to it, but the flames failed to catch onto the damp bark. Aestelle turned and saw the swarm of gargoyles was only moments away, hideous shrieks echoing across the rain-streaked skies as they folded their wings back to dive down toward her. She snatched the Sacred Arc banner from the saddle and ran over to the edge of the hilltop. Holding the banner up high above her head in one hand and waving her torch from side to side with the other, Aestelle sucked in a lungful of air and roared for all she was worth. The banner fluttered above her, the rich blue fabric rippling in the wind and rain as her chest burned with the exertion of the frantic ride and her desperate shouts for attention.

A horn blasted from the column of troops below her. The ranks of soldiers came to a halt and orders were bellowed out in the night as blocks of infantry and wedges of cavalry were wheeled in place to face the hill. More orders were issued from horns, and drums beat into life as three hundred Basilean soldiers reformed and prepared themselves for battle.

A smile spread across Aestelle's face as relief washed over her. The smile became a laugh and she threw the torch down to the ground, leaning forward to hold onto the banner pole with both hands as she dug it into the soft earth at her feet. She turned in place, knowing full well what awaited her.

Twelve gray-skinned gargoyles stood in a loose semi-circle around her, sharp fangs protruding from beneath their cruel, blue lips. Their grotesque, feminine bodies stood poised for attack, their clawed hands ready, and their blood red eyes fixed on Aestelle. Standing in front of them was a taller, more powerful and familiar figure. The red-skinned, raven-haired temptress she had spoken to at the massacred fishing village of Peleura stood in front of her lesser Abyssal creatures, her toned arms folded at her chest and her wings spread behind her back.

"Too late," Aestelle flashed a smile and a wink, "it's all for nothing now. You've failed."

"Too late?" the temptress narrowed her eyes and paced over dangerously, a coiled and barbed whip held in one hand and a curved sword held in the other. "You think that because you've alerted your pitiful little army that this is over? How many Abyssals do you think we have with us? Some token band, perhaps? We have an army, more than enough to crush your pathetic collection of barely trained soldiers! I did not come here to stop you signaling them, I welcome it! More souls for the fires!"

"You're lying!" Aestelle sang with a smile, unsheathing her sword from her back, forcing a false bravado to replace the terror clawing at her heart as she realized she was facing her final moments of life. "You haven't chased me all the way out here for nothing."

"Believe what you will," the temptress hissed, her tone sultry. "I am capable of mercy. Not much, but some small token. But for you? What was it you promised me? To maim me? Cripple me? I could have simply killed you. But you've annoyed me. So now I'm here to drag your soul to hell itself for an eternity of agony."

The temptress nodded to her hideous, gray winged minions. Aestelle charged forward to meet their attack, her greatsword held high.

*****

Any semblance of order in the defense of the portal stones was now gone. The top of the hill had descended into anarchy, a swirling and bloody melee of chaos and confusion. Isolated groups of paladins and militiamen fought back against the savage onslaught of Abyssal warriors as the scarlet-skinned demons continued to pour up over the edges of the hill from all directions.

Valletto stood within the triangle of the portal stones themselves, momentarily defended by a semi-circle of ten militiamen to one side and a frenzied defense by Tancred, Xavier, and Jeneveve on the other. He stared ahead, frozen on the spot, somehow the safest individual on top of the hill for a brief moment; but still the closest to mortal danger he had ever been in his life. His previous campaigns had seen him playing a supporting role from the very periphery of battle; certainly never close enough to see men and monsters disembowel and decapitate each other. The shrieks of rage and cries of the wounded filled the air, punctuated only by the clash of metal on metal as blades slammed against each other in the damp, night sky.

"Come on, man, do something!"

He realized that the chastising voice was his own. Narrowing his eyes in concentration, Valletto pushed the dread to one side and surveyed his surroundings. Abyssals continued to scramble up the slopes all around the defenders, threatening to envelop them at any moment. Valletto could do something about that.

Clamping both hands on his staff and holding it out in front of him, Valletto summoned arcane energies from his very core, feeling the surge of power grow within him and then extend out to the tips of his fingers. Sparkling light danced across his hands, white lines of energy swirling and spiraling around his arms as the power built within him. Valletto closed his eyes and concentrated harder on his surroundings, sensing the push of the wind, the moisture of the rain, the low pressure of the air over the water to the east. Diverting every drop of moisture for a mile in every direction, Valletto utilized his powers to draw the drizzle and rain in toward him to congregate rapidly in the air above his head.

Holding his staff up high, he released the energy in one powerful burst. The air rushed up above him, forming dark clouds directly above the northern slopes.

Summoning a second wave of energy, Valletto rapidly dropped the temperature of the air above. With the moisture suddenly and violently increased and the air dropped to near freezing, the clouds above let out a rapid monsoon of torrential rain. Valletto directed it onto the northern assault, turning the side of the hill into an impassible swamp of thick, slippery mud within seconds. Every demon attempting to clamber up was instantly cast down in the mud, slipping and sliding through the treacherous quagmire to tumble back down to the base of the insurmountable hill.

Satisfied that one of the four sides to the hill was now impossible to assail, Valletto turned his attentions to the east. Sweat pouring from his brow with the increased exertion of his efforts, Valletto summoned more moisture from miles in every direction, drying the air in the entire area to force the skies above him to utter saturation. Hisses of pain escaped through gritted teeth as Valletto forced the air down to its freezing point. Chilled to the bone, physically shattered by the toil of overpowering nature itself, Valletto held his staff high once more for the final ingredient. Drawing in wind from every direction, he sent a pillar of air shooting up into the soaked, frozen skies.

The skies flashed white and deafening thunder drowned out all other noise. Forks of deadly lightning spat down from the heavens straight into the advancing Abyssal guards on the eastern slope. Lightning tore through their ranks to burn vicious holes directly through the hellish monsters, dropping them lifeless and smoking into the mud of the hilltop. Fighting to keep exhaustion at bay, Valletto dropped to one knee and continued the onslaught of nature's elements for as long as he could, relentlessly assaulting the Abyssals as they drove headlong toward the peak.

*****

Orion battered the blade of his adversary aside, overpowering the Abyssal and casting its arm to one side. Seizing the opportunity presented by the opening, the paladin stepped forward and slammed his forehead down into the nose of the demonic warrior, snapping its head back and stunning it for long enough to drive his sword through its gut. The shrieking lower Abyssal writhed and clawed out at him as it stood impaled on Orion's sword, its agonized cries drowned out by the thunder up above as rain continued to pelt the two opposing forces atop the hill. Orion withdrew his sword neatly and cut a clinical strike down against his foe, cleaving open its torso, and sending it down into the dirt.

For the first time since the fight began, a felled Abyssal was not instantly replaced by another of the demonic horde, and Orion had a brief moment to assess his surroundings and how the battle was faring. Behind him, Valletto stood in the center of the portal stones, his magic having made one side of the hill unassailable while the deadly lightning he summoned from the heavens continued to wreak havoc and destruction on any creatures foolish enough to attempt to scale the eastern slope. With only half of the hill now open to the continued onslaught of Abyssals, the Basilean force was no longer surrounded and was able to rally.

"To me," Tancred yelled over the thunder and howling wind, "back to me!"

Orion stepped back toward where Tancred stood, flanked by Xavier and Jeneveve, arriving by their side just as Reynaud and Silus fought their way over from the southern edge of the hilltop. Dorn continued to command the surviving militiamen; perhaps half of the original number remained alive and fit to fight. Orion let out a breath and muttered a brief and regretful prayer as he saw Tantus lying prone and still amidst the carpet of corpses from both sides, his lifeless eyes staring unfocused up at the dark heavens above.

"Get back in line!" Tancred bellowed. "Face south! Valletto, can you take out another slope?"

The exhausted mage nodded and brought his staff up, but instantly sagged and dropped to one knee as his eyes lolled back in his head. Xavier broke ranks and dashed over to him, hauling him back to his feet and dragging him away from the next wave of Abyssals that cautiously advanced from the western slope. Orion turned to look down through the rain to the south, his eyes picking out the slope where Aestelle had run for. He had seen her a few minutes before, a speck stood atop the hill with a blazing torch in one hand and a fluttering blue banner in the other; he had even thought he had heard her crying out, but now all he could see was a flock of bats fluttering around where she had been. An instant later, his face dropped as he realized there was no way he could make out bats from this far away.

"Here they come!" Dorn yelled to his militiamen. "Up and at 'em!"

Orion followed Tancred as the handful of remaining paladins charged across the muddy hilltop toward the advancing creatures, their own lines made up of the ubiquitous lower Abyssals and the more dangerous Abyssal guards. The ragged militiamen crashed against the wave of demons, their halberds and spears jutting out to slash and stab at the unworldly warriors as they met. Perhaps two or three-dozen Abyssal monsters adorned in armor of spiked plates and armed with crude swords and axes threw themselves into the fragile Basilean line. Orion remained shoulder to shoulder between Tancred and Silus, rushing out to meet the charge of a line of black armored Abyssal guards.

The first monster met him head on, lashing out at his head with a double-headed axe. Orion leaned back to avoid the blow and brought his sword up to defend himself from a savagely linked series of strikes aimed at his chest and head. The attacks stopped as suddenly as they had started when Silus leaned across to exploit the briefest of gaps in the fighting, thrusting his sword through the side of the Abyssal guard's head. Orion was quick to seize the opportunity created and lunged forward to strike down the next Abyssal guard in line, now that its flank was left exposed and unprotected. He brought his heavy blade hacking down again and again, butchering the shorter creature and cutting great welts open in its flesh before it collapsed to the ground and was trampled underfoot as the fight continued to surge back and forth. Of the relief force sent to save them, there was still no sign.

*****

Twisting in place, Aestelle slashed her sword out at a third gargoyle that flapped viciously down to attack her, its inhuman claws tearing toward her back as she frantically batted it away with her blade. Mere moments seemed to drag on like hours as she stood her ground at the top of the hill, her discarded torch at her feet providing the only source of light in the night as the sea of bat-winged devils continued their tireless assault on her from every direction and angle. Every opening she thought she could take advantage of saw her rapidly being forced to switch back to the defensive as another of the gargoyles swooped down to attack with an ear piercing shriek. Every time Aestelle managed to link a flurry of precise strikes against one of her foes, enough to force it back and threaten to overwhelm its defenses, it simply flew away to be replaced by a fresh gargoyle, waiting for its turn to fight in the flock swarming above her head. All the while, the dark-haired temptress stood her ground several feet away, watching in silence as her vile minions continued to wear down their solitary prey.

Finally one of the foul, fang toothed gray demons fluttered in too close, close enough for Aestelle to strike. She swept up her great sword and sliced a vicious wound across the gargoyle's chest and was rewarded with an agonized shriek of pain and rage. Quick to capitalize, Aestelle grabbed one of the pair of throwing knives from the small of her back and flung it into the gut of a second gargoyle – the repulsive creature clutched at the blade buried in its bowels with both hands and dropped to the ground. Aestelle took a long step toward the felled monster, and with a single sweep, removed its head from its shoulders in a fountain of viscous, black blood.

Before she could return to a defensive stance, she found herself letting out a howl of pain as a clawed hand dragged razor sharp talons across her back, easily tearing through her leather armor and flesh alike. Angered, desperate in her realization that her time was running out, Aestelle grabbed her pistol from her side. She had wanted to save her single shot, her one definite opportunity to hit the temptress as there would be no time to reload, but her options were gone. Aestelle spun on the spot and brought her pistol up to aim at the gargoyle who had torn at her back – she leveled the gun at its head and pulled the trigger. The wooden handled pistol barked a staccato report and issued a great plume of white smoke, and the gargoyle's face disintegrated into a shower of black blood and bone as the lead shot ploughed through its skull and dropped it to the ground.

Shocked, perhaps even scared by the firearm, the swarm of gargoyles spread out away from Aestelle for a precious moment, long enough for her to concentrate on her divinity magic and press one palm awkwardly against her bloodied back and heal the worst of the wound. She doubted she would get another opportunity to use her magic again. As if reading her thoughts, the ten remaining gargoyles swarmed toward her again. Aestelle raised her sword and slashed out at them as they approached, forcing two of them back for a few moments before she felt simultaneous and agonizing tears at her left arm and right leg as the talons tore at her again. Her leg gave way and she dropped to one knee, helpless in front of the grinning, winged devils. Then the temptress attacked.

Two, perhaps three of the wailing gargoyles continued to flutter around her and slash out at her as the shapely, horned temptress leapt forward. The barbed whip cracked out and connected with Aestelle's face, tearing open the skin below one eye. She staggered to her feet and instinctively took a step away as she felt a slash across her back, reopening her semi-healed wounds. Dripping in sweat from her exertions, bleeding from multiple injuries, Aestelle forced herself back to the fight with a roar of rage and turned to strike at a gargoyle to her right, lopping off one of its legs at the knee and sending it whooshing away with a squeal of agony. The whip cracked again and the temptress struck Aestelle across one shoulder, tearing open a new wound.

"Who in hell did you think you were to tough talk me!" the temptress laughed as she took a step back. "You are done! Finished! I could have shown a shred, a sliver of mercy and killed you quickly! But now, all that remains is for me to drag you down to the Abyss for an eternity, an endless eternity of pain and suffering you cannot even begin to comprehend!"

Aestelle took her last knife from her belt and flung it at the temptress' face. With lightning fast reflexes, the demon woman turned her head but not quite quickly enough. The knife slashed against the side of the temptress' face, spinning her head and drawing an arc of blood as it swept past. The temptress let out a howl and turned to face Aestelle again, her right eye cut in two within its socket and leaking a trail of black liquid down her face.

"You talk too much, bitch," Aestelle forced a blood soaked grin across her face.

Yelling in fury, the temptress ran at Aestelle, who wearily brought her blade up to defend herself; but was instantly forced back under a furious onslaught of strikes by both whip and sword. She felt a slash across her midriff and the whip strike at her thigh but fought through the pain to smash the pommel of her greatsword into the temptress' face, breaking the demonic woman's nose. Then came the inevitable end.

The temptress thrust her sword into Aestelle's stomach, plunging the blade effortlessly through her body to emerge out of her back. Leaning in to press its face against hers, the temptress laughed maliciously as she lifted Aestelle's broken body off the ground. Aestelle used every last shred of her fortitude to will her limbs into life, to aim one last defiant strike, but her sword fell from her numb fingertips and her limbs refused to respond to her commands as blood flowed from the corners of her mouth. The temptress threw her to one side, pressing a booted foot against her chest and kicking her off the curved blade.

Her vision fading to a blur, Aestelle lay helplessly on the hilltop as the temptress stood victoriously over her, her surviving gargoyle minions gleefully flying around her after the unfair fight came to a close. She had fought countless battles in her short life and suffered a multitude of injuries, but never had the pain been so unbearable and never had it faded away to a numbness that she knew could only be the onset of death. Her eyes drifted closed as she prepared herself for an eternity of torment, never to see the mortal world again.

Then, behind her, three loud thuds in quick succession shook the entire hillside. Her world swimming, Aestelle forced her eyes back open and tried unsuccessfully to drag her broken body back up to her knees. The sky lit up, a blinding but soothing white sweeping through the night and casting long shadows across the hill. The temptress and the gargoyles looked up into the sky above Aestelle, their faces distorted in fear and panic as they stepped back away, clawed hands brought up to red eyes to shield themselves from the bright light.

Three towering figures, twice the height of a man, stepped over her and advanced a few paces toward the winged demons. The figures wore armor of shining silver that encased their bodies, save for wings of snow white feathers emerging from their backs. Each carried a colossal sword bathed in fire. Elohi. Angels of the Shining Ones, sent from the heavens themselves. The first of the trio of heavenly warriors swept his sword out in a great arc, catching one of the gargoyles and instantly incinerating it in an explosion of holy flames. The second Elohi surged forward in a burst of inhuman speed, thrusting her blazing sword forth to cut down a second gargoyle in a similarly spectacular display of fire.

As one, the winged Abyssals turned and fled, the one eyed temptress leading the rout. Aestelle heard the three angelic warriors converse in a language she could not understand, a melodic exchange of words as they turned and regarded her with eyes of pure silver-white. Eyes not unlike her own. The closest of the three, a woman of unnatural beauty with golden hair, dropped to one knee and held her hand out to Aestelle, offering her a smile filled with warmth and compassion.

"Take my hand, sister," she said softly, "it is not your time yet."

Aestelle again commanded her hand to move up, but her arm remained motionless. Her brow furrowing with sorrow, the Elohi leaned closer and gently took Aestelle's hand. The instant she did, a wave of calm washed slowly over Aestelle, instantly taking all of the pain away. She watched as a glowing halo of white moved from the Elohi's slender fingertips to travel down across Aestelle's wrist and up her arm. As it moved over her, Aestelle felt herself strengthened and reinvigorated. As if her soul was charged fresh, she suddenly found the ability to call upon her knowledge of divinity magic and send a pulse of healing power throughout her body. As she did so, she felt her arcane powers meet the halo of energy from the Elohi.

The glowing white ring continued to travel across her, moving over her wounds and leaving them healed in its wake. Aestelle watched in amazement as the ring eased across her arm, replacing the broken, torn, bloodied, and dirty limb with fully healed, cleansed, and refreshed skin. Her vision sharpened into focus; her hearing returned to normal, her heartbeat strengthened within her chest. Slowly standing, Aestelle felt stronger than she ever recalled. All weariness, all pain, any negativity within her body and mind had been expelled. She looked down on herself and saw her torso and limbs completely refreshed and untouched beneath her torn armor. She reached down and recovered her greatsword.

"Thank you," she said with the upmost sincerity to the Elohi as she bowed her head in respect. "Thank you so much."

And with that, the Elohi were gone. The three winged angels jumped back up into the skies and flew off to the north, toward the bulk of the Abyssal forces. Her body energized and strong, her mind and soul thankful and humbled, Aestelle recovered her pistol and banner and walked purposefully back to her borrowed warhorse.

Twenty-One

With a snarl, Tancred withdrew his sword form the guts of the lower Abyssal he faced, tearing open a gaping wound for the steaming innards to drop out of as the monster fell howling down at his feet. Yet again Tancred found himself alive, exhausted and facing the briefest in lulls as another wave of the seemingly ubiquitous lower Abyssal warriors was defeated. His breathing labored, Tancred quickly and apprehensively checked to either side to ascertain who still remained with him in the Basilean battle line atop the hill.

Orion stood to his left, soaked in blood, his narrowed eyes staring at the far end of the hilltop expectantly. Jeneveve knelt to his right, one hand holding onto her sword while the other clutched the Eloicon chained to her waist. Xavier had rejoined the battle, as had Valletto. Silus was the last remaining paladin, meaning that Reynauld had fallen against the last wave of attackers. While the stalwart paladins' numbers dropped only slowly, less than ten of the resolute militiamen remained alive. Their leader, Dorn, was not one of them. Only two men-at-arms remained standing.

The hilltop was carpeted with corpses; most of them the crimson skinned invaders from the Abyss, but regularly punctuated by the bodies of militiamen. The rain, summoned by Valletto, had eased significantly but continued to fall to make the ground treacherous underfoot. Tancred looked to the south and west, but still there was no sign of their relief force.

"What was that?" Jeneveve asked breathlessly.

The ground trembled a little underfoot as simultaneously a deep roar was issued from the slope on the far side of the hill. Tancred felt his pulse quicken as he fixed his eyes ahead, his metal clad hands tightening their grip on his sword. The ground rumbled again, and again Tancred heard the guttural grunting from the unseen side of the slope. A few nervous words were exchanged between Orion and Jeneveve. Then, appearing above the crest of the hilltop, Tancred saw the next foes they faced.

A huge, horned head with large, dim looking eyes loomed over the crest of the hill. The creature, easily twice the height of a man, continued to lumber up onto the hilltop. Clad in a loincloth of mail and fur, and armored with a few plates of metal and spiked rivets driven into its red, muscular flesh, the huge monster stared down at the remaining defenders. Holding a crude axe high above its head, it let out a deafening and prolonged roar as four more of the creatures stomped up onto the crest of the hill. The five hellish creatures – molochs – paced forward toward the defenders.

The final few militiamen broke and ran, their courage finally giving way to blind terror. With panicked screams, they turned and fled to the north side of the hill, disappearing down the slope to slip and slide down into the darkness of the night. Tancred shook his head. He could not blame them. Having seen molochs in battle before, the same terror gripped at his heart, but training, experience, and most importantly faith was on his side. He would stand his ground to the bitter end with his last paladins and men-at-arms.

"On my command, take them down!" Tancred shouted to his seven remaining warriors.

The nine Basileans stood in line as the molochs picked up their pace, their clumsy walks accelerating into lumbering sprints. With a combined, earth-shattering cry, the five scarlet behemoths lunged forward at the paladins and their single sorcerer. Wearily, Tancred delved deep within his spirit to summon the will for another charge. Caught out alone nearest the charging molochs, the last two men-at-arms bravely faced down the enormous demons. The first soldier was batted to one side like a toy, smashed off to plummet down the hillside and disappear into the night. The second soldier valiantly attempted an attack with his spear but was seized by the lead moloch, held high in one hand where the demon beast effortlessly tore his head off his shoulders with the other.

Seemingly from nowhere, a gap was torn in the clouds and a beam of pure moonlight shone through to paint the hilltop in an aura of white. Tancred looked up and saw three large, slender shapes fly down from the heavens, their bodies encased in graceful armor of silver and gold. The winged figures darted down and straight into the flanks of the charging molochs, slashing at them with swords of fire.

"Elohi!" Xavier exclaimed. "We are favored by the Shining Ones!"

"Forward!" Tancred shouted gleefully. "Strike them down!"

One of the colossal, ogre-like molochs was cut down in the first pass by the winged Elohi; the lead warrior striking a horrific tear across the monster's chest before a second angel flew in to lop off its head. However, the third Elohi was grasped at the ankle by one of the molochs as it flew over and plucked from the skies. The beautiful angel was dragged to the ground and thrown down heavily where, despite his best efforts to fight back to his feet, two of the immense, red demons hacked down at him with their brutal axes until the Elohi faded away into an aura of shining light. His immortal form temporarily banished from the mortal world and forced to return to the heavens to recover.

The paladins charged across the hilltop, their heavy greatswords held high to attack. Tancred saw Orion smash into the molochs first, jumping up to slice out and carve a deep rend into the arm of one of the hellish monsters locked in combat with a female Elohi. Xavier was next to arrive, but the second moloch in line saw the paladin's charge and rushed out to meet him head on, lopping down with its axe to slice a great wound across the veteran paladin's chest and send him crashing to the ground.

The same moloch continued its charge and hurtled toward Tancred and Jeneveve. Both paladins were experienced enough to recognize an unwinnable position and dived to either side to allow the charging behemoth to pass between them. Tancred quickly picked himself back up and returned to the fight, chasing the moloch down to thrust his sword into the creature's back before it could bring its clumsy body around to face him. The moloch let out a great roar of pain and swatted out at Tancred. Its backfist connected with the paladin's body, lifting him off his feet, sending him flying across the hilltop, and causing him to crash painfully into one of the portal stones. Groggily returning to his feet, Tancred looked up and saw Jeneveve immediately fall victim to a near identical attack, propelled through the air to come crashing down into the dirt a few feet from him.

The moloch was on him again, towering over him as a long, viscous trail of drool dripped from one side of its mouth, unable to close properly from an array of jagged teeth the size of daggers. Tancred brought his sword up, but the moloch, fresh to the fight and unhindered by wave after wave of combat, was somehow faster. His eyes narrowed and his teeth clenched in despair, Tancred frantically searched for the strength to bring his blade up into an effective guard to counter the hammer blow raining down toward his skull.

Lightning arced through the night sky, illuminating the hilltop and connecting savagely with the moloch. The lumbering demon suddenly stood upright, its eyes wide open in shock as its body convulsed and flailed from the deadly force of the bolt tearing through it. Agonized cries escaped its gritted, fanged jaws as the lumbering monster shook and quivered, steam rising from its blackening skin, until it suddenly exploded in a shower of blood and body parts, lumps of its flesh raining down around Tancred. He looked thankfully across to where Valletto stood a few paces away, swaying wearily but smiling in acceptance of Tancred's silent gratitude.

Up ahead, the battle fared well but was not completely one sided. The remaining two Elohi hacked down one of the molochs, leaving burning wounds across its body from their rapid attacks. Although well used to his aptitude on the battlefield, Tancred was still amazed to see a moloch fall dead at Orion's feet, the huge demon crashing down lifelessly as the tall knight stood to one side, his blood-soaked blade held at the end of a long, sweeping attack having somehow defeated the huge demon in one on one combat. Sadly, Silus of the Blades of Onzyan had attempted to replicate the feat; the final moloch wrapped a huge, powerful fist around the old paladin's body and lifted him high up into the air. With a macabre grin, the demon squeezed his hand and crushed the paladin, crumpling the thick plates of armor as if they were paper and forcing an agonized howl of pain from the brave warrior. Silus' final act was to lean forward and thrust his blade straight into the moloch's mouth and up into its head. Both demon and paladin fell down dead together, locked in a morbid embrace.

"Brother Xavier!"

Jeneveve shouted out in panic and ran to kneel by her comrade's side. The banner bearer lay crumpled where he had been struck down, blood flowing from his mouth as his eyes blinked in shock. Jeneveve placed her hands over his wounds and channeled her powers into healing; a hint of color returned to the aging knight's face to indicate the slightest of effects, but from Tancred's experience of battlefield wounds, it seemed she had done little more than delay the inevitable.

Tancred looked across the hilltop. The Elohi had disappeared as quickly as they had arrived; the molochs lay dead, and the seemingly endless wave of enemies had finally halted. Tancred stepped to move across to Xavier but was stopped as Orion grabbed him by his upper arm.

"Battlefield healing spells will not save Xavier's life!" he said urgently under his breath. "He needs proper aid!"

"You think I do not know that?" Tancred snapped, yanking his arm free. "I would do anything I could to help our brother, but the stakes are higher! If this hill falls, Basilea falls! Brother Xavier knew that when we started this fight!"

"Then get him out of here!" Orion growled. "Take him and find our relief force! Bring them to us before it is too late and this hill is in the hands of the enemy!"

"Do not spout such idiocy!" Tancred shouted. "I am not leaving you! I am not abandoning the defense of this hill, and I am not abandoning my last brother and sister! I will fight here with you! I will fall with you!"

"We cannot hold them off forever!" Orion exclaimed. "This is not about noble sacrifice, this is about stopping them taking control of these portal stones! One of us needs to get down there and direct our army to hold this hill! They are stumbling around in the darkness, oblivious to the threat to our nation's very existence! Lord Paladin, you need to direct them to this hill!"

Tancred let out a breath. It was not what he wanted to consider, even to hear, but he knew it was the truth. The relief force needed to know the severity of the situation.

"Sister Jeneveve!" Tancred turned to face one of his last paladins. "You must…"

"It needs to be you, Tancred!" Orion urged, planting a hand on his shoulder. "You are our leader! Go and lead! Get down there and take charge of this mess before all is lost! Go and do what you do best! Leave me here to do what I do best - dig my heels in and kill! I shall have Jeneveve and Valletto with me!"

Tancred looked across desperately at the other two. Jeneveve gave him a knowing nod, her face serious and committed. Valletto walked across and took a small, black pouch from inside his cloak.

"Give this to my son," he said to Tancred, "and tell him I loved him to my very last breath."

Tancred batted away the mage's arm with an impatient snarl.

"Do not talk nonsense!" he snapped. "I…"

The mage grabbed Tancred by the neck with a surprising force and dragged the smaller man over to meet him face to face. Tancred looked up into his tear filled eyes and saw such a pure, unadulterated anger and hatred that he actually felt fear.

"Give this to my son!" Valletto repeated with venom. "And you tell him I loved him to my dying breath!"

Tancred nodded silently and took the pouch. He helped Xavier up to his feet, taking one of the grievously wounded knight's arms around his neck. The relief force could only be advancing from the southwest. He turned and looked at the final three warriors. Jeneveve offered him a slight, sad smile. Valletto stared off to the south, toward the capital. Orion stood tall in the center, the very picture of the noble paladin ideal.

"Shining Ones be with you," Tancred said, his voice choked. "I shall be back as soon as I can."

The fate of the nation rested with the three soldiers Tancred left behind on the hilltop. The shouts, clashes, and din of battle had resumed by the time he was only halfway down the hill.

*****

The rear ranks of troops watched Aestelle warily as she approached, dozens of heads turning in unison as she rode past. The lead units were already engaged with Abyssal scouts, but even from behind the front lines, it was clear to Aestelle that the demonic skirmishers had been sent out with a sole purpose – delay the progress of the relief force. Dionne wanted the hilltop and its portal stones. Nothing else mattered.

Finding the force's commander was easy enough. A dictator, far more ornate in his choice of armor, banner, and retinue than Hugh had ever been, followed up behind the front few ranks of Basilean soldiers. The center line was made up of three blocks of legion men-at-arms, some forty men in each square, flanked by units of paladin knights on horseback, similar in size. With a second line made up largely of men-at-arms - some units armed with crossbows - the part of the force that Aestelle could see numbered at least two hundred.

Aestelle rode over to the dictator and dismounted by him and his inner guard of five heavily armored legion soldiers. The dictator, his features hidden behind a white helmet with gold trim that matched the rest of his impressive, plate armor, stepped out and looked her up and down.

"What are you supposed to be?" he demanded.

"Aestelle of Kurros, Dictator," she replied formally with a curt nod, content to show reverence to his rank but unwilling to display any more subservience than strictly necessary. "I was formerly a battle sister, but more recently I was a scout with Dictator-Prefect Hugh's force."

"What news?" the tall dictator insisted immediately. "Was that you signaling us from atop the hill?"

"Yes, that was me," Aestelle replied, "I was sent by Lord Paladin Tancred of the 15th Cohort, Order of the Sacred Arc. There is another hill just beyond the ridgeline to the northeast. Our only survivors are defending the hill. The Abyssals are going for the portal stones on top, and if they take that hill, they can open a path from the very Abyss itself. It is imperative that the hill does not fall."

"Oh?" the dictator tilted his metal encased head. "I am well aware of the portal stones and our direction from the Duma. But I have absolutely no proof that you are who you claim to be."

"Why in hell would I lie to you?" Aestelle snapped.

"You've signaled my forces into contact with the enemy, at night, in a valley. It is the perfect ambush site."

Aestelle let out a growl of frustration and turned away, running her fingers through her hair.

"Look, you stupid bastard, we're moments away from hell itself pouring into the damn Hegemony! Use your bloody head and listen!"

"Be you a peasant scout or an agent of the Abyss, I don't need to take insults from you!" the dictator signaled to his guards. "Take her away and have her restrained until this is over!"

Aestelle drew her greatsword the moment two of the armored legion guards moved toward her, stopping them dead in their tracks. She immediately regretted it.

"You are not taking me prisoner!" she spat. "Not after all we've been through! You have battle sisters in this force? Go and get one of them! I'll prove I am who I claim to be!"

"Put that sword down, now, or I'll have my men pin a dozen arrows in you," the dictator ordered.

Her fists clenched, Aestelle swallowed her pride and threw her sword down into the grass at her feet.

"There isn't time for this!" Aestelle urged. "The entire countryside is deserted, the whole population has fled! That means I am either an agent of the enemy, or the only one with real information to give to you. Either way, you need to ascertain who I am, and you need to do it fast! If you have any battle sisters in your force, bring one here!"

The dictator paused. The sound of fighting from the front line up ahead drew closer, louder. He turned his head and nodded to one of his guards. The man saluted and ran quickly off into the night. It was only a few moments before he returned with a tall, powerfully built woman of a similar age to Aestelle. The broad shouldered nun wore the standard fighting garb of a battle sister; a practical and light shirt and leggings, over which was a brown corset of armored leather, tall boots, and a hooded cloak. Her belt buckle displayed her rank as a Sister Superior.

"She claims she is one of yours," the dictator greeted the sister.

The nun looked Aestelle up and down, her face twisting to clearly display her disgust.

"Not a chance, Dictator," the nun folded her arms.

"*Salvatio arrivi*, Sister Superior," Aestelle greeted angrily, quoting the ancient salute of her previous order. "I am Aestelle, formerly of the Order of the Penitent and the Devoted."

Her words changed the Sister Superior's expression to one of caution.

"Rank and specialization?" the wary woman demanded, her powerful arms folded.

"Battle sister," Aestelle replied, "five years, standard battle line. One year apprenticeship, demon hunter."

"*Wei peramb enne lumio?*"

"*Wei indigiu relessio,*" Aestelle replied automatically.

"She's one of ours," the Sister Superior nodded to the dictator, "or, at least, she once was."

"Where is the hill?" the dictator demanded urgently. "Where are the portal stones?"

"Right over that ridge line!" Aestelle pointed to the northeast. "It is only minutes if you ride fast!"

The dictator's response was cut off as the galloping of hooves announced another new joiner to the conversation. Aestelle looked around and her eyes widened in surprise as she saw Tancred riding over from the north, his battered armor covered in mud and blood. Xavier sat on the saddle behind him, his face deathly pale.

"I need help!" Tancred demanded. "Aid for my brother!"

The dictator's guard immediately rushed to assist, carefully helping Xavier down from the saddle as the Sister Superior immediately set about using her healing magic.

"Tancred?" Aestelle called, pushing her way through to him. "What is happening?"

Tancred's eyes scanned past Aestelle for a moment before returning to lock onto hers in surprise.

"Aestelle? What are... it does not matter! I..."

"Tancred!" Aestelle clamped both of her hands onto his shoulders. "What is happening at the hill?"

"We still hold it," Tancred replied, returning to his senses, "but not for long. Three of our warriors remain. The rest are gone."

Aestelle took a step back in shock, sickness rising up to her throat as her mind raced through the possibilities of who was still alive and who had fallen. She beat down the urge to demand the names of the survivors from Tancred. Now was not the time.

"Why is the army still here?" Tancred demanded breathlessly as he watched the Sister Superior's healing magic at work on Xavier. "They should all be at the hill by now! You gave the signal, did you not? Orion said he saw it!"

"Oh, I gave the signal!" Aestelle spat. "But they're more interested in picking off skirmishers in a slow advance! I'm trying to tell them but they won't listen to me!"

"Now hold on there!" the dictator roared, pacing over to force his way between Tancred and Aestelle. "I don't know who you are, Paladin, but your scout here only arrived moments ago, and I'm acting on next to no information within a perfect ambush site! You expect me to risk the lives of three hundred men and women based off a few minutes conversation with a complete stranger?"

"No," Tancred replied wearily, "I expect you to sacrifice the lives of three hundred soldiers, if necessary, to save the lives of a million. If that portal opens…"

"I'm well aware of the implications, you little shit!" the dictator bellowed. "So don't you…"

Tancred's face transformed into a mask of fury and he lunged forward, wrapping his hands around the dictator's throat.

"Then move your army forward, now! My men and women are all dead! You hear? Dead! And if you don't do something, then this entire nation will fall and they all died for nothing! Act, you useless bastard!"

Two of the dictator's guards rushed across to drag Tancred off their leader, struggling to overpower the frenzied paladin. The dictator watched the struggle in silence before removing his helmet. He was a man of perhaps forty years, with cropped short white hair contrasting sharply with deeply tanned, leathery skin. He turned to face Aestelle.

"If the two of you are wrong about this, you'll hang," he said calmly before turning again to face his guards and aides.

"Orders!" he bellowed. "Front line to advance! Flanks! Break off the attack and proceed northwest at best speed! Do not stop for anything! Find the hill and secure its base until the infantry arrives! Messenger to the main force – move to our location immediately! Go!"

The dictator's orders were hurriedly repeated verbally down the line and then reinforced by a series of drumbeats and shrill trumpet calls. The four squares of men-at-arms began to advance steadily into the darkness, immediately pelted with fireballs from Abyssals secreted within the night as soon as they moved forward from their defensive position.

"You two!" the dictator pointed to Aestelle and Tancred. "Get back on your horses. One of you on each flank. Guide my cavalry to the base of that hill and hold it until the infantry arrive to secure it. Go! Now!"

Aestelle nodded and ran for her horse.

*****

Still atop Orion's hulking warhorse, Tancred galloped off along the left flank to catch up with the mounted paladins before they acted on their orders to advance at best pace. Well into the early hours of the morning, the night had somehow found a way to sink even deeper into blackness, although the air was warmer and drier – no doubt due to the arcane manipulations enacted by Valletto when he had played god with the elements to strike down and delay their Abyssal foes. Tancred patted the small pouch that Valletto had given to him for safekeeping, ensuring it was still securely inside his belt. Remembering the sheer emotion displayed by the sorcerer at their parting, Tancred vowed to himself to never have a family of his own. It could do nothing more other than hold him back.

To his right, the squares of legion soldiers were steadily advancing in the face of increased opposition. Tancred heard a low moaning up in the darkness ahead, and out of the shadows shuffled a mob of ragged, filthy bodies whom at first glance he mistook for undead. Rank after rank of stumbling, gray skinned men and women limped painfully forward toward the legion soldiers, rusted chains eating into their broken skin as moans of pure and utter despair, unlike any agony a mortal could comprehend, escaped their cracked lips. The mob, numbering at least fifty, stumbled headlong toward the center of the advancing Basilean force, bullied and beaten from the back by Abyssals armed with vicious whips. Tancred uttered a brief prayer for them – they were the larvae, all that was left of the mortal men and women who had been dragged into the Abyss for an eternity of torture or, perhaps worse, had deliberately ventured into the hellish depths to seek their own fortune.

Tancred urged the warhorse to greater speeds as he powered past the fight, watching over his shoulder as the larvae were whipped and beaten until they charged into the spears of the men-at-arms, where they were brutally cut down. Still, it slowed the Basilean soldiers to a complete standstill, and Tancred knew that this was all Dionne cared about achieving if he was to take the hill.

Skeletal trees flew past to either side in the night as Tancred continued the gallop across the valley toward the northeast. Up ahead, their armor glinting in the few rogue rays of moonlight that had managed to pierce the thick blanket of clouds above, Tancred saw a large mass of armored horsemen. He let out a breath and smiled as he recognized their colors and emblems – knights of the Order of the Sacred Arc; paladins of his own order.

"Brothers!" he greeted as he galloped to catch them up. "Who is in command here?"

From the head of the column of knights, a broad shouldered paladin turned his horse and trotted across to respond to the hail. Looking around, Tancred reckoned on some forty knights in the darkness around him. A force strong enough to crack a hole open in any enemy line.

"I am," the knight greeted, his voice gruff, "Brother Defender Artavius, 6th Cohort."

"Lord Paladin Tancred, 15th Cohort," Tancred returned the greeting. "The dictator has sent me to you to guide you to our objective."

"My knights are yours to command, Lord Paladin," the defender bowed his head in reverence to Tancred's rank.

"Good," Tancred accepted the gesture, "musician – form two units of two ranks, either side of me!"

A short knight from amidst the pack of armored men and women brought

253

a trumpet up to his lips and issued a short sequence of blasts, signaling the cavalry to follow Tancred's orders. Within only a few moments Tancred faced the advancing enemy with a unit of some twenty mounted paladins to each side. He took a few moments to survey the field of battle ahead of him.

Directly ahead lay the ridgeline that hid the hilltop and the portal stones from view. Pouring out from either side of the ridgeline along the valley floor, barely visible in the darkness, were Dionne's Abyssal hordes. The numbers were impossible to ascertain in the darkness, but Tancred judged there to be perhaps one hundred to either side of the ridge, quickly assembling distinct and disciplined units that defied their bestial appearance. The majority seemed to be taken from the endless ranks of lower Abyssals, forming units of similar size to the blocks of men-at-arms that advanced toward them from the center of the Basilean line. Among the lower Abyssals were less frequent groups of the far deadlier Abyssal guard and the dreaded, gigantic molochs. Above them were a few handfuls of the hideous, shrieking gargoyles, and in the second rank were flamebearers – lower Abyssals with the unearthly ability to conjure up and hurl balls of deadly fire.

"Brothers! Sisters!" Tancred yelled. "Beyond that ridgeline is a hill - atop the hill is a gateway to the very Abyss itself! Only three warriors guard that hill, and we must make it through to them! Basilea depends upon it! There is no time for tactical acumen; there is no time to minimize our losses! We charge, we charge headlong at our foes, and we fight through to reinforce those three brave souls atop the hill! Are you with me?"

A stirring, combined cry echoed through the night from the assembled paladins, renewing Tancred's faith in achieving victory. Pressing a hand against his Eloicon, he quickly and silently recited a prayer before unsheathing his sword and holding it high above his head.

"Charge!"

The deafening yells continued as the forty armored horsemen surged forward along the valley, their banners held high and proud and their trumpets blasting. The ground rumbled and shook under their thundering hooves, lances lowered along the front ranks to either side of Tancred. Up ahead, he picked out the weakest area he could see in the line of Abyssals to the northwest of the ridge where their infantry scuttled forward, only two ranks deep.

Balls of flame shot out from the rear ranks of the hellish denizens, momentarily illuminating the night before slamming into the charging paladins and sending a few of the brave warriors tumbling from their saddles, ablaze. Three hulking molochs turned and waddled away from the center of the enemy line, clearly intent upon standing against the new threat charging toward their weaker flank. Renewed cries were issued from the unit to Tancred's right and they surged ahead of him, spurring their steeds into a full charge. Through the narrow slits in his helmet, Tancred saw wooden splinters twirl and dance up into the air from the shattered lances of the front rank of knights. The molochs, mortally pierced by the long lances and the rapid speed behind them, fell to be trampled to a pulp beneath the dozens of armored horsemen.

"Left of center!" Tancred yelled above the thumping of a hundred hooves. "Take the lead! On me!"

Trumpets blasted to pass on Tancred's orders, and the unit to his left surged ahead of the paladins who had been momentarily slowed by the suicidal sacrifice of the molochs. Tancred positioned his warhorse in the center of the front rank, his heart pounding as the hill he had left his comrades to defend finally swam into view from behind the darkness of the ridgeline.

Clearly seen and assessed as a great risk by the enemy commanders, Tancred saw a fresh unit of heavily armored Abyssal guards charge across to stand firm in front of the lower Abyssals he had singled out in the line. It mattered not. Nothing could stop them now. Seconds away from impact, the men and women of the 6th Cohort shouted as one and couched their lances in preparation to strike. The line of black armored, fang jawed demons swam rapidly toward Tancred as he brought his blade up high and ready.

With a thunderous smash and a frenzied roar, the paladins tore into the lines of Abyssal guards. Lances splintered and crunched, metal tips tore through crude armor, and the front rank of Abyssals dissolved. A demon partially hidden beneath spiked armor and a horned helmet was the first to face Tancred; it simply disappeared as Orion's warhorse charged the Abyssal down, crushing it to a pulp beneath heavy hooves. Tancred leaned across in his saddle and brought his blade down into a warrior in the second rank, hacking into the shoulder to bring his sword emerging out of the Abyssal's opposite armpit to cut the fiend nearly in two.

The sacrificial unit of Abyssal guards was trampled underfoot and cut asunder by heavy blades, torn apart within seconds by the sheer ferocity of the paladin's charge. Tancred's lead paladins were immediately enveloped on both sides as lower Abyssals charged in from the flanks, taking the impetus out of their attack and swamping them with larger numbers. Paladins were dragged from their saddles by the nightmarish devils and savagely slashed to death as they lay helpless on the ground. The lead rank of paladins peeled back to defend their brethren, swarming through the sea of scarlet demons as casualties mounted on both sides.

"Push through!" Tancred yelled desperately. "Do not stop! Push through to the other side!"

A lower Abyssal leapt up at him and swung a notched longsword at Tancred's head. Tancred deflected the blow and brought his own sword down, splitting his adversary's cranium in two in a fountain of blood. Immediately, two more of the hellish monsters jumped forward to occupy the gap in the fight and attack him, forcing him onto the defensive.

With a sound like a hundred trees snapping at the trunk, the second unit of paladins charged into the flanking lower Abyssals. Isolated groups of knights smashed deep into the swirling melee, hacking and maiming their demonic foes as the balance was again turned in favor of the Basileans. Desperately eyeing his destination on the far side of the ridge, Tancred slashed down at the Abyssals swarming around his warhorse.

*****

As the thundering heavy cavalry rounded the corner in the narrow valley, the night was lit up. Ahead, from behind the southern edge of the ridgeline, Aestelle could see the blazing remains of the outskirts of Andro dominated by a tall fire raging up and over a mine pump house. The blackened, latticework beams of the tall building were still visible through the flickering, yellow flames; around the central building were a dozen smaller storage houses also melting away into the fire. Through the thick smoke and the hot, hazy air above the flames, Aestelle could see the hill where she had left the few survivors to defend the portal stones. They were close now.

Off to the north, Aestelle saw Tancred lead the left flank's mounted paladins into the fight, quickly disappearing into a raging melee at the edge of the ridge. The main fight continued in the center as the men-at-arms, supported by battle sisters, trudged forward to face the charging Abyssals of the enemy's main line. Two of the Elohi who had come to Aestelle's rescue earlier soared down from the dark heavens to land in the center of the Basilean front line, greeted by enthusiastic cries from the soldiers. But the right flank would not escape unscathed – Aestelle looked ahead and saw snaking lines of Abyssals weaving their way through the burning buildings to form a battle line to prevent the paladins from reaching the hill.

Aestelle was well aware that she was no knight. She could ride a horse well – and a gur panther for that matter – but she could not do what Tancred had done and simply assume command of a large group of heavily armored cavalrymen. Her role was to guide them to the hill to prevent any confusion on route. Nothing more. Orders were shouted and trumpets blasted up ahead, signaling formations changes that Aestelle did not understand. The knights broke away neatly into two units, forming pristine lines as the light from the flames ahead sparked off their immaculate armor, silhouetting their imposing forms against the backdrop of fire.

Digging her heels into Desiree's sides, Aestelle kept pace with the fifty charging paladins, Tancred's warhorse clearly eager and able to take place front and center of the stampede. Balls of fire shot out from the rear lines of the Abyssals, most sweeping harmlessly past the charging paladins, but some finding their mark and engulfing the noble horsemen and their steeds in flames. Proficient with a bow but certainly not able to shoot while riding, Aestelle took her pistol from her belt instead. One shot before a cumbersome and time-consuming reload. It needed to count.

The thunderclap of the lance charge connecting sounded from up ahead, and Aestelle watched the vicious assault suddenly slow to a near halt as the front ranks of knights ploughed their way through the Abyssal infantry. The second rank immediately peeled off and broke away to the left; Aestelle looked across and saw some twenty or thirty armor-clad Abyssal horsemen charging toward their flank, easily the equal of the Basilean paladins in fighting ability. The two opposing lines of horsemen met head on, smashing into each other and instantly merging into a bloodbath of slashing swords and smashing hooves.

Urging her warhorse forward, Aestelle moved up to catch the rear rank of the paladins, looking for an opening to move through and engage their enemy. The fighting fanned out as some of the paladins pursued Abyssals into the midst of the burning mining buildings, charging the demons down and hacking at them from above, or finding themselves surrounded and outnumbered before being dragged from their saddles to a painful demise.

Threading her way through the encumbered, heavily armored knights, Aestelle rode up to the fighting, wincing in the heat generated by fires raging around her. Cries of anger and agony rang around her as blades clashed into blades and cut through flesh and bone. To her left, a counterattack by a unit of Abyssal guards threatened to break the Basilean line; to her right, a spearhead of mounted paladins pushed forward to drive a wedge of destruction through the thinly spread lower Abyssals.

And then Aestelle saw it. Through the flames and smoke of one of the burning store houses, screaming hoarsely as it led a fresh wave of demonic warriors forward to face the paladins, Aestelle saw the temptress who had come so close to ending her life. All other objectives forgotten, all caution tossed unceremoniously to the winds, Aestelle kicked her warhorse into a gallop and leaned forward in her saddle. Barging her way through the flanks of an advancing trio of Abyssals, Aestelle rode into the flaming ruins of the storehouse, her eyes fixed on her prey on the far side of the burning building.

The vile temptress cracked her whip into the backs of the surrounding lower Abyssals, screaming curses at them and driving them forward in a frenzied charge against the stalling paladin horsemen. The thick smoke stinging her eyes and the acrid air burning her lungs, Aestelle charged through the building, her horse barging through the burning planks of the blackened walls to smash out of the other side only yards away from the temptress.

The demon woman's head turned to regard Aestelle as she galloped toward her. For a second, only a fraction of a moment, Aestelle saw bewildered surprise and even a hint of fear register in the winged monster's single remaining black eye. Aestelle brought her pistol up, took aim at the center of the temptress' chest, and pulled the trigger. The surprise in the lithe creature's eyes instantly changed to a snarl of rage, and it leapt into the air, propelled on its leathery wings to spring forward into an attack. Aestelle's pistol jumped in her hand, white smoke shooting from its barrel. The shot tumbled through the air, accurate enough, but by the time it had reached its target, the temptress was already off the ground. Instead of striking the evil creature in its chest, the pistol shot smashed into its hip, breaking bone and sending out a spray of black blood.

The temptress let out a shriek of pain as it continued forward, spiraling unsteady in its flight, but still managing to lash out with a booted foot to kick Aestelle viciously in the side of the head. Her head whipping back with the astounding force of the attack, Aestelle tumbled from her saddle and found herself dragged across the dusty ground, one foot still caught in a stirrup. Twisting to free her foot, Aestelle tumbled painfully to the ground but pressed herself instantly back up to her feet, drawing her greatsword from her back as she did so. The temptress stood only a few paces ahead of her, blood leaking from the gunshot wound in its hip and from the savage injury she had inflicted across its face in their last encounter. The fight continued around them as paladins and legion soldiers traded blows and mounting casualties with fanged and clawed demons.

"Literally cheating death!" the temptress spat, slowly twirling her sword in one hand and cracking her whip at her feet with the other. "What chance do you have now without your angels to save you?"

"If you've got the balls for it, why don't you stop bleeding all over the place and come find out?" Aestelle replied, tightening her grip on her greatsword with both gloved hands.

The temptress' arm shot up and the whip cracked out toward Aestelle. Holding out one hand, the whip wrapped painfully around her forearm but failed to tear through her leather glove; Aestelle quickly grabbed the weapon, yanked it across with all of her strength to drag the demon over to her, and punched the temptress square in the face. Its head snapped back, its one eye unfocused and stunned with the force of the blow. Aestelle leapt on her opportunity to take advantage of the opening and thrust her greatsword up into the demon's wing, slashing a massive tear in the leather skin and lopping off the end of one of the appendages. The demon let out a great hiss of pain and slashed out with its sword, catching Aestelle across the upper arm and spattering blood across the hot earth at her feet.

Her teeth gritted, Aestelle fixed a victorious glare at her opponent.

"You're not going anywhere with a bullet in the hip and half a wing missing," she grinned. "It's just you and I now."

With a doleful creaking of breaking wood, the tall pump house finally gave way and blazing timbers crashed down to the ground amidst the fighting. Too late, Aestelle mentally cursed herself for the moment's distraction, but the barbed whip cracked again to painfully wrap around Aestelle's thigh, and with a pull, she was flung down to the ground in a cloud of dust. The temptress was on her within a second, the razor edge of its sword bearing down toward Aestelle's throat. Snarling like a mindless animal, the mutilated temptress knelt on top of Aestelle, forcing the sword down with an inhuman strength as she desperately held off the mortal blow with both hands. The demon's bloodied wings flapped grotesquely above them as they both struggled with the sword, the temptress' superior strength showing with each slowly passing moment as the sword edge drew down toward Aestelle.

Realizing she was fighting a losing battle of raw strength, Aestelle quickly shifted beneath the frenzied temptress to move her body as far as possible from the path of the blade before rapidly letting go with one hand and jabbing a thumb into the temptress' mangled eye socket. The demon howled in pain but leaned in to clamp her fanged jaws down to bite Aestelle's wrist, tearing open a vicious wound. The attention taken off the critical sword lodged between them, Aestelle fought through the pain to grab the blade and push it back, forcing the edge to bite into the temptress' gut. The demon staggered back and Aestelle leapt up to follow, bringing one knee up into the temptress' groin before slamming an elbow into its face to smash into its broken nose.

Its face mangled and mutilated, a lead bullet smashed into its hip, and a sizable section of one wing hacked clean off, the temptress still would not fall. The demon lunged forward at Aestelle, swinging its sword skillfully down in a series of rapid thrusts and slashes aimed at her head. Aestelle fell back, ducking away and dodging most of the attacks while the tip of the blade managed to nick and cut at her with the few she was not quick enough to evade. Covered in sweat, blood, and dust, feint from the heat of the surrounding fires, Aestelle willed herself on to avoid the temptress' deadly attacks until she had stepped back to where she had dropped her own greatsword.

Quickly snatching it up, she brought her own blade in to deflect a strike from the temptress, parry a second blow, and then bat aside a third. She found her opening. With a hateful growl, Aestelle stepped forward and plunged her blade into the temptress' gut, thrusting it straight through the devilish creature. She twisted it to open the wound, planted a foot on the howling demon's chest, and then kicked it off her blade to fall back into the dust. Standing over her fallen foe, Aestelle leaned down to pierce the temptress through the chest, pinning the screaming, writhing demon to the ground with her sword. Black blood flowed from the temptress' mouth as Aestelle leaned forward, pulling her sword free before grabbing her foe by one of the horns on its head and yanking it up to its knees.

"I know you can't be killed by a mere sword, not forever," Aestelle hissed, "so I know in time you can come back here. When you do, I'll be waiting. You may think your kind hunts us, but I'll be hunting you. For the next hundred years, whenever you come back, I will find you. And each time, I'll make you suffer more than the last."

Aestelle brought her sword sweeping down to lop off the demon's head. Its body remained upright for a few moments, its torn wings flapping morbidly before it collapsed down. Aestelle picked up the severed head by one horn and held it high above her, yelling from the bottom of her lungs. All around her, lower Abyssals turned to see their leader decapitated and defeated. The demons began to break and run.

Twenty-Two

Victory was close now. It was a familiar taste to Dionne. His forces held the line against the Basilean vanguard, stretched out to either side of the ridge to the southwest, admittedly giving ground against the heavy cavalry on the flanks but also pushing forward in the center to maintain the pressure. The important thing was that the portal stones had been located and the defense of the hilltop was all but defeated. Now Dionne merely needed to move his smaller, portable portal stone to the larger static gateway to allow his agents to commence the ritual to open it, and Teynne would be able to bring his army through.

The only problem was that Am'Bira had the small portal stone, as she was the most skilled in its use to summon reinforcements from the Abyss, but she had disappeared into the vicious fighting on the southern flank, by the burning mining buildings. This caused only minor concern to Dionne; he had already dispatched a flock of gargoyles to remind her that her duties lay in supporting him, not prancing around the fighting to satisfy her perverse lust of inflicting pain. Once the message was through, the winged temptress would be back by his side in moments.

But for now, the most important job was positively securing that hilltop, and this had not happened quickly enough for Dionne's pleasing. This was why he had decided that a job of this magnitude was well worthy of his personal intervention. Having left the front line of the fighting, he now traipsed slowly up the hill toward the summit and the portal stones, the steep slopes causing him some difficulty as the fighting continued to rage behind him in the valley. His scouts had passed a message back to him that only a handful of enemy soldiers remained. One side of the hill had completely collapsed under a sudden burst of rain of cataclysmic ferocity, clear evidence that a sorcerer of no mean ability stood atop the hill. This was a concern.

The sound of fighting was also audible from the hilltop as he neared the summit; blades clashing against blades, angry shouts, screams of the wounded and dying. The sounds died away as his eyes finally reached the hilltop. His gaze fell on the portal stones; simple enough in their appearance to be somewhat anticlimactic but beautiful in their significance as a major junction in his road to overthrowing the evil of the Hegemon. The hilltop was covered in corpses; a veritable sea of dead demons littered the summit, clawed hands stuck up in the air like vicious, macabre trees shooting up through a field of long grass. A few isolated pillars of fire lit up

261

the night sky, no doubt resulting from attacks from an earlier wave of flamebearers. Perhaps fifty Basilean soldiers lay dead among them, bloodily hacked down by the ferocity of the repeated waves of Abyssals he had ordered to take the hill. They had nearly succeeded.

Only three Basilean soldiers remained. The closest was a huge paladin, tall and muscular, blond hair complementing his handsome features. Dionne had seen his type many times before – back in the legion, they called men like this 'Gymnasium Queens'; soldiers who spent all their time working on muscles to enhance their aesthetic appeal, but little time on developing their soldiering skills. They looked the part, they bragged to women about their skills and conquests, but they made terrible soldiers. Dionne was not worried by him.

The second soldier was another paladin; Dionne could tell she was a woman by her figure, although her features were all but hidden beneath her helmet. She had already noticed his arrival and watched him with nervous, exhausted eyes. Her fear spoke volumes. She did not concern Dionne either. However, after nearly thirty years of soldering, Dionne had killed many women on battlefields across Mantica. As much as he utterly despised killing women, the effect it had on angering male soldiers into doing something stupid was often a worthwhile consideration.

The final soldier was older than the two paladins, perhaps only a decade junior to Dionne. The man carried a staff in one hand, a blood-drenched sword in the other, and wore light armor. Dionne was well capable of besting any soldier in combat, but there was only so much he could do against magic. The sorcerer, like the two paladins, was already wounded and appeared exhausted. That was something. Dionne formulated a plan and decided on the best order to dispatch them. He felt the power of the Abyss washing through him, energizing him and strengthening him in a real, tangible way unlike anything that mere faith and courage had done for him before.

"He's here," the female paladin said, causing both of the other warriors to look across the hilltop at Dionne as he walked over to them.

He suppressed a smile as he watched them in silence. No doubt they believed that delaying would win them the battle, as their vanguard would soon be there to secure the hill. The truth of the matter was that the hill had already fallen; Dionne just needed to get close enough to the sorcerer to kill him, and every pace they allowed was just making his final job all that easier.

"You've done well," Dionne admitted as he picked his way through the sea of bodies to close the gap with his foes, "but it's over now. This is done. Run, if you want to, I don't wish death upon you. Just your Hegemon."

"We are not running anywhere," the tall, dashing paladin said wearily, "we see our duty through to the end. That is what a true soldier of Basilea does."

"You know nothing of a true soldier, boy!" Dionne spat, angry with himself for rising to the obvious insult just as much as he was angry with the young paladin for his impudence. "If you wish to die on top of this hill, be my guest!"

The tall paladin raised his sword and held it ready in both hands.

"Dionne of Anaris, formerly Captain of the Basilean Legion," he said formerly, "under the Duma's orders, I am authorized to arrest you and bring you to face charges of willful disobedience and dereliction of duty. Surrender your weapon."

The words cut Dionne to the very core of his soul. The audacity of the paladin, a boy who had not even been born when Dionne first volunteered to serve his country, added insult to the vicious injury. His honor insulted, his temper raging, Dionne let out a yell and sprinted headlong at the paladin.

*****

Whether it was exhaustion or the shock of finally facing his uncle's killer after so many years that froze Orion to the spot, he did not know. His sword held ready, he stared motionless at the legendary warrior sprinting toward him, swift in spite of his heavy, blue-black plate armor. From his right, Jeneveve dashed out to meet the charging warrior, bringing her own sword up to slash toward Dionne. Galvanized into action by his comrade, Orion leapt in to join the attack with a thrust aimed at the traitor's chest. With a speed unlike anything Orion had ever seen, Dionne countered Jeneveve's first attack, parried Orion's strike, batted aside a follow up by Jeneveve, and then lanced his own blade forward at Orion to force him to jump back to evade.

Orion darted across to the left to put space between himself and Jeneveve, forcing Dionne to divert his attention between his two foes. It appeared to make no difference. Linking a sequence of strikes aimed at Dionne's head, torso, and arms, Orion found his strikes parried and countered while the old soldier simultaneously defended himself from a series of strikes from Jeneveve.

"Get back!" Valletto called from behind him. "I can strike him down if you get out of my way!"

Orion did not care who took Dionne down, and he had seen the grizzly effectiveness of Valletto's lightning strikes – he needed no second prompt. Holding his blade up to defend himself, Orion stepped back in an attempt to give Valletto the opening he needed. Dionne merely followed him, hacking out at Jeneveve to force her on the defensive while slashing out at Orion with each alternative blow. Jeneveve let out a cry of pain as one of Dionne's strikes connected, tearing through the mail between her breastplate and hip.

Dionne did not let up. Stepping across to take advantage of the wounded paladin, he slashed out to catch Jeneveve across the neck and cut her a second time, forcing her to stumble back and fall away from the fight. Valletto rushed to step in, standing in front of Jeneveve to defend her with his own blade. Orion knew that the sorcerer did not have the skills to last long against the master swordsmen, despite a surprisingly spirited and agile defense he put up.

Summoning all of his might, channeling his willpower and determination into a renewed wave of energy, Orion lunged forward to aim his blade at Dionne's gut, diverting the attack into a strike to the head at the last moment. Dionne countered quickly, but Orion was quicker, arcing his sword around to sweep out at Dionne's legs and hack the blade deep into one thigh. The old soldier let out a cry of pain and smashed an armored fist into Orion's cheek, sending him staggering back in a daze.

Jeneveve was up again, fighting at Valletto's side as the mage's staff glowed white with the summoning of arcane powers. Dionne threw himself at the mage, slicing down with his sword to cut the staff asunder and send it clattering to the earth harmlessly in two halves. Even without his staff, the sorcerer bravely continued to attempt to assist in the fight, aiming a succession of strikes at Dionne's flanks. All were countered and a brutal cut hacked across Valletto's stomach as he attempted to jump back away from the strikes, dropping him to the ground with a vicious abdominal wound.

Jeneveve charged into Dionne, barging a shoulder against him and pushing him back away from the wounded sorcerer protectively. Orion returned to the fight, bringing his own sword down to clang against one of the traitor's studded pauldrons but without effect. Pained gasps forcing their way through his gritted teeth, Valletto stumbled back to his feet, one arm clutching at his bleeding abdomen while his free hand extended to shoot a blast of air into Dionne to knock him back away from Orion and Jeneveve.

Eager to take advantage of the opening the sorcerer had created, Orion dashed forward to resume his attack. His first blow connected with Dionne's head with a dull clang but failed to hack through his great helm. His footing unsteady beneath the onslaught of hurricane winds directed by the mage, Dionne stumbled back before falling flat on his back amidst the bodies and burning fires. Orion brought his sword down to hack at the prone warrior, but Dionne kicked his legs from beneath him, sending him rolling down in the dirt and dead bodies.

Jeneveve rushed over, whether it was to attack Dionne or defend Orion, he would never find out. Dionne propelled himself back up to one knee and thrust his sword out, plunging it straight through Jeneveve's chest. Orion yelled out in anguish as he clambered back to his feet, watching in desperate agony as Jeneveve dropped gently off Dionne's sword to fall to the ground, her lifeless eyes focused up at the stars above.

Orion ran forward and brought his blade down with all his might in a furious attack aimed at Dionne's head. The old soldier dodged the clumsy attack effortlessly and smashed the pommel of his sword into Orion's head, tearing open a bloody wound and sending him staggering back again. He took a few uncontrolled steps back before falling to the ground next to where Valletto had collapsed to one knee, still clutching his wound as blood trickled from one corner of his mouth.

Dionne stood over the two wounded warriors.

"Last chance," he said grimly, "just go. Paladin, take your wounded comrade and go."

Orion could do nothing. The three of them had failed to defeat the master swordsman, and with Jeneveve dead and Valletto wounded, he did not stand a chance. The appeal of the offer seemed so tempting, so tangible. At best, Orion could take Valletto to safety and have his wounds treated, meet up with Tancred, and come up with a plan to re-take the hill. At worst, he could run, escape with his life, and leave the pain and the mortal peril behind.

"We're not going," Valletto gasped as he struggled back to his feet, "we won't stand idly by and watch an evil bastard like you ruin these lands. We won't let your hordes of evil take the lives of the children who depend on us for their safety. We won't run."

Orion stood shoulder-to-shoulder with the wounded mage and nodded.

"He speaks for us both," he said, his eyes fixed on Dionne's.

The Abyssal soldier rushed at them. Another blast of strong wind from Valletto slowed the warrior enough for Orion to leap in to attack, his sword biting into Dionne's with a dull thud. The veteran warrior pushed him away and slashed out at Valletto, connecting the flat of his blade against the mage with enough force to send him staggering back over the lip of the hill to slide down the mud bath and disappear into the darkness below. Orion barged his shoulder into Dionne, using his superior size and strength to knock his opponent back to the ground.

He fell on top of him, slamming a fist into Dionne's face and denting the metal of his helmet with a loud clang. Dionne brought his head up to smash into Orion's, his metal helm connecting with Orion's bare head painfully. Undeterred, Orion brought his own elbow around to pummel Dionne again, striking his mouth and splitting his lip with a spray of scarlet. Both warriors rolled over each other in an attempt to gain the upper hand; Orion stronger, but Dionne more skilled and less tired by the night's battles. Eventually tumbling apart, both men staggered back to their feet and recovered their blades to face each other once more. Dionne looked down at a familiar object in one hand. His eyes widening in terror, Orion brought a hand frantically to his side. It was gone. His uncle's Eloicon was gone, its chain snapped in the fight. Dionne looked down at the sacred book in his hand before casually tossing it into one of the pillars of fire by his side. His heart thumping in his chest, Orion watched his last physical link with his uncle succumb to the flames and fade to nothing.

Blinking blood from his eyes, Orion tirelessly charged into the fight again. Dionne shifted to one side, bringing a knee up into Orion's gut to wind him and bend him over double before a fist slammed into his face and knocked him back down into the dirt. He looked up and saw Dionne stood over him, his blade held high over his head in both hands, his red eyes staring down at the felled paladin only a moment away from death.

An arrow thudded into Dionne's armpit, driving into his torso and sending him stumbling away with a howl of pain. Staggering back to his feet, Orion looked up and saw Aestelle pacing angrily over from the far side of the hill, throwing her bow and empty quiver to one side and drawing her greatsword. She pointed the elegant weapon at Dionne.

"I've already taken the head of one demonic bitch tonight," the tall woman sneered, "you're going to be my second."

With a roar, Dionne yanked the arrow out of his side and threw it away, fixing Aestelle with a rage filled glare.

"Look around you, you stupid old bastard!" Aestelle hissed. "The fight is lost! The paladins hold the foot of the hill! Your army is scattered! You've lost!"

Orion looked down the side of the hill. Some thirty mounted paladins were formed up at the foot of the slopes, wheeling their horses back around to face another wave of lower Abyssals who charged headlong at them from the ridgeline to the southwest. With a roar, the paladins hurtled out to meet the charge.

"Looks to me like things are still in the balance," Dionne said coldly, spitting out a mouthful of blood.

Orion placed a hand against his head and used the very last of his rudimentary arcane energy to heal the array of wounds across his face and crown. Wiping blood out of his eyes, the pain momentarily relieved, he felt focused and ready to fight again. Aestelle walked over to stand by his side.

With a defiant yell, Dionne charged into the attack. Orion moved in to meet him, sweeping past and dragging his sword across the old warrior's side, tearing a gash into the mail beneath his breastplate and drawing blood. Dionne continued regardless, batting aside a series of attacks from Aestelle before punching her in the stomach and slamming a fist into her face, knocking her to the ground.

Aestelle rolled acrobatically away and was back on her feet, a bloody graze across one cheek.

"You punch like an elf," she laughed at Dionne.

Breathlessly, the effort of the continued fight finally showing, Dionne ran at Aestelle again. Orion rushed out to intercept him, but Dionne met Aestelle first and rained down blows at her head like a hammer. One slipped through her skillful guard, ripping a wound open across her shoulder and forcing her back. Orion barged into the fight and slashed down at Dionne, slicing against his breastplate without success. Dionne again fought skillfully, tirelessly against two adversaries as Orion and Aestelle stood their ground, exchanging attacks and parries with their enemy as metal clanged against metal and vicious blades sliced out in deadly assaults.

Orion felt pain flare up through his leg as Dionne's sword cut into his thigh; a second later, Aestelle thrust her own blade forward to puncture a hole in Dionne's breastplate and through the side of his chest. Orion saw the smallest of openings, the briefest of moments for exploitation, and took it. He brought his heavy blade carving up and hacked through Dionne's arm, slicing it off neatly between the shoulder and elbow.

Blood spraying from the severed stump, Dionne staggered back and dropped to his knees as he yelled out in pain, his remaining hand pressed against the savage wound. Orion and Aestelle advanced to stand over him, looking down at the defeated warrior as his cries trailed away weakly.

"Kill him," Aestelle spat. "Kill the bastard."

Orion looked down at the helpless warrior. He remembered his uncle Jahus' hand frantically clinging to his arm, the strength fading and the grip loosening as his uncle's life slipped away. He thought of the anger and hatred he had carried with him for the decade since, for the thousand nights he had been unable to sleep, imagining the day he would finally avenge Jahus.

Then he thought of waking up under the care of the Elohi who had saved his life, of the revelation revealed to him regarding his own morality and the danger faced by his very soul. He thought of his promise to change. To do the right thing.

"Teynne..." Dionne whispered hoarsely. "Teynne, you bastard..."

"Kill him!" Aestelle repeated. "He murdered your uncle! He threatened our entire country, our entire people! Slit the bastard's throat!"

Orion thought of Jahus and considered reminding Dionne of what he did eleven years ago, of telling him that he was the squire who had watched the two paladins die on the mountainside. But it would make no difference. This was about justice, not vengeance. Orion lowered his sword and gently held out one hand to Dionne.

"Repent of your sins," he said softly, "and face your judgment."

With a snarl of pure hatred, Dionne snatched at his sword with his remaining hand and lunged forward at Orion. He had barely moved off one knee when Aestelle's sword hacked down into his neck to half-sever his head. He sank down off Aestelle's blade to take his place among the sea of dead bodies around the portal stones. Orion stared down at the corpse, partly unable to accept that this huge chapter of his life truly was at an end. He watched the body warily, almost expecting Dionne's corpse to transform into an Abyssal Champion and rise from the grave, a great claw emerging from his severed arm as fire spouted from his eyes.

Nothing happened. Orion turned and looked down the hill. The paladins, led by Tancred, charged down the final Abyssal warriors and slaughtered them. He felt a hand rest softly on his shoulder, and he looked across to see Aestelle's blood spattered face offer him a sad smile.

"Ri," she said quietly, "it is over now. He's gone."

*****

Dawn arrived in a blur of grays, color slowly seeping back into the world as the sun peered over the horizon to cast long shadows over the silent battlefield. Orion sat on the lip of the hill's crest, staring out to the east as the sun rose slowly and magnificently over the Low Sea of Suan, over the same islands and the same fishing fleets he had seen eleven years earlier as his uncle's squire. Soldiers moved silently across the battlefield, the valley, the hilltops, and slopes, dragging the hideous corpses of the fallen Abyssals to toss into the fires of the still burning mining town. The fallen of Basilea were arranged far more carefully, lined up respectfully at the foot of the hill for a proper burial when the time was right.

Below him, Orion saw Tancred working with a dictator to take charge

267

of the battlefield, to ensure the wounded were properly cared for and units were reformed to account for the dead and missing. Valletto was one of the wounded Orion saw below him, limping along with an escort of two battle sisters who had tended his wounds. The mage looked up at Orion and offered him a weak smile and a wave. Orion stood momentarily to salute him before collapsing back down to sit at the edge of the hill.

The only other wounded warrior he saw who he recognized was the solitary survivor of the men-at-arms who had first set out with them many weeks ago from the City of the Golden Horn, the legion soldier who had been smashed off the hill by the charging molochs. It was only then that Orion recognized him as the father of the children who had rushed out during the march through the streets when they had left the capital weeks ago. It made him smile with a warmth he could not remember.

Aestelle sat next to him on top of the hill as the sun rose. The two waited in contented silence for what could have been hours as the sun chased away the last remnants of darkness from the longest and worst night of either of their lives. As their energy slowly returned, they healed the worst of their wounds but remained physically and emotionally exhausted as they sat, covered in dirt and dried blood, as dawn broke. The clouds broke open and blue filled the skies above as the sun slowly rose, a gentle wind accompanying the cawing of sea birds to the east.

Aestelle stood and walked off after some time, returning several minutes later to stand over Orion. He looked up at her and saw that she was holding her sisterhood Eloicon. She offered it to him.

"I want you to have this," she said quietly.

Orion looked up into her eyes for several long seconds. She met his stare evenly.

"I cannot take that," he said gently.

"I want you to," she repeated, "I... cannot help but think of my actions on this hill. Of what I said at the end. I am thoroughly ashamed. You did the right thing, Ri. You offered mercy when I could not. You stood by the principles of the Shining Ones when I had only anger, malice, and vengeance on my mind. I would be proud if this Eloicon belonged to you. It can never replace the one that was taken from you last night, but at least it can be something. It can be from a friend."

Orion stood up and looked down at her. He stumbled for the right words but failed.

"I... thank you. Not just for this. Thank you for... well..."

"I know," Aestelle said with a soft smile.

He took the sacred book and carefully attached it to the broken chain at his waist. The sisterhood copy was smaller, lighter than that given to paladins, but it felt right. Orion felt his uncle would approve.

"Take care, Ri," Aestelle said, taking a step back away from him.

"You are leaving?"

"I'll see you at the capital," she said, "but I'm not going back with the army.

All that pomp and ceremony was never my thing. I need some time alone. I'll see you soon."

Orion watched her turn and limp over to where the horses had been gathered at the foot of the hill. She took the reins of her own horse and rode off to the south, soon disappearing from view.

"You did it, then."

Orion turned to see Tancred stood a few paces away. The short knight looked exhausted, his armor with its expensive accouterments was battered, tatty, and covered in grime. Orion smiled at the sight of his friend.

"We all did it," he exhaled. "We lost men and women far better than I could ever aspire to be; but between us, we did it. We stopped them."

Tancred nodded slowly.

"I think all those who fell would have done it nonetheless, knowing what the alternative was," he replied.

"I thought of running," Orion admitted shamefully. "I nearly did not see it through."

"We all think of running," the younger knight said, "every one of us. Any man who tells you otherwise is a liar or an idiot. But we did not run. We saw it through."

The weary young paladin looked up at Orion and flashed him a brief, sad smile as he rested a hand on his shoulder.

"Come on, friend. It is time to go home."

Twenty-Three

Bells chimed from every chapel, church, and cathedral across the entire City of the Golden Horn. Thousands of citizens flocked to the roadsides, lining the streets leading from the North Gate to the Royal Quarter. Colored banners were strung up across the streets; streamers were thrown from windows and rooftops, a thousand voices screamed and cheered on every street as the returning army marched home.

Beneath the baking autumn sun of southern Basilea, Valletto looked up into a cloudless sky. The familiar, dry, still air felt like a welcome relief after the harsher climates of the north, and the sensation of the Eriskosian climate finally sealed in his mind that he had truly returned home safely. Tancred rode at the very head of the victorious army, at the request of the Hegemon himself, atop his beloved warhorse Desiree. Behind him rode Orion, Xavier, and Valletto before the dictator then led the victorious vanguard. Trumpets blared and drums were beat from the musicians at the head of each column of infantry and cavalry, all but drowned out by the cheering crowds.

Valletto allowed himself a smile as he looked down at the small toy soldier in his hand. A simple, wooden carving of a paladin, carefully painted in blue and white by his son. It was that toy soldier Valletto had given to Tancred to return home. At least Valletto could do it in person now, thank the Shining Ones.

The journey home had been pleasant, surprisingly so, with gratitude showered on the soldiers at every town and village they passed. Valletto had become friends with Tancred and Xavier, but particularly close with Orion who regularly and awkwardly told him how much he appreciated standing with him atop the hill against Dionne. For Valletto, it was a memory he never wanted to revisit. He saw the impact the confrontation on the hilltop had made on the young paladin, but Orion did not speak of it. A veteran of many wars, Valletto was confident that Orion would wear the turmoil well enough, for now at least.

Tancred was more of an enigma to Valletto. It was obvious that he felt deep remorse over leaving the hilltop, even though his leadership in the valley was one of the decisive factors in their victory. The Hegemon certainly seemed to think so. Nonetheless, the regret was evident even though Tancred never voiced it. What was more confusing was his obvious and growing apprehension to return home.

Valletto wondered what on earth could be waiting for him in the capital that was more terrifying than facing an army from the Abyss.

As was tradition within the legion, men and women marching behind Valletto slowly began to break rank and run out to the crowds. Those with families to return to were at liberty to break off the march and leave their unit as soon as they saw their loved ones. It was one of the few Basilean military traditions that really stirred a chord with Valletto, even if it did leave returning parades looking somewhat skeletal by the time they reached their final destination.

The paladins and sisters had no such tradition; they would see it out to the very end. In this case, the very end of the procession was the palace itself, where Tancred had been summoned for an audience with the Hegemon. Such an honor for a relatively low ranking soldier was all but unheard of.

Valletto looked up and exhaled. A few dozen yards ahead, stood just a pace in front of the crowd line, his son Lyius looked frantically and desperately at the ranks of soldiers marching behind Valletto. The little boy had obviously scanned his eyes straight past the important men on horseback at the head of the column, never expecting to see his father there. As more soldiers broke rank to run out to embrace their spouses and children, Lyius looked all the more panicked and breathless. Behind him stood Clera, their daughter Jullia held in her arms. His wife's normally calm exterior had completely dissolved and the desperation in her face was nearly as evident as in their son's.

Valletto jumped down from his horse and walked slowly, hypnotically, across the street toward the screaming and roaring crowd line. His wife's eyes met his and her face dissolved into a tear stricken smile. She crouched down and pointed their son in Valletto's direction. His face joyous, the boy ran out as Valletto dropped to one knee to embrace him. His wife stood over them, her hand on his face as their infant daughter looked on in confusion. Valletto was home.

*****

The steps leading up to the palace's main entrance spanned wide enough to drive an entire army up to the grand, double doors sat beneath an archway of pure gold. A soft carpet of light blue, somehow kept impossibly clean despite being outside and exposed to the elements, covered the center section of the white, marble stairs. Tall pillars of smooth white ran up each side of the staircase, punctuated regularly with ancient statues of deities, saints, and heroes of legend.

The screaming of the crowds still audible from outside the thick palace walls, Tancred arrived atop the staircase to find High Paladin Augus waiting for him. Several yards behind Augus, a quartet of hulking ogres stood guard by the palace doors, their resplendent armor seemingly at odds with their harsh faces and terrifying reputation. Nonetheless, the guards stood rigidly at attention with a discipline that would make any race proud.

Augus walked out to meet Tancred, his face breaking into a smile.

"Welcome home, Lord Paladin!" the older knight beamed.

"Thank you, High Paladin," Tancred saluted smartly.

"No need to stand on formality," Augus replied with a wave of the hand, "there will be plenty of that when you meet the Hegemon shortly. It is needless to say, but I shall say it anyway. You have done Basilea a great service. Your bravery and leadership have made our Order proud."

"It was '*we*', not '*I*', High Paladin," Tancred corrected quickly. "We all played our part. Every man and woman from the detachment carried out their duty to the very last."

"I know," Augus nodded sadly. "I know. Our lost will be properly remembered."

Any response from Tancred faded from his lips as a familiar figure appeared at the far end of the gallery at the top of the steps and walked quickly over toward them. The newcomer was tall, with silver flecks at his temples and neatly trimmed beard, and broad shoulders covered by a cloak of rich crimson. The highly stylized leather breastplate and ceremonial short sword at his waist marked out his previous life in the legion.

"Tancred," the older man smiled, holding out his hand, "welcome home."

"Father," Tancred nodded respectfully, shaking his father's hand and noticing with some disappointment that he continued his habit of overpowering and turning his hand palm down during handshakes. Tancred looked up at the broad politician, their height difference reminding him of many cruel accusations regarding his parentage during his adolescent years.

"Tristen," Augus greeted, "good to see you."

"I had nothing but faith in you," Tristen continued to smile, "but even I shall admit that I did not envisage meeting you here, awaiting an audience with the Hegemon himself. You have exceeded all expectations."

Tancred opened his mouth to comment on expectations and accolades being very much secondary to the dangers averted and comrades lost, but a lifetime of high expectation and harsh discipline forced his mouth shut again.

"Yes, father. Thank you."

"I heard mention of a laurel ring being presented," Augus interjected. "Of course, I am not privy to any final decision, but I would consider that award feasible considering who you are about to be presented to."

"Laurel ring, be damned," Tristen scoffed, "my son just saved the Hegemony from complete and utter destruction! I would expect nothing less than a royal epaulette!"

"I did not save..."

"Perhaps," Augus interrupted Tancred's response, "but one must accept that being summoned by the Hegemon is honor enough. As paladins, it is our honor and duty to serve. We fight for good, not glory. Any decoration is gratefully accepted, but ultimately secondary."

"Nonsense!" Tristen flashed a friendly smile. "One singles out a worthy soldier for adulation. At least, that was how it was done in the legion in my day."

"Father, I did not save…"

"Quiet, Tancred, not now," his father held a hand up to silence him. "High Paladin, if my son does not receive the correct marks of respect for his leadership and devotion to this nation, I will be having some uncomfortable conversation with Gnaeus Sallustis."

"That may be…" Augus began, his tone calm and diplomatic.

"I did not save the Hegemony," Tancred declared, "hundreds of us did. I was one of many. We all played our part. If I did not do what I did, somebody else would have…"

"Augus, give us a moment, won't you?" Tristen said coolly to the High Paladin in a tone Tancred was well familiar with, a tone he had come to fear over the years.

The High Paladin nodded politely and walked over to wait by the palace's main entrance. Tristen turned to glare down at his son.

"Now, of all times, Tancred?" he said, his tone low and threatening. "You have the honor of meeting the Hegemon himself, and you decide now is the time to play humble?"

Tancred looked up to meet his father's glare but found himself transported back to the reprimands of his youth. He looked down at his feet silently.

"I've done the soldiering, Tancred," his father continued angrily, "I know exactly what it is like and I know exactly what you've seen. But a soldier's duty is to die for his country, which is why I did my minimum time to establish credibility as a politician and why you will do the same."

"Yes, father."

"Family is everything, Tancred. Family is infinitely more important than the comradeship of the military. Your family will take care of you when the military has spat you out and forgotten you."

"Yes, father."

"Your great grandfather elevated himself from pauper to knight. Your grandfather built on that status to build our entire family's fortune. I built on your grandfather's success to establish our name in the Duma. And now you will march into that palace and do your bit for this family by accepting the credit for leading the defense of this nation and get yourself out of that Order uniform. The paladins can do no more for you now. You owe this much to this family."

Tancred paused before answering.

"Yes, father."

"Good."

The huge doors swung open, allowing light into the reception hall. The cavernous room's painted, dome ceiling was supported by tall, thin pillars of green veined marble, while the center of the room was dominated by a life sized carving of a trio of Elohi, knelt in prayer, fountains of water spraying up to cascade down gently over their elegantly carved wings. Two lines of servants waited to usher

Tancred in to see the Hegemon.

Tristen gestured to the doors. Tancred nodded, turned, and walked smartly over to the vast reception hall as a thin, balding man with pale skin he recognized as Ferrien, another senator of the Duma, walked over to Tristen.

"You must be proud, Tristen!" the pale man greeted. "I hear rumors of a statue being commissioned in honor of the battle."

"As long as Tancred is front and center," Tristen laughed, "a statue might not be a bad thing."

Tancred stopped dead in his tracks. His temper flared up uncontrollably, rapidly rising to easily override the fear beaten into him by his father. He thought of the past weeks, of the immense, flame-eyed devils he had faced and the risks of being dragged into the depths of hell itself for an eternity of torment. His father suddenly did not seem so intimidating. He turned back and fixed his eyes on Tristen, Ferrien, and Augus.

"No," he said sternly.

"Excuse me?" his father stepped forward to challenge him.

"No!" Tancred spat venomously. "Nobody is building a damned statue of me! You want a statue? You want heroes? Jeneveve, Reynaud, Tantus! Those are the ones you need to honor and remember! Those are the ones who stood their ground and died for Basilea! Silus, brother of the Blades of Onzyan, add him, too! He fought with us to the end! If a statue is honoring anybody, it is them! And many others who died with them!"

"Now you listen here!" Tristen growled as he paced forward.

"Shut up!" Tancred boomed, stopping his father dead in his tracks, wide-eyed in shock. "I am still talking, father, so keep your damn mouth shut until I am finished! We honor our dead! They gave everything! Over a hundred of us left this city, and three returned! The least we can do is acknowledge their sacrifice and bravery, and do all we can to ensure they are never forgotten! So that is who will be on any statue which is commissioned, I insist upon it!"

The High Paladin and the two senators stared at Tancred in shocked silence. He could feel the awkwardness from the lines of palace servants witnessing the altercation from within the reception hall. It meant nothing to him.

"Now," Tancred continued, "I am going in that palace to speak to the Hegemon. You, father, I am not done with you! You wait – right there – until I am back!"

Turning on his heel, Tancred stormed angrily into the palace.

*****

A trio of brown chickens strutted across the ground outside the tavern, their clucks drowned out by the sound of merry music coming from within the building. The autumn sun was high in the sky, and the aroma of hops and olives drifted across from the fields behind the isolated tavern, the smells of summer still clinging to the atmosphere surrounding the country village.

Opening the door revealed a tavern like any other in the sunny south Basilean countryside; a rarely used hearth against one wall and a long bar running in an L-shape across the far wall; old and broken farming implements were pinned to the walls to add a touch of ambience, and an ancient and worn rug whose colors were long faded covered the age old timbers of the floor. Farmers nearing the end of their midday break finished their lunches and ales as serving girls collected their empty plates with polite smiles, stopping for brief conversations.

A gray mustached bard, as tall as a bear and with a belly that spoke of a fondness for ales and cheese, sat on a small stool by the hearth, a lute against one knee as his thick fingers played a succession of merry songs that complimented the laughter of the farmers and the serving girls, adding to the positivity within the country inn. The aging bard looked up as the two newcomers to the inn approached him. His fingers stopped playing their intricate tune, his smile faded, and his jaw fell open in shock.

"It... it can't be..." he stammered.

"Hello, Hayden," Constance smiled warmly, "it is good to see you, old friend."

His wrinkled eyes filling with tears, Hayden jumped up and embraced Constance and Jaque, pulling them in tightly and clinging to them as if he feared they would disappear. Her eyes closed in contentment, Constance held on to the old man, happy her journey to find him had come to a successful end. After a long pause, Hayden finally released his two old friends and took a step back to stare at them.

"I thought you were both gone," he gasped. "I didn't realize you made it home!"

"She's as tough as a bastard, and I'm a coward," Jaque explained. "It'll take more than hell's demons to kill us off!"

Constance joined the other two in a laugh before Hayden signaled to one of the serving girls.

"Constance?"

Constance turned to see Maya, Hayden's daughter, dash over excitedly.

"It's so good to see you!" Maya said as she embraced them. "Pa said... well..."

"He was wrong, thank the Ones!" Jaque grinned.

"Let me get drinks for you!" Maya nodded excitedly. "I'll be right back!"

Hayden sank down to his seat, gesturing for his friends to do the same.

"So," he began, still breathless, "what happened? You know, actually, I don't want to know. Those days were dark and I would rather forget. Seeing you both alive and well is more than I could have hoped for."

"Alive and recovering," Constance corrected, "but we needn't go into the details. So this is it? Your retirement? This is what you said you wanted."

"Aye," Hayden nodded, "I'm back here where I grew up, I'm here with my daughter, and I just sit here with ale and play my music. Life is good!"

"I think I may steal your retirement plan," Jaque remarked as he looked around the tavern, nodding in approval, "this was a good idea."

"So take it," Hayden said, "you're still young, Jaque. Learn an instrument and stay safe and happy for the rest of your life. Find a woman and settle down. This isn't a bad way to live."

Jaque exchanged an awkward glance with Constance. The smile faded from Hayden's cracked lips. He leaned forward to fix them both with an accusatory stare.

"So what's going on with you two?" he enquired, his voice low.

Constance looked back at Jaque. He shrugged uncomfortably and shook his head before looking out of the window.

"We're reforming the company," Constance said. "Tancred, the Lord Paladin, ensured we were paid very well. We're here to give you your share of the payment as well as catch up. But Jaque and I are equal partners now. We're not done with soldiering yet."

"Are you mad?" Hayden sighed, his expression one of utter disappointment. "You escape with your life from… from… that? And you want to go back for more?"

"It's all we know," Jaque offered, "it's not forever. But I'm not ready to stop. Not just yet."

"Look," Constance leaned forward, "I already know the answer, but I have to ask. We wanted you to know how much we value you. How much we respect you. We're going back to mercenary work and we want you with us. Equal partner, equal authority, the three of us run the company. What do you…"

"No," Hayden declared assertively, "not a chance. And that's me using my polite words. You two are mad."

"We had to ask," Jaque said.

"But for what it's worth, I'm glad you made that choice," Constance added. "I'll be happy knowing you're safe, and here with your daughter."

Maya arrived with three tankards of foaming ale, lowering them carefully down to the table between the three old friends.

"You pulling up a chair?" Constance invited.

"I wouldn't want to intrude."

"No chance!" Jaque grinned his gap toothed smile, standing to offer the girl his own chair before fetching another.

Maya sat down and looked across at the two newcomers.

"So," she said, "you staying here for long?"

Constance looked back at Jaque before turning to Maya.

"We're in no rush," she replied, "I think we can afford a few days here."

*****

The air was cooling slightly as the late afternoon sun dipped down to touch the tallest towers and spires of the capital, darkening the skyline dominated by the rich and complex architecture behind Orion. The coastal path leading west out of the capital climbed gently up to give a clear, unobstructed view south across the glistening, turquoise waters of the Sea of Eriskos, its smooth surface broken by lines of fishing boats and small trade fleets. His lumbering warhorse, Star, trotted gently up the dusty, undulating path, back up to fighting weight and strength after the rigors of the battles against the Abyssals. The familiar, powerful warhorse was a welcome return, but a sentimental part of him missed Henry, the farm boy's horse who had lumbered into his life following his recovery after the campsite battle. He smiled fondly. At least Henry was back home now, with the farmer's son who doted on him. And an extremely generous payment to the family as a reward, courtesy of the Order.

The last few days had swept by in a blur, each hour demanding Orion repeat his account of the events around Tarkis, the first battles, Hugh's murder, the campsite ambush, and the final battle against Dionne. His patience wearing thin with every repeat telling of the story, Orion was forced to debrief paladins of rising ranks until he found himself stood before Gnaeus Sallustis himself. The Grand Master of all paladins had warmly expressed his gratitude, but Orion's promotion came as something of a shock. Appointed Paladin Defender, Orion was presented an exquisite greatsword of shining silver, a precious alloy that allowed a weapon to be lighter and stronger than any conventionally smithed blade across all of Mantica.

Orion truly appreciated the recognition, but the first thing to enter his mind upon being formally presented his blade was also the first thing he did upon being dismissed from the Grand Master's company. He found Kell, his squire, and gave him his old sword, the very sword that had cut down Dionne and helped to save Basilea from invasion.

"You shall need a stout blade," he had told his squire. "I intend to put you forward for consideration for your spurs next year."

Orion could never expect Kell to suddenly warm to him, not after years of neglecting his training and taking his service for granted, but the grateful smile that Kell gave him looked to be a solid start. There was some positivity there at least, although Jeneveve's death in the final battle against Dionne was something Orion knew he would need address with Kell about at some point.

His nights had been torn apart by horrific dreams ever since his fight against Dionne. The fight itself did not leave any lasting mark upon his mind, nor did the confrontations with his Abyssal horde. It was something else, something new and unexplained that troubled his soul. A new feeling in his core, something missing. It dominated his thoughts whenever his mind was left unoccupied.

Up ahead, Orion saw his destination; a grand inn overlooking the south coast, its rooms and services priced to eliminate all but the richest of patrons. A main building housed a reception, eating hall, and bathhouse; while separate houses around the walled complex allowed lavish living conditions for those wealthy enough to enjoy them. Orion saw a lone horse outside the gate, with a tall, slim figure busily checking saddlebags.

Aestelle looked up as Orion approached. She wore a shirt of white silk to contrast her leggings of soft, black leather and a sash of deep blue around her slender waist. She offered him a smile as he dismounted his warhorse and walked across to her.

"Well, well!" she greeted. "A new aesthetic! I suppose this goes with the promotion?"

Orion wore a long coat of scaled mail with rich robes and a cloak of blue, and tall, thick pauldrons lined with gold to denote his new rank.

"It is a little ostentatious," Orion smiled uncomfortably, "but it is appreciated. Tancred wrote a long report on my conduct. I owe him for this."

"I owe him for this," Aestelle said, pointing to the rich accommodation behind her. "I was very well paid for my part. Shame that Tancred's first thought of me was one who desired payment above all, but I only have myself to blame for that."

"That is not true," Orion said as he stepped closer to her. "Have you not heard the songs? You are famed across the land now. The bards sing of you defeating the evil demon Dionne atop the mountain."

"They sing of you, Ri!" Aestelle laughed. "Or us, I suppose. I have to confess to being rather amused by the political requirement to change my portrayal in the songs to something more agreeable for the great-unwashed masses. 'A fighting nun, purer than driven snow,' I believe is my introduction. One assumes that is more inspirational to children than a money driven mercenary with a foul mouth and an uncontrollable wine addiction."

Orion failed to match her short laugh and smiled sympathetically.

"Those who know you do not think of you as such."

"Well," Aestelle secured the buckle on her last saddlebag, "speaking of those who know me, I have to go. Z'akke, an old salamander accomplice of mine, has taken an interest in our adventures. We are off to make sure that the undead menace we awoke trying to cross that ravine is not going to cause any trouble."

Orion nodded, trying to hide his disappointment. Aestelle turned to face him and looked up at him expectantly.

"Oh," Orion raised his brow, "I nearly forgot. I really could not think of anything as sentimental or impressive to give to you in return for your Eloicon. I am afraid this was the best I could do. Its color is the same shade as that of my Order. So you can remember us. Fondly, I hope."

Orion handed over the small sapphire he had bought and had drilled through to add to her collection of colorful beads in her hair. She accepted it with another smile.

"Thank you, Ri," she said gently.

"Do you have to go?" he found himself blurting out.

Aestelle's smile faded, and she looked off to the north as the coastal breeze whipped her blonde hair out to one side.

"It's what I do," she shrugged. "What else is there?"

"You could stay," Orion offered. "You could... I do not know... rejoin the sisterhood. They would take you back in an instant. Or... you could become a paladin. You can fight better than anybody I know! You can ride a horse in battle! Tancred could put in a word for you. You would only have to learn to fight in armor, and that is not so difficult."

Aestelle exhaled and narrowed her eyes before shaking her head.

"I don't take orders well, Ri," she replied, "I never did. That is why I left the sisterhood. I don't want to go through all of that again."

"I wish you would not go," Orion plucked up the courage to admit out loud.

Aestelle stepped closer, only a few inches from him, and looked up into his eyes. At that moment, she seemed more beautiful to him than ever before.

"Then give me a reason to stay," she said seriously.

His mind racing, Orion played through every possible scenario he could concoct in his head in a desperate attempt to find a reason to convince her not to leave. He thought of every role she could fill within his order, from soldiering to spying, scouting to instructing. None of them would satisfy her need to avoid the harsh oversight of authority.

"You are right," he conceded with a heavy heart, "it would never work. I have to respect who you are and what makes you happy. You are best living your life of adventure on the open road. I have to respect that."

Aestelle's eyes closed as her head sagged forward, an audible breath escaping from her lips. She took a step back and inhaled deeply before looking up at him again. She fixed him with a wide grin and a cocky wink before pressing a clenched fist against one of his shoulders.

"Take care, Ogre," she beamed, "you're a good friend."

Orion watched sadly as the tall woman vaulted back up into her saddle and dragged her horse around to face the road north. She looked down at him.

"You're a good man, Ri. Don't ever let anybody tell you otherwise."

Orion watched in silence as she kicked her horse into a canter and disappeared over the foothills to the north.

*****

Seated on a bench behind his house, overlooking the gardens extending away toward the fields to the east, Valletto sighed with contentment as he swilled his white wine within the delicate, stone goblet. His daughter, Jullia, waddled to and fro from a small barrel of water, experimenting with a succession of garden objects to ascertain whether they floated or not. His son, Lyius, sat on the bench next to him, an introductory text of beginner's magical spells open on his lap, his head rested wearily against his father's shoulder. Clera, his wife, sat on a chair opposite them, smiling in contentment as she watched them both in silence. Valletto returned the smile, so happy that even the pain in his slowly recovering abdomen could not take the shine off the moment.

Clera stood and wordlessly took Valletto's goblet back inside, returning after a few moments with a refill and a lit candle for the small table in their garden. She looked over at their daughter.

"I'll have to get her to bed soon," she said quietly. "It's a shame. I don't think any of us want this moment to end."

"I'll get this fellow tucked up in bed," Valletto nodded to his exhausted son, "but we can do exactly the same tomorrow."

Valletto turned to evaluate the best technique for carrying his son up to his room, but his thoughts were interrupted by a knock at the front door. He heard Hustas, his servant, walk along their hall inside to answer the door. There was a brief exchange before Hustas emerged from the kitchen door to enter the back gardens.

"A visitor for you, sir," he announced, "Paladin Defender Orion of Suda."

Lyius head shot up and his eyes opened wide.

"Orion?" he repeated. "The Orion? The one from all the songs?"

Valletto looked across apologetically at his wife as she grimaced at the sudden evaporation of any chance of getting their son to sleep at a reasonable hour. Valletto stood slowly, wincing as pain flared up in his gut.

"Thank you, Hustas," he said. "Could you get a drink for him, please?"

Valletto walked back into the house and to the small entrance hall, his eyes falling for a moment to the spot where he had collapsed down in despair at the thought of leaving his wife and children to join the hunt for Dionne. But that was over now.

Orion waited just inside the house, clothed resplendently in the new, spotless armor of a paladin defender. He turned to greet Valletto with an apologetic shrug. Valletto offered his hand.

"I am so sorry for arriving unannounced," Orion said, "especially at this hour, I was just on my way back from…"

"Please come inside," Valletto said. "You are always welcome here."

Orion walked into the entrance hall.

"I just saw Aestelle off," Orion said, "I had rather hoped she would stay."

Valletto nodded. He had seen the way they had both looked at each other on the journey home and was surprised that the mercenary had chosen to depart. Still, it was good to see Orion's response to the disappointment. He seemed a little sturdier, a little more content in himself after the hollowness he must have felt from finally slaying his uncle's killer.

"Come through to the garden and have a drink," Valletto offered. "The family are all out for sunset. They'll want to meet you."

Valletto led the paladin through his house and to the small garden. Clera rose and walked across to meet him.

"Orion, this is my wife, Clera."

"A pleasure," Orion bowed his head respectfully, "it is wonderful to finally meet you. Valletto spoke so highly of you while we were away."

"The pleasure is mine," Clera replied with a polite smile, "my husband tells me that you were one of the men and women I have to thank for his safe return."

Valletto winced at the words. When he had told her of his actions atop the hill, Clera had been furious with the paladins who had allowed him to fight by their side instead of protecting him. She had reminded him that sword fighting was not his strength, or his responsibility.

Jullia looked up at Orion momentarily from her barrel of water, but saw nothing of interest and returned to her task of dropping stones into the barrel. Valletto suppressed a smile, thinking of the day he would tell her that she once met one of the most famous warriors in the whole Hegemony and proceeded to ignore him completely.

"That is Jullia," he said to Orion, "and this is Lyius."

The small boy dashed across and looked up at the towering paladin in awe.

"You're Orion? You're the one who killed all of the demons?"

"Not... not all of them," Orion replied uncomfortably.

"Is that the sword you used to kill Dionne?" Lyius pointed up at the blade on the paladin's back.

"Lyius!" Clera snapped.

Orion looked across apprehensively at Clera. Valletto watched awkwardly as Lyius continued to stare up in wonder at the paladin. Orion looked back at him and then lowered himself to one knee, still towering over the small boy.

"I gave that sword to a friend. This is a new one. In fact, the only thing I have here that was with me when we were away is this old belt buckle."

Orion carefully unbuckled his belt and removed the gold plated clasp, holding it up in front of the amazed child.

"This buckle has been everywhere with me," Orion continued with a warm smile, "and I want you to have it. If anybody ever asks you why you are wearing a paladin's belt buckle, you tell them that Orion of Suda gave it to you. To say thank you because your father saved his life."

Valletto smiled proudly as his son's eyes widened in amazement.

"But there is one condition," Orion said.

"Anything!" Lyius gasped.

"When you grow up, do not be a soldier. Find yourself a safer job, something where you can help people. Your father and I became soldiers to keep people safe, so others do not have to. Do something better with your life than I did with mine."

"I will!" Lyius said as he accepted the buckle. "I promise! Thank you! Thank you very much!"

Valletto had long ago talked his son out of a future in the military, but he appreciated Orion's gesture nonetheless. He looked across and saw his wife look down at the paladin, silently mouthing the word 'thank you.'

Look for information on
Kings of War and Mantic Games at:

manticgames.com

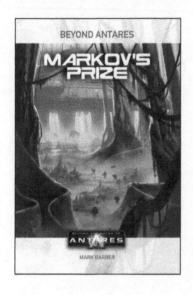

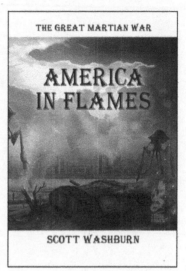

Look for more books from Winged Hussar Publishing, LLC
– E-books, paperbacks and Limited Edition hardcovers.
The best in history, science fiction and fantasy at:

www. wingedhussarpublishing.com

or follow us on Facebook at:

Winged Hussar Publishing LLC

Or on twitter at:

WingHusPubLLC

For information and upcoming publications